A
SCOUNDREL
OF HER OWN

A
SCOUNDREL
OF HER OWN

USA TODAY BESTSELLING AUTHOR
STACY REID

Entangled Publishing, LLC
10940 S Parker Road
Suite 327
Parker, CO 80134
Visit our website at www.entangledpublishing.com.

Amara is an imprint of Entangled Publishing, LLC.

Edited by Stacy Abrams and Lydia Sharp
Cover design by Bree Archer
Photography by Chris Cocozza and Period Images,
Malkovstock/Gettyimages, Kodochigov/Gettyimages
Interior design by Toni Kerr

Print ISBN 978-1-64063-768-9
ebook ISBN 978-1-64063-769-6

Manufactured in the United States of America

First Edition January 2022

AMARA

Du'Sean, always and forever.

PROLOGUE

LYNMOUTH, 1807

Someone was carrying her.

An exceedingly small someone, perhaps as small as herself, Ophelia thought groggily, her brain numbed and tired from the biting cold. Something important niggled in her thoughts but eluded her whenever she tried to catch hold of it. The person beneath her grunted, pausing for a few seconds before resuming their determined trek.

"Am I not too heavy?" she murmured into the crook of the person's neck, which smelled odd, almost like horses or wet puppies. Her hands around the neck felt heavy, the exertion to clasp them tremendous.

"Yer no more than…than a sack of potatoes, me gather," a little boy's voice replied in a sweetly lyrical accent she'd never heard before. "But do not let me go. Hold on tight."

She wanted to part her lips and reply, but the effort felt enormous, and her heart fluttered in panic. Her thoughts drifted hazily along, a heavy weight seemingly dragging her down. A whimper tore from her throat.

"I've got you," the little voice said, strain evident in the tone.

I'm freezing, she wanted to cry, but her mouth felt too numb. She wanted to stir, but there was a cold in her bones that felt like fire. It made no sense. How could she be cold but also hot?

The boy grunted, stopped, and heaved several harsh breaths. "I can make it," he muttered, stooping even lower and jostling her weight higher onto his back and shoulders.

Pain rushed through her limbs, and a great shiver racked her frame. He held her tightly, muttering what sounded like a curse or perhaps a prayer. Then onward he trudged. A light misting rain fell, and thunder rumbled in the darkened sky, a warning that more precipitation was on the horizon.

"I can make it," he whispered. "I can make it. I *must* make it."

He stumbled, then quickly righted himself, once again heaving her up higher onto his back. Ophelia grew aware of the breath sawing from the boy's throat and the sweat trickling down his face. She didn't fully understand, but the need to reassure this stranger welled inside. Though her throat felt raw, as if she had been screaming, she pushed out the words with great effort. "You can make it. I know you can."

Ophelia gasped, a black fright sweeping over her as the memory of her carriage crashing into a swollen river rose in her mind. She recalled her governess, Miss Kinney, saying the bridge that led to her parents' country estate was old and needed repairs, then the ominous sound of creaking wood cracking. The water had churned with fury and had dragged her along with the currents at a terrifying pace. She didn't recall much other than the screams of Miss Kinney and the footmen's and coachman's desperate attempts to reach Ophelia.

Frightened by the memory, she clung to him longer. She could not say how long the little boy trudged with her, but it felt like forever. Thankfully, the sun peeked from bloated clouds, and some of the terrible cold in her body eased.

"We are here," he said, panting with great effort.

He stooped very low, and Ophelia slithered off him, muffling her cry at the way her bones hurt. She stood, wobbling only slightly. The boy remained bent, as if he lacked the strength to stand.

She touched his shoulder tentatively. "Are you well?"

It took him a moment, but he finally said, "Yes."

Pushing to his feet, he faced her. The boy was rather small, bony even, and perhaps about her age—Ophelia had only turned eight years last month. His black hair was pasted to his forehead, and rivulets of water trickled down his hollow cheekbones. His body shook, and he clenched his fists at his sides as if to steady himself against the trembling. Sympathy squeezed her heart. "You are cold, too," she whispered, wrapping her arms around her body tightly.

A faraway look entered his dark green eyes. "You were in the river, and it was taking you away. I jumped in after you."

Ophelia had never seen eyes so vivid and lovely.

He shifted on his feet, and a pained grimace crossed his dirt-streaked face. "I might have worried me ma. I could hear her screaming as the water took us away."

"You are hurt."

"Just me back a little, and one of me foot. It'll get better."

"You should not have carried me; you are so very small," she murmured, hating that her lips trembled. "Though I am incredibly grateful. I shall repay your kindness, I promise."

His little chest puffed out. "I'm twelve. I ain't small."

"You are my size," she refuted. "And I am eight."

He scoffed, clearly affronted. "I am taller."

Barely, but she did not point that out, since it seemed to reassure him to think he was large and well-built. He shuffled around, and it was then she noted he stared at a cottage. It was very plain and had a thatched roof. With a sense of alarm, Ophelia also realized they were deep in the middle of a forest. She slowly turned, yet all she could see for miles was woodland. Why would this cottage be here in the middle of nowhere? "Is this your home?"

He gave her an incredulous look. "No. Our cottage is not this big."

She blinked, looking once more at the tiny hovel. He lived somewhere smaller and with his mama and papa? The idea was inconceivable. "How did you find it?" she asked, walking to stand beside him.

"By luck. I grabbed on to a branch and pulled us from the river. Then I hoisted you on my back and walked upstream. I canna tell how long I walked for, but my feet hurt."

He advanced on the cottage, and Ophelia followed. The door was locked, but he was very enterprising, for he went around to a small window that was opened, wiggled through, and unlocked the door from the inside.

"Come on in," he cried with a wave of his hand. "There is no one about."

Ophelia took her time and clambered up the few front steps, then entered the cottage. It was very tidy, with everything seemingly to be in one space. A kitchen, a fireplace, and a lone sofa that appeared sunken, as if the cushions were worn out. Then there was a bed to the far left, near the small window.

"Who do you think lives here?" she whispered.

He did not look up from where he was busy lighting the fireplace. "Maybe a gamekeeper."

Ophelia nodded, then coughed several times, rubbing her

aching chest.

The boy glanced around with a frown. "Are ye getting sick?"

"I feel tired," she replied and shuffled over to the sofa. It proved to be surprisingly comfortable, and with a start of guilt, she realized her damp clothes wetted the fabric.

"Go to sleep," his voice said from far away. "I'll take care of you."

Trusting him, Ophelia nodded. Her lids were heavy, and with a yawn, she slid into a deep sleep.

• • •

Sometime later, she jolted awake to the scent of something deliciously redolent in the air. The boy was not in the cottage, and Ophelia had a blanket over her body. Now she was warm and toasty. Pushing it off, she stood, swaying slightly. Hurrying to the door, she opened it and paused. The boy was in a clearing, something was spitted on a stick, and he was turning it over the fire. Whatever it was smelled wonderful, and her belly grumbled. She went over and sat on a log before him. "What is it?"

"A rabbit."

"You killed it?"

He hesitated. "Yes."

Oh! She didn't know what to say to that. "Were you afraid?"

"Of killing the rabbit?"

"Yes."

"No." He seemed to think about this. "Why would I be afraid?"

"Killing is bad and seems frightening."

He smiled, and she thought him a very pretty boy, even with all the dirt and grime on his face. "Not when it is to fill our bellies."

The boy jumped to his feet, ran back inside, and returned with the thin blanket. He wrapped it over her shoulders and then handed her a cup of water. Ophelia stared at the dented cup, never having seen a thing like this in her life. How utterly unusual. She took the cup and downed the water greedily. "Thank you—I was so very thirsty."

Mortifyingly, her belly rumbled.

"And hungry, too," he said with another broad smile. "That is why I hunted while ye were sleeping."

Ophelia smiled and tugged the blanket around her body, watching the rabbit turn over the fire and anticipating when she could eat it, thinking what a strange little boy he was. He knew how to light a fire, he was not afraid to kill rabbits, he could cook them, too, and he was only twelve.

How utterly extraordinary.

• • •

She was like a fairy in the stories his da had told him. Niall had never seen a little lady so beautiful.

Her skin was pale and soft, her eyes a deep golden brown, her cheeks dimpled when she smiled, and her hair black like raven feathers. It hung limply over her shoulders and down her back to her hips in a riot of curls. The mass of hair seemed too heavy for her body, but she tilted her head with elegance and smiled at him.

"What is your name?"

He cleared his throat. "Niall."

Her cupid mouth shaped his name. "Niall sounds perfectly lovely and special."

Something warm shifted inside him. "My grandmother named me. What is your name?"

Her little nose wrinkled. "It isn't anything special. It is Ophelia."

Niall frowned, not liking that she thought something about her was ordinary. Fairies were never ordinary. "We could make it special. Though Ophelia sounds beautiful to me."

Her golden-brown eyes glowed. "Special how?"

He thought for a minute. "I could call you…Fifi," Niall murmured, reaching out to tenderly brush a wisp of hair behind her ear, mildly surprised he was being so familiar with her.

Her eyes lit up with pleasure. "Fifi! I love it!"

Fifi it is, then.

Niall ensured she ate, and while she slept that night, he rested comfortably on the sofa, wondering how he would keep her protected or see her home to her family. He had no notion of where they were, and he had a cut under his foot that hurt like the devil. His ma, pa, and two younger sisters would be awfully worried. His ma's scream when he jumped into the water still lingered in his mind, the fright and pain in the sound haunting him.

Niall had to get back to his family soon, but he also had to protect Fifi.

"I'll find a way to take you home," he whispered in the silence of the cottage, dropping his head back onto the cushions of the sofa and closing his eyes.

• • •

The very next day, he took Fifi to a river so she could bathe with the rough bar of soap he'd found in the cabin. At first, she had colored violently and refused, but when he promised to turn his back and keep watch, so no one approached, Fifi waded to the shallow area and did her best. It had stunned him when she revealed that she did not bathe herself at home, and the entire experience had been oddly thrilling.

Niall walked as far as he could in one direction, hoping to see someone who could help them. There were no other houses, nor did he see the main house the cottage might belong to. One day turned into two, then into three, and now it was day five, and they were still together.

Niall was getting worried. His ma and da and his sisters must be worried. Fifi's parents must be just as anxious. And the bottom of his foot hurt more and more with each passing day.

They had just eaten roasted quail, and she yawned contentedly. Dusk arrived, painting the sky in vivid shades of amber. "I do not wish to return inside," she said a bit worriedly, scanning the forest.

"We do not have to."

She beamed. "Truly?"

"We can stay a few minutes longer."

Her richly colored eyes gleamed with delight, and she nodded happily. The chill evening air cut through her dirty gown, making her shiver. Niall removed his threadbare jacket and placed it over her small shoulders.

She wrinkled her tiny nose. "Your jacket smells weird."

He flushed as shame filled him. He did not wash as often as she did—perhaps once a week, sometimes longer in between. Niall bet at her home she washed daily and with rose-scented soap. His ma and da said there were people out there in the world who could afford such luxuries.

Something hot and burning curdled in his belly. "I will go for the blanket," he mumbled.

Her hands reached out and twined with his. "It also smells like you."

"Stink?"

Her eyes widened. "No. Like oakmoss. Like the woods we played in today."

Niall did not know what that scent was, but he liked how it sounded. She was also not pushing his jacket off her body but holding it close. Thankfully, it hung below her knees, protecting her from the elements. The cold bit at his bones, but he inhaled steadily, bearing it for as long as she needed to remain outside. The grass waved idly in the light wind, and against the pale night sky, the trees etched themselves in sharp silhouette.

"I have never been outside like this before," she whispered. "It is very dark…and beautiful. It's all *perfectly* wonderful, even though it is a little frightening. Imagine the creatures in the woods staring at us now!"

"Don't worry. I will protect you."

She lifted her face to him and smiled. "I know."

Niall's heart clenched at the surety of her response. *I'll always protect you.*

Her face scrunched in a tight frown. "You are cold, Niall." Ophelia scuttled closer to him on the log. "We can share. It is really big."

"My da gave it to me," he said softly, inching over to meet her.

They sat on the log, and she removed one of her spindly arms from the jacket. Somehow he wriggled a bit of himself into the jacket, too, and warmth and her unique scent of berries enveloped him. They stayed huddled like that, and despite worrying about his family, Niall felt an unusual happiness seep into his bones. Fifi started to hum softly under her breath, staring up at the velvet beauty of the night sky.

"Wot is that ye humming?"

"It's music for dancing. I've been learning these past few months."

"To dance?"

"Yes."

"Wot for?"

"It is important to know for when I am ready to marry."

Niall frowned. "Marry?"

"Yes. Miss Kinney says these are especially important things to marriage."

"You seem small to marry."

She smiled, and the beauty of it sent his heart to his throat.

"Miss Kinney says a young girl must prepare from now to marry in the future. I am not that small. Remember that I am eight years," she said, holding up the numbers on her hand. "Let me show you, Niall."

Fifi stood, dipped into a most graceful bow, straightened, and then started to dance, her dirtied dress swirling around her ankles as she pirouetted. He thought the notions of rich families were odd, but she looked carefree and lovely in her dance.

There was also a niggle in his belly that he could not brush away. "Fifi, wot age will ye get married?" Surely it wouldn't be *now*. He knew what married people did, kissing and the likes. He wondered if she knew. His ma and da were always kissing and hugging.

She paused in a turn. "I'll have my come out at seventeen or eighteen, and then I'm to marry Peter Warwick, the future Earl of Langdon."

Niall was astonished; this fellow was a nob. "You already know the gent yer to marry?"

"Mama knows it. I have not met him as yet."

Rich people were very odd.

A shadow passed over her face, and her gaze grew far away, as if she'd retreated into herself. She returned to the log and sat with a heavy sigh. The loss of her brightness made Niall feel cold. Reaching out, he used the knuckle of one of his fingers and gently tapped her nose. "Wot is it?"

"I miss my father. I miss home. Do you think they will find us?"

"Yes," he said bravely, though he was also scared. He was not familiar with these lands, and despite searching for hours daily, he did not see the path to take her to safety. "Your ma and pa miss you," he said reassuringly. "They will be looking for ye."

"My mama does not like me very much, I'm afraid. I am not certain why I thought of it just now."

"We've been 'ere for five days," he pointed out. "You miss her."

Large golden eyes landed on him with perfect gravity. "I suppose I do. I wonder if she misses me in return."

Niall didn't know much, but he was sure little girls were not supposed to worry about if their mothers loved them. "I bet she does," he said, feeling with every fiber of his being that it was important to reassure Ophelia that she was treasured.

"She does not hug or kiss me. My papa does," she whispered, a shadow of pain in her eyes.

"My mother tells me every mama loves her children, and Da says Ma is always right."

Her eyes widened. "Your mama sounds fanciful, and your papa…perhaps he is afraid of your mama."

They shared a smile at the idea.

"My mama loves me…and I miss her." To his embarrassment, his voice cracked, and he cleared his throat and squared his bony shoulders.

"What do you miss about your ma the most?"

"She 'ave the most beautiful voice," Niall said. "Da used to say Mama has the voice of one of the angels that went missing from heaven. She sings all the time, especially when she is cooking."

Her little mouth formed an *O* of surprise. "Your ma cooks?"

"Yes. Don't yers?" Perhaps that was why she was so tiny.

"No. We have a cook who does it, Mrs. Clovis. She is *very* good, and she always makes my favorite cake."

Before he could reply to that, she asked, "And does your da sing, too?"

"No, but he would make up stories. Lots of them."

A wistful sigh slipped from her. "My papa reads to me."

They shared another smile together, and strange but wonderful emotions filled the cavity of Niall's chest.

"I'll sing for you," Ophelia said, "and maybe you'll miss your ma less." Before he could muster a response, she started to sing, stealing all coherent thoughts from his brain.

Ophelia's voice was...pure and perfect. Not even his ma could rival the beautiful sound coming from a body this small. Niall stared at her, engrossed and enchanted. Each note felt as if it reached into his soul and stroked a part of him that he hadn't known existed, and the oddest thing happened to him. That phenomenon called love his da often told him about, the one that would happen when he was grown and met a lady, happened in this very moment.

He felt it. A wrench in his heart...painful yet hopeful, the urge to protect her always, the promise to make her happy forever. They all lived within him at this moment, and the dream he had for his future shifted.

His da had been hired on to be an estate carpenter for a squire in Lambeth: a great opportunity for their family to improve their living and for Niall to apprentice under his father. Yet at this very moment, that dream vanished like ashes in the wind. No longer did he want to be a carpenter like his da.

He wanted *more*...yet he wasn't certain what that more entailed.

"Why are you crying?" she softly asked.

He hurriedly swiped away the moisture from his cheek. "I ain't cryin'; boys don't cry." Then he took a deep breath. "Your voice is *beautiful*."

She grinned and clapped her hands, clearly delighted with his praise. "My mama does not like when I sing, and Papa says I must do it in secret."

Niall scowled. "That's stupid."

"I thought so, too," she whispered. "Do you think someone will find us?"

"Yes. But you do not have to worry, Fifi. Ever. I will protect you until we are found. I would never let any harm come to you—I promise it."

She stared at him as if she hardly knew what to make of his fervent vow. Niall could feel the tips of his ears turning red.

"You are the best friend I've ever had," she said a bit shyly. "I will protect you, too."

They shared another smile, but to Niall's mind, this one felt special. The small trinket he had made for her earlier, the one to cheer her up, unexpectedly took on a new meaning for him. Niall reached out. His fingers were trembling as he touched her cheek, but when he saw how dirty and rough they looked, he snatched them back. He didn't want to dirty her, and once again he felt that raw, burning shame that he was so different.

"I…I have something for you," he began haltingly.

Curious eyes assessed him. "What is it?"

Swallowing, he dipped into his pocket and fished out the ring he had made from twigs, green vines, and a flower. He held himself still as she stared at his gift with incomprehension.

"What is it?" she murmured, yet there was a throb of excitement in her tone, as if he offered her the world.

"It is a ring."

"I have never seen such an odd ring before," she said with a curious smile. "You made it?"

"Yes. For you." He cleared his throat, trying to sound mature, as how his da was always berating him to be. "It is my promise to you that…that I will…" *Love you*, he wanted to say, but the words felt too important and weighty to voice so casually. "I will take care of you forever. Will you marry me?"

Fifi stared at him with somberness, as if she understood the gravity of his words. Niall did not understand them fully, but he knew what marriage was—his ma and da. They were always together. Ma was always smiling at Da, even when they had no food in their bellies, even when they worked the farm till their fingers bled. Da was often singing to her, and they were always touching their mouths together. It meant family. It meant never being alone. That was marriage for Niall, and he wanted that with Ophelia for his whole life.

"Yes," she vowed with a solemn nod and the sweetest of smiles. "I will marry you, Niall."

His heart pounded as if it would leap out of his chest, and Niall even felt dizzy. It took several gulping breaths to reorient himself against the hope. "Yer sure?"

She nodded happily.

"What about Lord Peter…" He didn't remember the other name.

"I've never met him. I've met you, and you are *perfectly wonderful*," she said with a shy smile.

They laced their hands together then and watched the stars until it grew too cold to remain outside. Niall ushered her into the cabin and shoved all the wood, sticks, and bramble he collected earlier into the fireplace. After he stoked the fire, he turned to face her.

She was dragging the sole chair closer to the fire. Hurrying over, he helped, and they got it before the warmth. He went for the lamp, glad to see it still had some oil inside, and lit it.

"If you are hungry, I have some berries from earlier."

She nodded, then reached into the small bag she had gripped like a lifeline as the raging waters took her away, pried it open, and withdrew a thick leather-bound book.

"This is one of my favorite books. It is a bit damaged from the water, but it has all sorts of perfectly wonderful stories.

Would you like to read it?"

His throat closed, and for the first time in his existence he felt ashamed and frustrated of his lack of abilities. "I…I cannot read."

Her eyes flared with surprise. "I thought everyone knew how to read."

Niall cleared his throat. "Only…only mostly people who have lots of money. Those who are poor cannot pay anyone to teach them."

She thought about that for a few seconds. "Why didn't your da teach you?"

Niall flushed. "He…he doesn't know how to read, either. That is why he made up the stories he told me and Ma. He is particularly good; I bet his stories were better than those found in books."

She declared gaily, "I bet they were. Would you…would you like me to read to you?"

"Yes."

They huddled close to the small fire, the rain pelting the cottage, as her soft voice filled the room with the riveting tale of a little girl lost in the woods who encountered a secret magical kingdom. Niall was charmed by the animation of her features as she read her book and the way she changed her voice for each character. Despite his enchantment with the story, Niall's mind darted and whirled. Ophelia was a nob, Niall was sure of it. And he was…he was nobody.

"Is your father very rich?" he asked, interrupting her reading.

She glanced up at him. "Papa is an earl, and Grandpa is a marquess. Would that make him very wealthy?"

Niall breathed hard, and the heavy weight of despair

lodged in his guts. She was a nob herself. He'd thought her richer than he was for sure…

But not a real bleedin' lady.

"My da is a carpenter…a fine one but still a carpenter." And a poor one at that, barely earning enough to keep their family fed and healthy. How would Niall ever be enough to deserve her? He did not understand it, and he was a little lad, as she called him, but he was certain that Ophelia was his future.

"What are you thinking about?"

He inhaled deeply. "I was thinking when we would get married."

She beamed and glanced down at the vine ring around her finger. "Miss Kinney says only when I am seventeen or older can I get married."

He did the calculations quickly on his fingers. "I'll be one and twenty then."

She closed the book, excitement lighting in her eyes. "Wouldn't that be splendid? That way we could be friends forever. I heard Mama once say that marriage is until death. That means we live and grow old together forever. Like my grandma and grandpa. They are really old."

Niall nodded, and new lightness entered his heart. "I will work hard to ensure I can provide for you."

She beamed at him and, to his shock, reached up and pressed a quick peck to his cheek. She hadn't minded that dirt was on his face. Niall stared at Fifi wordlessly, his heart racing with an odd sort of joy. Not sure how to show his affection in return, he lifted a finger and gently tapped her nose with his knuckle. She giggled, and he hoarded that sweet sound deep inside him.

• • •

The next few days passed in the same manner. Niall would rise early and make his way into the woods to forage for game and edible berries. The woods in the forest were wet and would create more smoke than heat, and he worried that the small pile in the groundskeeper cottage would soon run out. He would painstakingly draw water from the well each morning to last them for the day and so she could keep herself clean. Niall had never been this clean, he too taking a bath every day instead of the once weekly he'd been used to.

Ophelia had also insisted on teaching him to read, and how he had blushed like a fool when she had praised him for learning his letters in half a day. Today they were learning to dance. It still astonished him that these were the things rich young girls did. Read and paint and dance, all in preparation to marry someone. Niall wasn't sure what those things had to do with a marriage, but Ophelia said her governess insisted they were most important.

And if they were important to her, he had to understand them, even learn to do them as well. That way they would be important to him as well. His da said it was important in a marriage that his wife was always happy, even if that meant he had to be wrong sometimes. Niall repeated that over and over as he went through the hateful dance steps, ignoring the throbbing pain in his leg that was now swollen.

"I've only just started learning," she said, her face adorable in a concentrated scrunch. "Mr. Bloomfield, my dance tutor, says that the minuet is a very elegant but a bit complicated dance. You are very smart, Niall; I am sure you'll understand it very quickly."

Almost an hour later, they were laughing like loons at all the mishaps they'd encountered.

"I have something for you," she whispered shyly.

Surprise lanced Niall. "Wot is it?"

She held out something crooked. Vines and flowers twisted together. It made nothing, really, but something fierce and wonderful filled his chest.

"It is my token for you. Perhaps it could also be a ring."

Niall swallowed. So that was what she was doing earlier in the woods.

A heavy press of an unknown sensation lodged in his gut. It certainly felt bigger than what his little body could contain. "I will treasure this always."

Fifi lifted up her hand to show his ring of vine and flowers on one of her fingers. Surely it must itch and prick her skin, but she had still worn it.

"Just as I will treasure your ring, Niall," she murmured with a shy smile.

The door opened, and they whirled around. A large man came to a shuddering halt upon seeing two children in his home.

Niall positioned himself protectively in front of Ophelia and lifted his chin. She pinched his arm, but he did not move. When she tried to skirt around him, he shuffled with her movements so that he was always in front of her. He grunted in surprise when she jumped onto his back. But he did not push her away, merely slipped his hands behind her knees and hoisted her up so she could hold on to his neck.

The man gaped as if he'd witnessed a circus act.

"Are you little Lady Ophelia, by any chance?"

She gasped and nodded eagerly. Niall narrowed his gaze on the man. "And who are ye?"

The man smiled disarmingly, removed his hat, and slapped it against his thigh. "I'm the groundskeeper of the nearby estate of Viscount Henry Rodrick. There is a large uproar in the area, and everyone is searching for the little lady."

"Even my papa?"

"And your mama," he said kindly. "They are guests at Viscount Roderick's home, and many have gathered, searching the forest for you."

She squeezed his neck tightly. "We are saved, Niall."

The groundskeeper did not look at him with warmth but with suspicion.

"Come on down now," Niall murmured.

Ophelia hopped down and skipped over to the chair to collect her bag and stuff her book inside. She paused, lovingly caressing her fingers over the worn leather. Turning to him, she held it out.

His throat closed. Niall knew how much she loved that book. "I cannot take it."

She hurried over to him, her matted hair curling atop her sweetly rounded cheeks. "Please. You are my best friend, and I so very much want you to have it and read every story compiled in it. We shall have great fun talking about it, I *promise*."

The man cleared his throat, tugging their attention.

"Come along now. We must get going before the rains."

The groundskeeper led them to a horse and took Ophelia up with him. She didn't appear happy about that and tried to wiggle down to walk with Niall. Finally the man grumbled and somehow seated them both haphazardly onto the animal before they set off.

At times they came down and walked, and it felt like forever before they cleared a copse of trees to see a large house in the distance.

"Is my papa inside there?" she asked, rubbing her eyes and yawning.

"Yes, little miss, he is."

She nodded and smiled down at Niall where he trotted tiredly beside the horse. After a time, she determinedly wiggled until she came down, slipped her hand between his, and they walked together. The groundskeeper protested, but she ignored him.

They reached the manor house, which bustled with frenetic activity. She must have been recognized, for two lady servants rushed inside, calling someone. A well-dressed lady and gentleman hurried outside, and when they saw Ophelia, the lady wilted against the man.

"That is my mama and papa," she whispered, squeezing his fingers.

As if she could not wait anymore, the lady broke away from the man and rushed over to them. The beautiful woman lowered her knees onto the ground, uncaring that she damaged her fine dress. Tears sprang to her eyes, and she held out her arms. Ophelia seemed hesitant at first, as if she did not know what to make of this show of affection and relief.

She glanced up at Niall, and it was then he noted her eyes also swam with tears. Letting him go, she flung herself at the lady, and they embraced fiercely. He could not separate the woman's sobs from Ophelia's.

"You are home," the lady said. "How I worried—we all worried…I've missed you dreadfully, Ophelia! Thank heavens you are home and safe!"

Niall stood there, looking around to see if he saw his ma or da. He gathered they were not here or had ever been with this search party. The lady parted from Fifi and looked at him. The large and handsome gentleman helped her to stand, and she smiled warmly at him.

"And who is this young man?" the lady asked.

Ophelia turned around and smiled her prettiest smile yet.

"This is Niall, Mama. He jumped into the river and saved me."

Both man and woman gasped. However, Ophelia merely continued. "He took care of me by hunting and cooked rabbits and birds on a spit. We will also be married when I am seventeen."

The gentleman choked, and the lady stiffened.

"I beg your pardon?" she said in accents so crisp, they almost sliced Niall.

"Yes," he said, wanting them to understand his intentions. His heart knocked frantically around inside his chest, but still he staunchly continued. "One day Fifi will be my wife."

"I find it incredible and brave that you were able to rescue our daughter. How old are you, lad?" the gentleman asked kindly. "Seven years?"

Niall pushed out his chest, the tips of his ears burning. "I am twelve years. I am old enough to understand our promise," he said earnestly, lest they thought him foolish and too ignorant. He sensed his success was rooted in approval from this large, imposing man. "Fifi and I will get married. She'll not have Peter Warwick, the Earl of Langdon."

The gentleman seemed to find some amusement in the matter, for he chuckled, but not the lady. She appeared affronted. Niall hoped that was the right word. His ma used it often, and it was always to describe when betters had *that* look.

"Come, Ophelia dear," she said, holding on to her daughter's hand. "A lady of your stature would not marry a gentleman of common origins but one of great wealth and consequences, a *titled* lord. You'll come to understand the full of it when you are older."

His heart started to thunder when the lady walked away with Fifi. *Common origins?*

Fifi glanced back and waved, her expression saddened. They were just taking her away from him, with no care that they were friends? His throat burned, and he hated that it felt like stupid tears.

The gentleman held out a few coins to Niall, but he placed his hands behind his back. "I...I doona want no money for saving Fifi." Never would he take money for her.

"You have the appearance of a starving flea-infested beggar. Can you afford to refuse this money, lad?"

A starving flea-infested beggar. The shame curdled deeper in his gut, but then he recalled the pride and dignity his da said a man, even a poor man, should always own. Holding the gentleman's eyes with his, Niall said tightly, "Yes. I'll not take no money for saving Fifi."

"Very well," the man said, arching a brow. "My servant here will take you to the kitchen and ensure something warm fills your belly. Then I'll arrange with the viscount for a carriage to take you...wherever your home is."

"Thank you, sir," he said respectfully, as his mother taught him.

The man made to turn away.

"Sir?"

"Yes, lad?"

Niall swallowed past the lump in his throat. "I promised... Fifi and I promised to marry each other, sir, and that we shall be great friends."

The gentleman smiled again, as if the entire situation was humorous. Niall was most assuredly serious, and it was his turn to feel affronted even if he was not better. He puffed out his chest, hoping to appear taller and more dignified than a starving flea-infested beggar. His da taught him to be a lad of his word. A man never goes back on his word. That would make him the worse sort of ruffian.

"I have no doubt you wish to marry her and be her friend. You are fit to be neither, and it is insulting that you believe you can. My daughter's husband will have wealth, power, and good breeding—all of which you lack. Learn not to want to pick the high-hanging fruit, lad, but always go for the one you can reach."

The man walked away, too, leaving Niall feeling hollow. "Fifi!"

A hand grabbed his neck and dragged him. Niall dug his feet into the gravel, the stone poking through his worn boots.

"Fifi!"

This time she heard, because she looked back just as she was about to enter the large home. "Wait for me..." he shouted, hoping she could hear him.

"Wait for me..." This time it was a whisper, a prayer, a hopeful plea.

Her mother tugged her inside, and the door closed with a finality that echoed through his soul.

Wait for me...

CHAPTER ONE

15 YEARS AND 6 MONTHS LATER.
BERKELEY SQUARE, LONDON.

Lady Ophelia Darby's fingers ran with swift grace over the grand pianoforte keys, playing a lively tune. Sensing a presence in the music room, she lowered her hands and twisted on the bench. The Marchioness of Shelton framed the doorway, a wide smile on her mouth. Her mother was an exquisite lady, and today she was garbed in a bright yellow gown that flattered her trim and elegant figure. Her light brown hair streaked with golden strands was no longer clasped in a tight chignon but flowed loosely past her shoulders in a riot of becoming curls.

As her blue eyes gleamed with happiness and a hint of tears, Mama looked many years younger than her actual age of five and forty. Most importantly, she no longer wore dark-colored gowns, nor did she appear wan and hopeless as she waited for her husband to die.

Aware of her own fingers trembling, Ophelia stood and fully faced her mother. "The doctors gave a good report?" she softly asked, renewed hope blooming through her heart.

"Your father…" Mama cleared her throat. "Your father has healed well. The doctors said *all* danger has passed, and he will eventually recover his vitality completely."

Relief swelled through her and burst forth in laughter. Lifting the skirts of her gown, she hopped over the bench.

"Ophelia, what wildness is this!" her mother cried, as if aghast; however, her eyes shone with laughter. "And you are without shoes and stockings, too! Impudent child."

Running from the room, Ophelia only paused briefly to kiss her mother's cheek. "Impudent *lady*, Mama. I *am* four and twenty."

Ophelia gripped her gown and dashed up the winding staircase, swiping away at the tears running down her cheeks. Upon reaching her father's bedchamber, she paused, swallowing down these peculiar feelings that darted through her whenever she met with him. Only two weeks ago, he had summoned her to his bedside to speak with her. She had greatly feared it was the last time she would see her father.

Her mama, the servants, and even Ophelia had anticipated the passing of the marquess with grim visages. Mama wept and prayed daily, and Ophelia often sat by his bedside reading and telling him of her day. Her papa had believed his death imminent, and because of that, he shattered the love and trust between himself and Ophelia by revealing a secret…or better, a truth. Since then, whenever they faced each other, she had to fight for equanimity and present a serene and determinedly untroubled countenance. Ophelia could not bear for him to see that the truth he had revealed still ravaged her daily.

She knocked and politely waited for him to respond.

"Come in, Ophelia."

She opened the door and slipped inside the large and airy bedchamber. Her father sat by the windows in a high wingback chair, a blanket covering his knees. He was wearing a purple banyan, but underneath, his shirt and neatly tied cravat were visible. He did not look like the powerful and robust marquess she'd always known, her papa who could conquer any insurmountable obstacle.

"How did you know it was me, Papa?" she asked with a smile, hurrying to his side and brushing a kiss to his cheek.

"Though I am sure you tried to practice restraint, I could feel the impatience in your knock."

Ophelia wrinkled her nose and sat on the chaise longue opposite his chair, curling her feet onto the cushions. When she was growing up, her father had lamented many times that her energy was entirely too boundless, that she did not know how to sit still, and even suggested that her impetuous temperament was better suited to a son, to which she had always rolled her eyes in the most unladylike fashion...no doubt confirming his assessment.

Running her gaze over him critically, she was pleased to note his color had improved and he seemed stronger. Since the affliction that had struck his heart, her papa had lost an undetermined amount of weight, grooves bracketed his mouth, and his skin was pulled taut over the elegant ridge of his cheekbones. Yet there was an inherent strength in his face that his ailment had not been able to reduce. A few more silver strands dotted his temples, but her papa was a man in his prime and retained his devilish handsomeness.

"The doctors have given a really good report, Papa. Mama is *very* happy. You will soon be dancing at balls with her and riding in the park again."

"That would please me," he murmured, his rich golden-brown eyes, identical to her own, lighting up.

Since his ailment, his marchioness had not been away from his side, refusing all callers to their home and canceling all her social engagements. Ophelia had taken over household matters with grim resilience, understanding her mother was too shattered to manage that responsibility.

"You will be taking walks with Mama soon, Papa."

"I daresay I shall, poppet. How I long to just hold your mother's hand between mine and walk about the gardens, listening to the chirping birds and the rushing waters in the fountains."

Her father smiled at her bare toes peeking from beneath her dress and her unbound hair resting against her hips. All the propriety she practiced outdoors in the company of others vanished once she rested under her papa's roof, and he had never forced her to conform to others' expectations. "Papa…"

Their eyes met, and it happened then. Ophelia's throat closed, and she simply stared at him, hating the burning sensation in her eyes.

"Why do you cry?" he gruffly demanded.

"I am not crying," she said with a stubborn lift of her chin, keeping those dratted tears from spilling over.

His hand that rested on the carved arms of his chair stilled. He sensed it, too, this uncomfortable strain between them.

"Will you tell me about her?" she asked hoarsely.

"No."

"Papa—"

"You do not need to know about her, *ever*."

Ophelia felt as if her whole solid world had evaporated in one breath. "Papa, what do you mean?"

His face was dark with emotion and wariness. "The marchioness has been a wonderful mother to you, and you have led a contented and happy life. Let us be enough!"

His command shocked her speechless. On his supposed deathbed, he had told her a truth that had destroyed her, and now Ophelia realized he never intended to reveal the rest to her. How naive she had been, waiting for the moment when he would share more.

"Tell me, Papa," she breathed. "Was she an awful woman? One who was unkind and selfish in her nature? One so terrible it is in my best interest I never know anything about her?"

"No. You are so very much like her," her father said, a faraway look entering his eyes, as if he disappeared into a memory. "Your voice is just as beautiful as hers...maybe even more. She too sang and played the pianoforte with incredible skill and passion."

Something inside Ophelia crumpled. "Then tell me about her, please, Papa! At least tell me her name."

Her father's eyes filled with tears. His throat worked, but no sound emerged. He turned his regard away, staring through the windows of the parlor for unending minutes. "Miss Sally Martin."

Her birth mother's name was Sally Martin.

"Papa—"

"No! What's done is done," he commanded hoarsely. "If not...if not..." His lips pinched, the words clearly heavy on his tongue and seeming unbearable to speak.

A sharp swelling pain rose up in her. "If not that you believed you were dying, you would not have told me," Ophelia said, a hot ache burning in her throat, such unknown emotions sweeping through her it took an enormity of willpower not to cry.

"You only told me to relieve the guilt on your heart. You wanted to go on to your rewards with a conscience no longer burdened by secrets and guilt. You would have departed this world at peace, but you would have left behind a daughter bewildered, hurt, and shocked, for the papa she loved and doted on had revealed a character that was flawed. You would have left me alone with such doubts and pain, such confusion I would have nowhere to turn. But you did not die, Papa. You *lived*, and I have so many questions. Please, I *beg* of you to answer them."

He closed his eyes, lines of pain and regret bracketing his mouth. "We will never speak about this again."

His tone was implacable, his eyes hard and shadowed, and it was the powerful marquess who stared back at her, not her doting papa. She met his gaze with seething frustration. "Papa—"

"Your mother..." Papa cleared his throat and gruffly commanded, "Your mother must not be troubled with this. We will not speak of it again, ever."

Ophelia understood then that whatever her father thought he protected—his wife's sensibilities, losing his daughter's love, having to face his own lack of honor—mattered more to him than the lingering confusion and doubts in his daughter's heart.

She stood, dipped into a polite curtsy, and rushed through the door. Once it had closed, she leaned against it, letting the hot spill of tears course down her cheeks. A tumble of confused thoughts and feelings assailed her. Since her father's confession, Ophelia had taken all the doubts and bewilderment, wrapped them in a tight ball, and pressed them deep down inside until they no longer tormented her. She had prayed daily with her mother that he would recover, for she loved him with her whole heart, and she was not ready to lose him.

Somehow, Ophelia had truly believed that once he rallied,

her father would have expanded on his brief confession and told her more.

"*Your…the marchioness did not give birth to you. Forgive me for keeping it so long.*"

Those had been his thin, whispery words, and how she had stared at him in utter bewilderment. "*But you are my papa?*"

"*Yes.*"

Her sudden, breathtaking anguish had wrestled with her shock. *Not my mother…*

She had tried to force her confused thoughts to order, for her parents had celebrated their twenty-fifth wedding anniversary recently. They had been married before she was born, so how could someone other than the marchioness have been her mother at birth? Those questions had spilled from her as she clasped his hands, and his only other response had been that she was the child of his mistress.

"*She did not want me?*" Ophelia had whispered, feeling little emotion because the absurdity of his story simply could not be true. It was the ramblings of a man in pain and confused by the tincture of laudanum.

Perhaps he *had* been muddled from the drug, but her father had murmured, "*I did not give her a choice. I took you even though she cried and begged me not to.*"

Then with a relieved sigh, as if a great burden had been lifted from his heart, her father had fallen into a deep slumber.

I took you even though she cried and begged me not to.

Everything she thought she knew about her father's honor, her mother's kindness, the love and happiness their family had been blessed with, shattered that day.

Ophelia had enjoyed her life and the bounteous fortune of being a marquess's daughter. She was doted on, given her heart's desires by her mother and father. But it had all been at the cost of someone else's torment, someone her father had used and left crumbled in the ashes of her pain.

She could not imagine having a child who was simply snatched away by the father, never to be seen again. Why had he done it? Ophelia struggled to reconcile that they had stolen her from her mother's arms when she was a squalling infant, without any consequences. But who would that lady be compared to her father? He was powerful. To be a mistress meant her Sally Martin would have little or no connections to the *ton* or wealth. She'd have no standing to resist or complain about a wealthy marquess.

Ophelia was haunted by so many questions.

Was Sally Martin still alive? How had she coped with having her babe ripped from her arms by her protector? Had she mourned and eventually picked up the pieces? Had she found another protector? Had she died from a broken heart? Who was she? Did she still smile…and also sing? Or had her song died when the marquess broke her heart so irrefutably? Did she still play the pianoforte with the same zest and passion Ophelia did?

With shaking fingers, she wiped the tears from her face and silently asked herself questions she had been afraid to ponder.

Are we alike in any other ways?

Her heart wrenched underneath her breastbone. Ophelia recalled a time in her young life her mother had found her presence unbearable. The marchioness had never hugged or played or read to her as Papa did, though how Ophelia had craved her mama's affections. Ophelia remembered how she would hide and watch her mother in her boudoir, wishing she could go to her and bask in her warmth and perfume.

Her mother had hated whenever she sang and danced in the long hallways of their country home, and the pain of knowing her mother rejected her had almost killed something inside of her. Her papa had tried to comfort Ophelia by telling her that she and her mama were simply different creatures. That one day her mama would start to hug and kiss her, too. She had not believed it, but then it had all changed when she had been found after several days missing.

"I understand it now, Mama," she whispered as she padded down the hallway to her bedchamber. "I was not yours, and a daily reminder of your husband's infidelity." *But it does not matter, because you love me now*.

That reassurance did not diffuse the wild grief and sense of loss that had settled upon her heart. Entering her room, she flung herself onto her bed and stared up at the ceiling. A wry chuckle escaped her. Only last month, she had teasingly said to her mother that they had nothing in common. Her mother was so delicate and proper, while her parents often remarked that Ophelia owned an uninhibited temperament that must be carefully disguised.

The marchioness had laughed along with her teasing, but there had been a touch of sadness in her eyes Ophelia had not then understood. But she had always felt herself different than her mother, who was charming, gentle, and wise beyond her years. Ophelia hardly thought herself much different than other ladies of the *ton*, even though Ophelia admitted she had little appreciation for inane chatter and malicious gossips, uncaring to make her existence be about the next ball or the latest *on dit*.

That was the reason it had been so easy and refreshing to be friends with several ladies who stood on the fringes of polite society and were mockingly called wallflowers—ladies who, despite being well-bred, were generally considered oddities. Even in that regard, she was not a perfect fit for their coterie. Ophelia was aware that as the Marquess of Shelton's daughter, she was never given a snub and was invited to all the society events that her friends were not. She was a wallflower by association, and no one in society dared refer to her thusly even as she embraced being one of the sinful wallflowers.

Pushing from the bed, she rushed over to the dressing table and sat before it, staring at her reflection in the mirror. "It does not matter who Sally Martin is. I *am* Lady Ophelia, daughter to the Marquess and Marchioness of Shelton."

Saying the words aloud did nothing to calm the terrible aching sensations burning deep inside her chest that felt too petrifying. Leaning forward, she pressed the flat of her palm against the glass. "Nothing has changed. Nothing. I am Lady Ophelia…nothing has changed."

To her distress, looking through the mirror, she noted the redness of her eyes and how incredibly pale her skin appeared. She closed her eyes, hating that she seemed so vulnerable and that it showed for everyone to see. Her papa had always complimented her strength, and she too had always relied on her fortitude.

Now is not the time to crumble. "And what is there to be afraid of, Ophelia?"

It was a question she could not answer, but she was most certain that she had to find Sally Martin.

Ophelia did not understand why that certainty blossomed through her, only that she would follow through. Still, she hesitated, torn by conflicting needs. Her family's wealth and reputation had secured her position in Society, and it was up to Ophelia to maintain it by never stepping out of line and disappointing her parents' efforts.

Her father expected her to obey his wishes, for she always did. *Always*. Even though she often teased them with her air of rebellion and spontaneity, Ophelia reined in her temperament when dealing with her parents' expectations. They loved her, and she loved them. Never did she want to disappoint or hurt them, and never had there been an instance where she flagrantly disavowed their wishes.

Closing her eyes, she promised to search for Sally Martin with utmost care of their position. What she could not do was simply pretend she did not know the truth of the matter.

I'll find you.

By any means possible.

• • •

Devlin Niall Byrne stared at the creature who strolled down King Street with all the leisurely grace of one who promenaded down Rotten Row in Hyde Park. Though this area was only a stone's throw away from St. James's Street, this side of the city was not for the likes of her. King Street was littered with undesirables—brothels, gambling dens, and cutthroats. Then there were men like him, walking the line between the fringe of polite society and the dangerous knifelike edge of the seedier underbelly of London.

A foot in each world meant Devlin belonged to none and his welcome in either territory was suspect.

That suited him, for he had learned a long time ago only to rely on his cunning and ingenuity.

The great beast beside him, his closest friend—a mastiff—rumbled low in his throat.

"Easy, Conan," Devlin murmured, biting the tip of his cheroot to reach down and smooth his pal's head. "Let's watch and see what is happening."

He took a deep drag of his tobacco, then allowed the smoke to curl around him, the twisting wisps disappearing into the night as the darkness swallowed it. Devlin and his dog watched the lady as she walked closer to the patch of darkness that securely hid their presence. Dipping into the pocket of the black cape she wore, the lady withdrew a piece of paper. Her dainty heels clacked on the cobbled stone as she walked under a fog-shrouded gas lamp, unfolded the scrap of paper, and read.

The lady was truly astonishing. Even without seeing her face and full raiment, Devlin knew her to be a lady of quality—and the finest quality at that. It was in her bearing. The set of her shoulders. The petite grace of her form, the soft sway to her rounded hips, and the elegance and shimmering sensuality of her walk.

A fine piece indeed.

And a foolhardy one. Movements twisted in the dark—men, truly creatures who should not bear the appellation, pushed off from the walls, slinked from the alley, and approached her. The lady remained oblivious, staring at the large red door on the opposite side of the road.

The Golden Tavern. What could she want with this disreputable pub?

He could not see her expression, but he felt her longing. With a wry twist of his lips at his whimsy, Devlin made to move on. Yet something inexplicably arrested his motions.

One of those creatures bent on robbery—or worse—reached her while the other slinked from another direction. The hood of her caped domino was violently pulled away from behind, the veil covering her features snatched off. A shocked inhalation sliced the silence of the night, and she whirled from the threat behind her, a perfect pirouette putting her some distance away from the men's lechery.

Another sharp sound hissed, silver glinted in the dark, and the blade she withdrew from the walking cane was held with confidence and steady grace. The men paused and exchanged a glance, no doubt wondering if a lady would know how to use the rapier and if they could disarm her before she did any damage.

"Ye won't be able to take two of us," one of the men taunted.

"Since you are so confident, lads, I invite you to meet your demise." She tossed her head, and a mass of black hair tumbled loose and fell in waves to her hips.

Devlin faltered into perfect stillness. Everything about him encased in shards of ice—except his heart. Only once in his lifetime had he ever seen hair that black, the sheen of raven's feather, with a bluish hue under the banner of midnight.

Only once.

He couldn't look away.

Thud. Thud. Thud. His damn heart was a huge drum pounding in his ears. She had been a hope he held on to for months, years, until he had begun to feel foolish in the extreme. Devlin had not allowed anything to impact him on such a profound emotional level since he had given up thoughts of finding her.

Hence his reaction now was startling…aggravating…and

uncontrollable. That was the part that bothered him the most. He could not control his heartbeat or the naked longing, which felt like it erupted through his very soul.

For her.

He lifted his cane and tapped it on the cobbled surface twice. That was all it took for the men who had shuffled closer to pause and withdraw into the shadows as if they had been summoned elsewhere. Confused, the woman twisted about, her weapon held at the perfect defense angle, the wind lifting strands of hair to curl around her cheeks. Devlin walked closer, hugging to the darkness of the night, his footfall as silent as a thief. He stopped when he was close enough.

Devlin made a deliberate noise, soft and barely discernable, and she whirled in his direction.

His world ended as a force robbed him of breath and would not give it back to him. Golden-brown eyes framed by long black lashes. Eyes that were swollen and a bit red, a testament to the tears they had recently shed. The palest of skin. A wide, lush mouth that was made for kissing. And smiling. And laughter.

Her beauty was the same—lush and provocative.

It was her. *Fifi.*

The only thing he could recall of that girl…the one who had changed his entire life. The one whom he had called for in his delirium as fever and pain had raged through his body. The one he had searched for but never found, not even with his connections and money.

It is you…

A fog of memory wafted through him, and the words danced in his head as if they were a song. *Wait for me…*

But he had stopped waiting, years ago, when the memory

of her had become a distant dream. Yet here she was.

He stood in the dark, watching as three footmen in livery ran toward her, fear on their faces.

"Lady Ophelia, please come with us! The marquess would skewer us if he knew you were here. Please, milady!"

He tucked away the name and carefully assessed the footmen, noting the designs of their livery and the shapes of their features. With this, he would be able to find the family to which she belonged. A stately carriage rattled down the street, and she hurriedly slipped the hood of her cloak over her head and went with the footmen. They knocked the carriage steps down for her, and with a last look behind her at that red door, she mounted the steps and entered the carriage. Devlin watched as it rumbled away, until he could no longer hear its wheels before he turned his attention to that door.

Something existed in there that was important to her.

Lady Ophelia…Fifi…I've found you when I was no longer looking.

"And what exactly should I do about it?"

Conan rumbled low in his throat, and Devlin replied, "I do believe you are right, my friend. Let us find out everything we can about Fifi."

Conan growled several times, and Devlin rubbed his head.

"Yes, it is the girl I told you about so many times."

A sound shuffled behind him, but Devlin did not startle, for he had long sensed Riordan O'Malley in the dark.

"You know," Riordan said drolly, appearing from the shadows to walk in stride with Devlin, "I cannot tell if the dog understands when you talk to him or not. He makes all the right noises at the right bloody time. Uncanny, that. Nor do I believe he actually told you to investigate the chit. *That* is all you, my friend."

"His name is Conan." Devlin patted his pal's head, who made an odd sound of pleasure deep in his throat. "We understand each other."

"Is that what it was, an understanding?"

They turned onto St. James Street, walking toward the notorious gambling den in which they owned considerable stakes—the Asylum.

At Devlin's lack of response to his prodding, Riordan asked, "Is it really her? The girl you spoke about from when you were a lad?"

Devlin's gut tightened. He had hoped his friend was far away enough in the shadows to have not heard him. He didn't want to think about what seeing her again meant. "Yes."

"What will you do?"

"She was a mere speck in my past. There is nothing to do."

"If that is the truth, why did your fingers just tremble?"

A raw hiss of annoyance slipped from Devlin, and he stuffed the offending appendages into the pocket of his great coat.

"I have touched a nerve," Riordan murmured provokingly. "I am now exceedingly curious about this lady."

Devlin shuttered his expression and made no reply. His friend must have sensed he was on edge, for he made no other provocative taunts, and that in itself was unlike Riordan. A quick glance at him showed a man lost in deep contemplation.

"You were gone for over three months," Riordan murmured. "It is good to have you back."

"I gather I was missed," Devlin replied drolly. "I had business in Ireland. It took longer than anticipated."

"Rhys was worried."

"I'm a grown lad. I can take care of myself."

Riordan grunted. "He wanted to celebrate with us before his wife went into confinement a few weeks ago."

"I missed it," Devlin murmured, soft regret flaring through him. "I took ma and da to Ireland. They longed for home and wanted to visit. Does he have a son or a daughter?"

Riordan smiled. "A daughter. She has his eyes."

"Has he retired from the dark side of the business?"

There was a contemplative silence from his friend before he replied, "Rhys certainly spends most of his time in Derbyshire with his wife and wee ones. I do not begrudge him such fine contentment."

A wife…children…a dream many men of their ilk hungered for themselves. Hope and happiness could be found within a family. Devlin knew that, having grown up with a father and mother who did their very best to provide for a son and two daughters. While many days their bellies had been empty of food, the house empty of coal to see them through the bitter winter, they had never been short of laughter or love. "Nor do I," Devlin said with a wry smile.

Riordan took a cheroot from his pocket, lit it, and started to smoke. "I cannot understand this penchant for walking. If we had hailed a bloody hackney, we would have reached the gambling house by now."

"Conan and I did not ask for your company."

Riordan drawled, "I suspect you wanted the time to think about your lady."

Wanting to sink under his friend's skin in the same manner he did to him, Devlin said, "Have you made an offer for Grace Tremayne?"

His friend stumbled as if he had tripped over something.

He shifted to face Devlin.

"What did you say?" he demanded raggedly.

Devlin arched a brow. "I know you want her. Only a fool would not be able to tell."

He raked his hands through his black hair. "*Hell!* Do you think Rhys knows?"

It was Devlin's turn to freeze. "He is your closest friend. Why would he object to a match between you and Grace?"

Riordan gave him an incredulous stare. "She is his bloody baby sister! You know everything he has ever done was to see his family elevated from the dregs...and I *am* the dregs."

Devlin had nothing to say to that, and they continued walking. Riordan O'Malley was the majority owner in the Asylum—one of the most profligate and powerful gaming hells known to London society. Rhys Tremayne, now Viscount Montrose, was a businessman who sold information on London's black market. Known as The Broker, for years he studied the men and women of England, high- and low-born, unearthing and collecting their secrets with great diligence, then traded that information when it held the greatest benefit.

Devlin had been one of Rhys's lads who slipped in and out of alleys watching, listening, and reporting back what he learned for a coin. So had Riordan. At one point they had diverged and pursued their own business interests but had always remained a close-knit group.

Devlin wondered if Rhys would truly hate the idea of Riordan with his sister Grace.

Hell. It was hard to say, but now he understood why his friend stayed away from the girl he stared at with such naked longing. Dragging on his cheroot, Devlin blew a plume of smoke to the overcast night sky. Wanting someone and endlessly longing for them was something he could identify with. Over the years, he had tried to envision the kind of beauty Fifi would have evolved into.

The reality of her far surpassed his foolish imaginings.

What would she think of him now? Devlin had changed from the small, weak boy she knew to…hell, he did not know what he was, except a simple man with simple needs even as he was lauded by his friend for his iron determination.

…*my daughter's husband will have wealth, power, and good breeding.*

The old memories washed over him, and a peculiar ache twisted through his heart. As a lad of twelve, he had packed his small belongings and made his way to London to seek work. Or anything that would make him become a man worthy of marrying a girl like his Fifi.

His mother's tears had not been able to stop him, and though brackets of worry had dug deep into his father's mouth, his da had given him a nod of approval. Devlin had only been in London for a few days before he realized he had wished a hopeless dream. Within another week he had been living on the streets, hanging with a crew of pickpockets, learning the trade of criminality, the pride and dignity his da had taught him mangling.

Shame had filled him, but so had a resolute determination to make it in this world. How else would he become a man worthy to marry Fifi? The criminal class had beckoned, the lure of making money irresistible. Then he had met Rhys Tremayne and Riordan O'Malley, two lads only a few years older than himself.

They had been hungry for the same thing and wanted to claw themselves from the gutter of poverty to the pinnacles of success. A friendship had formed, though Devlin had many times felt he stood outside of the bonds of brotherhood Riordan and Rhys had shared years before they met him. Devlin had been more of an observer of their camaraderie, barely engaging in their bantering and family gathering.

Rhys had done many things to include him, but Devlin's hunger to remake himself had seen him leaving their crew for days, sometimes months, seeking and searching, wanting to understand the complex world they lived in so he could conquer it.

When he explained this to his mother, she had stared at him somberly before finally saying, "*People like us can only belong certain places. In the fields. At the docks. In taverns. At the market. If you dare to, they will break your pride, trample your dignity, and kill your hope. Niall, you will splatter to the ground with no one to scrape you up.*"

She had warned him it was foolhardy to reach for heights that he did not belong.

Her words had reminded him of Fifi's father's words, but they had only emboldened him to push harder: doing all sorts of odd jobs, saving, teaching himself his letters, reading every scrap of paper thrown out by his supposed betters.

Devlin had been hungry, and he had consumed.

He now owned more wealth than he could spend in this lifetime. He understood the relationship between money and power enough to wield them when necessary to achieve his own ends. Good breeding would forever elude him. With Riordan at his side, as a lad of sixteen Devlin had learned to gamble, haunting the different gambling halls, studying the dice and the tables, learning how to weigh the risks against the rewards, learning to discipline his emotions and reactions so as to not make reckless mistakes.

By the time Devlin was eighteen, he had garnered a reputation amongst the different gaming halls. He did not lose. He picked the table he sat at with care and due diligence. He could not be goaded into acting imprudently. They hated when he entered their clubs and took their money, unentailed estates, lands, and even shares in a hotel he had won. He'd also learned that there was money to be made in the fighting pits and in investments.

Still he had felt it was not enough.

Devlin did not stop until he had amassed a fortune that rivaled most lords. He had taught himself to be cunning...and ruthless, a man who knew how to hold on to the things that were his.

Achieving them had been damn hard work...holding on to them was even harder. Now as a man of seven and twenty, he *should* be contented. Yet there was a nameless restlessness upon him that had seen him many nights standing in the dark of his bedroom, Conan by his side, the windows open as they stared at the beauty of the night sky in silence.

It felt as if he were simply drifting through life, with little compelling him to *live*.

With a scowl, he scrubbed a hand over his face. Devlin truly did not understand what more he needed or why he was so discontented.

Fifi.

He only needed to think her name, and the restlessness lowered its raking talons, giving him a measure of peace. A sensation that was impossible to know or understand scythed through him, stuttering his heart. Devlin faltered, and Riordan, preoccupied with his own musings, continued strolling along

St. James's Street toward his gambling club. Devlin turned around and stared down at the empty road. The wind gusted, and a discarded piece of newssheet danced in the air before settling under a streetlamp.

What should I do now that I've found you?

CHAPTER TWO

5 MONTHS LATER...

Ophelia frowned at the envelope the butler had presented to her on a silver salver. The crème parchment had a most unusual image affixed within the seal—a lady perched atop a lion. Using a letter knife, she slit the envelope open. Shock darted through her. It was a bank draft for ten thousand pounds, payable to her father, and drawn from Drummonds Bank, Trafalgar Square.

Ophelia lifted her head and glanced about the small and intimate parlor she had long claimed as her own, designed with elegant decor to suit her personality. Very carefully, she checked the address of the envelope once more. It had been franked to her.

She plopped without any form or grace into the sofa closest to her. Ten thousand pounds. A fortune! One that not even she could scoff away. There was a neatly folded note within the envelope beneath the bank draft. With trembling fingers, she flicked it open.

A song from you to me.

She dropped it as if fire had burned her. Leaning over, she retrieved that small piece of paper. What was the meaning of this? Hurrying to her feet, she escaped the small parlor and made her way down the hallway.

"Clarkson," she called to the butler. "Did you recognize the livery of the person who delivered this letter?"

Clarkson frowned. "I cannot say, Lady Ophelia. I saw the letter on the mantel with the others."

"I see." Ophelia whirled around, strolled down the hallway, and went into her father's study. Crossing the length of the room, she made her way behind his desk and sat in his chair. She tried to be deductive about the entire matter. The bank draft was made out to her father. Whoever sent it must know much about her father and his finances. Why else would they send money?

A song from you to me.

That seemed to Ophelia the service demanded for the money. The shock of that awareness robbed her of breath, for it meant whoever sent it also knew that Ophelia loved singing. Perhaps even knew she moonlighted in dangerous places she had no business being as Lady Starlight—a rising songbird of exceptional talent and beauty. As so many of the scandal rags touted.

No, no, no!

Breathing evenly, she reined in the panic. *Think calmly and logically, Ophelia.*

Only her closest friends Kitty, Maryann, Fanny, Charlotte, and Emma knew of her mad scheme, and even then, they only understood a part of it. Cosima, an exiled Prussian princess and another dear friend, had some idea why Ophelia daringly visited the singing taverns and opera houses. Perhaps this draft and demand for a song had nothing to do with Ophelia being Lady Starlight but had everything to do with her father needing money.

"Rubbish," she whispered, putting the bank draft onto his large oak desk. "Papa is a wealthy marquess. Why would he need money?"

Opening his drawers, she began a careful search. The bottom drawer was closed, and, dropping on her knees, she carefully lowered to the ground, removed her hairpin, and picked the lock. It might not work, since it was only last week she learned the skill.

With a snick, the lock opened, and Ophelia chuckled. She had to visit Maryann soon, and praise her for passing on her lock-picking skills to the other sinful wallflowers—a skill taught to her by notorious rogue Nicolas St. Ives, who had been stealing into her friend's bedchamber nightly. With a groan, Ophelia tried not to think on the madness of that and the great threat of ruination it presented to her friend.

The drawer opened fully, and Ophelia stilled. There were dozens of letters and bills from creditors stuffed into the drawer. Unpaid bills. "I do not understand," she whispered in the stillness of the study.

Some of the letters were demands for payments, bills owed from as much as three years ago. "This is not possible." She opened a few more letters until she could no longer ignore the truth. Her father's estate was in trouble, and he hid it from his family. Or perhaps only her; Mama and Papa shared everything.

She was about to close the drawer when she recognized a seal from Eton. After a slight hesitation, she reached for it. This seemed to be the headmaster's fifth letter requesting payment for her cousin's tuition and room and board. Robert was her cousin and—as her father's heir, since he had no son of his own—was taken care of by her father.

Yet it was plain as day his tuition was not being settled.

The most awful sensation twisted through her belly. Ophelia scrambled to her feet and stared at the bank draft once more.

Ten thousand pounds.

Suddenly, her palm dampened, and her heart shook violently underneath her breast. This money would help in settling some of the unpaid bills, especially the ones that were owed for more than a year. And also for Robert's tuition.

Many people sell their art. I would be no different.

"What am I thinking… This is outrageous."

Taking and using this mysterious money came with strings—dangerous ties that might wrap her in a web beyond her ability to maneuver. The feeling that her life would change, and not in a good way, should she dare lodge this bank draft beat at her senses. Who would send this to her and *why*? How did they even know her family faced financial difficulties when Ophelia herself had not known it?

Slipping the envelope into the deep pocket of her gown, she hurried from the study and made her way to the sun-room—the drawing room her father and mother favored. The door was closed, and she gently knocked, not wanting to rouse her father should he be asleep.

"Enter," he called.

Releasing a soft breath, she strolled inside the drawing room.

"Mama, Papa," she greeted with a smile, hurrying over to their side.

Her mother smiled brightly upon seeing her. "I thought you had taken a walk with Fanny. Are you back so soon?"

Ophelia dipped and brushed a kiss to her mother's cheek, who reposed on the chaise longue with a cup of tea in her hand.

"Fanny sent a note that she encountered an unexpected delay and must regrettably miss our walk. Instead of venturing out alone, I decided to stay indoors and read."

Holding tight to the odd twisting feeling inside, she faced her father, who sat in a high wingback chair, a blanket thrown over his knees. The gaze that stared penetratingly at her was a bit guarded.

"How are you feeling today, Papa?"

There was a flash of hurt in his eyes that once again she did not greet him with a kiss, and then his expression shuttered. Since his revelation to her about Sally Martin a little over five months ago, he refused to speak further about the past with her, yet it lingered in the air like a festering wound. Ophelia had not mentioned it to him since, but their relationship had been altered on a profound level.

"I shall be able to resume riding this week. It will be glorious indeed."

His recovery was slower than anticipated, and Papa had not yet resumed his normal duties. This was the first season he had not sat in Parliament. However, his cronies visited their townhouse frequently, and he had been very hearty in the debates that took place during their dinners. Ophelia sat on the sofa and accepted a cup of tea from her mother. She felt her parents' curious regard upon her, for it was not often she joined them in their morning routine of spending time together in this room.

Taking a careful sip of her tea, she glanced up. "Is it so odd that I am here? You are staring as if I am a creature!"

"No," her mother replied with a light chuckle, "but my darling, we know when you want something. There is a very stubborn lift to your chin, and we are merely preparing for how you are going to aggrieve our nerves this time."

Ophelia smiled wryly. "I do have something I want to ask,

but I…" The words were heavy and uncertain on her tongue—so very unlike her.

"Whatever is it, my dear?" her mother asked with a frown.

It was best to get on with it. "Are we in financial trouble?"

Her mother's eyes widened, and her father had turned into a marble effigy. Her mother's eyes darted to an empty space high on the wall, and it was then Ophelia noted a much beloved painting was no longer there. Her body prickled with cold. "You had to…to sell this painting, Mama?"

"This burden is not yours to bear," her father answered, holding up a palm to forestall Mama's reply. "Ophelia, you are a lady of clever and stubborn manners, but in this matter you will obey my words without question, or I shall be sorely vexed with you. I will have no compunction in ordering you to the country for the rest of the season, young lady."

"I see." Her voice sounded so terribly dry, she almost did not recognize it. "Do you wish for me to marry soon? Will this help matters?"

A smile softened her father's features. "Would you be willing to?"

Ophelia's throat burned as she recalled her promise to the other sinful wallflowers to be daring and wicked in her pursuits. Wasn't she already doing that by searching for Sally Martin as Lady Starlight? There was no need to be daring in matters of the heart, especially when she gave little thought to finding this elusive love. And despite her parents' lamentation about her rebellious ways, she had always tried to put their needs and desires above hers. "If a marriage would help our family, yes."

"I am glad to know you would do your duty should we wish it. However, it will not be necessary," her father said with a proud smile. "Your mother and I agreed a few years ago that when you marry, it will be your choice, and it must be a love match, yes?"

"Papa…"

"There are no buts," he said with steel lacing his voice. "Though I am curious as to why you believe we have money problems."

She wrinkled her nose. "I opened the bottom drawer of your desk and found all the creditors' letters."

"The drawer I closed with a key?"

"Yes, Papa."

He glanced at his wife. "Does our daughter sound contrite, my darling?"

"Not in the least," she retorted with a laugh, though to Ophelia's ears it sounded strained.

"Hmm," he murmured, stroking his chin thoughtfully. "We have indeed overindulged you. I fear it is too late for any lasting corrections, and I am entirely to blame for this lovely travesty."

Ophelia smiled, for it was a familiar refrain spoken by many aunts and cousins that the marquess's only child had been educated beyond the abilities of most gentlemen and was overly pampered. Her papa normally responded in a booming and pleased tone that it was love.

"Forgive my prying, Papa, but what about my dowry? Can it not be drawn from to settle some of the bills?"

At their silence, the truth of it sank into her bones. There was no dowry.

The situation was more dire than she imagined, and Ophelia was intimately acquainted with that stubborn flatness to her father's mouth. It was a look he grumbled that she wore as well as he did. Her father clearly believed this to be his duties and responsibilities, and he would discuss it no further.

Ophelia took a sip of the delicious brew of tea, her thoughts whirling. "There is a rumor about the *ton* that you… you have *increased* my dowry. Fanny said she overheard some whispers about it at Lady Franklin's musicale, and even a few scandal sheets speculated on my dowry, wondering which blessed fortune hunter will convince me to marry this season. I do know that this Lady O they refer to is me," Ophelia said with candor.

"A ruse, my dear," her mother said, an unfathomable emotion in her eyes. "A pretense that is unfortunately necessary until your father turns our fortune around."

Ophelia understood enough about society to know the appearance of money was just as important as having it. "Lord…the Earl of Langdon has asked me to favor him with dances and walks a lot recently," she said, putting down the teacup she had been holding before her like a shield. "I…"

"Have you fallen in love with him?" her mother interjected.

Love. "No, of course not. I barely know him."

"Young Lord Langdon has an income of thirty thousand pounds a year. You marrying him will not solve your father's financial problem. Marriage to the earl would be beneficial to you, my dear. However, while you might be provided for with a handsome carriage, a generous allowance, and many pretty dresses, a marriage without love is like spring in a barren wasteland."

After glancing fondly at her husband and smiling, the marchioness looked back at Ophelia. "Only marry a gentleman you *love*, my dear."

A raw ache expanded in Ophelia's chest. They had always put her happiness in their minds and hearts, and she appreciated and loved them dearly for it. Many ladies in society, and even a few of her friends who wanted the freedom to marry gentlemen of their choice, were unable to do so, for their families forced unsuitable matches upon them for money, connection, or sometimes power.

Her friend Maryann even now was desperately trying to escape marriage to a most unsuitable earl by casting herself to ruin and using Nicolas St. Ives—the very reprobate who had taught her how to pick locks—to do the deed. Another dear friend, Fanny, had wild plans of running away and hiding as a servant in an earl's household so as not to marry the old lecher who had actually paid Fanny's aunt an unmatched sum for her hand. He fairly bought her!

Yet Ophelia's parents would never force her to marry, a decision that seemed to grow the deeper they fell in love with each other. They were rare, lovely, fanciful creatures, and as she stared at the woman who had raised her, a profound wave of pain and regret blossomed through her. The marchioness had no notion that Ophelia knew she was stolen at birth. How could someone so lovely and kind reconcile her conscience with her husband stealing another woman's child?

The tide of familiar pain and guilt rose to choke her like thick smoke. The marchioness had given her so much love and understanding over the years, Ophelia *should* be contented. However, for the last several weeks, she had risked her reputation to locate Miss Sally Martin. Should the marchioness find out about this, it would crush her.

And what would her father say?

Concealing her distress, Ophelia rose. "I promised Kitty I

would write her a letter. I will see to it now."

"Is she not somewhere on the River Nile with her duke?"

"Yes, that is the most recent update."

Her mother smiled, for she enjoyed hearing about Kitty and how she had managed to have her most reclusive duke fall hopelessly in love with a known wallflower—not that she knew the full scandalous truth of their courtship. Ophelia swept from the drawing room and closed the door. Once outside, she could not move. Closing her eyes, she gritted her teeth and fought back the tears that burned behind her eyelids.

Her mother and father adored each other and did not care if people frowned upon how they doted on each other publicly. At her first coming out, Ophelia had shamelessly used their obvious adoration to secure a promise from Papa that she would be able to select her own husband. She'd also promised to wait for someone to love. Though for many years her parents had hoped she would marry Lord Langdon, to her surprise, they had been positively *thrilled* at the notion of her waiting to find her match.

Ophelia's eccentric interests, artistic sensibilities, and impetuous energy would not recommend her to be anyone's wife. Or so her mother groused several times over the years—even though she had done so with little gravity and more with fondness, lending support to Ophelia's wishes. But Ophelia had come to this realization herself when she had come out at eighteen. Every gentleman she had walked with showed very little interest in her peculiarities, some even scoffing whenever she spoke with animation of her great love of music, art, and literature. They did seem captivated by her beauty and dowry.

It was by choice she had remained unattached. It wasn't

that she did not want to love someone or eventually marry, but no one compelled her heart to shake or inspired her to hunger for more. Since her debut, there was only one gentleman she had ever flirted with and allowed for the possibility they might one day marry—the Earl of Langdon.

He was handsome and gallant; however, despite their long-standing acquaintanceship, Ophelia felt no romantic sentiments whatsoever toward the earl.

She would have doubted the existence of this passionate love if she did not observe it in her parents, and if her friend Kitty had not fallen hopelessly in love with the Duke of Thornton. Maryann also wore a similar look whenever she talked about Nicolas St. Ives. So this love existed. Perhaps one day Ophelia might encounter it, and then she would embrace it wholeheartedly.

If she were to marry, Ophelia would want that gentleman to be her friend, one in whom she could confide anything. Would any gentleman understand that Ophelia was a bastard even though she had been raised with the advantages of a legitimate child? Would that gentleman understand that she wanted to find the woman who birthed her to know what became of her? Would she be able to talk about this strange sense of loss and pain she felt at never knowing Sally Martin? Did she have siblings? Or other aunts and uncles? Was she a lot like Sally Martin, or were they different?

Shrugging away those haunting questions that had revealed no answers, Ophelia wondered what her next possible step was now that she had confirmed her family was truly burdened with financial difficulties. What should she do about this strange offer? Dipping into her pocket, she reached for the bank draft.

Do I dare?

That the sender hid their identity said to Ophelia it was a gift offered for a diabolical purpose.

Princess Cosima was the only confidante Ophelia could dare to ask about this. Cosima was not a member of Ophelia's intrepid sinful wallflowers coterie, but Cosima had become a dear friend to Ophelia over the last few months. Quickly searching for quill and ink, she dashed off a note and instructed the footman to deliver to a particular home in Russell Square. Ophelia then called for the carriage and her lady maid, Hattie, and made her way to Kensington Gardens.

Several minutes later, she descended the carriage with the aid of the footman, then went to the section of the garden, a private area, where she often met Cosima. A soft breeze whispered through the trees, carrying with it the scent of jasmine and roses. She sat on a stone bench and waited. It did not take long for her friend to arrive, and Ophelia grinned, truly happy to see her. Cosima wore a gown of rose-colored silk trimmed with lace and a hat with plumes of flowers slanted rakishly atop her dark red hair styled in a fashionable cut.

"Ophelia, once again you sent a cryptic and most intriguing note," Cosima said, coming over to kiss her cheek.

They sat on the bench, and Ophelia sighed gustily. "That is because I received a most cryptic gift. I am not sure if I should even call it such!"

Cobalt blue eyes widened. "I am intrigued."

Ophelia handed her the note and the bank draft. Cosima stilled, a flash of worry darkening her eyes before her lashes lowered.

"You know who sent it," Ophelia whispered. Suddenly her

heart started a wild dance beneath her breastbone.

Is it you?

Devlin Byrne—a man who lingered in the shadow of Ophelia's footsteps, yet a man she had never met. Several weeks ago, it was this phantom gentleman who had sent Princess Cosima to Ophelia's side as a favor. That had shocked and bewildered Ophelia for days, but it had never occurred to her to refuse his largess, for it was he who paved the way in the underworld, a force that protected her from all manner of undesirables as she walked freely through London's dark and seedier pathways without fear of discovery or harm. Whenever she brazenly moonlighted as Lady Starlight, it was as if she took a noonday stroll in Hyde Park.

His protection permitted Ophelia to ask discreet questions about Miss Sally Martin, a young girl who once lived in Luton, Bedfordshire—one who had danced and sang privately for many wealthy men. A woman who had eventually become the celebrated mistress of the influential and powerful Marquess of Shelton.

Some remembered her; others pretended ignorance. All were tight-lipped with information about Miss Martin. She had vanished, as if the sum of her life had been reduced to a plume of smoke that wafted away with no evidence that it had existed. Ophelia had known Mr. Byrne's protection would come at a cost, even though Cosima had denied it and called it a kindness. Ophelia had scoffed at that bit of rubbish and waited for demands to fall at her feet. But surely this could not be it *months* later? And how was giving her ten thousand pounds for a single song equitable?

"Is it…is it him, Cosima? Devlin Byrne?"

Her friend did not reply, and a tight silence fell between

them. Ophelia's thoughts raced. Since he had inserted himself into her life, she had made it her business to find out about him, paying keener attention to every mention of his name.

Devlin Byrne was a man who stood on the very edge of respectable society, with his close associations and rumored partnership with a most notorious gambling den. It was said he had fought more than one duel, developing the reputation of being a crack shot and a man who did not give second chances.

The times he had been mentioned in the newssheets had been sparse. They freely speculated on his money, for he was an exceedingly wealthy entrepreneur who had been grudgingly interviewed by *The Morning Chronicle* on the state of the financial district and the terrible economy of the poorer class.

His views on the reforms that were needed had been insightful, controversial, and profound. His arguments that there should be equal rights to education and mobility among the classes had not sat well with the lords of society. She recalled her father in one of his political meetings suggesting that this man—who clearly was not "*one of them*"—could not truly understand the reasoning and presentations from political and economic elites if he were used to the gutter.

The cheers from her father's cronies had been raucous in their approval, even though Devlin Byrne's dogged rise to wealth and influence in the society had been remarked on frequently by their very set. They had been outraged that a piece Mr. Byrne wrote had been featured in the famous *Political Register*. It had been shocking to everyone that Cobbett had allowed a guest article, but, given his many criticisms of the government, Ophelia had not thought it so odd. The viewpoints had been similar.

Her father and his cronies speculated about Mr. Byrne's family and his background, which was shrouded in much uncertainty—was he a Scotsman, an Irishman, half-British, a mongrel? His uncertain origins did him no favor amongst the *ton*. One scandal sheet had said his family and connections were unworthy of any mentions, thus making the man himself unworthy of the *ton*'s regard and admiration.

"Will you not answer me?" Ophelia asked softly, aware of the slight tremble in her voice.

Cosima sighed. "Possibly. I *cannot* say for sure. However, I do know if it is not Devlin who sent this to you…it cannot be someone from our world, or someone who knows Lady Ophelia and Lady Starlight are one and the same."

Some of the awful tension knotted in her belly loosened. "Why not?"

Cosima's eyes held hesitation, as if she were unsure of how much to share.

"Please tell me," Ophelia urged.

"No one from our world would dare approach you. Is Lady Starlight not his proclaimed woman?"

Ophelia stared at Cosima as if seeing her for the first time. Ophelia turned her words over, assessing them from all angles, and only arrived at one inescapable truth. No one would dare approach her like this in a clandestine and suspicious manner in fear of Devlin Byrne's reaction. That evening weeks ago, when the sky had been painted in hues of vermillion as the sun lowered, the snow falling on the ground to cover the villains' footsteps who approached sneakily, someone had overheard her scandalous declarations.

It had not been the first time a footpad or dubious men

had approached her. But it had been the first time she felt not even a smidgen of fear. For Ophelia knew by then she had the protection of a mysterious benefactor.

"*Do you know who I am?*" she had tossed out recklessly when a man with rotted teeth approached her, his two friends edging closely behind.

Without giving him a chance to respond, she'd curled her lips in a sneer and said, "*I am Devlin Byrne's woman. Do you dare?*"

That man had faltered, his gaze cutting from left to right in clear dismay. Then he had bowed and hurried away from her. She vaguely recalled a low, masculine laughter, and a large dog strolling behind her.

Oh God. How utterly absurd and...wonderful.

Ophelia had only been using his name and the suggestion of an intimate connection to scare away those men. She sat there, amazed and very shaken. "He is very influential in his circle. Is that it?"

Cosima met her eyes, a peculiar gravity in her regard. "Devlin Byrne is respected for his business acuity, his ruthless shrewdness, and..."

"And what?"

"He is *very* protective of you," Cosima whispered, curiosity and perhaps a touch of envy rich in her blue gaze.

Ophelia stiffened and looked down at the note.

A song from you to me.

Dear God. A fresh and dreadful thought occurred to Ophelia. What if...what if all of this...this protection he offered from the shadows, this money he submitted on a silver platter, was a carefully constructed lure to trap her?

But lure her into what?

Surely it could not just be for a single song.

Ophelia was worried, for she found him vaguely disturbing and a compelling character. She thoroughly loathed that she was also intrigued.

Who are you, and are we to finally meet?

"Are…are you not his lover, Cosima?"

Cosima's eyes widened before she laughed, the sound tinkling and lovely. "I was not aware the gossips wondered if Devlin and I were lovers. How positively crass. Can a lady and a gentleman not be mere friends? Must the waters be muddied with such idle talks?"

Ophelia flushed, for it was in her loftier circle—the one Princess Cosima was excluded from—that they whispered these rumors behind their fans. Even her dear friend Kitty had asked if the exiled princess was not Mr. Byrne's mistress. Shame burned through Ophelia, and she touched her friend's shoulder. "Forgive me for even asking something so nonsensical. I do not even know why I asked it."

Cosima grinned naughtily and waved her hand. "I am not offended because I have flirted shamelessly with him. A great waste, I am afraid. That man is like a block of wood. Nay, some wood might have more feelings. He has no idea what flirting is." She assessed Ophelia with curiosity glinting in her gaze. "Are you going to accept the money?" Cosima asked.

Ophelia hesitated. "No."

"You should."

"Surely I cannot."

"Then you have nothing to worry about. Tear up the draft and ignore everything."

Ophelia stood and lifted her face to the sky. "I believe that is what I will do."

They walked arm in arm along the garden paths, chatting and indulging in light gossip, a thing Cosima adored. Especially if it was about lords and ladies of the *ton*. Though Ophelia tried to relax and put the bank draft from her thoughts, it was as if it burned a hole in the pocket of her carriage dress, taunting and tempting her.

Her father was still in recovery. Where would he get the money from to start repairing the estates? This money would only help so far, but even the servants of their townhouse had not been paid a wage in months! And they had families of their own but remained steadfastly loyal to the marquess.

Oh, what should I really do?

CHAPTER THREE

The very day the bank draft was handed over to Mr. Hunt, her father's steward, with careful instructions on the bills to settle, a note arrived at Berkeley Square, addressed to Ophelia. She stared at it as if it held a small viper that would spring out and sink its fangs into her skin as soon as she opened the letter. The envelope held the same insignia on the seal as the one that had held the bank draft.

It was from the same man.

The power it suggested shook her. This man had known exactly when the steward of their household made use of the money. Ophelia had held on to that bank draft for a little over two weeks, staring at it almost nightly yet denying its existence in the day. She had overheard the housekeeper meeting with the butler, speaking about how best to reduce the staff while maintaining the appearance and dignity of the marquess and his marchioness.

Not while she managed the household, Ophelia had determined, informing Mrs. Barrett no one was to be fired, but all unpaid wages overdue for almost a year would be settled.

Flipping open the note, she sucked in a wondering breath.

A carriage will arrive for you at 7 p.m. Wear the dress and the wig. You will be taken to the Asylum.

There was no return address—no room for protest or negotiation.

The Asylum. This man was outrageous. That gambling den was one of great notoriety. Ophelia was being sucked into a world of intrigue, and every instinct within her warned her to flee. The ordinary and the mundane were safer.

Boring most assuredly, but *safer*.

A shaky laugh escaped her, and how Ophelia hated the thrill that went through her heart. That decided thrill spoke to the edge of impropriety and indecency she had been living in for the past few months. It spoke to the part of her that no longer found satisfaction with the life she endured. And that was what she did daily: endured disappointment, frustration, and anxiety, often mired in dark, confusing feelings she did not like or understand.

Ophelia longed to go back to the girl who laughed, danced, and sang with gaiety. The girl who loved the seasons in town and found them to be jolly fun, even as she danced and walked in the park with a few gentlemen, knowing she had no plans to marry unless she fell in love. Fanny and Maryann noted the strain, for they delicately probed. How she wished she had confided in her wallflower friends; they were remarkably close and shared many secrets and triumphs. A hot lump rose in her throat, along with burning shame. To admit to anyone of her bastardy, and the lack of honor in her father, felt unbearable.

She tentatively opened the large box that had arrived with the note. *Oh!* A dark golden blond wig of exquisite quality and a gold filigree mask laid inside. The wig was similar to the one she wore the few times she acted as Lady Starlight. Inside the other box was an icy-blue gown made of the finest quality, together with dainty silver dancing slippers.

Every instinct warned her the author of the notes was Devlin Byrne. Oddly, Ophelia found comfort in that belief. This was not a man who wanted to harm her. Surely he would have done so a long time ago if he had ill intentions. Perhaps singing the one song would be worth it.

"Can I really do this?" she whispered in the emptiness of her bedchamber.

Being alone with this man for the timespan of a song. Five minutes was worth the benefit to her family. Though many things could happen in five minutes. *Such as ravishment.*

Her parents would possibly collapse if they ever learned the shenanigans Ophelia had been up to. With a pang, she acknowledged how much she had changed since learning about Sally Martin. With a groan, she dropped her forehead onto the box. If not for her cousin Robert, her father's heir, being sent home from Eton, she might not have had the temerity to summon the steward and hand over the bank draft.

Ophelia had checked the books secretly, waiting to see what her father did to turn around their fortunes. The only things that seemed to have happened were more bills getting added to the drawers, and some of her mother's precious items disappearing. Such as a diamond necklace gifted to her by a Russian princess and a painting by Rembrandt. The sums fetched for those items still had not been able to dent their financial problems.

Even more infuriating, she did not see where the monies had been applied to servant wages and creditors more important than the milliner and her modiste. Her father was even now contracting a small gazebo with a stone fountain of Neptune at the back of their townhouse so he could sit and admire the birds on sunny days with his marchioness. Worse, her father still shut her out of those meetings with his steward and lawyers, only imparting what he believed necessary for her management of the household.

How could Ophelia refuse so much money when her family had need for it? And what about the repayment? Could one really place dignity and pride before her family's comfort and her father's heir's future expectations?

"Just a song," she whispered. "Then why is it so scary?"

If this mysterious man was Devlin Byrne, he did not own a reputation of being licentious. He was dangerous but not dissolute. He was a known lover of the arts, extravagantly supporting amateur but extraordinarily talented painters, musicians, and novelists. Perhaps he wanted a singer to add to his coterie.

"Please let this man be Devlin Byrne," she muttered.

The ridiculous irony did not escape her.

Shrugging aside the doubts and fears, Ophelia soaked in her bath for a long time, then, with the help of her lady's maid's discretion, dressed in the gown, which contoured to her body quite flatteringly. All her curves seemed more pronounced, her décolletage on lush display. Her black tresses were pinned in a coronet and the blond wig fitted to her head. It was styled in a chignon, with several curls kissing her cheeks and shoulders. Staring at herself in the cheval mirror in her chamber, Ophelia thought she have never looked more… sensual.

Nerves plucked at her heart, and, taking a deep breath, she allowed her maid to help her slip on the gold filigree half mask and a dark blue pelisse. Tugging the hood of the pelisse over her head, she walked down the stairs, confident she would not encounter her mother or father. Since her father's ailment, they retired to their chamber at the same time each night, no doubt savoring the time they had left with each other.

Stepping out into the cold night, she noted the large conveyance awaiting her. Footmen in no discernable livery knocked down the steps, and Ophelia ascended the carriage. Inside was elegant, well-lit, and comfortable. The carriage rattled off, and with each clack of the wheels against the cobbled stone, the knot in her belly drew tighter and tighter.

"This will be no different than singing in one of those opera halls or taverns," she whispered, clasping her gloveless hands together. "One song. That is all." Leaning her head back against the squabs, she recited the song in her head over and over, and the manner in which she would sing it.

Sooner than she anticipated, the carriage stopped, and she leaned forward to part the curtains. They were on St. James's Street. That she had not expected. The carriage steps were knocked down, and Ophelia released the curtain. Reaching up, she touched her face to ensure the mask was securely fitted. Then patted her wig. No one would recognize her as Lady Ophelia.

Taking a quick, steadying breath, she descended the carriage, surprised to see an elegantly dressed lady in a mask approaching her.

The lady paused close to her. "Lady Starlight?"

Ophelia almost laughed. She swallowed down the sound that would surely have a hysterical edge and nodded confidently.

"This way, please," the lady with the blue-and-green mask said with a smile.

She led her to a large oak door that opened as if an invisible force had commanded it. Ophelia stepped into sin and decadent luxury. She handed her coat to the majordomo, glancing around as she walked farther inside. The decor was one of elegance and luxury. Blue-and-silver carpets covered the floor of the long hallway, and swaths of silver-and-golden drapes twined themselves around massive white Corinthian columns. The dim, firelit interior of the club made it impossible to identify anyone, though several ladies wore glittering masks. Sounds of laughter and music filtered on the air, and as Ophelia walked behind the lady, an unexpected bite of anticipation coursed through her veins.

I am in a gambling hell.

This news would have to be shared with her friends first thing tomorrow. How shocked and delighted they would all be. Especially Charlotte and Fanny. Another large set of double doors opened, and they stepped into an enormous room, at least the size of two ballrooms merged into one. The glitter of the chandeliers seemingly lit by a thousand candles, the dazzling array of lavishly and beautifully dressed ladies, the self-indulgence and excess, and the raucous sounds of laughter assailed Ophelia's senses.

In this room, dozens of tables were scattered in an organized sprawl, and many gentlemen recognizable to Ophelia sat at tables playing faro, Macao, whist, and vingt-et-un.

"This way," the lady said, leaning closer to be heard over the facile laughter and chatter.

Ophelia followed her through the crowd, aware of the many eyes upon her body. Staring straight ahead, she almost missed an opened door, the gateway to a ballroom. Several couples danced the waltz, but much more scandalously, as their partners clung so close it bordered on indecency. She was riveted. Her heart jolted upon seeing Nicolas St. Ives, Marquess Rothbury amongst the dancers; however, Ophelia faltered when she noted his partner.

Dear God, Maryann!

Others might mistake her, but Ophelia knew her friend, and how many ladies about the *ton* would wear their spectacles perched atop their masks? An ache formed in her throat when she observed the way that rogue held Maryann to his body. It *was* indecent…but there was something very tender and possessive in his stare.

Please be careful, Maryann.

Looking away, Ophelia continued onward, down a long, silent hallway. A few weeks ago, she and her friends had met at Maryann's home for one of their usual gatherings. Something had been different that night, and it was Maryann who had stood and dared everyone to be wicked in their pursuits, reaching for the dreams in their heart. Ophelia had been unable to say she was already being daring in her search for her mother, but something inside her had awakened at those words, and she too had felt the awful emptiness that had lingered in her friends. Surely the sums of their lives were not balls, more balls, perhaps a few picnics, and then marriage and children if they were fortunate enough. Something seemed amiss, and that aching void in her heart and soul yawned even wider.

"We are here," the lady said, opening a door.

Ophelia swallowed, pushing aside all nerves, and stepped inside. The room was empty. The door closed behind her with a soft thud. There was a stage, raised on a dais, and it was lit with several candles and a lone chandelier. She walked over to it, quite aware of the largeness of the room and that no one was about. She had assumed there would be an audience. Halfway to the stage, she faltered, awareness rippling down her spine. There was someone else in the room with her.

There…near the stage but in the shadows. A large animal was sprawled at their feet. A dog or a wolf. Half in the light and the next half in the shadows.

A song from you to me.

So an audience of one, then.

Butterflies erupted in her belly, and her heart jerked so fast Ophelia feared fainting. She would never forgive herself if she did something so silly and miss-ish.

What the devil is the matter with me?

Ophelia continued to the stage, going up five steps before she turned around, her gaze searching for him. He was barely discernable, sitting in the center of the room in a large armchair. He was indolently reposed, a cheroot in his mouth—she could see the red spark at the tip with each drag. One of his hands rested casually on his knee, and in that hand was a glass, with perhaps whisky.

Ophelia stared at him, quite aware that he must be staring at her, too. She almost did not know where to begin. Should she ask for an introduction? Should she rush from the stage and go to him to demand to be told what was happening?

A song from you to me.

Ophelia swallowed. Just a song, and then she would leave. Immediately.

She almost chose one of the songs she had performed previously at the opera house and the tavern as Lady Starlight. Something either operatic or lively and upbeat in the manner of folk songs. Something simple and without tension…without feelings.

Yet as she stepped closer, it was the song she had written last night as she lingered in the shadows of her doubts about everything that came pouring out. As a soprano singer, she had often been praised for her powerfully dramatic renditions. Ophelia stared at the man in the dark and sang in a manner unique only to her—slow, sultry, powerful, and sensual.

Waking up in shadows, a tempest trembles in my heart
Listening for your voice in the rain and the wind streaming
No answer I hear, and how long the night can be apart
I fear to reach for you, but you come as I am dreaming
Seeking to touch your face, but you vanish in the dark night
The world is a storm, so I'll follow you through the cold
Then you're standing before me under the silent moonlight
Trembling with fear, shall I rush to you? Can I be so bold?
Like frost drifting endlessly as I float in wind's power
Do not leave me, my darling, everything will be right
Dreaming as the moon shines down on the night-blooming flowers
Together in dreaming the gentle winds succor our flight.

Tipping her head to the ceiling, she sang the other two verses, dimly aware of the wetness against her lashes. The song died from her lips, and her hands dropped to her sides to hang limply. Terrifying sensations crashed against Ophelia's senses when the figure stood, the shadows around him dancing and twisting. He said nothing, but the large beast by his side also rose, and they prowled together toward her.

Ophelia's heart jolted, for she was distressingly aware they were alone in this room. Another step, and the light from the candles caressed his features. Almost lovingly. Something warned her nothing with this man would be harmless—even her very virtue might be in danger. Simply because of the raw pulse of want that burst inside her body when he stepped fully into the light.

He had high-sculpted cheekbones, a strong patrician nose, and a full, sensual mouth. His black hair needed trimming, the strands of it curling around his cravat. Something tumbled inside of her, the feeling so fleeting it vanished before she could allow herself to assess the sensation.

There was an air of keen alertness about him and a sense of recognition deep inside her.

But Ophelia was certain she had never met this gentleman in her entire life.

It would be impossible to forget such a man.

They stared at each other, and to her mind, it was as if he waited on her. *To do what?* She felt a sharp thump of panic, and that annoyed her greatly. She was not the nervous sort, not given to fits of vapors or rattled nerves. That was why she could be here, in this club, singing for this stranger.

"Who are you?" she finally whispered, unable to bear the silence any longer, stepping down from the dais.

Instead of answering, he took another step toward her. There was an indefinable air of self-assurance about him quite uncommon to a man of his class. Ophelia did not jerk or betray any sort of anxiousness that the hem of her dress brushed his polished shoes. A rigid, breathless silence filled the space between them. No man of refined sensibilities would presume to stand so close to a lady. Or stare so boldly at her. And she was quite determined to appear unflappable.

His gaze lowered to her fingers, and she fought not to curl

them. That had been one of his odd requests: that she wore no gloves.

"You hid your talent well. The few times you sang as Lady Starlight, you were singing subpar. Why?" he asked on the harsh note of some emotion she couldn't identify. "Do you sing now for a lost lover? Or because you hunger for one?"

Ophelia recoiled, shocked. But perhaps she should not be. The words of her song had been unspeakably scandalous, and she had poured the pent-up emotions that churned her up daily in her words. If she had sung so at a musicale, polite society would have thought her ruined. She had to make a conscious effort not to bite her lip. "It was but a song."

His eyes—a dark yet vivid green, burning beautiful, stunning in a face of flawless masculinity—rested on her face and stayed there. "A gloriously beautiful one."

The reverence in his tone warmed her. Careful to only show an expression of civil politeness, she said, "I daresay you should feel as if you attained ten thousand pounds' worth and shall dare make no more demands on my time."

His eyes kissed over her skin like a sharpened blade. Ophelia was actually afraid to ask his identity once again.

"I never heard a voice as pure…or as sultry and sensual as yours. You have a gift."

"Thank you." For she could think of nothing else to say.

"Did you write this song?"

"Yes."

Another stretch of silence passed, barely endurable. Ophelia felt uncertain. Should she leave? Surely, they could not just stand here, staring at each other. Confused laughter tickled deep in her throat, and she bit the inside of her lower lip. It was important to remain unruffled at all times.

My very life…virtue…and all my sensibilities might depend on it.

Quite dramatic and overwrought, but she would allow for the slip, given the highly unusual nature of this situation. What even was the situation?

He shifted slightly, patting his dog's head. "When?" he finally asked.

When had she written the song? "Does it matter?"

"Yes."

She lifted her eyes to his face in a questioning look. "I…I wrote it last night."

"Where were you?"

A startled smile bloomed on her mouth, and he stepped back as if shoved. The dog growled low in his throat, and her heart started that dratted thumping once more.

"In my chamber," she admitted softly.

"Were you sitting before a desk, or were you in your bed?"

He was the oddest creature, and it baffled her that she indulged him with a reply. "In my bed."

Another shift, this time casting his expression in the shadows from the mounted lamps. "In the dark…under the covers, or were you sitting on the coverlets, quill and paper resting on a pillow?"

"I crafted it in the dark…in my thoughts…until I memorized each line."

"Ah, so these are words that speak to the very heart of you."

A feeling she had never endured before erupted inside her chest. "I supposed they do."

"I am captivated. Why did you write this song for me?"

Ophelia tilted her head to one side and gave him a shrewd glance. "For you?"

His hard, brilliant, and beautiful emerald eyes gleamed. "Yes."

"Your audacity leaves me breathless."

"It does not negate the truth that you wrote this song for me."

She choked back a laugh, but still some of it trembled on her lips and filled the air. "I daresay songs of flowers and pretty milkmaids would have bored you silly and perhaps made you feel cheated. I simply wanted to create words that might appeal to a man of your rumored jaded senses. Nothing more."

"Consider me now titillated."

"Who are you?" burst from her before she censored her thoughts.

A chiding expression settled on his face. "I presumed you knew, given you are familiar with my tastes."

Ophelia did not like the intimate way he lingered over those words; it felt perplexingly obscene. This man before her wanted more than a song. The awareness settled over her like a dangerous, smothering blanket. "It is ungentlemanly to ignore my question."

"Forgive my lack of manners—Devlin Byrne at your service." These words were accompanied by an exaggerated but very graceful bow.

The piercing tension in her stomach eased, and a soft breath shuddered from her body.

A barely-there smile touched his mouth. "I have never seen anyone relieved upon hearing my name before, particularly not a lady of quality. Dread…doubt…fear: those I am intimately acquainted with. I believe I am doubly titillated. A new state for me, if you are wondering."

He must be one of those rich, eccentric fellows people sometimes whispered about with a sense of awe and fright. For they were unpredictable, and anything the *ton* found unpredictable *was* unquestionably dangerous—and a little bit captivating. "I am merely relieved I am not dealing with another bounder. One is enough."

"You are safe with me, always."

That odd promise did even odder things to her heart, and she brushed aside the warm feeling with an irritated snort. "One may smile, and smile, and be a villain," she drawled mockingly.

From the dark humor that lit in his eyes, Ophelia saw that he was familiar with Hamlet and all of his musings on treachery and villainy.

"You do think me naive—a simpleton, perhaps—to believe in such a promise from a man of your ilk, a man I do not know."

"I think you are an iridescent flame unlike any I have ever seen, one I cannot help coveting."

Oh God! Holding on tight to her composure, she made a chiding, *tsk*ing sound. "We are ever striving after what is forbidden…"

A very faint smile curled one side of his mouth. "…and coveting what is denied to us," he said, ending her quote from Ovid. "Ah… so our story will be a forbidden lovers' tale, then."

Forbidden lovers? Those words drifted over her skin like fire, unsettling her composure entirely. It was her turn to take one…two…three steps away from him.

Forbidden lovers?

His gaze skipped over her body, lingering in places a man of respectable conduct had no right looking. Every dip, every hollow, and every curve felt the caress of his eyes as he probed. Ophelia was most aware the gown he had sent clung enticingly to her curves and revealed the swell of her cleavage. Hating that her heart quickened, she said, "You are no gentleman to so blatantly…" Her lips closed over the words.

"To so blatantly admire your sensual beauty?"

"I came because I was most handsomely rewarded for a song. No other reason," she murmured huskily, feeling disposed of her usual calm and rational thinking.

Something in the air felt perilous. That strange feeling caressed her skin like the sharpened edge of a blade.

"I will leave now, Mr. Byrne," Ophelia said, taking a few more careful steps away from him.

"Will you?"

That drawl hooked low in her belly and pulled, shaking her laboriously acquired air of indifferent civility. Worse, she could not dismiss the impression that this man was amused by the entire affair.

"Yes. I *must* leave." Because there was something frightful inside her that actually wanted to stay. To ask all the questions that had plagued her these last few weeks as she pondered his identity and bank draft.

Ophelia whirled around and hurried away, aware that the only noise echoing in the room was the *clip-clop* of her heels on the floor. Her hands on the latch, she stopped, twisted her head, and looked around. He was barely visible from her current position, but she was certain he had not moved. Mr. Byrne merely watched her with a hand resting on his dog's head.

Her breathing had become agitated. She felt herself slipping, sliding into his net. Turning around, she walked back to him, stopping at a careful distance.

"I have been able to visit so many places unmolested because of your protection. For five months, I lay in the darkness of my room and wondered about you; it had become a torment. *Why* have you been helping me? How did you know I...my family needed money and that I would be tempted to act with recklessness and visit you here? Why would you only demand a song for such a fortune?"

He stared at her, seemingly unmoved by her outburst. There was a hint of something hard...almost sensually cruel about his handsome visage. That impression she could not dismiss, and the longer Ophelia stared at Devlin Byrne, the more her heart trembled.

Another familiar chord struck inside her, and once again the pit of her belly felt warm. Her reaction was most astonishing. If she possessed any wisp of rationality, she would turn around and rush from the room, forgetting she had ever been here. And she did just that. Turned around, hurrying at such a pace it was almost as if she ran. Another day, another time, should they meet again, she would ask those questions. Right now, every instinct inside her warned her to flee.

"Fifi."

She was instantly riveted. Such a small word to make her breath stop.

Her feet faltered, and her entire body shuddered as she felt her heartbeat stutter. Again and again. Ophelia slowly turned. "What...what did you call me?"

Surely she misheard.

He walked toward her, stopping at a respectable distance. "I did all those things because you are Fifi."

The years fell away, and for a brief moment, so fleeting she might have imagined it, she saw them sitting on a log, staring at the beauty of a midnight sky. "*Niall?*"

His head dipped in a brief nod of acknowledgment.

"So you are not Devlin Byrne?" she mumbled foolishly.

"A man reinvented cannot keep the same name."

She wouldn't have known what to reply to that even if she could. Speechless, she stared at him. Was he really the boy she had spent those several days with in the woodlands that had appeared enchanted? The memory had stayed with her for a long time, but she had forgotten him as life drifted along the path set for her at an alarmingly fast pace. She had not thought about him in years…and here he was before her, seemingly having never forgotten about her.

The feelings that tumbled through her were too strange and complex to name or even understand.

I did all those things because you are Fifi.

"I do…I do not know how to repay you," she whispered, searching his expression.

"I paid to listen to the pleasure of your wonderful art. I am not owed."

Her heart gave an appalling leap. Why had he chosen to approach her now, when he had known of her existence for months? The question hovered on her tongue, but she did not voice it, wary of the answer.

"I missed you," she said, shocking herself—and clearly him. "For days…weeks…months…I missed you."

Then I was forced to forget you.

Those enigmatic eyes touched her face, and while he did not return her sentiments, he paused, one side of his mouth kicking up. That small smile changed his expression from chilling insouciance to exquisitely charming.

"Fifi, I would like you to meet Conan. Conan, say hello to Fifi."

To her astonishment, the massive dog sat on his haunches and lifted his front paw.

Ophelia took it, amazed that his paws were almost the size of her hand. "A pleasure to meet you, Conan."

The dog purred low in his throat.

"He feels the same way."

Ophelia smiled, unsure what to do with the sudden warm feeling rushing through her. Devlin Byrne was Niall.

"We meet again, Fifi."

"We meet again, Nia...Devlin. I am astonished I am here with you. What are the odds that we would find each other? I thought I would never see you in this lifetime."

"Fantastical odds, I'm sure," he said with a dry bite. "But here we are."

There was something a bit chilly in the gaze that skipped over her body once more.

"Are you trying to be discreet?" she asked archly.

"No."

"Just rude?"

He smiled, and Ophelia almost forgot how to breathe.

"You are *terribly* handsome. Unsettlingly so. And so *tall* now," she said with an almost nervous laugh. If not for the eyes, she would not think Devlin Byrne and her Niall the same person.

Devlin looked so befuddled, she couldn't help smiling.

"No one has ever told you that before?"

"I believe you are the first lady to compliment my appearance."

Unexpectedly, her heart squeezed. "I think I like that."

"Do you?"

"Yes. Perhaps I shall be your first in many things."

In the silence, the words seemed to echo. Ophelia had no blasted idea what she meant; the repartee had just fallen from her tongue. However, his gaze sharpened, and something cunning yet carnal moved in the depths of those eyes. When he smiled, she felt undeniably provoked.

She sniffed. "I suppose there is a naughty innuendo your mind is turning around?"

Humor lit in his eyes. "You are not at all like other girls, are you?"

"Of course I am. We all have a bit of madness in our hearts; we've just learned to hide it. I admit I might sparkle a little brighter because, according to my father, I have been overindulged." *Or perhaps it is that bit of Sally Martin hidden inside of me.* Her breath caught at the errant thought.

He stared as if he did not know what to make of her.

"We are in accord," she said in a voice of careful nonchalance.

He veiled his eyes briefly with his long, dark lashes. "About what, I wonder?"

"I do not know what to make of you, either. You are an exceedingly rare creature I am not sure if I should run away from."

The words seemed to surprise another barely-there smile from him. Ophelia did not trust that smile. The quickening of her breath and heart also suggested something very remarkable. This absurd conversation made her feel alive and inexplicably more aware of herself in a way she had not been in months…years.

Devlin was so still…and watchful. "I brought you a gift,"

he finally said.

She stared at him, dumbfounded. "A gift?"

"Yes."

"Whyever would you do that?"

"I knew we were going to meet eventually, and soon."

"You were so sure I would take the money?" she asked.

"No. I had another, far more reliable plan."

"Which was?"

"It is better not to say." His tone was laced with cynical amusement.

She stared bemusedly at him, nefarious ideas swirling in her mind. What other means could he have used to persuade her to visit him in this place of notoriety and sin? "Did it involve kidnapping?"

"More like gentle persuasion. There is a remarkable distinction there."

A delicate shiver went through Ophelia. "Do you find this conversation at all odd?"

"No."

She was flummoxed at the surety of that reply. Perhaps he had peculiar discourse in this vein daily. "What is the gift?"

"A goat from Ireland. A wee one, really, only about a month old."

She looked up at him warily. "A *goat*?"

A small frown flickered on his face before his expression was quickly rendered inscrutable. "Is this an inappropriate gift for a lady of your station?"

"More baffling, and I believe that would be to *any* lady."

"What is wrong with a baby goat? It is alarmingly...fluffy and...fantastical."

Ophelia started to laugh, vaguely recalling a conversation

they had years ago, when she said if she should own any pet, it would be a goat. Nay, it *had* to be a goat, or she would be forever forlorn. How dramatic she had been as a child. The sense of absurdity evaporated, and a curious sensation wrapped its arms around her body. The powerful, enigmatic man standing before her really *was* Niall. And from the glint in his eyes, he knew he was being outrageous. Did he really have a baby goat, or did he jest?

"This gift was meant to be a bridge of sorts," he murmured.

A part of her understood it. So many years and distance separated them, but this "gift" would have been a reminder of their connection, of their past shared laughter and wishes. How profound and special their brief friendship had felt. An ache crowded her throat as she stared at him.

What did it mean that they were reconnected? Simplistically put, they were gossamer silk and rough sacking. Hades and Persephone. From different worlds with different interests and different futures. What did they have in common but a past that was almost forgotten?

"I missed you as well, Fifi. From the moment that door closed."

It struck her then that, despite the hint of danger that practically glowed around him, he was candid about his feelings, unashamed to express them to her.

Who are you now, Niall, and why do I want to know?

Unexpectedly, the night did not feel so scary anymore. He did not feel so dangerous anymore.

And perhaps I am being sillier than I have ever been in my life.

CHAPTER FOUR

The rough clearing of a throat brought Devlin out of his reveries and out of the past he felt stuck in since he had delivered Ophelia home. The carriage ride to her father's home had been filled with hesitant and curious silence. Neither of them had broken it, and she had simply sat beside him, stroking Conan's fur with the delicate tips of her fingers. Even when she had exited the carriage, she had not turned around, and once more the door had closed on a silent wonder.

The emotions that had been awakened were real and tangible. His life before tonight had been nothing but feeling hollow, as if his existence was already exhausted with nothing new to inspire wonder.

Then her.

Before tonight, he'd had enough of loss and useless hope. Over the years, all that nonsense had been replaced with ruthless pragmatism. There was no disappointment in emptiness; yet, with just a smile, he felt a small drop into that well, and it resounded deep within him. This was a weakness that he would have to carefully guard against.

A violent feeling leaped through him. What kind of man was he to be so weak over one damn woman? Devlin abhorred weakness, and it was something he had excised from his life years past when he had reshaped himself into the man he was today.

Devlin gritted his teeth until they ached.

"Whose death are you plotting?" Rhys Tremayne, Viscount Montrose, the man everyone in their world called The Broker, drawled.

Devlin's mouth tugged, but he buried the smile. "No one. I was merely thinking."

"About Fifi?"

He considered his friend with an arched brow. "Riordan told you."

"Some. He was very succinct. I believe he was leaving it up to you to decide what to divulge."

With clipped brevity, Devlin filled him in.

"Are you certain Lady Ophelia and your Fifi are one and the same? Fifteen years have passed."

"I have been certain for weeks."

Rhys intently studied their chess game for several moments. "I had always wondered why you were so protective of Lady Starlight. You rediscovered her ages ago. Why the hell are you just now making your move?"

Devlin smiled and moved a piece across the chess board. "Everything takes calculation."

"Not love."

He froze. "Have a care with your words."

"Why?"

"I do not love her." *Not anymore.* "That was a young, ignorant boy's foolish idea."

It annoyed him to recall the boy he had once been, idealistic, full of unrealistic dreams. He had been a fool who thought he was in love when he had barely understood the concept. Fifi was not the only woman in the damn world. When he had relinquished the idea of her, he had told himself that he had simply built up a fantasy around it…her…them, and he could dismantle the entire ridiculous affair by cutting her from his heart...from his hungry, tormenting dreams.

Keeping his expression inscrutable was no easy feat.

"Then what are you, if not in love?"

"You are overthinking the matter," he said with a derisive scoff.

Rhys dealt him a skeptical glance that said he saw the truth Devlin hid.

"I still recall that every backbreaking labor you did at the docks, you said it was all for *Fifi*," Rhys said in a tone rich with mockery and amusement. "You were a lad obsessed."

"Love and obsession—fruits from the same poisoned tree," Devlin drawled caustically.

"They are different, my friend. Very different."

Devlin said nothing, his efforts fiercely concentrated on the game. Or better, recalling every moment of the reunion he'd just had with Fifi. One thing had become inescapable to Devlin: she had not thought deeply of him once or the promise they made to each other after the door closed on his plea to wait for him.

While he...everything he had made himself to be, had been to make himself worthy of the lovely black-haired girl who had stolen his heart.

Who would I be if I had not met you, Fifi?

A farmer...a carpenter...a dockside worker. Not the young fool whom he had tossed in the fires and reshaped with brutal clarity of purpose. To be good enough for a girl his mother told him was the figment of his delirium. A dream to find succor in because of his poverty. A dream of pointless hope even if she were real.

"I am certain I spoke of providing for my family. My sisters and parents," Devlin said drily.

"It was always…and I mean *always* Fifi first. You were thin and weak, yet you pushed yourself with a single-minded determination that damn well scared me at the time. And now it means nothing?"

Impatient, he passed a hand over his face. Why was he allowing Rhys's words to rattle him so?

"Was it not errant idiocy?" he demanded harshly, lifting the bottle of whisky directly to his mouth. "I was nothing but a foolish boy who spoke of foolish hopes." He took a burning swallow before handing the bottle to Rhys, who also took a swig.

"I do not think it wise to dismiss hope so foolishly. Meeting her gave your life a different meaning. And that made you the man you are today."

Devlin grunted, for a moment lost in the memory of those early days, working any and all jobs, saving for something grander. An opportunity. In the lives of those who were poor, there was nothing grander than a chance for something else. His chance had been Rhys, who gave him the job of a secret collector, pulling him from the drudgery of being in a gang.

Rhys leaned over, scrutinizing the chess board. "I know you, Devlin. I can see the gears in your mind turning. Admit what you are plotting."

He allowed himself a slight smile. When he had joined their gang at the age of twelve, he had been the youngest and the wettest behind the ears. Rhys Tremayne had been like an older brother, one who had been able to see through a lot of careful walls Devlin constructed around himself.

"She was here tonight…and she sang for me," Devlin admitted, as if that explained everything.

"Ah. Riordan told me you had some very specific request about a particular room. He had to direct men to set a stage, decorate it in swaths of green and cream, and even set the lighting to illuminate only the stage. I spent a few minutes telling him you were not a madman."

A fleeting smile touched Devlin's mouth.

"Was it worth meeting her like that?"

"Have you ever heard her sing?"

"Once. If I did not love my duchess with my entire heart, I would have stolen her at that moment."

Devlin grunted but could offer no rebuttal. Her voice was dreamlike.

His friend hesitated slightly. "Your Lady Starlight is the daughter of a powerful marquess. That cannot be taken lightly."

"I seem to recall that you brought a duchess here more than once."

Rhys grunted and made no comment on the lady who was now his cherished wife. Rhys made a move, and Devlin contemplated sacrificing his knight.

"I do not want to see you tangle with the marquess and get hurt. My advice is to walk away from her."

Blasted hell. Months ago—five, to be precise—he had made a promise to keep his distance, for there was no future with her. She was forbidden to him, a sweet apple perched on a branch he would never be able to reach. Then he had heard one little rumor, and that vow had faltered.

He had faltered.

As a man who prided himself on self-control and discipline, the ease with which he had abandoned that promise to walk away from her had shaken him to his core. Then when she sang for him—those old dreams, those gnawing, unrelenting cravings, had once more erupted inside and reawakened a foolish wish. Pure unguarded joy had also leaped in Fifi's gaze when she recognized him as Niall. "I cannot let her go."

"Devlin—" Rhys began in a warning tone.

"Even in my dreams," Devlin clipped, interrupting a warning that was useless, for he would not heed it. "Fifi visits me there nightly, in such bright images. All of that time in the cottage, I remember now so clearly. You asked me why I took months to approach her. At first I was content to simply extend my protection to a girl I knew briefly."

"A girl you wanted with everything inside of you," Rhys pointed out.

"I know it," Devlin murmured, his fingers tightening over a bishop. "I wanted to protect her from the vagabonds on the streets, and also from penury. Seeing her again reminded me of the old dreams, but I am a damn sight older and wiser than that foolish lad. How could I still want to marry her? Protecting her without revealing myself was enough. Then…"

At his long silence, Rhys frowned. "Then?"

"Then a few weeks ago, Princess Cosima mentioned that it is on the tongue of everyone that Fifi might marry soon…to an earl, one Lord Langdon."

"Hell," Rhys said, leaning back in his armchair.

"Everything I thought I had let go…" He scrubbed a hand over his face and released a wry chuckle.

Being this close to her, speaking with Fifi, revealed she still possessed a part of him—that piece which had believed in the whimsical nature of love. Devlin loathed to admit it, but she still fucking owned it when he thought all sentimentality had been eradicated from himself. If not, how would his heart still beat harder at the mere sight of her?

Should he not be in control of his body, if it was in his possession?

How could his heart thunder, make his body feel weak when the corners of her eyes crinkled in a smile? How could she make sweat bead on his brows when she tipped her head and laughed?

"Devlin—" Rhys began.

He slashed a hand in the air, cutting off his friend. "I have fought for everything I have ever wanted. I am a *fighter*. Should I let her go without trying? That is the damn question that has been on my mind. I know the odds are stacked against me; I know I will never be able to force society's acceptance. But it is Fifi's acceptance I want. How can I walk away without trying? Failure or success, I will damn well try first. That way I shall live without regrets."

And I will not falter.

Rhys contemplated for long moments, and Devlin did not rush to fill the silence.

It had been thoughts of marrying Fifi that had driven Devlin to reshape himself, and he had worked brutally hard to do so, all with the dream of becoming worthy of her. He couldn't pinpoint exactly when he had given up hopes of ever finding her—when exactly he had realized they came from different worlds and even if he found her, he would never be seen as deserving of a marquess's daughter.

He *had* let the idea of her go.

Until he learned he might lose her forever.

It had damn well gutted Devlin. The notion another might soon be kissing and loving Fifi. Another man might be responsible for her laughter and joy. Another man might give her children. It would be another man's duty and care to protect her.

Devlin had felt like someone had punched a hole inside his chest and ripped out his fucking heart. A long-interred hunger had risen to the surface and tormented him for the night. Devlin had not slept, and when his mirror had reflected back to him the ravaged face of a man in doubt, he'd acknowledged that old dream was finally now within his grasp.

How could he walk away without trying?

He had weighed the risks and probabilities and deduced his chances of success were slim to none. However, such low yield had never stopped him before. Devlin had learned to be persistent and tenacious, always willing to fight for what he wanted. Sometimes it was not the outcome that made the man, but the journey. And he was willing to walk this journey and invite Fifi along. Thus he had scrawled the words, *A song from you to me*, and set everything in motion.

"I am only accepted in the upper circles and in my duchess's life because I managed to wrangle a title from the powers that be. I gave up many secrets for it. *Many*. Worth millions on the black market. What do you have as leverage for her father to accept you?"

"Nothing," Devlin said icily, recalling the man's promise years ago about the type of man his daughter would marry.

He was not a person of refined breeding, nor was he educated to the standards of most gentlemen. He had not attended Cambridge or Oxford like gentlemen of quality. He had never traveled beyond England and Ireland. Many gentlemen often spoke of their grand tours across the continents, their treks to Egypt and Prague, their dashing swaths cut across Rome and Italy with their ribald tales of singers and actresses. He had not learned to make small talk seem charming and of importance.

Devlin's edges were rough and would forever remain unpolished. The fires that had forged him were not the ones that cared about gentlemanly mannerisms. In the company of her friends and family, Devlin would always be found lacking.

"You have not told me why it was imperative we meet tonight. Is it wooing tips you're after?" Rhys asked, tacitly changing the topic.

"I want everything you know on a Miss Sally Martin."

Rhys stilled, a frown marring his handsome countenance. "As an investor…hell, part owner in our venture, all the secrets and information we collect are yours."

"Sally Martin is not in the books. I have been asking discreet questions about her, and I have gotten nowhere."

"Who is she?"

"I do not know. However, she is important to Lady Ophelia. It is the reason she risks her reputation and safety."

Rhys nodded. "I will set my team on it."

"D-do you have any?" Devlin asked.

Rhys arched a brow. "What?"

Devlin cleared his throat. "Wooing…courting tips."

Rhys grinned, and Devlin scowled. Grabbing up a few of the chess pieces, he tossed them at a now-chuckling Rhys. The man saw everything through the lens of love since marrying his wife, the young and lovely former Duchess of Hardcastle.

"Save it," Devlin said. "I do not want to hear anything about love at the moment."

"You are planning on seeing her again, aren't you?" Rhys murmured.

Devlin ignored him, but his heart already answered for

him in the erratic way it started to race. *Yes, I'll be seeing her again*. The only thing he was uncertain about, a state he did not like, for he was a man of surety, was how Lady Ophelia— *Fifi*—would react to his pursuit.

Would she run, or would she be intrigued?

Devlin stood, grabbing his coat, hat, umbrella, and walking stick, which held a hidden blade.

His friend also stood. "Where do you head to?"

"To see Mrs. Ashely."

Rhys stilled. "Your paramour?"

Devlin donned his coat. "My friend."

Rhys made no comment but observed him with a measured stare. Conan stood and padded over to him, and, with a brief dip of his head in his friend's direction, man and dog departed through the back entrance of the gambling hell. Devlin enjoyed walking, and almost everywhere he went in London he walked with a cane or a large black umbrella in one hand, with Conan trotting faithfully by his side. He kept a town carriage, and one for country traveling. He even owned a barouche and a landau. Devlin had never used them. He simply preferred walking, whether it rained or the sun shone.

Now he had at least an hour's stroll to make to a particular townhouse where Mrs. Jane Ashely lived. When the rain started to fall, he opened his umbrella, ensuring it covered his pal appropriately. Conan could be fussy about getting wet.

A little more than an hour later, Devlin entered the bedroom of his lover. She was tying the belt of a silky robe around her waist, her blond hair tumbling about her in waves. As he stood watching her, she peeked at him from beneath her lashes. Her inviting stare held no appeal, and he scrubbed a hand over his face.

"I will await you in the drawing room." He couldn't explain the feeling of wanting to be out of the bedchamber.

Ignoring her astonished look, he turned about and made his way downstairs. She was practically on his heels, entering the drawing room as he poured whisky from a tumbler into a glass.

"I did not expect you tonight, but I am pleased you are here," she said with a warm smile.

He stared at her, and that wide smile faltered as her gaze roved over him. Devlin was not sure what she saw in his eyes, but her throat worked on a swallow, and she looked away from him for a long moment.

"You've come not to indulge in pleasure but to end our… friendship."

"Yes."

Her flinch was subtle, but he caught it. There was no room for artful and manipulative phrases to make her feel better. They had always been honest with each other—not only lovers but friends.

"Have you found her, then?"

It was his turn to flinch.

"I have always known you would end our liaison once you found your Fifi."

"I mentioned her only once."

A wistful smile curved Jane's mouth. "It was *how* you mentioned her, Devlin."

Jane padded over to the sideboard and poured herself some sherry. There was a sadness in her hazel eyes that he did not like to see. He had never promised anything but the pleasure they found in each other's arms and the security she found in his wealth.

"Is she a lady of quality?" she asked, tossing him a probing stare.

"Yes."

"Top quality or bottom quality?"

Devlin did not understand Jane's distinction, but he supposed a marquess's daughter would be at the very pinnacle of quality. "Top."

Her face softened in a glance that was almost pitying.

Devlin arched a brow in silent response.

Jane took a deep breath. "Though you are wealthy and have garnered influence in some circles, you will be considered beneath her in *every* regard, Devlin. Surely you know this."

The truth of her words stabbed deep in his stomach, leaving a burning sensation inside his body. Of course he was not good enough.

"I know it," he said drolly, almost with a measure of amusement.

"Then why do you plan to try?" she asked almost pleadingly.

"I do not know what my full plans are in relation to her, so how could you discern it?" he asked, aware of the cutting edge to his words and unable to temper them.

"May I…may I ask who she is?"

"It does not matter."

Her lips pinched. "Do you think she will love you?"

"I am not looking for love."

Her eyes widened. "Are you going to marry her? Is that it? To consolidate more power in society?"

Dark amusement wafted through him. "Her family would never consent."

She emptied the glass of sherry in one swallow and lowered it to the table with a decisive *clink*. "Then why are you ending our liaison?"

Devlin stared at this lady who had offered him many comforts for the past three years. His first and only lover. As an older widow by six years, she had taught him much, but most of all, they had been friends. She had earned his honesty.

"When I think of bedding you now that I have found her... it feels like I am betraying something," he said. He held up a hand to forestall her reply. "I intend to pursue her to be my lover, and I will not do that while having another lover."

Many men had several lovers and mistresses together, but that was not Devlin. Such unfaithfulness either in thoughts or actions disgusted him.

Her expression once again softened. "I should not have asked you just now if you planned to love her. You already love her."

He stiffened, suddenly angry with himself for letting a fleeting moment in time, a blip in his existence, define so much of himself. That others could fucking perceive it and misinterpret. And that he could not walk away now, even believing his chance of success was less than five percent. He had gambled with worse odds before, he ruthlessly reminded himself.

"Do not be foolish. I do not love her." What he had felt had been through the lens of a boy who hardly understood himself, much less love. What in God's name was love? He *wanted* Fifi. That much he knew, for it was a burning hunger he could not ignore or deny. How could he allow himself to become once again mired in the emotions that had ruled him as a lad? They had no place in this moment, nor would they in the future.

He had to be smart about his pursuit. Damn smart or he might find himself shattered against jagged rocks. If he let himself become too entangled, Devlin knew with a chilling certainty that Fifi had the power to cut him deep, flaying his flesh open to reveal bone.

"Nor will I entertain any more discourse about her. That is not why I came, Jane." Devlin walked over and handed her a roll of paper tied with a ribbon and an envelope.

With a curious frown plucking at her brows, she opened it and gasped. "What is this?"

"You always spoke about living in a cottage by the seaside, growing your children away from the city. That is the deed to your cottage."

Jane stared at him as if she did not know what to make of him. "You have also provided a dowry for my daughter, a trust for my son, and enough money for me to live in comfort for the rest of my days." She casually dropped onto the sofa. "Why would you do this? This is too generous of a parting gift."

"Do you wish to find another protector and live as his mistress?"

Her throat worked on a swallow. "No."

"Then take it, Jane." Devlin walked over to her, tugged her to her feet, and pressed a kiss to her cheek. "Thank you for your friendship."

She hugged him fiercely, and after a slight hesitation, Devlin returned her embrace.

"Thank you," she whispered in the crook of his neck. Tears wetted his skin, and he drew back. With an embarrassed chuckle, she wiped them away.

"Farewell, Jane."

From the look in her eyes, Devlin sensed she wanted a

more pleasurable and lasting parting. He turned around and walked out of her life, aware of her stare against his back.

Stepping into the night with Conan, Devlin strolled down the street toward his townhouse in Mayfair.

"Why does it suddenly feel complicated, Conan?"

His dog growled and bounced his large body against his master.

Who would I be if I had not met you, Fifi? If I had not lost my damn senses and rushed to London?

Devlin wasn't sure why he had found Fifi again, when for the past few years he had all but given up on thoughts of ever finding that little black-haired girl. Happenstance and several accidents of circumstance had allowed their paths to cross once more. After that night he rediscovered her on King Street, Devlin waited for months in the shadows, discreetly observing her whenever he accidentally crossed her path, which happened several times.

The first had been a day at the British Museum. She had been alone, save the two footmen who followed for her protection. How forlorn Fifi had looked as she walked the long halls, pausing every now and then to admire a piece of history. She seemed to adore ancient Greek art. Devlin had scandalously stared, studying her, hoarding every laugh and smile, collecting her smallest habits and gestures, admiring her kindness and the way she interacted with others.

The second sighting of her had been in another suspect part of the city. She had used his name and reputation to scare away a few footpads. He'd liked her daring, especially when she'd declared she was his woman. Those words had unlocked him, jolting desires and hungers awake that he had never felt in his life.

The third instance had been at the botanical garden. In a quiet spot, she had cried her heart out and said a soft prayer asking for help in finding Sally Martin.

Hating the thought of her venturing into the seedier parts of London without the proper protection, he had sent a friend to her side. Princess Cosima. That way, he would always be abreast whenever she visited. Whenever Lady Starlight performed— only four times since she donned the moniker and identity of a songbird—he had watched every performance.

The crowd never applauded when she finished. The silence was always hushed. But they stood. In awe...and shock. For her voice was most enchanting.

"Who is she?" always rippled through the throng in hushed whispers. Desperate men who always fancied that they had just fallen in love would try to chase her when she left the stage. His power and connections always saw that the path before her was like the parting of the Red Sea. He'd ruthlessly broken a few bones so it was understood that she was precious.

Nothing and no one troubled her.

Except whoever this Sally Martin was.

All those meetings had been happenstance, mere coincidences of fate. To Devlin's mind, it had astonished him that she seemed to appear everywhere, when for fifteen years he had not caught a glimpse of her shadow.

Now that he had revealed himself to her, would she be brave enough to take his hand when he held it out to her?

Ice formed in his gut as he recalled Jane's warning.

...*you will be considered beneath her in* every *regard*...

A humorless smile curved his mouth. *The dice have been cast. I will see it through to the end.*

CHAPTER FIVE

Two mornings later, it was impossible to sleep or even pretend to. Groaning in frustration, Ophelia kicked the coverlets from her legs, rolled over, balled her fist, and thumped her pillow as hard as she could. A measure of satisfaction filled her, and it would have to do for now.

With only one meeting, Devlin Byrne invaded her dreams as though he had a right to be there. How could she have dreamed of the man? And worse, it had been a frightfully intimate dream, one in which he had kissed her mouth with carnal thoroughness.

"Ugh," she groaned, pressing her face even deeper into the softness of her pillow. "Why am I dreaming of kisses!"

His eyes were so lovely and perhaps a bit lonely. Her heart gave a strange stutter. Whether he was the devil in disguise luring her to ruin or an ordinary man, Devlin Byrne held her interest as no one ever had. She tried to pull her thoughts into some semblance of order. Today she intended to meet a lady who had claimed of knowing Sally Martin. Ophelia could not afford the unexpected distraction of Niall…*Devlin*!

Ringing for her maid, she quickly dressed in a fashionable day dress of yellow taffeta with a cinched waist. Donning her hat to tip rakishly atop her artfully styled curls, Ophelia tugged on her gloves and collected her pelisse. She would call upon Cosima, then make a change of clothes at her home. To remain undetected while she searched for Sally Martin, Ophelia had thought it prudent to leave a set of disguises at

Cosima's house. Hurrying down the stairs, she asked for the town carriage to be prepared. That would take at least fifteen minutes for the order to be taken to the mews and the carriage drawn around the front. She would use the time to check in on her mother and father, as she had missed them at breakfast, a repast they always shared together.

Knocking on the drawing-room door, she entered, noting only her mother was there. And the marchioness was staring at a large box, shaking her head.

"Ophelia?"

"Yes, Mama," she said, walking over.

"There is a goat in this box."

She skidded to a halt as if she had slammed into a wall. "A *what*?" Good heavens! Her voice came in a high, unflattering squeak.

"A goat. It came for you."

Her thoughts madly whirled. "A goat?"

"What is this about a goat?" her father asked, strolling into the room, immaculately turned out in the first stare of fashion and ready to spend the day with his wife.

"There is a goat for Ophelia in the box," her mama said disbelievingly.

Her father blinked. "A goat?"

"A goat," she repeated.

Why was it all beginning to sound like a scatterbrained folk song?

"Why a goat?" he asked with a puzzling frown, plucking the note her mother held out.

Ophelia covered her face with a hand to mask her laughter. She was going to skewer Devlin Byrne.

"Is this a lark from one of your friends?" he asked, casting her a sideways glance. "The note says, 'Admit that Barbosa is charming. Alarmingly so. I took the liberty of naming him.' I gather you know the sender."

"Yes, Papa," she said, fighting the blush determined to climb her cheeks with all her will. "Recall there was a time I...I wanted a..."

She faltered under his probing stare.

"Why are your cheeks red?"

This had her mother whirling around, finally taking her attention from the goat that must be in possession of three horns and red glowing eyes.

"Well," Ophelia said, mortified that her cheeks grew hotter. "There is a goat."

"And it is causing you to blush so frightfully?"

"I've heard goats do that. Especially the baby ones."

Her father stared at her for several seconds, then shifted to look at his wife. "Are you hearing this, my dear? Goats have been known to inspire blushes."

Bless her mother, who erupted into peals of laughter. Her father made a noncommittal grunt, and she hurried over to the box and peered down. It was the tiniest creature and most lovely. He was mostly white with black spots. He was fluffy... and fat...and incredibly adorable. Warmth blossomed through her, and she stooped, reaching out to touch his fur.

"Are we to keep this creature in the house?"

"Yes, Papa," she said, laughing, not understanding the way her heart was squeezing. "Please do not forbid it! We'll be withdrawing to the country soon, and I trust Barbosa will be happy in Derbyshire."

Her father muttered something unintelligible, and her mother offered him some soothing nonsense. Ophelia would have to leave careful instructions to her maid for bedding and a litter box to set up in her room for him. And perhaps milk and lettuce as his food for now, until they understood each other's likes and dislikes. And daily baths, perhaps.

She had no notion of how to take care of a baby goat.

Ophelia stood and almost fidgeted under the stares of her parents. Her mother's eyes were bright with curiosity and something unknown to her, and Papa's own were suspicious. She groaned silently.

"We are heading to Kensington Gardens, and perhaps the museum after. Would you like to accompany us?"

She paused, swallowing at the hopeful note in her mother's voice. It was most uncomfortable to look at her father, who carefully stared beyond her shoulder. He had been slowly venturing out, and this would be the third invitation in recent weeks. Ophelia had gently turned down all of them. Distress burned through her veins. "Yes, I would like to accompany you for the day," she said, pushing aside all thoughts of Sally Martin and the lady she had planned to meet.

The tension leaked from her father's shoulders, and there was such a relief in the smile he gave her. There would be another day to travel discreetly to Wardour Street. Today, her father and mother needed her. And perhaps she needed them, too. This distance between her and Papa could not be maintained, not when they had been so loving and open their whole lives.

Her mother smiled brightly. "Well then! Let's be off, shall we?"

. . .

Ophelia returned home with her parents about three hours later. They had not made it to the museum, for the stroll in the garden with the numerous stops to speak to a fellow peer or acquaintance had tired Papa greatly.

"There are a few letters for you, Lady Ophelia," the butler said as she handed him her hat and pelisse.

A quick glance down the hallway showed her mother escorting her father to the drawing room, and they had not heard Mr. Clarkson. Her mother was frightfully inquisitive and would want to know who sent a correspondence and what it might entail.

Ophelia already recognized the bold scrawl that had franked the letter to her.

Devlin.

Her heart started to skip and dance beneath her breast-bone. Another letter was from a Bow Street investigator she hired, surely concerning the lady she was meant to meet today to learn about her mother. Taking the envelope, she rushed up the winding stairs to her chamber. Once there, she went over to the windows and opened them so the air might cool her cheeks. Tearing the first envelope, she quickly read. Miss Fenley had to leave town for a week and would not be available to meet. Ophelia groaned, thinking it fortunate she had not made the journey today or it would have been in vain. Opening the second envelope, she reached for the note and stilled.

Dance with me. A waltz.

Those words stole Ophelia's breath and set her heart to racing. There was also another bank draft for ten thousand pounds, once again payable to her father's account. Stunned, she tightened her fingers around the papers, her knuckles turning white.

"Whatever are you thinking, Niall?" Ophelia whispered. "Ten thousand pounds for a dance!"

Where would they even dance? Would it be once again after this money was lodged at their bank that another set of instructions followed? She did not understand his reasoning, and there was a part of her that did not want to understand him at all.

Liar, a soft voice inside whispered. She wanted to know *everything*. How had Niall, a simple country boy who could not read, become Devlin Byrne? A restless feeling encompassed her, and suddenly she wanted the comfort and advice of her friends. Perhaps she would call upon Fanny or Maryann. Perhaps it was time she shared with them some of the things that had been heavy upon her heart.

Hurrying down the stairs, she faltered in the hallway, thoroughly shocked to see her mother running with a newssheet flapping in her hands. A smile tugged at her mouth to see the marchioness appearing so mussed and out of sorts. "Mama, whatever is wrong?"

"Ophelia!" she said, skidding to a stop, only to grab her arm and drag her into the drawing room, where the marquess awaited.

"My dear, what has you so breathless?" he said, opening his eyes, which had been closed.

He looked weary, as if their outing had thoroughly worn him out. Her mother waved the newssheet, clearly too aghast to speak. Ophelia plucked it from her hands, knowing instinctively that it was the society mentions she should look for. For a precious moment, she could barely breathe.

"Someone tried to kill Maryann?" Ophelia asked, her heart roaring.

"It is a most dreadful scandal, and everyone...I mean the entire *ton* is atwitter. This was only printed in the afternoon editions, which is why we heard no mention at the gardens." Her mother pressed the back of her palm to her forehead. "It is most ghastly!"

"What in God's name are you saying, Florence?" her father demanded, evidently appalled. "Why would anyone act in such a dubious manner?"

"If I can credit what the newssheets are saying, an earl wanted to somehow hurt Lord Rothbury, and the bacon-brained notion was to shoot Lady Maryann in a ballroom full of people. I still cannot believe it to be true, even upon Lady Danby's vigorous insistence and account, which arrived in a letter just now!"

Fighting the fear tearing through her heart, Ophelia dropped the paper on the small rococo table. "I have to leave, Mama and Papa. I must call upon Maryann at once."

"Now you wait a minute, young lady," her father said sternly, a concerned furrow about his brows. "From your mother's tone, this scandal will be far-reaching and might have severe ripple effects."

"I know it," Ophelia whispered. "Which is why I need to leave immediately. Maryann will need my support."

Her mother stiffened. "Until we understand the full extent of the situation, it is best you... It is best you do not call upon Maryann for a while, my darling. Just until we understand fully the way the wind blows."

Ophelia was momentarily speechless in her surprise. "Mama, surely you cannot mean it!"

"The full scandal is not yet printed! It seems there was also a violent declaration of love, and there might be a child. All of this is according to Lady Danby, and if she knows it, every drawing room in London also knows it!"

Ophelia hesitated, torn by conflicting emotions. "Forgive me, Papa, but I am unable to obey you in this matter."

She felt their profound shock at her stance—and why not? She was an obedient daughter who showed her love by always listening to their advice.

Ophelia sighed. "Papa, please understand. Maryann is one of my dearest friends." Then she headed for the door, bracing for her parents' rebuke.

"You will have a care for this family's reputation in every action of yours, young lady," her father said. "We allow you much, but never forget it is because we have faith and trust in you. Do not abuse it."

She swallowed, and her fingers dropped from the latch. "I will be *very* discreet, Papa. I always take into my care the things you ask of me. And I will do so again, but do not ask me to abandon my character by ignoring one of my dearest friends when she is in need."

Ophelia opened the door and hurried down the hallway. She winced to hear her father's shout that they had indeed indulged her willfulness echoing through the door. He might just banish her to the country for this.

Blowing out a sharp breath, Ophelia did not waste the time to call for a carriage. Hurrying down the streets of Berkeley Square, within a short fifteen minutes, she was knocking on the door of Maryann's townhouse. The butler opened the door, his craggy yet still handsome face creasing into a warm smile.

"Lady Ophelia, very pleasant to see you."

"Good morning, Thompson." Hurrying to untie her bonnet

and pelisse, she handed them over. "Is Lady Maryann in?"

"She is in the back gardens, my lady."

"No need to announce me to the earl and countess. I will make my way to the gardens." Intimately familiar with her friend's home, Ophelia hastened through the front drawing room, which connected to the ballroom, opened the terrace window, and slipped outside. She almost ran on the graveled pathway around to the back, only to skid to a halt.

Maryann was seated on a stone bench, appearing quite lovely in a green gown, her dark brown hair hanging loose to her back, the sun glinting off the red streaks like burnished copper. Her friend was humming.

"I expected tears, at least!" Ophelia said, rushing over to a very startled Maryann.

"Ophelia," she gasped. "I did not anticipate you."

"After the commotion of last evening's ball?"

Maryann pushed her spectacles atop her nose, a nervous gesture Ophelia was well acquainted with. "It was most awful!"

They hugged briefly, and Ophelia drew back to scan her friend from the top of her head to the tips of her shoes. "You arc well, then?"

"I had such a huge fright…but then it also ended gloriously."

"Gloriously?" Well, that was the last thing she expected to hear from Maryann. "Are all your senses intact?"

She nodded, her green-brown eyes sparkling with something decidedly naughty *and* happy.

Ophelia wilted under the tide of relief. "I assume the scandal sheets went ahead of themselves and printed a most ridiculous story. I do hope your father will demand a retraction and sue—"

"Well, most of it is arguably correct." Maryann wrinkled her nose. "I sent a footman to buy as many papers as he possibly could. I have a copy of *The Times*, *The Morning Chronicle*, *The Spectator*—"

"Maryann," Ophelia said gently. "You are rambling."

"Well then, depending on the paper you read, most of it is true."

They spent several minutes chatting, during which her friend filled her in on the entire sordid tale. "I am sorry that Nicolas was hurt," she said when Maryann stopped.

A soft smile touched Maryann's mouth. "Nicolas is well. He was here a few hours ago. The doctor gave a most excellent report."

Nicolas. The manner in which Maryann lingered on his name had a tight ache forming in Ophelia's throat. "You love him," she breathed.

A wide, brilliant smile curved Maryann's mouth. "Oh, yes, very much."

"Even with his dastardly reputation?"

"I daresay I love him even more for it."

"You must not leave me in this terrible suspense any longer, or I shall be very vexed with you, Maryann!"

As quickly as possible without becoming overwrought with emotions, Maryann told her what happened. "I cannot believe any of it," Ophelia said, once again hugging Maryann to her.

Hand in hand, they returned to the bench and sat. "A bounder truly threatened to take your life, and then Nicolas St. Ives, London's most notorious rogue, declared to this bounder that he would…repay life with life because he is so violently in love with you?"

Maryann laughed, her hazel eyes gleaming with rich delight and love. "Yes."

"You are beyond scandalous," Ophelia said, shaking her head. "What did your mama say? Are you banished to the country? Should the other sinful wallflowers plot and mount a daring rescue?"

Maryann's cheeks pinkened. "No. Nicolas came by earlier. We are getting married by special license in a few days, and then we will hie off to the country until society finds their next favorite scandal to chew on. Oh, Ophelia, I love him so much! And he loves me with the same intensity."

"Maryann, I am so happy. First Kitty, and now you have found great happiness!" Ophelia hugged her arms around herself tightly. "Are we addle-brained to recklessly chase after wickedness?"

Devlin's brilliant green eyes floated in her thoughts, along with that sensual slant to his lips.

"No, I daresay we are brilliant for chasing our own paths." Maryann hesitated. "I was at the Asylum…the night before last. I heard you singing."

Ophelia's heart jolted. "Yes, I…"

Her friend touched her shoulders. "That man in the room was Devlin Byrne. We have heard many rumors about him, and he has a very dubious reputation. But I suspect he is your slice of wickedness."

Ophelia looked away, lifting her face to the sky. "I have no notion what he is. Our…friendship, if I dare call it that, is very unusual."

"Have you…have you been friends for a long time?"

In halting accents, she shared everything with Maryann, unable to hold it inside anymore.

When she glanced at her friend, Maryann had paled. "The marchioness is not your mother?"

"Yes."

"Good heavens. I cannot credit your father would conceive of such a scheme or that the marchioness would go along with it." Maryann sent her a sympathetic glance. "Have you any fortune in finding any news about her, about Sally Martin?"

Ophelia bit into her lower lip to stop its trembling. "None. I admit I do not know what to do. I have hired a Bow Street runner to aid me in investigating, but in five months he's had nothing to report. He gave me an address of a lady, Miss Barbara Fenley, in Wardour Street who performed with Sally Martin, which is great progress. I've made arrangements to visit Miss Fenley and ask her about Sally Martin."

"When will you call upon her?"

"She is not available until next week. It is frustrating, but I must be patient."

"We all thought you donned the persona of Lady Starlight because you loved singing so much, but it was all to find her."

Ophelia nodded wordlessly.

"And you have deliberately used Devlin Byrne's name… said that you are his lover to walk freely in London's seedier districts."

"Yes," she said softly. "I did."

Maryann sniffed and cast her friend an admiring glance. "I do recall you were the one to plant the idea that night when we were at your father's house stealing his whisky and getting tippled that we should be wicked and daring to get the things we want. And it was you who coaxed Kitty the most to pretend to be the fiancée of a duke not about town! It was all because you were doing a similar chicanery!"

"Yes, but my scheme will not lead to love like it did for you and Kitty."

Maryann's expression softened. "Do you want that? Love?"

Ophelia hesitated. "I do know that, should I marry, I want to admire, respect, and have great affection for that gentleman. I've had several seasons, and I have not met a gentleman who captured my regard. If I cannot feel some…I do not know, passion or interest for someone, I also know I shall be contented if I never marry."

"There is no happiness in being alone." Maryann looked about the gardens, leaned forward, and whispered, "That is because you know nothing of the pleasures of the flesh."

Ophelia gasped. "You and the marquess have anticipated your vows?"

Maryann grinned cheekily. "Many, *many* times, and let me tell you, it is bloody *delicious*!"

After a beat, they both started to laugh at their scandalous topic of discourse. "Coupling is delicious?"

"Oh yes," Maryann murmured dreamily, pushing the glasses up her nose.

Ophelia stared at her friend in shock, never dreaming when Maryann had set out to be naughty it had gotten that far without the benefit of marriage. And why not? A pulse of something unfathomable tumbled over inside Ophelia, and the breath that left her mouth was shaky. "I am not sure whether to be proud or scandalized."

"Be both," Maryann said with a wink, and they both chuckled.

She stayed almost an hour with Maryann, laughing and chatting, bemused and a little bit frightened that thoughts of Devlin Byrne and that coupling was *most* delicious did not depart from her mind—not once.

CHAPTER SIX

That evening, Ophelia stood on the terrace of Lady Newby's ball, feeling listless. She'd only attended to lend support to Maryann. After last night's debacle, her name and Nicolas St. Ives were on the tongues of everyone. All her other sinful wallflower friends—Fanny, Charlotte, and Emma—were in attendance to rally around her, if necessary. Except Maryann had not shown.

Good for you, Maryann.

No doubt the throng expected her to be here, appearing meek and apologetic or more desperate to be enfolded back into their good graces. Ophelia grinned, loving the idea of her friend being so rebellious.

"Lord Montrose and Mr. Devlin Byrne."

Ophelia jolted, spilling a bit of the champagne on her gloves. "Drat," she muttered, very cognizant of the sudden fluttering low in her belly.

Had Devlin Byrne really just been announced, or had she simply thought of the man so much that she'd imagined it? Trying to see over the heads of the throng was no small feat. Glancing about to see the best pathway to walk close to the receiving line, she paused. More than one guest wore an expression of horrified amazement. A few ladies appeared tickled pink, and several gentlemen's shoulders had stiffened.

She knew he titillated some in society because of his staggering wealth and having more than a hint of danger around him. In the expression of many ladies, she now saw fascinated awareness.

Suddenly he was there, standing with Rhys Tremayne, Viscount Montrose. The two men were dashingly handsome and very much out of place in a ballroom setting. Ophelia did not understand it, but they seemed...dangerous. He really dared to appear at a ball uninvited. Ophelia had never seen the man in such a setting before, and he fitted oddly yet also perfectly.

Do not let your imagination lead you astray tonight, she silently chided herself, unable to stop staring at Devlin. He was dressed in unrelenting black, including his shirt and silk waistcoat. The only splash of color was a dark red neckcloth at his throat. An expression of chilling insouciance settled on his face as he surveyed the ladies and gentlemen in their fineries.

Viscount Montrose said something to him, and after Devlin nodded once, the viscount walked toward Lord Livingston. Devlin stood there alone, and no one approached him. Yet he did not appear uncertain as he idly scanned the faces in the ballroom.

Who was he searching for?

His face was an unreadable mask as his gaze skipped from face to face as though taking the measure of each person who stared at him. Others dismissed his presence as if he were a speck that was not worth their attention. Many looked nervous. They were familiar with him, possibly having done business with the man. But what was clear to Ophelia was that they did not like him in their domain.

"I cannot credit that Lady Newby would dare invite him!" a hushed whisper said.

"Perhaps the countess had little choice in the matter. I've heard a tidbit that her son owes an alarming amount of money to the Asylum."

"Never say!" another voice gasped dramatically. "He *black-mailed* her for an invitation? He is clearly *not* a gentleman."

Ophelia was quite aware those who owned that appellation thought of him as nothing more than a mongrel trying to climb the ranks and insert himself in a place he could never belong. Unexpectedly, his gaze touched upon her, moved on, then swung back to her almost immediately, stillness setting into every line of his body.

There…I've found you, his stare seemed to say.

A powerful force seized her throat, robbing Ophelia of breath.

Dance with me.

Did he hope for her to dance with him *here*? Good heavens! She had truly thought he would have required a private setting similar to when she had sung for him. He was outrageous if he thought she would accept him so publicly.

To society, she was a lady of propriety and reputation and all other sorts of perfect nonsense that did not reflect the true heart of her. Ophelia understood that their reputations mattered a great deal to her family. There had been no scandal attached to their names going back two generations. Or so her father liked to brag.

In all her interactions, Ophelia was careful to maintain the proper polite civilities and not be too familiar or flirtatious with a gentleman. Dancing publicly with a man like Devlin, to her parents' minds, *was* the beginning of a scandal that might taint their family's name for years.

Yet as he drifted closer she did not turn away and cut him. *This is Niall.*

Ophelia returned his stare, painfully aware of her

suspended breath and the erratic beat of her heart. Someone came up beside her, and a quick glance revealed it to be Fanny, garbed in a most becoming gown of green and black organza.

Flicking open her fan, she placed it artfully above her mouth. "Are you aware there is a man over there staring at you?" Fanny asked, outrage filling her voice. "I hurried to your side to save you, for you were returning his stare just as foolishly! I admit he is very handsome, but do have a care for your reputation."

Ophelia did not have the will to laugh. "That man is Devlin Byrne."

Fanny's head snapped in his direction before she brought her gaze back to Ophelia. "He is still staring at you. The man has no decency! Why is he looking at you so?"

"I believe I owe him a dance."

Fanny made a choking noise, but her eyes gleamed with curious delight. "I see. Will you dance with him here?" she asked deftly behind her fan. "It will start a scandal. I fear many in this room know who he is. Do you see how they are looking? And the gentlemen are deliberately ignoring his presence. No one has greeted him, Ophelia."

Fanny sounded suitably mortified on his behalf.

"I do not think he will approach me without an intro—" Suddenly, Ophelia's thoughts crashed and shattered into a thousand pieces.

"He is coming over!" Fanny waved her fan with agitated vigor. "*Good God*, is he not aware of the etiquette?"

"I do not think it is us he is... Oh, dear!"

Devlin cut a direct swath to her, his long strides graceful, owning in every languid step the confidence of a man uncaring of what others thought of him, a man also fully aware of his power and how to wield that influence. It alarmed her that she found him so uniquely compelling. Ophelia's fingers tightened around the champagne glass.

Lifting the flute of champagne to her mouth, she emptied the contents in a long swallow as he arrived at their side. As if he were a magician or a dark conjurer, all the senses in her body awoke. Ophelia was acutely conscious of the shock of excitement that shimmered through her at being this close to him. She could feel the eyes of several guests on her shoulders, crawling over her skin like a swarm of ants...the kind that bit and devoured.

"Lady Ophelia," he said, bowing most charmingly, the corner of his mouth tugging into a daring half smile. "Will you honor me with the upcoming dance?"

Something hot and uncomfortable shivered low in her belly. The night she sang for him, most of his features had still been cast in shadows. It was only now, under the brightness of hundreds of candles, that she saw the scars. He had a cut above his left eyebrow, a thin scar on his cheek, and a deeper one under his chin. Yet, oddly, those little imperfections only gave him a more handsome, rakish, and unquestionably dangerous air.

Ophelia had not granted anyone a dance for two seasons. Her name had made the scandal sheets for it, and matrons had given her frowns of severe disapproval. But after being out since she was eighteen, dancing had become a routine she had not cared to indulge in anymore. Instead, she had preferred to stand on the sidelines with her other wallflower friends and laugh and chat through the night.

To permit Devlin Byrne to dance with her now *was* courting scandal.

He straightened from his bow, and in his eyes, she spied the dare. With a jolt, she realized he had come fully prepared for her to deny him. He was aware that no lady in attendance would ever risk her reputation by dancing with him.

"I thought you would prefer a private setting," she said softly, carefully eyeing him.

"Do you want to be alone with me?"

"No." She cleared her throat. "I merely thought our next meeting would have been like the first...private."

"I will arrange it."

"You are already here," she said quickly, not trusting that sudden spark in his eyes.

She snuck a glance at Fanny, who was busy looking anywhere but at them. The flush on her cheeks suggested their whispered conversation was not hidden from her.

The orchestra struck up a waltz while it seemed as if everyone in the ballroom held their breaths. An awfully intense sensation twisted low in her stomach, Ophelia's heart pounded, and her breathing turned rapid as a sense of unalterable consequences beat at her—but she did not turn away from him. She dipped into a curtsy and lifted her hand to his. A few gasps reached her ears, but she looked nowhere except at him.

Shock flashed in his eyes for the briefest moment before his expression became inscrutable.

They walked out to the dance floor.

"Your fingers are trembling," he murmured, the cadence of his voice ragged and a bit uneven.

Their gazes collided, and for the briefest moment, the intensity of his expression frightened her. Ophelia swallowed, and then she became aware of it...and more.

"So are yours," she whispered.

He rested a strong, powerful arm about her waist and swept her into a world of pure delight. A quick ripple of laughter escaped her as he spun her in a graceful twirl, caught her about the shoulders, slid their elbows together, and moved across the span of the ballroom with pulsing energy and something unexpected sparking between them. Those keenly watching noted her laugh—the lack of proper decorum, the intimacy it suggested. Speculation gleamed in several eyes. In the periphery of her gaze, she saw a young gentleman furiously scribbling on a piece of paper after observing them. There was no doubt the man was a reporter and this dance would be splashed in several scandal sheets tomorrow.

"You dance beautifully," she said, staring up at him.

"After your lessons in the cottage, I had another good tutor."

"Who?"

"Jane Ashely."

Ophelia's heart twisted unexpectedly. "The widow of Sir Archibald Ashely?"

She was familiar with the lady, having seen her about town and at a few balls. They had never spoken before, but Ophelia recalled that she had a remarkable stature, was beautiful, and had a lovely smile.

"Yes."

"Why did she agree to teach you?"

"I asked her."

A mere request, with no money offered. It suggested an intimacy that robbed her of breath for the feelings it roused within Ophelia's breast. They clawed up from her belly, ugly and uncertain. Was this jealousy? The notion so startled her that she missed a step, but he was quick and graceful in spinning and drawing her back to his side, so the keenest observer would have missed her *faux pas*.

"Why did you learn?"

He wasn't the typical gentleman about town who was invested in knowing the dance styles for when they ventured into wooing a lady on the marriage mart.

"For this moment."

The words were simple and without any deep inflection, but his eyes gleamed with hidden knowledge.

"And what moment is that?"

"To dance with you, Fifi."

Do not call me that, she wanted to say, not liking how it made her feel. Shy and so uncertain about the dip in her heart, the wild flutters in her belly as if birds were trapped there. Ridiculous, of course. What did she have to be shy and flustered about?

His rough murmur pierced her like a well-aimed arrow. "What nonsense," she said, searching his expression. "You could not have known we would meet again, that you would ask me to dance, and that I would say yes."

"I could not have known it, but I hoped to meet you again, so I plotted for it."

Plotted. Such a diabolical word. For a breathless moment, she could only stare at him, recalling his promise in the cottage years ago. "Did you learn all the dances I prattled on about?"

"And a few more."

The memory of how excited she had been in describing the many dances she had to learn for attending balls rose in her thoughts. Niall had been more…aghast when she had begged him to be her pupil. A clear image formed of them, he with his dirt-streaked face spinning her around in that small cottage until she grew so dizzy they had taken a tumble. How they had laughed and laughed, as if falling to the floor was the best thing that could have happened.

The memory lingered in the air like smoke; the remembered joy curled around her heart and stroked it with tendrils of emotions. Something she couldn't identify, something she couldn't understand.

Wait for me…

The memory of that desperate plea cut her deep. "You make little sense to me," she whispered, rattled.

He made no reply but spun her in another graceful glide. It truly felt wonderful dancing again, and suddenly she was glad it was with him. That curiosity she had tried to bury stirred. "Where do you call home when you are in London? I am assuming you have a place here?"

"I have a private room at the Asylum."

"I'll certainly not visit you there."

His curious, emerald eyes blazed with a cold, penetrating intelligence. "You plan to call upon me, Fifi?"

"I cannot foretell the future," she replied flippantly, though flutters went off in her belly. "I do like to be armed with information. What if I need to see you one day? However do I reach you?"

Something unfathomable flashed in his eyes, and his fingers imperceptibly tightened on her gloved hands. "Grosvenor Square," he said gruffly. "I recently purchased a townhouse there."

"What number?"

Twirling her deftly, he leaned close and inhaled deeply

before saying, "Thirty-six."

"I see. Are your sisters here in town?"

"No."

"If I recall correctly, Sara should now be about one and twenty, and Gwenn nineteen. Are they affianced or married?"

He slanted her a curious glance. "I am surprised you recall so much about them."

"I remember our conversations."

"And I was so certain you had forgotten about me the instant the door closed. I am corrected."

Ophelia stared at him, bemused by the shadows that touched in his eyes just now. Forgotten him? "I would be a liar if I say you remained in my thoughts all these years. But I did not forget you, Nia...Devlin," she said softly. "I never forgot that you saved me...that you were my friend. Since we've met again, each night I close my eyes I see our time at the cottage."

The dance ended, and a pang of disappointment filled her. She had barely had a chance to converse with him. He led her back to Fanny, who watched their arrival with uncensored inquisitiveness. Devlin bowed to Fanny, then to Ophelia, and melted away in the crowd.

"Is he leaving?" Fanny gasped.

"It appears so," Ophelia replied drily.

"The man is *outrageous*. Does he not know what will be said about how he came, only danced with you, and then left?"

"I doubt he knows how ridiculous our society can be or the sort of rumors they will assign to his actions."

Ophelia saw the Earl of Langdon making his way through the crowd in her direction. Swallowing her groan, she looked for an avenue of escape. He would want to dance with her, possibly even make a demand as to why she refused him twice since the season but danced with a man with a questionable reputation.

"I am going to leave early, Fanny," Ophelia said.

"You do look a little pale," her friend said with a worried frown. "You should go. I will seek out Emma and Charlotte. They are by the refreshment line."

They briefly hugged, and Ophelia hurried from the ballroom, breathing a relieved sigh when she noted the connecting hallway was empty of any guests. A hand grasped her elbows. Her heart slamming into her throat, Ophelia whirled around. "Devlin, I thought you had left!"

"Not yet. Follow me."

Without awaiting her reply, he tugged her down the long hallway, and she looked around frantically to ensure they were alone. "I am not Lady Starlight here," she said. "We have to be careful, and where are you taking me?"

"Dancing."

"Where, in this cluttered library?" she muttered when he led her through a room that had all sorts of artifacts on the ground, sofas, and desk. She had heard that Lady Newby's husband was some sort of collector.

"Outside."

Ophelia looked toward the wide-open windows and hurried over. "You mean for us to climb through?"

"Yes. Did I not teach you this at the cottage?"

She pinched his arm, and he mock growled, startling a low laugh from her.

"I am a *lady*. We do not sneak through windows into dark gardens with men we barely know!" Yet she was so awfully tempted.

"I am wounded, Fifi," he drawled. "Are we not friends

about to become forbidden—"

She hurriedly slapped her hand over his mouth, acutely aware she stared at him with wide eyes. "Do not say it," she whispered. "You are unspeakably outrageous!"

Forbidden lovers.

God, he made her want things she should not think about. Not now. Perhaps never.

Perhaps she was more like Sally Martin than Ophelia had anticipated, reckless in her desires. She closed her eyes against the errant thought. Devlin's mouth moved beneath her palm, and his teeth nipped her gloves. She lowered her hand, not trusting the ache twisting through her belly. It was an ache of want for the very forbidden things he hinted at.

Knowledge gleamed in his eyes, one that hinted of mockery and an awareness that she did not understand. The silence grew hushed and thick.

"Let's go, Fifi," he said, swinging a leg over the sill and climbing over.

She did not hesitate to follow him, and he gently placed a hand around her waist from outside and tugged her through. This back part of the garden was dark, and even with the half-moon, she could not decipher Devlin's expression. Ophelia was reckless being like this with him, yet she did not flee from his presence.

He drew her deeper into the alcove.

"I feel as if you are kidnapping me."

"Your feet are happily skipping along."

Ophelia choked on her reply, for he was no longer holding on to her hands, and she *was* following him through the darkness.

"Do not lose courage now," he chided. "Will you dance

with me, Fifi?"

When had he moved to stand behind her? His hand rested on her hip, and she gripped the skirts of her gown until her fingers ached. Ophelia could hear her own heartbeat and the sounds of the night, and she was extraordinarily aware of his hand, strong and warm, on her back. Of the darkness of the back gardens. Of the scents of rose and jasmine on the night. Of her heartbeat and her tongue. Of the strength of his arm beneath her gloved fingers. That he had stolen her from the hallway like a wicked thief in the night, and she had recklessly gone with him.

She turned in the cage of his embrace, setting her hands on his shoulders. This was how it should have been. A dance from her with him, private and alone.

"When I questioned why we danced publicly, it was not a suggestion to do this," she whispered.

He tugged her to him, so scandalously close a gasp of denial rose in her throat.

"Upon reflection, your suggestion had merit."

It felt natural to dip with him, to allow him to lead her in the gentle but somehow sensual and provocative movements of the waltz. They danced for several minutes, the strains of the violins spilling out into the night air for their music, but somehow it was also to a tune of their own making. A song of temptation, perhaps. He evoked feelings within her that no one else had ever stirred, and ones she had never dreamed of feeling. This felt too soon…too perilous.

Then, on a long, shaken breath, she asked, "Niall…what do you want from me?"

He thrust his fingers into her upswept hair, tilted her face to his, and dragged her against his body. "This," he muttered harshly. "I want *this*."

How she wished his expression were visible to her. Ophelia could feel the waft of air so close to her mouth, and she inhaled the mingling of their breaths. He held her there against his body, her face upturned, his mouth precariously close to hers, until the uncertainty and hunger built in equal measure. Until she reached up with shaking fingers to see how close his mouth was to hers.

It is right there.

She closed her eyes on a silent gasp. Ophelia placed her fingers in the space between their mouths, and he bit them — the pain running through her fingers felt...haunting. *Dear God in heaven.*

A slow, languorous ache rolled through Ophelia, settling in that secret place between her thighs. A part of her she had not known existed awakened, the greedy desire clenching low in her belly. It frightened her, the newness of this feeling. The unexpectedness of it. She stepped back, almost stumbling in her haste. He caught her against him, and a whimper lodged in her throat at the touch of his powerful body against hers, the scent of his warm masculinity.

Forbidden lovers.

Ophelia wrenched from his arms, whirled around, and walked away. She half expected him to pursue her, but he did not. Hurrying back toward the path, she stopped when a soft moan, then a feminine laugh reached her ears.

"How naughty you are, Henry," a breathless voice whispered. "But we must return inside!"

She swallowed a groan of frustration. Lovers were on the path before her, blocking her discreet return to the ball. A low murmur of a gentleman followed, but she could not discern his reply. There were more rustling sounds and what sounded like a panicked gasp.

"Henry! Stop. You are *ruining* my gown."

There was more rustling and frantic panting. Ophelia's face flamed, and she glanced back at the darkened pathway behind her. To return to Devlin would be to surrender to a temptation she did not understand. He did not fit into her life, and even if he was a slice of wickedness, she would not dare make him her whole.

"Stop, please!"

Ophelia turned back to the lovers' voices.

"Henry, please stop. I do not want this!" the lady sobbed, sounding frightened. "Henry!"

Ophelia hurtled toward them, anger and a dash of fright surging through her veins. Under the pale moonlight, she barely discerned a tussling couple in the grass. She could not identify them, but the man was atop the lady, who struggled and sobbed.

"I believe the lady told you to stop, Henry," Ophelia said coolly, clenching her fists at her sides. "It is not the mark of a gentleman to ignore a lady's wish, but that of a blackguard!"

The man jerked, pushing to his feet and spinning around. The sobbing lady tried to stand, and Ophelia hurried over to help her. To Ophelia's great alarm, the man grabbed Ophelia by the shoulders and dragged her back. She slapped his hand, and when he reached for her again, she balled her fist and slammed it toward his mouth. It landed on his chin, and pain shot up her arm.

Ophelia cried out and recoiled.

He reached for her, anger contorting his features. "You damn interfering—"

The man's word choked away as an arm came around his throat and dragged him toward the darkened pathway. *Devlin!* An odd fright tore through Ophelia's heart. She whirled to the lady, who stood there trembling so badly her teeth chattered.

"We will need to go inside and discreetly tidy up," Ophelia said, wincing at the pain in her fingers and wrists. "Your hair needs to be re-pinned, and your dress checked for any tear."

"Jemma," someone frantically whispered in the distance. "Jemma, are you out here?"

Suddenly, Ophelia knew it to be Lady Jemma Darlington, a reigning beauty and society darling of the season, and Ophelia knew who had been courting her these last few weeks. The bloody, spoiled, bacon-brained blackguard!

"I must go. My sister looks for me," Jemma said, wiping at her tears. "Please do not...please..."

"You may be assured of my discretion," Ophelia said gently. "Should you think about it, I am also out here in the dark gardens without a chaperone. Both our reputations would be damaged if I spoke about this encounter."

Lady Jemma thought for a minute, then nodded. "Thank you."

"I would also urge you to end all associations with that... gentleman."

Jemma's lower lip trembled, and another sob came from her. "I feel after this I will be forced to marry him."

"Do you want to?"

"He was...he was very frightening just now. I cannot..." Her shoulders shook under the weight of her silent sobs.

"I doubt he will inform anyone about his dishonorable and callous behavior. You must tell your father or brother so they might defend your honor."

"No! Should my father know of this…he will surely insist I marry him. Please do not say anything."

"You have my word," Ophelia said, hating that Lady Jemma was right. Her father would indeed force her to marry the bounder who acted in such a disagreeable manner. Because that was what any lady would want after being frightened witless: to endure the rest of her life with a man who owned a clear disregard for her wishes and sensibilities.

"I must go," Jemma muttered when her name sounded once more. Skirting around Ophelia, Jemma hurried toward her sister's voice.

Ophelia gripped the skirts of her gown and ran toward where the bounder had been dragged. Only a few paces in, she stopped. A spark of red in the dark drew her attention. It was Devlin, and he was smoking a cheroot.

"What have you done with him?" she asked, making her way over to that beacon.

The scent of something tangy wafted on the air.

"He is trussed up and awaiting me."

What did that mean? Muffled sounds came from a corner a few feet from her, and she gathered that the blackguard was somewhere close by. Ophelia grabbed Devlin's arm and tugged him away to another section of the gardens so they could not be overheard.

"I believe that gentleman you have trussed up and gagged is Lord Henry Forsythe. He is…he is a duke's son," she said, wincing at her apologetic tone.

"One who is ill-mannered and a brute and was about to strike you," Devlin said, his tone mild and bored.

Yet something about it had that black fright sweeping over

her once more.

He took her hand in his and tugged the glove off, lifting her hand close to his face for inspection. But, unfortunately, the half-moon barely provided any light, so she did not understand what he searched for.

"You ran to that lady's aid without any thought of your reputation."

"Is that censure I hear?"

"Yes. You are not allowed to put yourself in harm's way."

"Yet here I am with you outside in the dark, quite beyond the bounds of propriety with a man referred to by many as shrewdly ruthless."

Of course, he chose to ignore that pithy reply. She scowled at him, knowing he could not see her.

"Next time you are in such a situation, you wait and assess the surroundings to see how they could help you, instead of hurtling into the fray. If he had hit you, he would have lost his hand. Duke's son or not."

Ophelia believed the implacable promise in his tone, and it frightened her. "Do not speak so! You are not a peer…should you hit a gentleman, you can be…you can be sent to prison for it."

His low chuckle was mocking. "Worried about me?"

"Unspeakably so," she whispered, knowing the powers of lords within society. The laws were made by them, for them. "Will you un-truss him?"

"After I have given him a small lesson on how to treat the treasures we are given."

"Dev—"

His finger on her lips cut off her words.

"I'll not kill him, and this duke's son who would attack

women without any fear of consequences will return home intact. I promise you, however, he will always remember tonight's lesson."

"You are outrageous," she hissed, gripping his jacket, then with a soft cry releasing him to shake her hand.

"And you are hurt," he said, gently rubbing her knuckles.

She dropped her forehead on his chest, inhaling deeply. He glided his fingers over hers, searching and gently probing. The feel of his bare skin against hers was shocking. All at once she was aflame. When had he taken off his gloves? "Devlin?"

"Hmm?"

"I must return inside immediately."

He ran his fingers carefully over each of her fingers, down to her wrist, the callus tip of his fingers evoking a most rousing sensation.

"This one is swollen." With a tender brush of his lips, he kissed that finger.

Oh...Lord.

Ophelia caught her lower lip between her teeth and bit hard, hoping the small sting would center her. He turned her hand palm up and placed a warm, open-mouthed kiss to the center. Then, with provoking deliberateness, he kissed the pulse at her wrist.

"I have it on the highest authority that kissing wounds better does not work," she muttered, thoroughly cross with her reaction.

"Your voice is trembling, Fifi."

Ophelia's heart began a rapid hammering. Her cheeks burned, and she was grateful for the darkness. It was not only her voice that shook, but it also felt like tiny tremors were exploding throughout her body. *Fireworks.* And he seemed entirely unmoved. The utter wretchedness of that awareness brought a tight ache to her throat. Was it that she wanted him to be just as affected by their closeness?

He touched a spot, and she flinched, saving her from coming up with a response.

"Here?" he murmured, tenderly pressing.

"Yes."

"It is not broken or sprained."

"How can you tell?"

"I am familiar with broken bones."

How bland his tone was, yet it hinted at hidden pain. "Yours?"

"Yes."

She was aghast. "How?"

"I worked in a fighting pit for a few years, and there were other circumstances."

She couldn't imagine what he meant. "What other circumstances?"

He stilled. "I will tell you another time."

His calloused thumb rested against her wrist, sending another wave of heat through her.

"Your heart is beating rather fast, Fifi, and you are trembling."

Ophelia closed her eyes against a wave of embarrassment. "I'm not quite sure what has come over me. It must be the night's air."

Tugging her fingers from his, she stepped away from his closeness. Suddenly she felt like she could breathe again without filling her body with impossible cravings. She did not bid him good night or warn him again from hurting a duke's son. Ophelia simply had to get away.

So she left without looking behind, painfully conscious of the feel of his stare against her shoulders. Every instinct warned her that Devlin Byrne was not a man she should become entangled with in *any* form. The boy she had met back then and liked so much no longer existed. There was no justifiable reason to maintain a connection with him.

None.

Yet her heart did not want to listen to reason, for it danced and skipped in anticipation of when she might see him again.

CHAPTER SEVEN

Devlin poured himself a glass of brandy and sat down on the sofa instead of behind his desk to read an investment report. Conan jumped onto the cushions and sprawled his large body on the sofa, resting his paw and head against one of Devlin's thighs.

Idly he stroked his back while he read the notations his man of affairs had made on the expected returns. Several minutes later, he lowered the papers with a grunt of irritation. His concentration was disturbed. His body was on edge, yet he was denying himself release. After leaving the ball last night, he had delivered that bounder at his father's townhouse still trussed up, his cravat tied over his eyes. Devlin had reacted to Fifi's worry and had kept his identity a secret and his actions very circumspect. No one would know he had a hand in the entire affair. It was not the lesson he'd wanted to impart, yet one could hope the humiliation of being found tied on the ground in that manner by the servants would teach the man a lesson.

He had thought about sending Fifi a note but had refrained after seeing their names linked in the society page of at least three different newssheets. Dancing with Fifi had been interesting. Devlin had anticipated her cutting him dead, yet she had lifted her chin and not looked away from his challenge. Her actions were worthy enough to send the *ton* in a fit of distemper, yet she had not flinched away from him or their anticipated reaction.

The young girl he remembered had been brave, the woman even braver. His intrigue was stoked to even greater heights. And when they'd danced, he had seen the awakening sensuality in her gaze. Fifi wanted him.

His body…his damn fingertip remembered every place he had touched her.

The door opened, and he slammed it shut on his thoughts. Glancing up, he saw Poppy hobbling inside. He did not rise or make any offer of assistance. Miss Poppy Dobson was fiercely proud and independent and would twist his ear should he dare to treat her as if she were less because she had lost a foot.

"You are home," she said with a smile, which quickly disappeared when she noted he only read with one lamp.

Using her crutch, she went over to the other lamp and turned up the wick before moving to sit on the sofa facing him. With care, she placed the crutches to her left.

"I hired a new maid today," she said, patting the cushion to her right.

Conan left his side and bounded over to her. Dog and woman greeted each other in a series of coos and growls.

"Another one?"

This was the third new maid Poppy had hired in the past month. She acted in the capacity of his housekeeper because she stubbornly refused to live on charity. Poppy was like a sister to him, and he felt extremely fortunate to have her present in his household.

"Yes, I… John said when he saw her in the market, she had bruises on her arm and a man chased her."

John was a young lad who served as a footman.

"She was scared and crying."

A chill of violence brushed against Devlin's senses. "Who

was this man?"

"John did not say, but thankfully he brought her home."

Poppy sighed.

The heaviness of it had him tossing the investment papers onto the desk in the far corner. "What is it?"

"The girl, her name is Mary, and she believes she is with child. The rumors will… They will talk about us for hiring a maid who is pregnant."

"I suspect it was her employer?"

"Yes. A Sir Henry Clarke," Poppy spat, looking away into the fire.

"You did the right thing. However, I think we should send her to one of my other estates in the country. There she will be safe, and the staff will take care of her. Send instructions to Mrs. Hagley in Dorset to care for her and ensure physicians and midwives attend to her. The girl should be kept on and be given a salary during her confinement."

Poppy smiled at him, and the radiance of it eased some of the cold tension in his gut. Sir Henry Clarke would be taught there were consequences to preying on those who worked in his household and had little to no power to resist his advances.

"There is something else," Poppy said. "Mr. Baker came by today with several reports that he marked as urgent. Did you see them?"

Devlin assessed the bright spots on Poppy's cheek and the nervous way she clasped her hands together.

"Did something happen between you and Noel?"

Her wide eyes swung to his, and she looked ready to collapse. "Why would you say so!"

"You are blushing, Poppy."

"You wretched man!" she burst out.

Devlin leaned forward with a frown. "If he acted improperly and scared you, I will gut him," he said, recalling the many times he had caught his man of affairs staring at Poppy. Though the man would also always ask after her, and whenever she entered their presence, he treated her with the utmost care and respect. Poppy, in turn, avoided him as if he were a bug. The situation almost amused Devlin, but if Noel had hurt her in any way, he would painfully regret it.

"No, it isn't anything like that. He…he…" She looked away, her throat working on a swallow. "He asked me to marry him."

She said this without looking at Devlin, but he noted how her fingers gripped the skirt of her dark blue bombazine gown.

"Why does that shock you so much?" he murmured.

Her head whipped around to meet his gaze. "Did you hear me, Devlin? Mr. Baker asked *me* to marry him."

He smiled at her with amused affection. "I heard you. You are a lovely, intelligent woman. I am only surprised he took this long."

Her lips parted, but no sound emerged.

"It would be an unthinkable disgrace to accept. I am no one; how could he, a promising barrister, wish to marry me?" she demanded with an incredulous laugh.

Devlin hated to see the tears glistening in her eyes. Yet, she was strong enough to not allow them to spill over.

"Poppy—"

"My mother was an orange cart seller. His father is a well-known magistrate in Cornwall. What is he thinking?"

Devlin had met Poppy when he saved her from a lord who thought her less than himself. His back tingled in remembrance of the whip slicing into his skin. A whip that had been meant for a young girl of ten years old. Devlin stared at Poppy, noting her sheer loveliness. Though she was three and twenty, she appeared wiser than her years, a result of knowing the harsh side of living like himself. She owned a buxom beauty, with vibrant golden hair and soft gray eyes, and she loved the scent of fragrance soap. Devlin bought her dozens over the years. He had taught her to read as he learned, how to dance as he learned, and how to fence.

"Noel is thinking that he admires you and wants to make you his wife."

"We do not belong. We are not from the same world."

"I am fucking tired of hearing that particular line."

Poppy gave a small, frustrated exclamation. "Is that why you danced with Lady Ophelia last night? Because you forgot we do not belong to *that* world or with them?"

He stilled.

"I read the scandal sheets, Devlin," she said softly, looking at him worriedly. "What are you doing?"

"It's Fifi," he muttered gruffly.

Poppy's eyes widened dramatically. "She...*Fifi*?"

"Yes."

"Oh, Devlin, she is a marquess's daughter."

He found for a moment he had nothing, nothing at all, to retort. Then, "You say it as if it is a tragedy."

"Well, isn't it?"

"No. Women of quality bed men like me all the time. The danger of waltzing close to the forbidden," he said with a sarcastic bite.

"And that is all you want?" Poppy asked tartly. "To bed her?"

"What else could I possibly want?" he asked icily, ignoring that nameless fucking hunger that seemed to rest upon his soul. "You do not ever have to worry about her and me. I am not a fool, Poppy; you know that. My wants are simple, and once they are satiated, I move on."

"Devlin—"

He leaned forward even more. "Do you love Noel?"

"I would *never* marry a nob!"

"He's not a nob. He is one of *us*."

"Is he?" she demanded rawly. "He never lived on the streets or in stews."

"True. Neither is Noel Baker proud, cruel, nor believes himself better than us. He is a second son set to inherit nothing from his father, and he came to London and clawed and fought his way, just like us, Poppy. He is a brilliant man of affairs and will make a formidable barrister."

Her lips trembled, but that she did not protest gave Devlin hope she might not let fear and prejudice destroy the possibility of a future. One of them deserved to be damn well happy, and that should be Poppy.

"Do you hold any affections for him? Surely there is something to make him ask."

She flushed a telltale shade of red, and her eyes slid away from his. Devlin thought of all the time Noel spent within this house, in this office without the presence of Devlin. Poppy, as his housekeeper, would have often been present. They would have been alone many times.

"I bring nothing to him," she said, "I—"

"You have a dowry—"

She gazed at him with dazed eyes. "I beg your pardon."

"I have always planned that you might want to get married one day," he said gruffly. "I started putting away for your dowry when I was eighteen. I always meant to tell you when you seemed open to it."

She glanced down at her missing leg, and when she looked back at him, a lone tear spilled over.

"I have a dowry," she said again as if she truly did not understand it. "I am your housekeeper. I am not—"

"You are my family, Poppy. You are not just a housekeeper; you know that. You run this house like a general, you help me dictate my letters, and you even help assess my investment reports. You like to keep busy, and whatever you ask of me, I have granted it. Do not believe for a minute I consider you less than either of my sisters."

She stared at him for a long time before a watery laugh escaped her. "Tell me about this dowry."

"It is twenty thousand pounds, shares in a mine, and a seven-bedroom cottage in Lincolnshire."

She set one hand to her bosom as if to still her palpitating heart. "Does Noel know about this?"

"No. Nor do you have to marry for your inheritance to be yours."

She started to sob. Devlin shifted and went over to her, nudging Conan and taking his place on the sofa. His dog yawned and padded over to sprawl by the fireplace. Devlin became aware of the fact that she was trembling. Without a word, he placed his hand around her shoulder and drew her slowly into his arms.

"I love him, Devlin," she gasped. "I do love him."

"Then fuck all the fear you are feeling," he said with crude gentleness, "and marry him."

Poppy laughed and rested her head on his shoulder. "Thank you," she whispered.

Anytime, he thought as he sat there and simply held her.

• • •

Ophelia did not run away from uncomfortable situations, as they would only chase after her. Of course, it was her papa who had taught her that. Yet she stood outside the drawing room, wishing she could turn around and escape this confrontation with her parents.

Her papa was shouting. Her mother's more modulated tone would not soothe his ire. There was a third voice, softer than her mother's, one Ophelia could not discern.

"She danced with that man!"

"It is nonsensical to be this upset about the matter when you are still recovering, my darling. And do recall your account is from the scandal sheets. We must wait to speak with our daughter before making any assumptions."

Ophelia closed her eyes. *Yes, I danced with him, Papa. In sight of everyone, and then again, alone in the dark.* And it was there she learned how much she desperately wanted him.

She knocked on the door and entered with a smile that faltered when she saw her cousin Effie standing by the window with a cup of tea in her hands.

"Effie!"

Her cousin smiled brightly, her beauty lighting up the room as if the sun had decided to appear from beneath the unexpectedly overcast clouds.

"Whatever are you doing here, Effie? I had not thought to see you until Christmas. I thought you were off to Bath until then?"

Her cousin flicked a quick, discreet glance to her parents, and suddenly Ophelia understood.

"You've asked Cousin Effie to chaperone me?" she asked, incredulity rife in her tone. "Mama, I am four and twenty and, according to many scandals rags, a spinster."

Ophelia had been afforded many liberties this past year, and it was because of her age and the trust her parents afforded her. Of course, when she went shopping with her friends, she would take her lady maid and footmen along, but she had to forgo any chaperone at society events this season. She stiffened as an understanding dawned. Ophelia and her parents had a tacit agreement. Since she was a little girl, they'd allowed her the freedom to be herself, with the understanding that all those freedoms *must* be private. Last night, she had broken that agreement.

Despite her love for them, for the first time in her life, she wondered how long she could live with such a restraint. Her future could not be living with her parents and dancing to attend to their expectations. There was so much more. Love and laughter and children.

Oh God, am I being silly to wait for love? What if she never found it—what then?

Shaking away the alarming questions rousing in her heart, she asked, "Cousin Effie and I are practically the same age, Mama."

"Cousin Effie is nine and twenty and a widow," her mother said gently. "And you must think of her more as a companion, not a chaperone."

"Mama—"

"After last night, what did you believe would happen?" her father demanded, a scowl darkening his features.

"I merely danced with a gentleman at a ball. It does not warrant any security or speculations," she said, walking to sit on the sofa.

"A gentleman, you say," Papa thundered. "Devlin Byrne is not a gentleman, and he is not from our society! It is ill-judged to think a man can crawl from the gutter and strive to sit above his natural place."

Ophelia swallowed down the sick feeling that entered her stomach. "And where is Mr. Byrne's natural place?"

"Not at a ball, and most certainly not dancing with my daughter," he spat, "casting shade on her reputation to be associated with the likes of him. This man is unequal to you in every respect and very much unqualified to so much as hold a conversation with you. What would he even dare speak to you about? You are more educated than he is."

Ophelia felt a ripple of guilt, for she knew these words were not enough to keep her away from Devlin. She did not ascribe to her parents' prejudicial nature, nor did she believe being born into a blue-blood family made her better. Ophelia was certainly *not* better, and her father should know this. From the little she had been able to learn, Sally Martin had been a poor country girl, only with great beauty and wit. Was her father forgetting that she was not fully blue-blooded?

"Formally, I might be," she said softly. "However, given that Mr. Byrne has wealth that is rumored to rival most peers and can pen such political letters that inflame society, I daresay he is a man of equal wits and intelligence, Papa, and it astounds me you would ignore such accomplishments."

"Your defense of this man is unacceptable," her father snapped.

Cousin Effie sent her a sympathetic smile. They did not argue often, or at all, and Ophelia did not like the awful feelings stirring low in her belly. Most profound was disappointment. "You taught me to be kind to others, Papa, but you are now angry that I did not cut Mr. Byrne directly?"

"Kindness must be rendered to others who are deserving," he coldly said.

"And what has Mr. Byrne done to make him undeserving? He was born poor but worked diligently to shape himself into the wealthy industrialist he is today. Is the natural order that he should remain poor for his life? Is that why most of the bills that support education and workhouse reforms for the poorer class are never passed? Lords of your elevated standards cannot bear to share their wealth and knowledge?"

Her father stared at her as if she were a creature dropped from the ceiling. "You dare?" he said in a low, angry tone.

"Come, my dear," her mother said, standing and placing a restraining hand on her husband's arm. "Do not be angry. Recall the doctor said you are not to display any excessive emotions. It is not good for your heart."

Immediately, the hurt digging its claw deeper inside Ophelia eased, and concern rushed through her. She stood and hurried over to his side. "I do not mean to aggravate your heart, Papa."

He grunted something beneath his breath, but she caught "*spoiled rotten*," "*willful*," and "*locked in her room without food.*"

Ophelia chuckled, peeking up at him. "Papa, you would never lock me in my room without food. Who would obey? Certainly not the staff. They *adore* me."

He spluttered, and she brushed a kiss across his cheek. He froze, and it was then she realized her actions. Her throat tightened with emotions. Since he had shattered the faith she had in his honor, Ophelia had not been this affectionate with her father. Hope kindled in the gaze that stared at her, and to her mortification, she felt tears prick behind her lids.

Forgiving him was inevitable, for she loved him. But not now—not when he remained closed and refused to tell her of Sally Martin even though he must know it lay heavily on her heart.

Drawing back, she said a bit hoarsely, "I promised Fanny we would visit Hatchards today."

"I'd ordered a few books. Be a dear and collect them for me," her mother said with a small encouraging smile. "And do ensure you take Cousin Effie with you."

She shared a glance with her cousin, who seemed to be holding back her laugh. Ophelia smiled and said, "Yes, Mama."

She walked away, not liking the gamut of emotions running through her heart.

"Ophelia?"

She faltered at the steel lacing her mother's tone.

"Yes, Mama," she said without turning around. She would hate for them to see the vulnerability she felt in her heart evident in her expression.

"Should this Devlin Byrne approach you publicly again, for any reason, we expect you to act according to your position in this family and within society. That man must not be entertained in any manner, for he is not… He is not of our set, my dear, and simply not acceptable. You must take care not to be callous with our reputations or do anything that will put yourself quite beyond the pale."

Another stretch of silence passed, barely endurable. Ice congealed in her chest, then exploded. But the shards burned.

Whirling around, she said, "Devlin Byrne is the boy… He is the little boy who saved me from drowning years ago. The one who carried me on his back for miles without rest. The boy who hunted in unfamiliar woods and fed me. The boy who told me stories of his home when I was sad and frightened. The boy who took me home to you. Should I repay his kindness by pretending I am better than he is?"

Her mother swayed, and her face had paled. Uttering an incredulous laugh, she glanced up at her husband. "That child... He is Devlin Byrne?"

"Yes," Ophelia said.

"That is why you danced with him? To repay a kindness?"

"That is a part of it," she answered truthfully. "I believe he wants to be acceptable to the *ton*, and Mama, all it takes is the sponsorship of someone noteworthy. I had hope that dancing with him would signal to the *ton* he is not some elusive monster come to steal their peace but merely a shrewd, respectable businessman."

If she had expected that knowledge to soften their prejudicial stance, Ophelia was corrected when her father's mien grew even more austere.

"Then it is evident what game of his is afoot, and it will not be countenanced. And by whatever silly means you find this hard to understand, you *are* better than that unknown mongrel."

"Papa, I do not—"

"He wants to marry you," he said, interrupting her protest.

"Marry me?" Now it was her turn to laugh, and she did so without tempering herself. "Papa, I am most certain you have mistaken the matter. Mr. Byrne simply asked for a dance." And a song. *And I have accepted thousands of pounds from him.*

Dear God. If her parents knew it was his money she was secretly using to save their estates and to pay the wages of their servants...

"That was the last thing that boy said to me, young lady. That he would marry you."

She sighed exasperatedly. "Well, marriage takes two. And Papa, that was over fifteen years ago. I assure you that very naive promise we made to each other is long forgotten."

Her mother stood shoulder to shoulder with her father in support and said firmly, "You have repaid Mr. Byrne's kindness by dancing with him once. That was an acceptable nod, and it must be enough. Consider the matter now finished."

Dipping into a quick, respectful curtsy, she bid them adieu and escaped the drawing room with Cousin Effie on her heels.

"Allow me to retrieve my pelisse," Effie said, touching her shoulders gently. Effie held her gaze for a long moment as if reading her innermost thoughts. "I gather you need someone to speak with now."

Ophelia shook her head. "I would prefer to not speak about Mr. Byrne."

Worried brown eyes skipped over her features. "Are you certain? Even I was alarmed when I saw the mentions in the newssheet."

"There is no need for any concern. It was but a dance and mild discourse." *And the very beginning of my fall from the tedium of life and into the fires of temptation.* Ophelia winced. "I will await you in the carriage."

The fingers that set the hat atop her head at a rakish tilt shook fiercely.

As she walked down the hallway and allowed the butler to help her slip on her pelisse, Ophelia couldn't help noting that her heart once again danced a wild, impossible rhythm that felt like a song of dreams in her head.

CHAPTER EIGHT

Another coincidence of fate.

That errant thought drifted lazily through Devlin's mind as he stood at the window of the bookstore, discreetly looking at the ladies walking along Piccadilly. Only one had arrested his attention, however. He would know the curve of her lips, that pointed chin, and her delectably petite shape anywhere. He had a well-stocked library at home and often walked along Piccadilly to visit the bookstore to peruse their latest intake. This was the first time he had ever encountered Fifi.

She strolled along with two ladies, laughing gaily, uncaring that she did so publicly with her whole face. She appeared quite exquisite in a fetching dark yellow pelisse and a walking dress a shade lighter. Her fetching bonnet was titled rakishly atop her raven-black curls, with several tendrils bouncing about her forehead and cheeks. One of the ladies said something to her, and she covered her mouth with her gloved hand, hiding her obvious delight.

A young lad ran up to them, and when one of the ladies attempted to run him away, Fifi placed a restraining hand on her arm. Dipping into the pocket of her reticule, she withdrew a coin purse. Devlin tensed and, gripping his umbrella, moved toward the bookstore's entrance. The boy, who could be no more than eight years, grabbed the coin purse and darted away. How shocked and befuddled she appeared, then, to his surprise, she laughed, as if she had not been robbed. One of her elegant companions waved a parasol at the young thief and gave chase with two footmen following at her heels.

From the quick movements Fifi made with her hands and the insufferable arrogance writ large upon her other companion's face, he discerned she was not pleased with Fifi's reaction. Devlin smiled. In his experience, nobs never took lightly someone robbing them. In truth, they could be merciless about it. That Fifi remained unaffected showed her generosity of spirit.

With a smile, he went to the small counter and collected his order. Over the years, once he'd learn how to read, it had become one of Devlin's favorite pastimes. Fifi had instilled in him a love of the written word, and to date, his favorite pleasures were the Brothers Grimm folklore stories.

The proprietor eyed Conan a bit skeptically but did not order the dog to leave the bookstore. A few of the patrons had also sent them arched looks, but Devlin ignored them. His dog was well-behaved and would never cause a ruckus inside the establishment.

Taking his wrapped package, he hurried outside, noting that it had started to rain. The sky hung dark overhead, the clouds a deep blue gray that threatened rain. Fifi looked skyward, and so did her friend. The other who had chased the pickpocket had yet to return. Thunder rumbled distantly, and the ladies hurried their walking. Devlin held back, wondering if she would notice him. Without warning, the sky opened, and the rain fell in earnest.

Fifi's lady friend, a woman of refined elegance, dashed in a mad run toward the large store beside the bookshop. Several other pedestrians hurried for cover, and a few even hopped into their parked carriages, which rumbled away. A footman dropped some packages he carried for his lady and was met with a severe rebuke. His lady employer did not pause to help the footman but hurried out of the rain.

Fifi did not rush from the rain but stooped to help the harried-looking footman collect the packages with a smile.

Devlin admired her independent nature, kindness, and utter loveliness. But the thing he still loved most was her incredible smile. As a boy, he had thought it felt like sunshine.

It still bloody did.

With quick strides, he went over and picked up a few packages and handed them to the man.

"Thank you, milord," he said, bobbing to Devlin.

He did not correct the man's assumption that he belonged to that set. Many merchants made the same error, given his wealth and the understated elegance of his tailoring. The footman hastened away.

"Oh, dear, I am awfully wet!"

"Allow me to offer some shelter from the rain," he said, opening the large umbrella over her head.

She stilled and slowly lifted her head to meet his regard.

"Oh!"

Devlin was intensely aware of Fifi's scent and the lush diminutive form of her body when she stood this close to him. A slight tremor of response went through her, suggesting she sensed the raw need pulsing through him. He reined in his response and shifted the umbrella closer.

"May I walk you to your carriage?"

Her throat worked on a swallow. "It is parked some distance away."

Glancing up and down the street, she noted it was very empty. They were the only ones standing there in the wide, empty street, the rain pelting the heavy umbrella. Devlin saw that she was worried for her reputation, and despite the heaviness in his gut, he understood. He bowed slightly. "I will bid you a good day, Lady Ophelia. However, please allow me to leave my umbrella with you."

· · ·

Ophelia faltered in the act of dashing toward the bookstore's awning, where several maids and footmen lingered. All the ladies and gentlemen had ducked into the various shops along Piccadilly to avoid the sudden downpour. She noted that Cousin Effie had run into Fortnum & Mason and would not likely come out soon.

"I cannot take your umbrella," she said softly. Tendrils of water ran from the brim of her hat onto her cheeks. "I have a sturdy constitution. A little rain would not harm me."

His mouth curved, and he dipped into a slight bow. "Then I bid you good day."

When he made to move off, she said, "Where is your carriage parked?"

God. She really did not want him to leave.

"I walked."

"From your home?"

"I enjoy walking."

Swallowing, she stared at Devlin, painfully aware they were the only ones now standing in the streets. "Perhaps you should walk me to my carriage. My maid was determined to chase a little boy who took off with my coin purse, and my cousin is inside a shop sheltering."

"You do not wish to shelter in place with your cousin?"

Propriety and the expectations of her parents dictated that

she should. "It is more palatable to be in my carriage's warm confines than a store that is surely packed with those hiding from the rain."

Do you want to start a scandal? was the errant thought that floated through Ophelia's awareness before she dismissed it. There was no one about, and the umbrella was large enough to hide their features should anyone try to look at them through the sleeting rain.

He nodded, and they walked toward her carriage in the distance, the rain muddying her boots and the hem of her pelisse. Today he was dressed elegantly in a coat of blue superfine, a waistcoat of silver with darker gray trousers over shining boots. He was the perfect picture of a gentleman until one glanced at his face. Despite his arresting handsome visage, there was a hardness in his eyes, a permanent cynical curve to his mouth, and a proud, arrogant tilt to his head, as if he stood in judgment of the world he stared at.

Ophelia shuffled closer under the umbrella and was instantly overwhelmed by the solid, unyielding strength in him. Desperately aware of him, she glanced at the package he held close to his chest.

"You collected books from Hatchards," she said, smiling, recalling a time when she attempted to teach him his letters.

"Yes."

She snaked another sideways glance at him before hopping over a puddle. "What titles?"

"*The Village of Mariendorpt* and *Travels into Several Remote Nations of the World. In Four Parts. By Lemuel Gulliver, First a Surgeon, and then a Captain of Several Ships.*"

"My friend Fanny wants to read *The Village of Mariendorpt.* It is not in the circulating library as yet. I intend to purchase her a copy for the outrageous sum of three pounds!"

"I once heard a nob say it is a good thing that books are expensive, for it prevents those in the lower classes from becoming infected with unsuitable ideas for their station," Devlin replied caustically.

"How outrageous," she said, wrinkling her nose.

"It is. One day, however, it will change, and reading will be available to all."

"Do you believe so?"

"Yes."

She liked his self-assurance and thought that men like Devlin should have a voice in making laws. Not only titled lords. Conan rushed forward, jumping into several puddles, streaking his wonderful coat with mud. Something about the dog's obvious happiness with the rain delighted Ophelia, and she laughed. "Conan is incorrigible and such a beautiful beast," she murmured, watching the dog frolic in the rain. "What breed is he?"

"He is a Bullmastiff."

"Has he been with you long?"

"Five years."

"He is happy."

"And *very* dirty. We shall have a hot bath together."

"You take baths with your dog?" she asked, aghast and also amused. She dearly tried not to imagine a naked Devlin in a large copper tub.

"My tub is rather large."

Ophelia laughed, then hurriedly covered her mouth with her gloved hand. "Surely I cannot believe you."

"It is such a shame to cover your smile," he said.

"Ah, but you do not realize the scandal it would cause

should I dare laugh in so unfettered a manner." She shuddered mockingly. "The vulgarity of it would see me as the main topic of conversation for a week." Ophelia peeked up at him again. "What happened to the duke's son?"

"Young Lord Henry Forsythe arrived home safely without any bruises."

"Thank you."

His gaze skipped over her lips before he looked away. "Did you know that Herodotus was coined the father of history by Cicero?"

"I did very poorly with my Greek lessons," she said, staring at him and noting the way his gaze dropped to her mouth, then glanced away. "I suspect because you want to kiss me, you spewed a random fact. How was it as a distraction tactic?" Ophelia had meant her words to be teasing, but they came out a touch too breathless.

"Did I?"

"Yes. It is particularly charming."

"I admit I have grown hungry for a taste of your mouth. Exercise in restraint is not my strong point."

Ophelia was unprepared for his provocative words and the sensual quirk to his lips. Heat flushed her entire body, and she glared at him. Or attempted it but ruined it by grinning. "There is something very wicked about you, isn't there?"

His eyes were bright with wry humor. "Do you want to explore it?" he asked silkily.

Temptation slid against her skin like a honeyed blade. *Forbidden lovers…*

"Do you hear the music in the raindrops?" she asked, employing distraction. "I hear it against the umbrella…and how it falls against the ground. Even in the *clip-clop* of our shoes, I hear a melody."

"Then sing a song to it."

"Do you plan to sing with me?"

"God, no. I still sound like a croaking frog."

"You were not that bad."

Unexpectedly, he waved a hand and did this quick tap with his feet in a dance and warbled a few lines. Ophelia was astonished, and then she was delighted. Grinning like a loon, she hurried to keep pace with his outrageous tapping and singing in the rain. She repeated his lines in a song that quivered to the beat of the slashing rain, shocked to discover how free and simply wonderful she felt in the moment.

He faltered, and when she met his eyes, her song died.

"Do not look at me so," she begged. "Please."

Devlin had been fashioned by Lucifer to tempt her. All the warnings from her mother about gentlemen of his ilk who seduced and discarded maidens roiled in her mind. But that seemed too unsavory a way to look at their situation, unlike the mutual satisfaction hinted at by *forbidden lovers.*

Her carriage came into sight, and she paused, slowing, not wanting to reach it so soon.

"Is that your carriage?" he pointed out to her.

"I'm afraid so. Is it wicked of me to wish I did not have to return to my gilded cage?"

"Very, but I am glad you do not want to rush away from me, Fifi. Do not worry—we will meet again."

As they neared the carriage, he opened the door and kicked down the step for her to enter. Their eyes met, and he doffed his hat and bowed slightly to her as she climbed aboard. A footman had rushed to help and closed the door, sealing her inside.

Devlin smiled and then turned and walked on with Conan at his heels.

• • •

A kiss from you to me.

The shock of those words almost sent Ophelia straight into a faint. *The damn scoundrel.*

After not hearing from him for almost a week, was this truly the note he sent her? It also did not escape her attention that she had teased him in the rain about kissing. The man had clearly pondered upon it and came up with this. She opened the second envelope with trembling fingers to see what he believed a kiss from her was worth. Everything else before had been ten thousand pounds, extraordinary sums by any standard. But she had not thought he would have dared overstep the tentative bonds of friendship that had rekindled.

Memories of how he had held her when they danced, the intensity of his stare, and the dreams…those *silly*, persistent dreams that came to her nightly. She fooled herself into thinking only a peculiar friendship lingered in the air. There was so much more, and Ophelia was not afraid to face that he attracted her in a manner no other gentleman had ever done before.

I would have kissed you without an incentive.

Flushing, she tossed down the note, hating to look at the amount of money offered. Rubbing her chest, she padded over to the fireplace and held out her hands, wanting to warm the icy chill that had encased her body. Was this how he conducted all his relationships? Something had to be offered to receive something in return. Did he only perform transactions? Was nothing driven by impulse, and want, and desire?

Annoyed with herself for wanting to look at the bank draft, she marched to the music room and sat before the pianoforte. She started to play, closing her eyes. A deep study of the estate and the ledgers every day for the last week showed extraordinary loans that Papa had taken out over the years. Forty-five thousand pounds in one instance, then six years ago another fifty-eight thousand pounds. Their estate pulled in a generous income, and most went to pay these loans with little going toward the upkeep of the mills and country estates that relied on tenant farmers.

Clearly, Papa's heart illness for the last several months had done him no favors. Ophelia had observed they were still unable to make the accounts in the black, but in the ledgers and letters, she saw no plans to show how her father would rectify the matter. She had tried several times to total their indebtedness and, whenever she thought she had discovered the whole, found another debt or loan that needed to be paid. And her father continually refused to discuss it with her despite her attempts.

A kiss from you to me.

In the secret recesses of her dreams where wanton wickedness lurked, she had thought more than once about kissing Devlin Byrne. But not like this. Not for money!

Blowing out a frustrated breath, she continued playing with vigor and passion, losing herself in the piece. As a lover of music, she found the sound of songs in almost everything— the swaying of the trees as the wind whispered through the leaves, the gentle babbling of a brook, the chirping of birds, the ping of rain against the windows, the clatter and *clip-clop* of heels on cobbled surfaces and parquet floors. Everything had its own rhythms and melodies.

Sometimes even as she lay in bed unable to sleep, Ophelia would find the notes of a melody in the stillness of the night. She would hum, and words and musical notes would dance on the bed canopy and in the air, so vivid was her imagination. Whenever she thought of Niall...Devlin Byrne, the sensations that cascaded through her were like a song thrumming through her soul, aching to escape its confines.

A melody would play inside her, at first a sweet hiss, a slight stutter as if there was uncertainty, but it never stayed in that low note. The melodies she felt were dark and slow, sultry, tempting. Her fingers danced over the keyboards, and the words of the song she had written for him hovered on her lips but did not fall. Ophelia closed her eyes, allowing the music drifting from the pianoforte to tug at the long-buried desires. Behind her closed eyelids, the notes she played danced and twisted as if truly alive. Right at that moment, she heard his voice in the darkness—the start of a gentle breeze.

A kiss from you to me...

A discordant sound startled her, and she snapped her eyes open.

"Forgive me. I did not mean to startle you," a low voice said.

Ophelia stood and turned around to see Peter, the Earl of Langdon, his golden hair shining like a halo under the rays of the sunlight.

"Lord Langdon!" A quick glance behind him showed their door had been left ajar, but she saw no servant or her mother. "Did you call for me?"

"Your mother did not want to disturb your playing, and neither did I. She has left to hand the roses I brought over to a servant. I gather she will return soon."

Ophelia felt a new wariness come over her. "I see."

He came toward her, and she skirted around the bench to keep a respectable distance between them. He ran his fingers over the keys of the pianoforte, producing a lively tune.

"I do not see any music sheets. What piece did you play? I have never heard it before, and it was beyond lovely."

"I wrote it."

"*You* wrote it?"

She smiled at his surprise. "We ladies are an accomplished lot, you know."

"I've also heard you have a more than pleasant singing voice."

When she shot him a startled glance, he said, "Your performance at Lady Trumbell's musicale was spoken about for weeks."

"That musicale was last year, my lord." The earl flushed and tugged at his cravat. Was he nervous? "Lord Langdon, I—"

He smiled in that charmingly boyish way of his. "Please, Ophelia. I daresay we are friends. I have asked you many times to call me Peter."

"Peter," she said softly, walking over to the large windows that faced the gardens. "I had no notion you would call upon me today."

"I was driving my new curricle in the park, and I suddenly felt inspired to stop by and invite you to a drive out."

Ophelia turned and leaned her back against the wall, pinning the billowing drapes in place. Peter had asked her to marry him last season, and she had gently declined. It had stunned him, for he was a most eligible catch, and he had clearly thought his suit would be acceptable to any lady he chose to honor with an offer.

This was the fourth time he had called on her within the last month, not to mention the dances he asked for at balls. She had walked out with him at Hyde Park last week, and they had spent a lively hour discussing horses. A very passionate topic for him, but admittedly she had not been bored. She enjoyed his amiable manners, and he was very handsome and kind. However, Ophelia did not want him to believe there was a chance she might accept his proposal should he renew his offer. She simply had no tender feelings for him.

"You are staring at me in a rather frank manner," he said with a slight chuckle. "Is my cravat undone?"

"I am a frank sort of girl," she said with a slight smile. "I was merely lost in thought for a moment."

"And what thoughts were those, if I might be bold enough to inquire?"

She hesitated, and his gaze sharpened. "I thought this felt like it could be the beginning of a courtship," she said candidly.

"And you object to the idea?"

"I still have no wish to marry at the moment. Your efforts would be in vain, my lord."

"And if I wanted to wait on you, Ophelia?"

She stiffened, a stricken feeling stabbing at the heart of her. *Wait for me…*

"Whyever would you say this? I have not given you any hope that I have any tendre for you. There are many ladies far lovelier and more accomplished than I am who would be thrilled to be your countess!"

The way he stared at her was baffling. His expression was tender and almost loving. To her thoughts, there had been nothing in their interaction to suggest any passionate feelings on her part. Or on his!

"You are not in the first blush of youth as others, but you are beautiful. You are agreeable, dignified, and quite lovely on the inside and out. Why would I not want you as my countess?"

"I am not sure what you have heard—"

"It is what I have observed," he said with a charming wink.

Ophelia laughed. "I am not at all agreeable!"

"You also own the loveliest laugh I've ever heard. The thought of listening to it for the rest of my life is rather pleasing."

She stared at him, stunned and discomfited. "Peter—" she began.

He held up a hand. "I swear I did not call on you today to unsettle you. Would you like to see my curricle?"

"I suppose I would," she said kindly.

His eyes lit with pleasure, and as she collected her shawl and hat, she couldn't help noting that Effie was conspicuously absent to act as a chaperone and the smile on her mother's face was absurdly pleased.

Ophelia dancing with Devlin had really unsettled the wits of her parents. Her mother was matchmaking, clearly with the hopes her daughter might fall madly in love with the earl. Cousin Effie and perhaps Papa were in on the scheme. The freedom from their machinations she had enjoyed for so many seasons was coming to an end.

In her parents' mind, a wolf had stepped into her path, and they must save her before she was devoured.

Bollocks!

CHAPTER NINE

Upon returning from the park with Peter, Ophelia did not indulge her mother, who wanted to know every detail of their outing. Instead, she quickly excused herself, pleading a slight headache, and rushed to the privacy of her room to read the second note. The entire time she had laughed and chatted with the earl, admiring his new curricle, it had burned a hole in her pocket, taunting her.

A kiss from you to me. That was all she'd been able to think about.

Closing her door firmly, she dipped into the pocket of her day dress and retrieved the envelopes. Ophelia turned over the other folded note she had ignored earlier. This time, there was no money, and relief pulsed through her—though it was quite short-lived when she read his words.

One kiss, five thousand pounds.

Two kisses, another five thousand pounds.

Three kisses, another five thousand pounds.

And if you grant me a fourth, the total sum before double.

Perhaps with four kisses, Fifi, I shall stop thinking about kissing you.

"You scoundrel," she gasped, her fingers tightening over the paper. He would so casually pay thirty thousand pounds for four kisses. Her entire body shook with mortified heat. What manner of nonsense was this, and did he really own such a fortune?

Angered in a manner she did not understand, Ophelia

called for the carriage to deposit her at Grosvenor Square. She was careful to don her blond wig and a dark green silk pelisse with its frog fastening. Walking down the winding stairs, she paused at the soft call of her name. She gripped the banister and looked up. Cousin Effie lingered in the hallway, a book pressed against her bosom.

"Are you heading out?"

"Yes. I plan to call upon a friend."

Effie seemed indecisive, then her lips firmed. "I will be there in a few minutes."

Frustration surged through Ophelia. "Effie, it is too absurd! I am not a fresh-faced chit that needs to be hovered about. I appreciate your dedication to the task Mama set before you, but I'll not accept your hypocrisy."

Her cousin gasped, outrage parting her lips.

Ophelia held up a hand to forestall her reply. "I went out just now with Lord Langdon, and you were conveniently absent. I will not await you. I will be home in two hours."

Hurrying down the stairs, she went to the front parlor to await the carriage's arrival. Cousin Effie might have gone for her mother, and Ophelia braced for an argument but was quite relieved that neither showed. A few minutes later, she entered her family's carriage and was rattling away to Grosvenor Street. She gave specific instructions for the carriage to park two homes down from number thirty-six. So righteous in her indignation, it did not occur to Ophelia to wonder if a man as busy as Devlin Byrne would be home at three in the afternoon. Only after she knocked on his door and glanced about the streets did the idea float through her thoughts.

"Drat," she muttered, about to turn around when the door opened.

The butler stood at the door, his expression one of comical amazement. The man looked up and down the street and even lifted his face to the heavens.

"My good sir, are you wondering if I fell from the sky?" she asked crisply, bemused by his incredulity.

He drew himself up sharply. "Forgive my startlement, but my...my...there has not been a visitor in... We have never had a lady visitor. Have you called at the right address, my lady?"

"Is this the home of Mr. Devlin Byrne?"

The butler caught his splutter and assumed a mien of professionalism. "Yes, my lady. But he might not be home to you...my lady."

"Please inform Mr. Byrne that Lady Fifi has called about an important matter. You will see me to whichever lower room has a fire, and tea and cake will do nicely," she said with a smile, hoping to put him at ease.

Clearly, the man was flustered.

"Of course. Right away, my lady."

Ophelia did not hand over her pelisse when she entered. The butler ushered her to a tastefully decorated drawing room where a fire already roared in the hearth. The room was pleasantly warm and smelled like roses.

She did not have to wait long before the door was flung opened.

"Did something happen? Are you safe?"

Ophelia spun around at his rough, urgent demands. "I am well," she said, fighting back the ridiculous heat climbing in her cheeks and the warmth blooming in her heart at his concern.

A dart of awareness prickled along her skin. She had

interrupted Devlin's dressing.

He looked so darkly handsome and splendid, his silk shirt open at the neck revealing the corded muscles of his throat, the fine wool of his trousers accentuating the slimness of his hips and the muscles in his legs. He was without shoes. Or stockings. She had never seen a gentleman's toes before—not even her father's. An odd thought to have, and Ophelia hated that she was flustered.

His dark green eyes, filled with alarming savagery, rested upon her. "Why are you here? Did someone hurt you?"

At her lack of response, Devlin prowled over to her and took her chin between his fingers, tilting her face up to him. His touch shook the ground beneath her. *Bare skin to bare skin.* The feel of his finger against her skin...callused yet gentle, was an imprint she felt to her bones.

What if the pads of these fingers were to coast over the softness of her body? Ophelia wrenched away from him, putting distance between them and her shocking thoughts. "No one hurt me. That is not why I am here."

He made a sharp, slicing sweep of his hand. "I did not expect you to *ever* show up here. Tell me what has happened."

Suddenly, she felt foolish to have barged into his home. "I..." She laughed. "I...upon reflection, I can see my visit was entirely unnecessary. Please forgive my intrusion. I should return home right away."

His expression closed. "Not until you tell me what urged you to come here."

Blowing out a sharp breath, she tugged open the drawstring of her reticule, fumbled around, and withdrew the envelope with the notes. "I wanted to know: what is the absurd meaning of this?"

He looked briefly, chillingly amused before his expression once again became inscrutable. "My note was clear."

Her stomach did a frightening little flip. "I assure you I am not understanding the matter."

"I was offering you money for kisses."

She widened her eyes, genuinely shocked by the infuriatingly casual admission. "I do not want your money," she said, tossing the note to the ground. "I am guilty of accepting such outrageous payments for a song and dance...but *this*!"

"I offended you," he said in soft contemplation. "That was not my intention. Please tell me how I might remedy the situation."

"I am not a doxy! To offer me money...for a kiss..." Her chest lifted on the harshness of her breathing. Now she understood the burn that had lived inside her chest since reading his note. She was angry that he could so coldly offer money for something she foolishly yearned for. There were little feelings within him while she...while she could not stop thinking about the press of his lips to hers. "I am not a damn doxy or courtesan for you to pay for a kiss!"

He stilled. "Would you have given it willingly...without incentive?"

Yes! erupted in her mind, but she caught it in her throat. "That is entirely beside the point."

Her expression must have betrayed her words, for knowledge of her wanting him flashed in his eyes. With profound sadness, Ophelia noted he was shocked. Had every relationship of his been cast from transactions and bargains? Did he not trust that she could desire him for more than what his pockets offered?

He walked over to her; nay, he prowled as the sensation of

being hunted blossomed through her entire body. Yet Ophelia did not move but lifted her chin to meet his gaze with a defiant toss of her head.

He skimmed his fingers over her cheek, almost tentative in his exploration, very much at odds with the savage carnality of his expression. His gaze searched every nuance of her features as if he was trying to imprint something on his mind. "Tell me the truth, Fifi. If I had asked for your mouth as if asking for a dance, would you have given it to me?"

There was something sensually crude about his words, the almost cruel slant of his mouth, the dark desire flaring in his eyes that brought forth a flush to her cheeks. There was a low arousing thrum at the base of her spine, a musical note of lust that was intent on blossoming throughout her body. Its melody felt dark and complex.

Ophelia admitted then she was wildly, outrageously attracted to Devlin Byrne.

If this was wickedness, she wanted it…to swallow it whole and let it consume her. Just for a moment in time.

Her racing heartbeat was spilling all her secrets, for surely he could hear it, and within its erratic beat, Devlin would discern the wild hunger burgeoning for him. Dangerously, brazenly, *weakly*, she wondered how it would feel if she reached out to touch the fullness of his mouth. Tipped on her toes and kissed it. She felt an exquisite awareness of him, a sensation never felt before in her life. Her breasts swelled with languorous heaviness, her breathing fractured, and the unfamiliarity of her reaction frightened Ophelia.

Nothing in life should be this intense. She swallowed. "I…no…I…"

The few gentlemen who had tried to steal kisses from her

had been gallant, quoting poems and subtly drifting closer to her. Ophelia had always danced away from their reach, entirely disinterested in their practiced seduction and flirtations.

If I had asked for your mouth…

There was nothing practiced about that raw demand, nothing suave and charming. His callused thumb found its way to her mouth, and he gently rubbed that thumb over her bottom lip. "What if I had simply taken it, hmm? Would you have recoiled from me…and frantically scrubbed my taste from you?"

Tendrils of alarm and excitement speared through her stomach.

No. I would lick my lips in the hopes I would never lose your taste.

Ophelia felt as if she were falling from a high cliff, for she knew, without a doubt, Devlin Byrne would kiss her before she departed his home. Her heart was a pounding mess, and her knees were weak. It was more than that; butterflies wreaked havoc with her stomach.

"What if I should take your mouth now? What would you do, Fifi?"

"Take? You may only taste me if I am willing to permit it."

A rough, low groan came from him even as admiration lit in his eyes, and he lowered his hands. "Do you want the money?"

"My mouth is not for sale," she said with an unexpected spurt of black humor. "I daresay there are ladies you can purchase for a pittance."

"It is you I want, Fifi."

There. The mask of indifference cracked, and the desire she spied sent a frantic thrill through her heart. "And is that the only way you know how to go about it?" she demanded pertly. "To offer money for intimacy?"

A shadow darkened his eyes to emerald. "Ah, you mean I lack the finesse of a gentleman."

"Yes," she said. "There is no subtlety or art to your flirtation."

"Is that what you want, Fifi—subtlety?" he drawled bitingly. "Flowers, poems, and long walks?"

"A wholly unremarkable experience for you, I can tell."

"What a tart tongue you have," Devlin murmured, his eyes darkening with amusement and something terribly lascivious. And that very look called to something wild and improper inside of her.

"I never said I was one of your *tonnish* men, Fifi. I am simply a man wanting his woman…"

"I am not your woman!"

He took her chin between his fingers, bent, and kissed her lightly on the corner of her lips. "A man wanting a particular woman with every breath in his body and foolishly thinking money was the way to do it. I've never had any hand at courting."

She tried not to blush or fidget at his slow, measured, and very sensual appraisal.

"Is that what you are doing? The song…the dance…the thousands of pounds, *courting* me?"

His regard was intent and unreadable. "If I were?"

Her heart stuttered. "For marriage?"

He tapped the tip of her nose. "How aghast the lady sounds."

His words were laced with indifference, but his eyes

bespoke emotions she could not fathom.

"It is mere surprise, not dismay." Ophelia was unable to stop staring at him. The very notion that he might truly wish to marry her was simply outrageous and so…wonderful. *No… no…not wonderful; it cannot be wonderful.* Devlin did not love her, and she certainly did not love him. Worse, her parents would never suffer their union. The embarrassing nature of such a connection would see her father using all his power and influence to cast Devlin Byrne from her life and their society. Ophelia did not want to imagine to where he would be hurled—in Newgate on fabricated charges or the bottom of the Thames.

Its mere contemplation was frightening, for it showed how little faith she had left in her father's honor. The marquess was a man of power.

And so is Devlin, a little voice whispered.

Dear God. Ophelia gripped his hands at the wrists. "Devlin—"

"I urge you to be at ease, Fifi. I am not a fool in love with stupid…impossible expectations," he murmured with rough amusement. "Wipe the fright from your eyes."

"Then, if marriage was not your expectation, what do you want? Friendship?" she said tartly. "One with kisses?"

"Yes…and *more*. Then perhaps we will walk away with the memory to keep us both, hmm? Or perhaps we will stay together and damn everyone else to hell."

"You are the devil," she cried, perfectly interpreting the gleam in his eyes and the low, dangerous ache that rolled through her body.

"Ah," he said on a hum of rich pleasure. "That means you are very close to giving in to temptation."

Wickedness was plentiful within the gentle purr of his voice. A desperate ache went through her. "And that is what you wanted? *Four* kisses?"

"A taste of you might succor me for a lifetime. How was that for me being poetic?"

Ophelia laughed, surprising herself with how very provocative she sounded. "A credible attempt."

His eyes gleamed, and there was a touch of humor in his gaze. He *liked* it. This back-and-forth between them.

Amidst the laughter, a slender, delicate thread of something impossible wove its way into her heart...her very soul. It was more than the comfort she felt in their past connection, and it was more than friendship. It felt blazingly close to... Oh, God, she could not say it...she could not think it. A liking. There...she *liked* him.

"I do not want to lie to you," he murmured, his gaze intent on her face. "Ever. I do not want to pretend to be someone else when I am with you, Fifi. I was not...raised as a gentleman. Do not hold me to those standards I might never understand. Know I would never hurt you or allow a hair on your head to be hurt. I would not lie to you. Nor would I ever show you discourtesy. Even with the years between us, I know you to be precious."

She briefly closed her eyes, searching deep in her heart for all those reasons to flee from Devlin. She was wading into dangerous waters, and she had no knowledge of how to keep herself from drowning. There was a roaring sound from a distance, as if wind rushed down and swept her upward with dizzying force, crushing all objections before they were formed.

"Then tell me with all honesty. What do you want from me,

Niall?" she whispered.

"I would give all the money in the world for a taste of you, and to have that taste every morning and every night. Fucking stupid, but there you have it. I am courting you to my bed."

Good heavens.

Unable to be alarmed by his crudeness, she swallowed. There was an awful weak feeling low in her belly. It was almost as if she wilted against the door. "You are courting me to…to your *bed*?"

"Yes."

Forbidden lovers.

Devlin wanted her in his bed. Something elusive curled inside Ophelia, heating her entire body, especially that secret place. "I do not think my friends would approve."

He lowered his head so that his mouth hovered near hers. "Is that a yes, Fifi?"

"You are a madman," she whispered.

"That is not a denial."

Even if she had tried to step back, she couldn't have; desire had hooked itself low in her belly and tugged her toward him, toward madness. Her stomach dipped, the sensation strange, but it felt as if she were falling, down and down and down, the way it was in dreams and hopes and nightmares and everything terrifying and electrifying. Very slowly, very deliberately, giving her all the time to resist, Devlin threaded his fingers through the dark strands of her hair, brought his mouth down to hers, and kissed her. Her entire world contracted to the heat of his lips pressed to hers…their sensual softness, the hot flames sparking under her skin.

Oh God!

She tried; Ophelia dearly tried to hide her reaction but

abysmally failed. That soft whimper was an admittance of desire. The tentative way she stroked her gloved fingers over his exposed throat was a confession of the yearning she felt for him.

Her entire being ached with want.

Devlin Byrne was like the gambling den he associated with…sparkling, extravagant, *forbidden*. Accepting his kiss was surrendering to the things Ophelia craved in the dark of night. The very thought weakened her knees. And, deep in the pit of her stomach, an ache bloomed. Her heartbeat surged in recognition of the desires she kept hidden, and with a sigh of wonder, she parted her lips.

Ophelia surrendered.

CHAPTER TEN

Sweet heaven.

Devlin touched his mouth to hers, teasingly light. She made a soft, inarticulate little sound that utterly captivated him. He wanted to sink into this illicit embrace and devour Fifi, yet he was so very careful as he framed her face between his hands, as if she were the most precious thing he had ever touched in his life. Never before had Devlin felt this much sensation, this much pleasure from a kiss. The fragrance of her perfume drifted through his senses. Soft, feminine, subtle, yet also bold. He gently teased her lips apart, nipping at her lower lip, teasing his tongue along the closed seam of her mouth.

Ah God, just this little taste of her made his head spin. Her lips were so soft, delectable, and tasted ripe as berries. He did it again, and she froze, then moaned softly, rising on her toes to meet him, her slender arms encircling his neck. His chest cracked open. Everything hard inside of him weakened.

He *was* kissing Fifi.

Years of bottled need rushed through Devlin, filling him with a depth of craving that scared the hell out of him.

He gently bit at her lower lip before soothing the sting with soft kisses. Her mouth yielded to him. Those lush lips parted on a gasp, and she sweetly moaned when he swept his tongue through her mouth. The taste of her hit his system, hot and intoxicating, making him drunk with need and desire. As Devlin chased the tart and sweet flavors on her tongue, his cock rose hot and turgid against the fall of his trousers. He had yearned for this, dreamed of it, but nothing compared to the reality of Fifi.

You are truly in my arms, Fifi.

His famed control spun away from his grasp. Arousal rode him hard, and with each whimper and sigh she released, he lost a bit more of himself. Devlin wanted her beneath him and sheathed on his cock with disquieting urgency. Holding his passion in check after months of longing was torture of the keenest sort. He gripped her hips and dragged her up against his body. Their hips fitted, and he knew she could feel him against the opening of her thighs, hot and heavily aroused.

Devlin swallowed her soft whimper, a sound of alarm yet also arousal. Her hands tightened around his neck when he started walking with her. Within a few strides, he spilled from the drawing room and down the hallway, causing Fifi to make a startled sound into his kiss…but she did not pull away.

The stairs to his bedchamber felt much too far away.

Devlin opened the next door, grateful to see they were in the smaller library on the ground floor. There was a desk. And a chaise longue.

She sighed into his kiss when he placed her on the large desk. Without releasing her mouth from his sensual assault, he nudged her legs wide and stepped between them, allowing her thighs to cradle him intimately. She hooked a leg around his thigh, drawing him even closer. Devlin felt like he held a storm in his hands. His Fifi was wild and beautiful in her eagerness, crackling with sensuality.

She tasted like hope but also like sin.

Devlin could not stop touching her. She had a tiny waist,

curving hips, a sinfully rounded backside, and a soft, inviting bosom. And Devlin ran his hands everywhere, touching, kneading, and then softly caressing. He did not give her a chance to protest but ruthlessly seduced her until she panted and ached with want of him. He slipped his hand between her legs, coaxing them apart even wider, so he could touch the softness of her thigh. He dragged his fingers up, the incredible heat of her beckoning him closer to her quim. His knuckles brushed against her drawers, and she yelped, wrenching her mouth from his.

"This is not a kiss," she gasped, shaking in his arms.

"No?"

"You scoundrel, you know this to be ravishment," she said huskily.

He smiled faintly at her choice of words. Devlin had learned to be ruthless and cunning in getting what he wanted, and that extended to Fifi. As he stared into her widened eyes, the oddest sensation wrenched through his heart. There had been an artless wonder in her kiss. Had he frightened her with his intensity? Taking a deep, steady breath, he reined in the brutal need pummeling his body. His hands were shaking, Devlin realized as he cupped her delicate chin and swiped a thumb over her swollen lower lip.

"When you visited my home so daringly, did you not once consider ravishment a possibility?"

A sound he could not interpret slipped from her, and a pink flush rose into her cheeks. "I most certainly did not expect to find my derriere on top of a desk, my dress pushed to my knees, and my hat on the ground while being kissed senseless."

Her tone was one of mild rebuke, but her eyes were

intent…searching…daring.

"Your hands are free," he pointed out, lowering his hand from her face. "You could slap me for my…unpardonable behavior."

She appeared stymied for the briefest of moments. Fifi lifted her hand; he tensed in anticipation, but her contact was featherlight, the press of her palm against his jawline, and she stared at him with accusing eyes. How he wished her hands were not encased in gloves.

"I wanted your kiss, and even now, I do not want to wipe away your taste," she murmured. "I would be a hypocrite to pretend otherwise."

Her words razed his heart. *I do not want to wipe away your taste.* She had not been disgusted at all by their torrid kiss. A knot he hadn't realized constricted his gut loosened in slow increments.

Do you want me as I want you, Fifi?

Possibilities started to tumble through his thoughts, and an awareness dawned. She wanted him with such intensity, her response scared her. His impression of the woman before him was quiet strength, boldness, and impetuosity. But now Devlin could see something else in the depth of her golden gaze.

Uncertainty. Vulnerability. And undisguised craving.

Suddenly, he was afraid to move—afraid that he would frighten her away. "Fifi?"

"Yes?"

"You know what I hope for… What do you want?"

Her lips trembled before she bit deeply into her lower lip. "I am going home."

The knot in his gut retied with a vengeance. What had he expected? That the innocent daughter of a marquess would instantly declare that she wanted an affair with him after one kiss? He made to step back from her, but her fingers tightened on his shoulders.

"Are you to take four more kisses?" she asked tartly, an undeniable fire in her gaze. "Was that not the extent of what you wanted? Four kisses?"

The extent of his want? How little she comprehended. Black humor washed through him. "I am tempted, but alas, I must show restraint." When everything in him screamed to take her and bind her to him by all means possible. Rubbish, of course. He wanted Fifi badly, but Devlin needed her to want to be with him.

Her eyes searched his. "Was I not a good kisser?"

Doubt from Fifi? That he had not expected. "Kissing you was beyond anything I have ever experienced. I am not taking…"

He smiled at the sudden fierceness of her expression.

Devlin cleared his throat. "Your pardon, Fifi. I…took your offer and kissed you, but because of your innocence, I will not…ah…take any more offers."

There. That should satisfy the outrage darkening her eyes.

"You expected a tart, then. That is your reason for kissing me so salaciously?" she asked with a mocking smile.

"No."

Her eyebrow arched in amusement. "Then why should my innocence ruffle your feathers?"

Her hands slipped from his shoulders to rest on the desk, bracing her weight from falling backward. Devlin could have stepped away, but he didn't, liking the provocative position of her on his desk, her legs splayed to accommodate him in that delightful space between her thighs, and her tousled, wide-eyed sensuality as she stared up at him.

"I clearly liked it," she murmured, still searing his expression in that curious manner that was entirely endearing. "Considering only honesty will lie between us, tell me: why do you hesitate?"

He gently tapped the tip of her nose. "The kisses I wished for…they were not all meant for your *mouth*."

She lifted a hand and touched a fingertip to his lower lip. Fifi's expression was thoughtful, her eyes gleaming with sudden deviltry. "Where else did you want to kiss me, if not on my mouth?"

He went still, keenly aware of the longing in her stare. Such open, naked hunger and a touch of fright. *What do you yearn for, Fifi?* The plan to tread with care unraveled. He would treat her like the woman she clearly was, one who knew her desires and boldly…perhaps recklessly chased them.

"My first kiss was always to be on your lips; the second, right above the pulse fluttering on your delicate neck; the third would have been long, deep, and wet against your cunny. The fourth, too. Then, with the fifth, I would take your mouth again."

Shock widened her eyes, and she shoved him away from her. He moved easily enough, and he caught the word "*reprobate*" as she muttered under her breath. His Fifi hurriedly tidied herself without looking at him, then sauntered from the small library without a farewell, closing the door decisively on her way out.

He couldn't help smiling and then chuckling. Devlin had evidently mortified her sensibilities. She was such a curious creature. A beautiful blend of ladylike propriety and a blazing impetuous flame. Served her right for turning his damn senses upside down by merely showing up at his house and—

His thoughts careened and crashed when the door was flung open and she framed the entrance. Her cheeks were rosy and so damn pretty, her eyes bright with heat and laughter. So, he had ruffled her sensibilities and also amused her. "Ah, so you've returned for—"

"What is a cunny, Devlin?"

He choked on the taunting words he'd been about to say.

"Did a fly get into your mouth?" she asked, her eyes gleaming even naughtier.

Did she know and mean to test him? Surely not. "A…what?"

One of her shoulders lifted in an elegant shrug. "What is a *cunny*… Where is mine, which you are going to kiss so long and deep? It was explicitly distinguished from my mouth, and I am curious."

This time the choking sound came from behind her.

Devlin glanced beyond her shoulder and muttered a curse. Riordan O'Malley stood there, staring at Fifi as if she were a creature with a horn. She glanced over her shoulder into the hallway. Her cheeks blazed as she looked at Riordan.

"I beg your pardon; I did not hear someone enter. From your expression, I gather you know what it is?"

Sweet merciful Christ. Before Riordan could answer, Devlin said, "It is a place on…behind your elbow." He raked his fingers through his hair. "It is said to be sensitive."

Riordan sent Devlin a wickedly amused stare, achieved a creditable bow to Fifi, and then continued down the hallway to the study. How the hell had he forgotten he was meant to meet with his friend to discuss business matters?

Fifi frowned. He could see the cogs turning in her brain. Devlin's heart galloped when she entered the room fully, closed the door, and sauntered over to him with a provocative stroll.

Looking him in the eyes, she smiled. "Devlin?"

"Yes?"

"Where is my cunny?" she asked with precision.

The laughter that came from Devlin surprised him. "Do you really want to know?"

She bit into her lower lip, a nervous gesture, but she daringly lifted her chin. "To be sure, it did occur to me it might be something wildly improper. Though it seems common enough knowledge. I want to know…"

"Because?"

"Because I like your kisses," she said with a soft smile. "And I may very well want all of them."

She robbed him of breath with those words.

That black humor swept through him once more. "You'll not slap my face when I demonstrate."

She glanced down at her elbows. "What…you mean to kiss my cunny now?"

Sweet merciful heavens. The image slammed into his mind so fast it was a miracle he'd not collapsed: Fifi spread wide for him, her plump sex wet and glistening from the licks of his tongue. Devlin cleared his throat. "No," he murmured, hunger clawing through him. "I mean to touch it."

"Oh."

Was that disappointment he heard? "Unless you want me to kiss it now?"

Say no…say yes…fuck, I am twisted around.

"Of course not," she said and delicately cleared her throat, then lifted her shoulder in an elegant shrug. "A…touch will do, or you could just tell me."

Devlin stepped close to her…then closer still. For some reason, she stepped back until her shoulders were flush against the door. When there was no more avenue for retreat, she lifted her chin and glared at him. He chuckled, and she grinned sheepishly. Devlin slid his finger along her delicate jaw, down to the soft hollow of her throat. Beneath his touch, he could feel her pulse quickening. He lowered his hand even more, and she stole another quick look at her left elbow.

"Look at me."

Her gaze snapped to his. Holding her stare, Devlin carried his hand down, barely touching her but ensuring she could feel the impression of him through her clothes. Her face flushed a beautiful pink when he rested the weight of his hand briefly on her stomach.

Her lips parted, but no words came when he slid his hand down more until he cupped her sex through her skirts. Her eyes flew so wide it was a wonder she did not faint. Her hands jerked upward, but it was to grip his shoulders. The devil riding him, he dipped his head and placed his mouth to her ear. "This…Fifi…this is where I want to kiss. This is your cunny."

He flexed his hand, and she squeaked. Devlin could feel the heat from her fierce blushes.

"Oh, God," she gasped, a violent tremor going through her.

He rubbed his fingers…his palm against her, and she moaned, the sound hot and wanton.

"This is also your velvet sheath, fruitful vine, muff, vagina, cunt, quim, pussy, Venus's honeypot. All the same, sweet… tight…hot place, Fifi, I want to taste."

Fifi's fingers dug into his shoulders, and she rose up on her toes as if to escape the feelings. "A colorful choice of words that were clearly invented by the male mind," she whispered, her voice heavy with arousal.

He had done that to her. The heady feeling went through his body. "There are more," he drawled with mock heat. Then he flexed the heel of his palm. This time she bit her lip to hold back her moan, and a pink tongue darted and licked along her bottom lip.

"More?"

"Aye… Crinkum crankum has always been a personal favorite for its sheer ludicrousness."

Surprise shot her eyes wide. "Crinkum cran…"

Fifi giggled. For an instant, he was completely fascinated. Devlin caught the infectious sound with his mouth and kissed her deeply, sliding his tongue to twine with hers. Devlin knew he was being wicked, provoking her so. But he wanted to touch her. God, he wanted to drop on his knees, part her legs, and lick her, suck her, and drive her mad with passion. Breaking their kiss, he breathed raggedly.

Through the layers of her clothes, he rubbed her with the heel of his palm, arousing her to fever pitch. Her forehead fell forward, and her teeth clamped onto his shoulder. Devlin grunted at that bite. He flexed his fingers again, feeling for that slit, knowing he found her clitoris when her entire body shuddered.

He waited for a protest or for her to shove him away, all his thoughts centered on the heat against his palm, that erotic bite on his shoulder. Tension coated the air, and something passed between them—a mutual pulsing ache of sheer want. But neither wanted to break the perilous aroused silence to discover exactly what was happening in this moment of madness.

He rubbed her over slowly, with precious aim so the heel of his palm dragged against her clitoris until she quaked in his arms. Her teeth bit deeper into his shoulder, and he flexed his hand against her sex, reveling in the heat against his fingers. He rubbed her mons, making sure to drag his fingers slowly over where he imagined her clitoris might be. He was rewarded with the sweetest, hottest moan he'd ever heard. That sound whispered over his cock and then tightened around it like a fist.

Ah God...to truly win this woman with this flaming sensuality as his. What a futile, impossible dream.

He ruthlessly cut the doubt away before it could dig its poisonous talons into his thoughts. Fifi clutched his upper arms, seemingly unable to speak. And he caressed her over and over, until she arched against him, until sweat beaded on her brow. Her hands slid from his jacket and around his neck, where she held him to her in a tight embrace. And Devlin never let up on his wicked caress of rubbing her plump and heated quim through her dress.

"Devlin!"

Her voice sounded fractured...shocked...and hoarse with desire. He would not let her release. No...the first time Fifi found release would be in his arms, sheathed on his cock, or when he placed her cunny on his tongue. He gently lowered his hand, holding her to him as the soft shudders left her body.

She made a low sound of frustration, and he tenderly stroked his fingers over her hips, soothing her. "If my fingers **did this** with so many clothes between us, imagine what a kiss would do on your naked—"

She reared back and slapped her hand over his mouth. His

Fifi was shaken, and a foreign tenderness softened something inside of Devlin. It was clear to him she did not pleasure herself, nor had she ever felt or done anything in this regard. Something possessive slithered under the surface of his skin, and he had to breathe deeply to steady himself against the feelings.

He was going deeper. That was not supposed to happen—not until he was certain she would take his hand and step forward with him. *I am sliding deeper.* A warning alarm went off in his head, but he still stood there, not wanting to move away from her. Devlin was tempted to swing her into his arms, mount the stairs, and ruthlessly seduce her into spending the day and possibly night with him in bed. Fifi was teeth-achingly, sensually formed. Pleasure in her arms would be unlike anything he'd ever experienced. She would blush with her entire body, but given her adventurous and impetuous nature, she would still split those legs wide, maybe even help him by using her delicate fingers to spread the lips of her cunn—

"I'll box your ears," she murmured huskily, her cheeks blooming a fierce red.

He arched an inquiring brow.

"Whenever you are thinking wicked deeds, your eyes darken." She removed her palm to trace the curve of his lips with trembling fingers. "And these curve…but it is not really a smile, is it?"

To his shock, she tipped onto her toes and caught his bottom lip between her teeth. She bit him, and he hissed at the erotic sting. "Was that my punishment?" he asked.

"For your utter shameless effrontery," she whispered.

And he understood. He had dragged the carpet from underneath her feet without any warning. To touch her with such carnal intimacy, to provoke a response she had never felt before.

"It is more like what utter shameless *pleasurable* effrontery," Devlin murmured, brushing his mouth over her wildly fluttering pulse. "One that should be rewarded, hmm?"

Even though her entire body was blushing, she surprised him by smiling and tossing back her head. "*I* was a willing participant in that shameless debauchery. What more reward could you possibly want?"

The conceited arrogance thrilled and amused Devlin. "I like a lady who knows her worth...and you, Fifi, are worth kingdoms."

"My vanity is delightfully flattered," she murmured, amusement shining in her golden orbs. "You are a dangerous temptation, Devlin Byrne."

"'Tis one thing to be tempted, another thing to fall. Will you fall with me, Fifi?"

A bold, provocative question, but he had never been the kind of man afraid to face anything, whether they be demons or hopes and dreams. She lifted a hand to his jaw, her eyes serious and considering. Those stroking fingers slid to linger on his jaw before dropping off. "Temptation," she whispered. "The fiend at my elbow."

An answer that only showed they both knew their Shakespeare. Perhaps her quote was more revealing. She saw him as the damn devil...a fiend of the worst sort, enticing her down a dangerous and ruinous path.

Fifi placed a hand flat against his chest. That was enough for him, and he stepped away, giving her the space she needed. They stared at each other for long silent moments, then, without saying another word, she turned, opened the door, and hurried away from him. Devlin chuckled before blowing out a sharp breath. He waited a few minutes for his arousal to subside before leaving the room toward his study. Riordan was patiently waiting and had availed himself to the decanter of brandy.

His friend lifted his head from the report he read and smiled. "I—"

"She is not open for discussion." Devlin dropped himself into the wingback chair opposite Riordan and went right to the heart of the matter. Lifting his chin to the pages of the report Riordan had taken the liberty of reading while waiting, Devlin said, "What do you think?"

"A bold undertaking, setting up such a well-equipped boarding school for the poorer class," he said, taking a sip of his whisky.

"More like a boarding house."

Riordan nodded. "I like that their education will be tailored like those nobs and will also be opened to lads and lasses. It will take a lot of money and dedication."

"I have the money," Devlin said, tapping his fingers on the surface of his desk. "Dedicated people can be hired. I've already secured top-notch tutors and governesses for the school in Chatham. It is small and can only hold up to thirty-five children, and that is because I want each child to have their own room. The house will be equipped with a music room, ballroom, drawing room, fencing, and boxing rooms, and a stable so they might learn to ride."

Riordan chuckled. "I still recall when we learned to ride. It was a ridiculous sight, us grown men afraid of horses."

Devlin grinned, recalling he had learned at nineteen, and it had taken immense courage for him to mount the damn horse after seeing his friends dumped on their arses several times.

"I never thought I would see a man outrunning a horse determined to bite his arse."

Devlin laughed. "I merely outsmarted it, and I am still at a loss why it tried to clamp its damn teeth in my backside."

Riordan stood and went to the side mantle to refill his glass. "I will contribute handsomely. It seems I have too much money lying around. Many lads and lasses in the stews will be wary of the opportunity. They steal for their families to live. Perhaps we could even set up a fund to pay a generous stipend during their studies. That way the little urchins won't worry about picking pockets or whoring for their families when they could be learning."

"Good. Now tell me about this new venture you think worthy of investment. What are the potential yields and the risks?"

Riordan arched a brow. "Are we really not to talk about—"

"So help me…" Devlin began on a warning note.

The door was shoved open, and a young lad of about ten with a mop of reddish-brown hair spilled into the room with an overly exuberant Conan nipping at his heels.

"Conan!" William cried, his light blue eyes alight with happiness. "This dog be a big brute who likes to play. He keeps bouncing me over, but Poppy says that is because he loves me."

He sent them a toothy grin as he dashed to plop himself onto the sofa, making space for the dog who hopped up beside him. The rascal who once worked as an orange seller to assist his ma had little to no manners and had all the markings of a tiny genius. It was by chance Devlin had caught him trying to pick his pocket on Fleet Street a couple months ago. Of course, he had not turned him over to the authorities to be imprisoned or hanged. In the boy's eyes, he had seen a reflection of himself and even Poppy—that defiant vulnerability and a fierce hunger for more.

William's wit was sharp. He had taught himself his letters and how to read from discarded newspapers and the rare books he found. More likely, he stole the books during his time as a chimney sweep. His ability for arithmetic was far in advance of most upper-class boys of his age, particularly for someone without any formal learning. Devlin had no notion how to interact with a child who had the crafty mind of an old man, but William had become his companion of a sort. He even paid the lad an astronomical sum of twenty pounds per month to simply chatter in his ears and to also keep Poppy company.

It had been a sight that day when he had strolled into the Asylum with a small boy on his left side and his beast of a dog on his right. They had sat at a vingt-et-un table, and an hour later, the boy had won a thousand pounds. Devlin had looked around and thought of the money the lad could make to lift his family from the edge of poverty and misery they lived in. But something inside had also warned him to provide another opportunity. Perhaps with education, William might be more than a gambler. He could be a fine barrister, a banker, or even an investor.

The extraordinary inequalities of wealth between those in the *ton* and the other classes had pushed Devlin to invest in charities and businesses that would provide more opportunities to folk who barely earned wages to keep themselves, much less a family.

Devlin had taken the boy under his wing, determined to

shape his innate intellect in a way that would pave a future far more prosperous than an orange seller or a damn pickpocket or a gambler who could lose everything at the toss of a die. He wanted to enroll the lad into Eton College or Harrow School when he turned thirteen. And after William's five years receiving that proper education, Devlin would pave the way with his money…or by blackmail if necessary, for William to attend Oxford or Cambridge.

He chuckled, thinking of how that would outrage the nobs. They might march to take his head then. Boys from William's class—Devlin's class—were only destined to work the fields or, if they were very lucky, to secure some sort of apprenticeship. Many young girls and boys of the lower class were capable of being more than servants, selling themselves or cheap wares on the streets, and polishing their betters' boots. But the aristocrats and those who made the nation's laws were horrified that they might rise above their class. In Devlin's mind, they withheld quality education from those below them simply to keep their status quo of being filthy rich and supposedly better.

Devlin had long lost the need for the approval of those who considered themselves "better." The aristocrats were not better. In his experience, they owned more depraved hearts and selfish desires than those of lower classes. What he had learned about them had killed the burning desire inside him to be just like them. That desire had been born because of Fifi. It had died because he saw their callous and cruel sides, their belief they were owed the world and they could trample on anyone for it without any consequences.

He'd had a friend who died for stealing a loaf of bread to feed his family. That friend had only been thirteen years of age, but they hanged him without an ounce of mercy in their hearts. He had seen ladies of great wealth walking down the street, sidestepping children holding out their hands pleading for a coin. He had seen lords with vast wealth and influence fight to deny a bill that would relieve the burdens of the poor and make life better. And that betterment probably only meant being able to keep their family from starving. He had seen a drunken earl run down an orange seller, and no justice was meted, for he was a lord and the cart seller and her two children were insignificant in the earl's eyes and the eyes of his peers.

They didn't give a damn. And it was up to men like him, Riordan, and Rhys—who knew what it was like to be in the gutter and the stews—to do whatever they could to help. That was why they were working to improve things for some of the children who were suffering the same poverty that they had dragged themselves out of. Their prospective school and other plans were all intended to give opportunities for the poorest children to succeed in life and so support their own families. Even with the enormous wealth Devlin and his friends had amassed, they could only do so much. It was merely a drop in the ocean of poverty, but it was a start.

They had no illusions that they were being especially benevolent and certainly did not see themselves as philanthropists. It was more that they were thumbing their noses at the social elite who had tried to keep them down. Devlin's resentment of the British class structure was something he acknowledged, but rather than seek to become part of the ruling class, he sought to work against it by lifting others to prosperity. It might not change the system, but gradually it would whittle away the inequalities that ignored the masses living in misery while the *ton* paraded their affluence.

If more upstarts like them gave back to the communities they had sprung from, then perhaps it would dent the complacence of the nobs and make them realize that the inequality of life could not be justified.

CHAPTER ELEVEN

It had been a couple days since Ophelia fled a particular townhouse on Grosvenor Square, low, masculine laughter following her departure. The man was a scoundrel. A wicked, vexing, provoking, wonderful scoundrel. And he wanted her in his bed, possibly to do all sort of delightfully wicked things to her cunny. With a groan, she admitted she had never thought in the absence of a suitable gentleman to marry, she might indulge in an affair with one who attracted all of her senses.

Spending time with her father at the British Museum; coaxing her mother to attend the Covent Garden, where they watched a delightful opera performed by the incomparable Fanny Corri-Paltoni; even attending a ball last night with Cousin Effie did not sufficiently distract Ophelia's thoughts from tumbling recklessly down a forbidden path. She had an exhausting day shopping with Cousin Effie and Princess Cosima. They visited Rundell and Bridge, seeking a diamond choker with matching earbobs for Cosima, then toured several shops along Bond Street.

The outings should have stilled the restlessness plaguing Ophelia, but as the days passed, she was thinking of Devlin Byrne *more*, not less. Laughter and low murmuring of conversation swirled around her, but her concentration was frazzled. And that irritated her, for she was not the kind of woman to be so easily befuddled. She was certain of it. In three days, she was to visit Wardour Street to see Miss Fenley. Ophelia was not familiar with the area, and she would need to have her full wits about her.

"Are you well, my dear?" her mother said. "You are awfully quiet."

Lowering the fork that still held a piece of succulent veal speared on its tip, she said, "I fear I am poor company for dinner this evening. I have a slight headache."

"The sun was intolerable today, and you wore that little flip of a hat instead of a bonnet that would have afforded you much more protection," her mother said with a sigh. "You do appear frightfully flushed."

Cousin Effie turned concerned eyes to her. "Do you still have plans to attend Lady Bloomfield's ball?"

"I'll send my regrets," Ophelia said, pushing back her chair to stand. "Mama, Papa, if you'll excuse me. I believe I shall retire to bed early."

Dipping into a respectful curtsy to her family, she hastened from the formal dining room and made her way up the winding stairs to her chamber. Her maid helped her remove her clothes and the pins from her hair, tumbling the heavy tresses to her back. Then she sat while her hair was brushed to make it shine, the traditional one hundred strokes. Clad only in her chemisette, Ophelia sprawled on her bed, staring at the ceiling, unaware of the creeping darkness as night blanketed the city, unable to sleep.

She was caught in a quandary and at a loss on how to proceed. Avoiding thinking about it was not a solution, and as the last few days proved, her problem only lingered in her thoughts, waiting to haunt her while she slept. She had always been decisive, chasing after what she wanted. Her mother often bemoaned that her wild energy would be her ruination. And for the first time, Ophelia felt her mother's worries might prove correct.

Her thoughts were indelibly captured by Devlin Byrne.

When his lips touched hers, Ophelia had ceased to remember that he was the forbidden fruit. His fingers had evoked sensations and wicked yearnings that must be wrong but had felt so existential. It had felt like the rays of a thousand suns caught her skin.

So her sex was her cunny...and he wanted to kiss it. The idea was too scandalous to contemplate. How would he do it? Through her drawers, or would he remove them...his mouth and tongue to her bare skin?

As if I would ever allow myself to be so reckless with you...

Worse, she had no current notions of how she could ever face the man again. She had embarrassed herself by fleeing as if the devil himself chased her. His low, masculine laughter had followed her, taunting her all the way home.

She wanted revenge.

She wanted to kiss him again and again.

She wanted...

Ophelia blew out a sharp breath, curved her body around her largest pillow, and buried her face against its softness. His kisses had felt good. *Extraordinarily good.* Her lips tingled, and Ophelia lifted her shaking fingers to a mouth that still wore the impression of Devlin Byrne. She licked her lips, and she swore she tasted him still—a hint of whisky, something evocative. She couldn't say exactly what it was about him that drew her; she knew only that she was irrevocably drawn, perhaps to her detriment.

Unexpectedly, she felt a surge of envy for what Kitty and Maryann had experienced. Not for marriage or even love, but for a connection that filled them with sensations that did not encompass loneliness and uncertainty. Ophelia craved to feel that intense, forbidden thrill of his touch…of his kisses. "What am I to do?" she whispered.

The barely lit chamber provided no answer.

I want you…

She lifted one hand to the valley between her breasts and lightly stroked down her quivering belly. Drifting her hand lower, she rested her fingers lightly above her mons, warmth working through her entire body. Her hand drifted lower and lower still until she touched the very place he had rested his palm with such surety. She felt a flood of heat, and a curious shock moved through her body.

Forbidden lovers.

For a moment, Ophelia allowed herself to imagine being clasped in Devlin's embrace. She would take her fingers and thread them through his dark hair. She would be brave…and wicked enough to press her body against his as he stroked and molded the shapes of her breasts, hips, and then once again caressed that secret place between her thighs.

Her palm turned hot and damp. Her fingers shook as the temptation to stroke herself rose in her fevered thoughts. The remembered feeling of his fingers rubbing her…cunny flushed her entire body with delicious heat. The sheer intimacy and trust she had placed in Devlin had been toe-curling, freeing, and like nothing she'd ever experienced before.

With a guilty groan, she admitted to herself she wanted to feel his body atop hers, heavy and strong. She wanted to indulge in all manner of delightful naughtiness with him.

I barely know him! To have such a longing was nonsensical.

Her thoughts lingered on those days in the cottage. They had been two children scared witless who had forged a connection in their determination to be brave. Friendship, trust, and a bond had been formed, and not once had Ophelia thought herself better than him. In fact, with the little she knew about marriage, she had thought Niall perfect. For he cared for her. In his own way, he had loved her truly, and all of her little self had adored him.

She remembered the days she had buried her face in the pillows and sobbed her little heart out. The despairing looks her mother would give her father. And the insensitive means they had used to distract her from thoughts of a poor boy who had no role in her life.

His wild, determined cry before that door had closed clung like a phantom ghost in her ears. *Wait for me…* Ophelia had unintentionally waited. Now there was a chasm between them, one of class and prejudice. To even pursue their friendship now felt like a distant hope that might never be attainable.

Only if I let it.

Agitated, she sat on the edge of the bed, curling her toes into the soft carpet. "What am I thinking?"

Society would skewer them if she dared to align herself with him in any way, and she would not have her parents' support. "Hang society," she muttered crossly, standing to walk over to her windows and look down in the back gardens.

Everything she longed for seemed unattainable, and the stumbling block was her own judgment. Irritation snapped through Ophelia, for, like her friends, she loathed that her life was not controlled by what she wanted but by the condescending, boorish, bigoted, unjustified opinions of others. A soft bleat had her hurrying over to her bed to scoop up Barbosa, who tried to stand on shaking legs. Holding him close to her chest, she padded back with him over to the windows.

She cuddled him close to her chest, inhaling his lavender scent. Ophelia had insisted her companion be given daily baths in scented water, to her mother's annoyed shock. Even her maid and several other servants seemed to have fallen in love with the baby goat. Her mother was a tougher nut to crack, while her father was at best indifferent to his presence.

"What am I to do with the desires in my heart, Barbosa? They will not leave me be."

Another soft bleat came from him, and then he caught the edge of her chemisette between his teeth. Ophelia laughed and snuggled him even closer. Then the ghost of Kitty's words whispered to Ophelia.

"We will have to be wicked, improper, and terribly scandalous."

"Improper and scandalous," she whispered with a smile, tapping her finger against the glass. "And why not? Did we not promise to take what we wanted and live for ourselves, that it would be marvelous to be wicked?"

The ghost of Maryann's voice joined in the arguments for giving in to temptation.

"We must be daring and take what we need instead of waiting, wasting away on the shelves our family and society have placed us on."

Something unlocked inside of Ophelia, and a pulse of vibrant awareness scythed through her. She rested her forehead on the cool windowpane, welcoming the swell of something intangible but decidedly free blossoming throughout her body.

Unexpectedly, she laughed and covered her face with her palms.

• • •

The very next morning, as if the devil had known she dreamt of him and temptation for the long night, he sent her a note. Cousin Effie, who waited a few paces down in the hallway, threw Ophelia an inquisitive glance.

"You looked flushed, Ophelia. Are you unwell?"

"On the contrary, Effie, my heart is enlivened. I… It is a letter from a friend. If you will grant me a moment, I must read it and pen a reply before we head for the park."

Without awaiting Effie's response, Ophelia darted around and hastened to her private parlor. She wrenched the door open, then entered, closed the door, and leaned against it. With slightly shaking fingers, she tore into the envelope.

Another elegantly scrawled note.

Have dinner with me.

There was a quickening low in Ophelia's belly, a thrum of anticipation throughout her entire body. No money was offered, and sweet relief rushed through her. When she sauntered from the parlor, the sound of the pianoforte playing pulled her to the music room. She went over and sat beside Effie, lightly skipping her fingers over the keys until she found the perfect piece to match her cousin. They played a duet for several minutes until their songs ended.

"A much lighter and livelier piece than what you played this morning," Effie murmured.

Ophelia glanced at her cousin, who watched her with piercing curiosity. "I thought the household abed."

"I could not sleep and went to the kitchen for some milk. It was on the way back to my chamber I heard you playing. I peeked in on you, and you were so intent you did not even hear me. For the life of me, I cannot imagine how that little goat lay on the carpet so peacefully."

Ophelia chuckled. "Barbosa loves my playing."

"What a ghastly name."

"How disagreeable of you to say so. It is lovely," she said tenderly.

Cousin Effie touched her shoulder. "I can tell that a gentleman sent you that note."

Ophelia's breath hitched. "Effie—"

"I can also tell that you like this gentleman—absurdly so. You… The instant your fingers touched that envelope, it was as if you'd awakened from sleep."

"Surely not," she replied, mortified to be so obvious in her tendre.

Effie grinned. "Your mother will be pleased when it is announced; only yesterday she mentioned how much she wished for you to marry and settle into your own home, even though they left the decision in your hands. I know your reckless heart and that gleam in your eyes intimately. I urge you to be careful that your evident affections do not lead you to marry in haste."

It felt as if a fist closed over her heart. "Effie…"

"Yes?"

Unable to speak past the ache in her throat, she pushed a smile to her lips. "I would like to visit Hatchards to collect a few books I ordered last week. Will you accompany me?"

"Yes."

"Effie?"

Her cousin frowned at the tightness in Ophelia's tone. "What is it?"

"I would have your confidence on a matter of grave importance."

Effie gently touched her arm. "Please be assured of my discretion."

"I am searching for someone. A woman by the name of Sally Martin." No recognition sparked in Effie's eyes, and Ophelia released a slow breath. "Since Mama is determined for you to accompany me about town for a more correct appearance, there are a few places I will traverse that might alarm your sensibilities. I promise you that it is safe, and for now, that is all I can tell you."

"I gather you will not stop these visits," Effie said somberly. "Even if I make an objection?"

"I will not. It is very important to me. A friend has also invited me to a dinner party. I might attend," she said softly. "I am not certain if I shall accept as yet."

"Then I shall accompany you if you accept," said her cousin simply with a smile. "Dinner parties are always delightful."

"Thank you, Effie." Ophelia hugged her, unable to explain the emotions rising inside at her cousin's unflinching support.

Perhaps she might tell her of Devlin, and Effie could help her to resolve the unrelenting cravings that beat in her heart for the man. The butler announced another letter had arrived for Ophelia. With a frown, she took it, breaking into a wide smile when she saw that it was from Maryann. Hurrying into the parlor, she used a letter opener on the envelope.

$\cdots$

Dearest Ophelia,

Nicolas and I are getting married in a few days' time by special license in the family chapel at his principal estate. I am sorry for the short notice, but promise me that you'll come. My heart is already breaking that Kitty will not be here to witness my happiness. Please travel down as soon as possible so we can spend some time together. I've also invited Fanny, Charlotte, and Emma.

Love, Maryann.

P.S. The address is Delacree Park, Wiltshire, and the wedding will be at ten o'clock.

• • •

A hush settled over the small intimate gathering of friends and family as the bride appeared. The groom, who had waited with an absolute stillness that had been remarked upon, jolted, a sensual smile curving his mouth. His bride, Lady Maryann Fitzwilliam, soon to be the Marchioness of Rothbury, appeared enchanting. She wore a fashionable cream gown that flattered her slender yet curvaceous figure. The hem was trimmed with delicate seed pearls, and her head was covered with a long cream veil in priceless Chantilly lace upon which a small diamond tiara was set.

Ophelia leaned backward from where she sat cramped together on a hard pew in the small chapel belonging to Nicolas St. Ives' country seat. It was a beautiful old building that, as part of his family's personal estate, had not been devastated by the Tudor desecration of religious buildings. It was simple in design but had such depths of history. Ophelia breathed in the fragrance of incense and the arrangements of roses that scented the chapel, and she could not imagine anything more perfect.

A wide smile curved her mouth as her dearest friend hovered in the arched entrance of the chapel and stared at the man who loved her with every breath inside him. Maryann was flushed, her eyes bright, her countenance one of pure, unguarded joy.

"How lovely she looks," Cousin Effie said wistfully. "I've always thought her a little mousey with those spectacles she wears, but today she is…"

"Maryann has always been beautiful," Fanny said with loyal sincerity, her eyes glistening with tears.

"Oh, my," Charlotte said, clasping her hands together. "Would you look at the marquess's face?"

"The man is scandalous," Effie said stiffly. "He looks like he wants to eat up his bride."

Glancing at the marquess, Ophelia froze, her stomach flipping alarmingly. When she had danced with Devlin…when they walked in the rain…and when they kissed. *Devlin looks at me like that—as if he wishes to consume me.*

That thought was a revelation to her.

An unknown tempest brewed in her breastbone, and chaotic longings tapped inside Ophelia's heart, the rhythm feeling like a song. She wanted to be kissed, to be held in a lover's embrace, to be stared at with such poignant longing and care. Not just by any lover…by Devlin.

I want Devlin Byrne.

"I truly think *eat* is too tame a word," Emma said, two spots of color high on her cheekbones. "The man has no shame!" Yet her tone also reflected longing and envy, a feeling Ophelia understood.

"Maryann is blushing," Charlotte said, a glint of mischief appearing in her blue eyes.

"She is glowing, isn't she?" Emma said with a sigh. "I swear I need to find something to be wicked about. That seems to be the way to secure well-sought-after gentlemen. First Kitty snagged a duke, and now Maryann a marquess."

Ophelia, Fanny, and Charlotte laughed softly and shared an amused glance with one another.

"I wish Kitty could have been here," Fanny said. "It would have been perfect to have all of us sinful wallflowers together."

Ophelia also noticed how Charlotte glanced at Lord Sands, who sat on the opposite pew, a marquess in his own right and a man their friend seemed to long for. As if he felt Charlotte's gaze, he suddenly turned his head, his obsidian eyes capturing her friend's regard. The man had the reputation of being a dangerous flirt with no intentions to marry. His lips quirked, and even Ophelia gasped at the provocative carnality in that expression.

Charlotte quickly looked away, her pale alabaster skin turning a delightful pink.

"Well, she could have at least removed those spectacles for today," Effie grumbled, but there was a peculiar wistfulness in her voice that had Ophelia looking at her closely.

Effie's cheeks were pale, and her eyes held a touch of remembered pain. She had married at nineteen to an earl who had always treated her with kind consideration and love, only to have lost him in a reckless carriage race, along with a companion who had later been revealed to be a mistress of his.

Effie hadn't completely forgiven him for the scandal that had swept through society afterward. That was five years ago. Although a widow, Effie was still so very beautiful and elegant with her pale blond hair and glistening brown eyes. Effie could have remarried but had not done so. Ophelia had asked her once if it was because of how much she had loved her husband, and Effie had merely smiled and brushed it aside.

A string quartet leaped to life, playing a beautiful song for Maryann to proceed down the aisle. Maryann took a deep breath and, as if she could not wait, she broke into a small run, at which her waiting groom chuckled.

"Why, I never!" Effie gasped, staring at her, utterly aghast. "She is markedly impulsive."

"Be quiet," Ophelia murmured. "You are only here because of me. And it is because Maryann is so…free and decided about what she wants that Nicolas St. Ives adores her."

Her cousin harrumphed but remained silent for the duration of the beautiful ceremony.

Have dinner with me.

At Devlin's remembered words, Ophelia felt as if a dream awoke inside of her. She had been undecided before, afraid of being too tempted by Devlin Byrne.

That aching dissatisfaction she had allowed herself to feel for so long reared its head. Whenever she was with Devlin, Ophelia felt as if she lived. She never felt that she had to slip on a mask of perfection, no matter how small their interactions were. A faint stirring of anticipation went through her, and in that moment she understood so much why Maryann had urged them all to be wicked and daring and free and to hunger after the things they wanted.

Life was not limitless… It would invariably end, and the idea that she might never experience something as beautiful as she witnessed cut her to her soul.

Yes…I want my very own slice of wickedness. Ophelia might not have found the love she once dreamed about, but it felt as if she had found that thing that might make her hunger to live a little. To take the leap and discard her anxiety about whoever that might disappoint. She closed her eyes briefly and only saw a darkly sensual smile and brilliant green eyes.

Yes…I'll have dinner with you.

• • •

According to Devlin's calculations, they would arrive at his home in Rochester, located on the outskirts of the city, within an hour and fifteen minutes. Riding alone with Ophelia for said time would certainly be interesting. At their few encounters so far, he'd quite enjoyed bantering with Fifi. There was something about her droll, witty repartee that made him long to simply lie with her under an oak tree and talk. He wanted to know things about his Fifi, and perhaps they could start with his carriage drive.

Not my Fifi, he reminded himself. Not his anything. *Not yet*.

It made no sense for him to be hopeful when he could not anticipate success. He might kiss her again, and she might slap him across the face for his improper advances. He might be acting like a fool, pursuing her to his bed. But he would be a damn careful fool. It was that easy to slide back into the old dreams he'd built up around her, despite that the reality of the woman was nothing like what he had envisioned. Fifi was unpredictable, and he liked that. She was a lover of life, and he saw that in the beauty of her singing, but he hungered for more than just her splayed beneath him. Devlin wanted to know her likes and wants, and what made her smile, what made her frustrated. He wanted her friendship. And he wanted her as his lover. He would not be stupid enough to dream of her being his wife.

"Imagine my sisters' faces when they meet her," he said to Conan, rubbing him behind the ears.

Devlin told himself it was the petty need inside him to see his family's faces when he made the appropriate introductions that urged him to make said introductions. Leaning against the squabs, he heard when the steps were knocked down and a soft murmur to his footman.

Fifi entered the carriage sheathed in a golden dress, which clung alluringly to her curves, a matching pelisse, and black gloves encasing her slim hands. A small hat perched atop her midnight dark hair had been swept up in a simple chignon, with artful curls kissing her cheeks and shoulders. She wore a string of black pearls around her throat and matching earrings in her ears. The simple yet fashionable cut of the gown accented her small waist and all her generous curves, and Devlin had to look away for a moment.

Only a moment.

Her eyes seemed to laugh at him, and he arched a questioning brow. She winked, the motion so quick he almost missed it. Devlin inhaled deeply. Some faint scent clung to her, a teasing hint of honeysuckle and…something far more elusive to his common senses.

Another young lady dressed in a lovely blue gown was assisted into the carriage. She was incredibly pretty, with her hair coiffed in a fashionable style. This unknown lady appeared shocked to see him but quickly gathered her composure.

A third lady entered the carriage. She was young and dressed in a serviceable gray dress. She dipped into a quick curtsy when she saw him and lowered her eyes. The ladies sat opposite him, one audaciously staring at him with a slight smile about her mouth, the other sneaking discreet glances that volleyed from Fifi to himself. The young maid determinedly looked through the small slit in the curtains. Luckily, his conveyance was large, elegant, and up to the standards of carriages owned by important lords.

Devlin curled his fingers over the head of his cane. "You were to come alone."

The unknown lady sucked in a breath at that brash pronouncement. Conan, who reposed beside him, *woofed* his greeting, then went back to resting his jowls on his paws. Devlin idly rubbed his head with his other hand.

"Though I am four and twenty and a veritable spinster, if I came alone, I would be taken for a lady of questionable character should anyone find out," Fifi said with sweet sarcasm. "I am obliged to invite my cousin Effie, who has been tasked to be my chaperone."

"Your chaperone?"

"Unfortunately, the impropriety of my daring to dance with you in such a public fashion made it a necessity. We unsettled my parents' considerably unflappable composure." Ophelia chuckled lightly, as if she found the notion of a chaperone amusing. "I thought it prudent to also have my maid accompany us. Cousin Effie, allow me to introduce my friend Mr. Devlin Byrne to you. Mr. Byrne, Lady Ephigenia Deidrick."

He had never understood this notion of chaperoning by betters. He and Fifi would engage in discourse, and this lady would sit there and pretend she did not hear a bloody thing. Worse, this cousin was discreetly assessing him from the top of his head to the polished tips of his boots.

Tucking a wisp of hair that had escaped its elegant chignon behind her ear, Fifi settled comfortably against the squabs.

"Lady Deidrick," he said, dipping his head in a brief bow. "A pleasure to make your acquaintance."

"Mr. Byrne," she replied with a crisp smile and chilling civility. "When my cousin informed me of our outing to

Rochester, she gave no indication a gentleman would accompany us. I do hope by the end of this…dinner, I can say it has been a pleasure."

He had nothing to add to that, but he dipped his head to the maid. "It is a pleasure to meet you."

The girl's eyes widened as if she had not expected him to acknowledge her presence. Her cheeks pinkened, and she dipped her head and returned his greeting. The little miss then removed a book from the pocket of her dress and started to read.

His surprise must have shown.

"My friends and I decided months ago to teach our maids their letters and how to read. Our first act of rebellion," Fifi said with a provocative smile.

Devlin leaned back against the squabs. "What were you rebelling against?"

Fifi's eyes gleamed with a defiant spark. "Society. Our set can be ridiculous at times."

Devlin stared at her for several moments. "How have you been, Fifi?" *Since we last spoke…touched…walked in the rain…kissed.*

Her cheek took on a rosy glow, and her eyes shifted from him briefly. "I have been quite well. Barbosa and I get along famously."

"Why did we meet at an inn?"

"My friend Lady Maryann is now the Marchioness of Rothbury, having married by special license only two days ago. I am on my way home from the wedding."

"I glimpsed a bit of their story in this morning's papers. London's most scandalous couple."

Fifi nodded happily, and a faraway look entered her eyes.

It reminded him of the days he would walk along the beaches of West Dunes, thinking of her and wishing their paths would once again cross. Back then, hunger had been a living entity within his soul. Now it was muted. Waiting. Watching. Or so he told himself, not liking the raw throb pulsing through him. There was so much he wanted to say to her, to ask her. Hell, he wanted to draw her onto his lap and kiss her senseless.

"My family will be present at our dinner."

Her eyes widened. "It would be most lovely to meet them." A small smile touched her mouth. "I never thanked you for my goat. Thank you, Devlin."

An odd sound came from her cousin's throat, no doubt at Fifi's familiarity.

"He is Mr. Byrne to you, as you are Lady Ophelia to him," her cousin said tightly under her breath and in a very disagreeable tone.

"How absurd," Fifi said. There was a stubborn pride in the set of her small chin. "Devlin and I are friends, and as such, we've dispensed with formalities while we are amongst other friends."

A swell of admiration went through him. He liked her lack of pretension.

Acting on rare impulse, he dipped inside his pocket and withdrew a small leather-bound book.

Surprise widened her golden-brown eyes. "Is that... You still have it?"

"I've read it many times."

She laughed and blushed a little, clearly flustered. "I am not certain what to say."

They shared a secret smile, and her cousin chose that moment to delicately clear her throat. Devlin tugged at the damn cravat that felt like it was about to choke him. The young girl seemed engrossed in the book, and the cousin seemed to find Conan fascinating, but he suspected they were keenly aware of every word that passed between him and Fifi. He was incapable of diverting his attention from Ophelia, an observation her lady maid and cousin noted, to his irritation.

Devlin closed his eyes, leaned his head back, and settled in for the journey.

He had to admire the ladies. It passed in a silence that almost felt companionable. Except he could feel their stares upon him, all with a different intention. Only Fifi's gaze he savored, especially when he caught her ogling his body. He winked. She blushed and looked away, a naughty smile curving her mouth. The chaperone gasped and clenched her gloved fingers while staring at him more wrathfully.

The chaperone would be a problem. He wondered darkly how he could do away with her.

"What villainy art thou plotting?" Fifi murmured after more than thirty minutes of silence.

Devlin cut his gaze to her chaperone and then attempted to share with Fifi his most villainous look. Her eyes twinkled, and he thought then they were the deepest brown and prettiest he'd ever seen. Of course, despite her lowered lids and pretense of sleeping, Lady Effie harrumphed.

Several more minutes passed before the carriage turned into a stately driveaway. Fifi brushed the carriage curtains aside, and her lips parted on a soft gasp of surprise.

"Is this your home?" she asked, her tone filled with admiration.

"Yes."

"It is beautiful!"

That had her cousin peering outside as well. The lady, however, refrained from sharing her opinions.

They drove along a graveled driveway lined with towering elm and beechwood trees up to the main house, a large manor designed in the Tudor style that had been refurbished with a more modern turret, arched windows, and entrances. The land-scaped grounds were exquisitely maintained and stretched to romantic vistas enlivened with a ruin in the distance and ele-gant plantings. A small lake edged with weeping willows and other trees was inhabited by a profusion of water fowl, includ-ing a pair of swans that continued their stately way across the water, ignoring the new arrivals. Devlin had purchased this es-tate from an earl who had badly needed money to help restore his principal estate. It never ceased to amaze, how many nobs squandered their fortune at the gambling tables and ran their estates to the ground with their vices.

The carriage rolled to a halt, and he dismounted first with Conan, then assisted each lady down.

Fifi's gaze drank in the large mansion, the sweeping lawns, the gardens, and the woodlands. "What a splendidly situated lake."

That his estate could impress the daughter of a marquess filled him with an annoyed sense of pride. Devlin made no reply to her admiration and ushered Fifi and her cousin inside while his butler led the lady maid below stairs.

"I believe my family awaits us in the drawing room," he murmured, waving them toward a door down the long hallway. He knocked on the door, opened it, and stepped back, allowing the ladies to precede him inside.

His two sisters, who were standing by the windows, their heads bent together in close confidence and giggling, whirled around.

"Niall, you are home!" Sara cried, hurrying over.

She paused long enough to dip into a curtsy for his guests before flinging herself into his arms. He held her to him, returning her hug. A fierce rush of love went through him.

His younger sister strolled over more sedately, her curious gaze on his guests.

"Lady Ophelia Darby, Lady Ephigenia Deidrick, allow me to present my sisters, Miss Sara Byrne and Miss Gwenn Byrne. Sara…Gwenn, meet Lady Ophelia…Fifi, and her cousin Lady Ephigenia Deidrick."

His sisters froze, their expressions ones of comical dismay and shock. They dipped into the appropriate curtsies, but their attention was wholly on Fifi. Amusement rushed through him when Sara tossed him an accusing stare.

"You lie!" she declared passionately.

He lifted a shoulder in a casual shrug, went over to the wingback chair, and lowered himself into a relaxed sprawl. He stretched out his legs and leaned back in the chair, crossing his ankles. His repose clearly offended this Cousin Effie, no doubt for its lack of refined posture. He had seen many gentlemen sit, like they had something large stuck in their arses and it might explode should they relax their shoulders and cross their legs above their knees. Devlin smiled at her, and she flushed, looking away.

"Who are you?" Gwenn demanded, staring at Fifi.

CHAPTER TWELVE

Before Ophelia could reply to that taut question, Miss Gwenn followed up with another quick, impatient demand, her lovely green eyes flashing. "How much is my brother paying you?" Gwenn asked impertinently.

Ophelia frowned. "I... Paying me for what?"

"To pretend you are her!"

"Who?"

"Fifi!" the two girls chorused.

Confusion rushed through Ophelia. She slanted a quick glance at Devlin. That familiar ironic smile appeared at the corner of his mouth.

"I *am* Lady Ophelia. Dev...Niall and I are friends. However, he is the only person who calls me Fifi. I have never shared my moniker with anyone else."

She felt Effie's stare, but Ophelia did not look at her. Effie did not approve of this dinner simply because the invitation came from Devlin. Ophelia thought it ridiculous, even though she appreciated her cousin's discretion in accompanying her. Surely, upon reaching her own home, she would receive an earful of Effie's concerns.

Miss Sara wore a black scowl that could rival any of Devlin's. The lady was lovely, with a mass of sable hair caught in an elegant chignon. Her frame was willowy, and she stood a few inches higher than Ophelia. Miss Sara, Miss Gwenn, and Devlin all shared the same beautiful eyes. Sara's eyes were now narrowed in curious contemplation. "Fifi...is shortened from Lady Ophelia?"

"Yes."

"Look, Sara," Gwenn said, her eyes widening. "Her hair is as black as a raven's feathers. Eyes as golden as whisky. And skin as unblemished as a peach. I think it is really her."

Ophelia flushed but was even more riveted by the red stain sweeping up Devlin's strong jawline. Was that how he had described her to his siblings?

"I am still not convinced," Gwenn said, folding her arms. "What is his favorite food?"

He scowled. "Come now, girls, let's pretend we know how to comport ourselves in the presence of—"

"Porridge sweetened with honey and cinnamon. His palate has probably evolved, but at the time it was porridge," she said softly.

Devlin jerked, then faltered into remarkable stillness. She felt his stare, but she did not look his way, holding the regard of his sisters.

"His favorite color," Sara whispered.

"Golden-brown…" It was only then Ophelia realized he had chosen his favorite color to be the one that matched her eyes.

"Before he was entranced by the lightning spark from your golden orbs, his best color was blue," Gwenn said, laughing, clearly entertained by this turn of events.

"I am now beginning to think this dinner a mistake," Devlin said, tugging on his cravat.

"His full name?" Gwenn asked, her eyes still narrowed suspiciously.

"Devlin Niall Byrne, though when I first met him, he was simply Niall."

"Are you still not convinced, lass?" he said gruffly, standing to walk over to his Gwenn and playfully chucking her under her chin.

Gwenn tucked a fist on her hip. "*No*. I am not convinced. She might be a charlatan whom you've brought here merely to unsettle us."

He raked his fingers through his hair, casting his sisters a black look. Neither seemed intimidated.

Sara folded her arms across her chest and pinned Ophelia with a gimlet stare. "When Niall took you by the river after that first night in the cottage, there was a large tree, and it looked strange, as if the trunks and massive limbs undulated. Tell me what happened."

"You do not need to answer," he said at her silence. "My sisters are conducting themselves outrageously."

Ophelia stared at his profile, noting that his shoulders were tensed and his expression was one of chilling austerity. Did he believe she had forgotten them, that their time had not also been etched indelibly in her mind...forever?

"Niall walked over bravely, telling me to stay away, that he had sworn to protect me. I was a bit skeptical there was any danger from a tree trunk, even an odd one, but I ran from the water to his side. We walked hand in hand—very bravely, I might add—to that tree. We did not understand what we perceived, for the massive trunk did not look brown but held a multitude of colors, from the floor of the tree, up covering almost every limb."

He turned sharply to regard her, and Ophelia could not decipher his expression. But her heart twisted upon itself and started to beat an uneven rhythm. "Yellow, blue, purple, brown, and those colors waved with the wind. Of course, we had to feel it. There was some back-and-forth argument on the merit of actually touching something so strange, but I won. We reached out together and stroked the trunk, and thousands of butterflies took flight into the sky. They swirled around us…magical and *utterly* beautiful. We stood there; our heads lifted to the sky as they fluttered about. I was convinced the forest was enchanted…Niall was more amused and awed, but he indulged my ideas and agreed it *was* magical."

Silence fell in the drawing room.

"You remember," he said gruffly.

"Every moment. We climbed a tree together, and somewhere out there, across the great landscape of England, a rather large and impressive willow tree bears our carved initials."

"I do not think she is fake," Sara whispered.

"I am not fake," Ophelia said with a wide smile. "And I am very pleased to meet you."

Her cheeks heated under Devlin's unflinching regard. It felt…almost indecent. And they were in front of company. A quick glance at Effie revealed she stared at Ophelia with appalled shock and dawning awareness. A throat cleared, and Ophelia whirled around to see a lovely couple standing in the open doorway.

"I declare our Niall has really brought you home to meet us, Lady Fifi," the gentleman said, his accent lyrical, his tone filled with warm humor. This man was tall and wiry and quite handsome. His hazel eyes gleamed with mischief and his smile…oh, that charming smile was the same as Devlin's. At once, she saw Niall as he would appear thirty years from today, and it was a most pleasant view.

"None of us believed my lad when he rambled that he had

saved a fairy and lived with her in an enchanted cottage," he said. "We thought him quite mad and often teased him over the years about this beautiful imaginary creature he met. It is a pleasure to meet you, Lady Fifi."

"Da, properly she is Lady Ophelia," Sara said.

Ophelia smiled and dipped into a deep, graceful curtsy as if she addressed a duke. "How very nice to meet you, sir."

His eyes widened, and he rushed over to her. "Please, Lady Ophelia, I am no one to curtsy to," he said on a deep bow.

She canted her head. "On the contrary, sir. You are Niall's da."

His eyes warmed and flared with approval.

A sniff tugged her attention to the lady who walked over. Niall's ma. She was beautiful, and all her children had inherited her lovely dark green eyes, which gleamed with pleasure.

"Lady Ophelia, it is very lovely indeed to meet you. I...I..." She broke off on a laugh and turned to look at her son. "We all owe you a large apology, my lad."

He angled his head most arrogantly. "I believe you do."

Gwenn poked him in his belly and then cried out when it seemed his stomach hurt her hand. Ophelia swallowed the laugh, a warm feeling blossoming through her body. His family was happy, and it was because he had worked so hard to ensure they lived so. A rush of fierce pride filled her. The boy who had rescued her had been so thin and dirty, so in awe of the size of the cottage, and he was now a wealthy and influential man in England.

His parents greeted Cousin Effie, who thankfully seemed charmed by Niall's da's roguishness, though whenever she peered at Devlin it was with careful suspicion. After a few more minutes of pleasantries, they were led to the dining room. A plump woman of indeterminate age carried out trays of food with another young girl assisting her. The table was laden with wonderful dishes. Steamed lobster, glazed salmon, roast beef, smoked trout, and pork loin stuffed with prunes and apples. No footmen served courses, and the family dined quite informally by passing dishes to one another, laughing and chatting with great vigor.

Devlin's father's manners were charming and humorous, and Ophelia found herself laughing several times at his anecdotes. Even Effie smiled a few times, the rigid decorum she wanted to maintain melting away. Ophelia also couldn't help noticing the careful manner in which Mrs. Byrne watched her—as if she did not trust Ophelia's presence in her son's life.

It was a decidedly odd experience, when in truth it was his presence in her life that posed the danger to her virtue and reputation.

Almost two hours later, Ophelia found herself outside in a most charming gazebo not very distant from the main estate. She'd left Cousin Effie playing the pianoforte for Gwenn, who sang an Irish ballad. Picking a petal from a primrose, she gently plucked at the flower. Soft footfall had her heart leaping in anticipation. She turned around and blinked.

"I see that you expected my son," Mrs. Byrne said with a smile, pulling her shawl tightly around her shoulders.

"I did," she said honestly.

"He left the music room shortly after you did. However, he made his way toward the woods."

She looked in the direction Mrs. Byrne pointed with a small frown.

"Whenever my lad feels troubled, that is where he goes,"

she said, coming to stand beside Ophelia.

"Troubled?"

"Aye…you trouble him."

Ophelia's heart jolted. She had not expected this bluntness from his mother or the piercing way she stared at her. "I…I have given him no cause to worry."

A soft, mocking laugh escaped her.

"You are my son's *a ghrá mo chroí*," his mother said, pinning Ophelia with a steady gaze. "Is he yours?"

"I…I do not know what that means."

"From the way he looks at you…touches you, do you not understand it?"

At her shocked silence, his mother sighed most aggrievedly. "You are going to break my boy."

The absurdity of the idea was almost too much to contemplate. He was the rakish scoundrel seducing her to his bed. All the risks were hers. "I… You mistake the matter," she said hoarsely. "He is my friend… I would not hurt him."

"Is that all he is to you, my lady? A friend?"

Forbidden lovers.

"Yes." Her heart stuttered in denial, and an acute longing rose inside her like a great swell, threatening to choke her. Flustered, she looked away, toward the towering skyline of the woodland.

"Several years ago, I watched my son fearlessly jump into a swollen river that had washed a little girl away. We all thought we had lost him. I thought I had lost my only son." A faraway look entered Mrs. Byrne's eyes. "I fainted and was abed for days. How I prayed that he lived. And then one day his da found him out in the fields behind our cottage. He was blistered from being under the sun. He was fevered, and beneath his feet he had a cut that was infected."

Ophelia pressed a hand to her chest. "Infected!"

"Yes. He told us a very likely tale of rescuing a young fairy and staying with her in a cabin, protecting her. The entire time he protected her, he had a cut under his foot from a stone in the river."

"No," Ophelia whispered, her heart aching, recalling how fiercely protective and comforting he had been to her. So many nights he had sat by the bed and sung for her when she had pitifully wept for her papa. All that time, he had silently suffered. "He never mentioned it."

"Because my lad's only thought was to keep you safe, even from worry. He told us of a groundskeeper rescuing his fairy. And that a servant from the home she had been delivered to took him as close to home as possible. They did not have the kindness to carry him all the way home to us. It was a blessing his da worked the fields that day."

Ophelia felt like she couldn't breathe. "Niall…was dumped in a field. That was his reward for saving me?"

Mrs. Byrne sighed. "His journey home would have been left in the hands of a servant. He was less than that servant and clearly a burden. Our boy was gripped in a painful fever for days. It was thoughts of you that brought him through the crisis. And when he woke, all he spoke of was this Fifi…how he would one day marry her."

Ophelia drew a deep breath, trying to calm the wild pounding of her heart.

"My son left home at twelve to make himself a man worthy enough to marry this girl we all believed a figment of his delirium. By the time he was fourteen, he was imprisoned."

Ophelia recoiled. "No!"

"Yes." She gripped the wooden balustrade on the gazebo. "We thought he would die in that terrible place."

"Why…how did Niall…*why*?" Ophelia's throat closed.

"Because he *had* to become wealthy, and that desperate drive pushed my son to the very brink of death and back. So many days I cried, for when I closed my eyes all I saw was him crawling on his belly, bloodied, and beaten, reaching for something that he could never attain. And I had no way to pierce his resolve. He was very decided on his path, and I believe it was all for you."

"No," Ophelia whispered. "I…"

"My son is unlike anyone I have ever met. He is very driven—sometimes, I fear, to his detriment. He is ruthlessly protective when it comes to the ones he loves. And he is not afraid to love. Never that. And when he does…he does it fiercely and with his whole heart. I urge you to remember that, Lady Ophelia."

Mrs. Byrne tilted her face to the sky. "He never stopped pushing, even when we told him that you were worlds apart. A fine lady like yourself would never accept someone who lived in the stews, who lived inside a dank, cold…and violent prison for two years with God knows what manner of vileness happening to him. He is someone who walked on the edge of criminality, who made money by barbarically fighting with his bare knuckles. He has known hardship. He has known pain. And I am worried, for I see how he looked at you throughout dinner and in that music room. He did not let it go! Why would a fine lady of quality such as yourself even associate with my boy?"

Mrs. Byrne's tone had turned accusing.

"He is my friend."

"Is he?"

"Yes. I would never hurt Devlin."

Ophelia walked jerkily to sit on the gazebo bench, the primrose petals a mangled mess in her hand. She could scarcely comprehend the circumstances that had shaped Niall into the man he was today, or the determination that allowed him to walk this path. That burning hunger for something everyone told him would be out of his grasp.

Suddenly, she saw him, walking a thousand miles through harsh weather, small arms lifting heavy crates by the docks as he labored brutally under sunshine, rain, and snow. She envisioned him hurt, feet bloodied and infected but unable to rest for fear of harm coming to her. She saw him, fiercely defiantly crawling…fighting…enduring two years imprisoned. And at the end of his path, there she stood.

"So you do have some feelings for him," his mother murmured. "You cry for him."

Startled, she lifted her hands to find her face wet with tears. "I…"

Mrs. Byrne sighed. "You are both fools."

With that cryptic reply, she walked away. Ophelia hastened down the steps of the gazebo toward the woodlands to which Mrs. Byrne had pointed. Gripping the skirt of her gown, she lifted it so she would not trip and ran toward the forest. A well-worn path made itself evident, and she followed it for several minutes until it opened into a wide-open clearing.

Her breath hitched.

A cottage waited there—one that was painfully familiar. Devlin was nowhere to be seen. Ophelia did not understand what drove her, but she walked across the lush lawn, passed a cluster of artfully arranged stones up to the small steps of that cottage and opened the door.

Inside was clean, well fragranced, and quite lovely. The bed was very grand, with finely carved bedposts and silk hangings and a canopy. A large, beautiful rug was before the hearth. It was almost a replica of their cottage, but this was larger, cleaner, and tastefully decorated.

Ophelia's fingers trembled when she walked over to a table close to the fire and picked up the book of children's stories she had given him.

How long had it been? Sixteen years? And while it appeared to be well read, it was carefully, lovingly preserved.

Wait for me...

Had he really cried those words when the door had been closing? For so long they had echoed in her thoughts and dreams.

Ophelia sensed his approach and his regard upon her body in the same manner she could sense her heartbeat in her throat. The familiarity of everything was bizarre. "You built a cabin similar to the one that provided a safe haven for us."

"Yes. Is it as you remember?"

Ophelia did not face him. She couldn't, not in this moment, not with this peculiar vulnerability roiling through her heart. "Perhaps. It feels just as peaceful. More beautiful, I think. Why...why did you build it?"

A low chuckle sounded. "More so in defiance of everyone who insisted you were not real."

Silence fell, and she stood there, staring down at the book, gasping at the realization that her vision was blurred...by tears.

"Are you ready to return to town?"

"I think I would like to...lie on the grass and stare at the night sky." Something they had done several nights as children.

There was a pregnant pause. She could feel him thinking.

"Alone?" he asked gruffly.

Oh, God. "No."

A soft, wordless murmur came from him, and from the corner of her eyes she saw him gather the large rug by the fire, tug a blanket from the bed, and then go outside.

Reckless. She should insist they return to town immediately. The carriage ride would be an hour or more. And she had this much freedom because her parents trusted her to act with good sense in regard to their standing and position at all times.

Niall is my slice of wickedness…

Lowering the book to the table, she whirled about and went outside. Farther away from the cottage than she had thought, he had spread the rug on the grass and then the blankets atop. Somehow, he had carried cushions and pillows, too…and a lone lantern, which barely provided any light against the encroaching night.

He walked toward her, and how her heart danced beneath her breastbone. Devlin reminded her of a large, sleek panther, predatory and dangerous. But also utterly magnificent. The manner in which he observed her so keenly, so thoroughly, as though he could unravel whatever mysteries she presented, unnerved Ophelia. She was not mysterious in the least.

Her feet took her slowly forward, step by step, as if directed by a force she could not control. It was then she noted his air of dishevelment. Devlin had discarded his jacket, waistcoat, and cravat, and she could see the beat of his heart underneath the thin linen of his shirt. She breathed in the scent of the man, all warmth and masculinity, a heady musk overlaid by spicy soap. The top buttons of his shirt were open, and not only could she see his throat, but there was also a golden chain around his neck with the ugliest pendant Ophelia had ever seen.

It was the ring of vines she had given him years ago. She simply stopped and stared at him, beyond words—but not feelings. They crashed over her senses in dizzying waves of surprise and bewilderment. The most troubling and profound sensations were the tremble in her heart and the tight, twisting ache in her belly. No; it wasn't an ache but heat. A fire that spread and blossomed upward, rushing down to gather in her fingertips. Ophelia was certain should she touch him, all that fire would somehow leap to him and burn them alive.

Her thoughts whirled, the whimsy and fanciful nature of them almost amusing. But she could not smile. He stared at her, his eyes dark and shadowed.

"You kept it," she whispered. All these years, he had kept that stupid, childish promise ring from her.

His mouth twisted in a rueful grin. "I presume you discarded yours."

Her throat went tight, and an unfamiliar sensation lodged inside her chest. It felt suspiciously like yearning. If he only knew the truth. But she would not speak it. For he might read more than what she intended, when Ophelia hardly understood herself in this moment.

"Let down your hair," he murmured.

Her cheeks went hot; her throat and belly, too. She should ask why...perhaps say no, but Ophelia lifted her hand, removed the small hat perched atop her curls, and dropped it to the grass. Plucking the pins from her updo, she removed them until her hair tumbled to her shoulders and down her back in loose waves. She placed the pins in her upturned hat so they were easy to locate.

Longing lay naked in his eyes, and it undid her. "I like the way you look at me," she softly confessed. The words had come from a hidden part of her she'd never before acknowledged, the part that hungered to be touched, to be vibrantly alive, connected to something that inspired desire, to be unchained from responsibility and duties, to be free from guilt and doubt.

"And how is that?"

"Like I am…precious, maybe. And at other times like you want to gobble me up. No one has ever considered me with such licentious sweetness."

His low, pleased chuckle stroked sensually over her skin. Devlin took a few steps closer. "And you are not afraid, hmm?"

"Of course not!" Toeing off her shoes, she glided her stocking-clad feet against the grass. It was not enough. She wanted to feel the small prickles against her skin.

"I remember you loved to walk in the woods in bare feet."

She grinned, dipped slightly, tugged her gown to her knees, and removed her stockings. They too were discarded in the grass.

"We are not children anymore, Fifi," he drawled, walking closer.

"It feels just as magical," she said, recalling that small boy who had encouraged her to be fearless and adventurous as they raced barefoot through the woods. It had been glorious to dirty her feet. To stomp in mud puddles, climb trees, chase rabbits, and bathe naked in the stream. For those nine days, Ophelia had been someone different.

I always feel…different with you, Niall.

He removed a flask from his pocket and tipped it to his mouth, where he took two long swallows. He screwed on the cork, then tossed the small bottle to her. She deftly caught it.

"Are we to become drinking companions?" she teased, absurdly pleased.

No other man of her acquaintance would have thought to invite her to drink so casually.

She opened the cork, tipped it to her head, and took several small mouthfuls. The heat that slid down her belly warmed her from inside out. Ophelia tossed it back to him after a few more swallows. When he placed the flask back to his mouth, his eyes closed, and he clearly savored the drink. Or perhaps the taste of her mouth that she left behind.

Humor filled her upon noting the careful distance they placed between each other. He edged toward the lake, and she followed, keeping that respectable space. He noted it, too, and they shared an unexpected smile. Something passed between them, hot and tremulous. They did not speak it, but somehow, she knew he had the same thought as her. Should they reduce the space between them...draw closer to each other, they would suck away that open breathable air and would surely burn themselves in a reckless passion.

It was there in the shadows of his stare—as if she were the answer to all the secret dreams and cravings he'd ever owned. And she felt the answering call deep inside her heart...her body. The touch of his gaze on her skin was possessive... carnal...and so delightfully wicked. Ophelia was torn between two impulses: to run away from the raw, aching sensation that had hooked low in her belly, tugging her toward him, for it felt too powerful...too terrifying to explore. Or to surrender to her desire to be with Devlin.

She recalled that the small cliff had a waterfall, which gushed into a river. How she had wanted to leap into the water but had been too afraid.

"*My da says life must be lived, for we get the chance only once. I ken this is what he means, Fifi. Doing the things that make us afraid but also make our heart do that weird dance.*"

His face had been so fiercely beautiful and intense as he stared at her.

"*I'll jump with you.*"

Ophelia had scoffed, her little heart so hopeful that she might be brave enough to step off the cliff. "*What happens when we both perish together?*"

He hadn't looked afraid at all, and Niall had smiled. "*Then we'll bloody perish together.*"

She had giggled, then run for the edge and shouted for him to catch her. His hands had slipped into hers before they tumbled off the edge into the water.

A dangerous thrill burst in her heart, and tingles raced over her skin, raising gooseflesh. "Niall?"

"Yes?"

"Catch me," she murmured and allowed herself to once again tumble over the cliff.

CHAPTER THIRTEEN

Ophelia launched herself into Devlin's arms, and he instinctively caught her against his body. Her soft weight fell against him, her slim hands encircled his throat, and her legs hooked scandalously around his hips, the skirts of her dress riding high to her thighs. He glanced down and almost expired on the spot. Devlin gripped her hips, holding her weight easily, painfully aware that she had removed her stockings, and he could feel the heat of her skin against him, the warmth between her thighs on the front of his trousers. This close, he could not escape the savage beauty of her under the moonlight, with her mass of hair tumbling around their bodies to her hips.

"Do you recall carrying me like this through the woods?"

"I believe then you were on my back, your arms choking the life from me."

Laughter bubbled up from her throat. "I had good cause."

She looked wildly desirable, her raven hair spilling over her shoulders in ripples of midnight waves. *Ah God*. He felt so weak to her. "I never saw those spiders, and I searched to vanquish them for you," he replied drily.

"They simply hid from your eyes," she said, her eyes gleaming with laughter.

Her small smile made his heart beat a little faster. "And what is your excuse for jumping in my arms now, Fifi?"

He waited for her to admit she was falling into the dangerous mire of allurement.

She leaned in toward him, her eyes somber and searching, at odds with the deviltry that purred from her lips as she said, "Naughtiness."

Ah, I see. An ache of want settled low in his gut, and he wondered if he would have the will to send her home with her virtue intact. Unless… "Have you had a man before?"

If she answered yes, he might dump her in the bloody lake, after getting the man's name to gut him later.

Her eyes sparkled with provoking humor. "What is it to you? I am sure you've had a woman or two."

The silence pounded and stretched, yet neither spoke. "Fifi?"

"Hmm?"

"Do not test me."

An inelegant snort echoed in the night air, mocking the primal feelings crawling up from his belly. "Who is he?" He was going to kill the man slowly and with pleasure.

An impish grin curved her lovely mouth. "Who is who?"

"For God's sake, woman!"

She laughed, the sound light and teasing. "I've never had a lover, Devlin."

"Then say so. Do not tease me."

She slipped a hand from behind his neck, confident that he held her weight from falling to the ground. Fifi lightly touched the bridge of his nose. "Why not?"

"I cannot bear the thought of you in another man's arms."

"And I must bear the thought that you've had women?"

The soft words were a crushing fist against his heart. *Hell.* Regret iced through his insides. "No," he said quietly. "One. Not women."

A tiny frown appeared between her winged brows. "You've had one lover in all your life?"

"Yes."

She ducked her head, the curtain of her hair briefly hiding her expression. "Is she your lover still?"

"No."

Their gazes collided. In hers, he spied relief. "Why not?"

"I ended the liaison the night you sang for me."

She trailed that lone finger down to his lip, and he noted that it trembled. Her touch was so soft and light it was scarcely a breath of sensation, yet it hooked into his gut and pulled with ruthless intensity, toward her...always toward her. The jolt in his body was savage, arousal curling through him.

Fifi sparkled. She tempted. Devlin hungered. *Fuck*. His heart trembled. There was something wild and bewitching about her. Something enchanting...and untouchable. At this moment, he felt a rare feeling of being unworthy of Fifi. Much like his friends, he'd learned to cloak himself in a mask of civility, some semblance of breeding, and eloquence. But it did not take much to see the coarseness beneath the surface of that manufactured elegance. He had done things—shameful, ruthless things—to get where he was today.

She was so damn beautiful. She was too elegant for him, too refined, too ladylike. He forced himself to take a deep breath and then exhale slowly. "It is best we start our journey back to town."

He needed to bloody well think. Rethink his approach. Re-strategize. And he damn well could not do that with her so close.

She rubbed her thumb over his lower lip, delicately parting his lips so she could wet her finger. Hot, urgent desire stirred inside him, the powerful need touching a raw nerve. *Remember to progress slowly...woo her, not ravish her*.

"I do not wish to leave as yet."

He nipped that thumb, wanting to punish her for making him crave her so much. "It is late."

"It is barely nine p.m. When I am at balls, I leave most times at three or four a.m."

"Is that where your parents think you are?"

"They believe I am at a small dinner party at my dear friend's home. It is expected that I will return home late." Her lush red mouth curved deliciously. "*Very* late."

Bloody hell. For a wild moment, Devlin forgot to breathe. "Where is your cousin? I expected her to be a hound at your heels sniffing."

"You do know I am four and twenty."

"So you have said before."

She removed her thumb, blew at where he bit, and then licked his taste from her fingers. Devlin almost dropped her on her arse. His cock rose on a painful pulse of want. The teasing, wretched minx!

"Cousin Effie is aware of the truth."

"And what truth is that?"

"As many whispered behind their fans, I am long in the tooth, on the shelf, no longer in the blush of youth. I am not required to observe the proprieties and rectitude of gentility as much as ladies younger than myself. She will not chase after me but respect my need for space."

Dark humor rushed through him. "A woman as lovely as you are is considered long in the tooth?"

"And a wallflower," she whispered, as if she shared a secret. "There is nothing worse than a long-in-the-tooth wallflower."

At least she seemed amused by the ridiculousness of that idea.

"You could have told your family you visited my parents' home for a dinner," he said, watching every nuance of her expression.

Her lip curled in a delicate scowl, and her eyes glinted with mysterious allure. "You are the danger that lurks unseen in shadowy corners, masked as a handsome and debonair man." She touched her fingertips to his cheek. "Even a spinster…a long-toothed wallflower can be irrevocably ruined by being associated with you."

"I would not want you ruined and cast aside by your society." The instant the words stumbled from his mouth, he tasted the truth of them. He had been so damn busy thinking about his desires, he did not pause to consider the impact on Fifi. Though he did not respect many nobs for their selfishness, it was still the world she had grown in—the only one she knew. They would need to discuss a plan on how to deal with those from her world who might want to hurt Fifi for her choices. He would repay hurt with hurt. Perhaps it was best to keep that part to himself. Devlin sensed she had a compassionate heart.

"It is my risk to take."

"And what do you earn in return?"

There was a hitch in her breathing.

He knew he pushed her, but he wanted to understand without a doubt why she was with him. When he'd sent his invitation, he had not offered money or any form of coercion. It had been a request born of hope and hunger, and she had replied, astonishing every sense he owned.

"I would never be how I am with you now with another, Niall," his Fifi said, a curious ache of want in her tone. "I am not afraid to be alone with you. I am not afraid of the risks…

in truth, I do not think of them, for I am too busy relishing this…being myself with you, with no fear of reprimand or judgment."

Her trust cut him open—he wanted to bear her down to the carpet of grass and devour every inch of her delectable body. If she stayed here with him…alone, with nothing but the darkness of the night known to hold secrets and whispered temptations, he would take her, and damn all consequences.

"Fifi—"

"Let's stargaze, Devlin," she said with a smile that crinkled the corners of her eyes. "The last time I had the pleasure of simply staring at the stars was after we dared jump in the river, chasing waterfalls and fishes."

He walked with her over to the rug and blankets, biting back a groan when she shimmied off him. With a gusty smile, she tossed herself onto the blankets, staring upward, her hair fanning about her. Devlin lay beside her, careful that they did not touch. He felt aching and hungry and empty. The stunning creature who had reduced him to such a state reposed beside him, wistfully staring at the velveted blackness of the sky. He slid his hand across the grass. Just a touch. Just once, and he would content himself with that. His finger brushed against hers, and she stilled. He felt when she shifted her head on the blanket and stared at him. Carefully masking his cravings, he turned his head, and their gazes collided.

Hers were bright with something naughty yet sweet.

"Are you foxed?"

She snorted, the inelegant sound surprising him. "I have had whisky before."

"Really?" he asked drily.

She slipped her fingers through his, the move casual, but

his heart slammed against his chest. Did she realize her actions? Devlin curled his fingers around hers, in the event she thought she would take back her clasp. He was far from ready to let her go. Perhaps he never would be.

Pushing those thoughts from his mind, knowing how ruthless he could be when he pursued something he wanted, Devlin directed his attention to her words.

"Us sinful wallflowers often pilfered Papa's whisky. We have been tipsy more than once, and I assure you, I am far from that. I simply feel…languid and so warm."

"Sinful wallflowers?"

"Hmm, my friends."

Wallflowers. That silly sobriquet. "I suppose society would say they are long in the tooth as well?"

"Or some such nonsense." The hint of laughter had quite vanished from her eyes. "I would love for you to meet them. There is Kitty, who is now a Duchess; Maryann, who is married to Marquess Rothbury. There is also Emma, Fanny, and Charlotte. We are the dearest of friends, and we have promised one another to stop letting life pass us by because others have their own notion of how we should live. Existing at the will of others is rather unpleasant, so we are determined to live by *our* own wants and desires."

A notion he rather admired and one that explained why she was here tonight. So he was a part of her wants and desires. Dark pleasure hummed through him. *One step closer.* From what he understood about society and the strictures it placed on young ladies, it was rather an extraordinary thing they had decided. "Your depth of unhappiness must have been profound."

She made a sound that was a cross between a snort and a

hiss. Devlin had no idea what the hell it was, but it brought a smile to his lips.

"Can you imagine the audacity of everyone directing our lives? *How* do they imagine this is acceptable? Since we were girls, we were told how to walk, dress, behave, and lord forbid how dreadfully improper it is should we have any original ideas of our own. We are always rebuked for daring to do anything outside of their expectations. Well, we were all annoyed…"

A slight hiccup interrupted her, and Fifi gave a breathless small laugh. "Society has a rigid opinion on the fun we may have and the men we are to marry. Imagine that society considers that if we do not agree to behave exactly as they decree, we are *ruined*. How can I be ruined…no longer suitable to speak or dance with, no longer suitable for elevated company, if I simply dare to exist within my own dream? It is so outrageous it is almost laughable."

"So you all decided to pursue wickedness?"

She must have heard the incredulity in his voice, for she laughed again.

"No. That is simplifying matters. We will pursue what we want. It is our life, is it not? Our happiness? I doubt the engine of society will crumble should we pursue the yearning in our hearts instead of doing what we are told. If the path to that happiness just happens to be wicked…well!"

"And what are your pursuits that are so dastardly it would send society into a swoon?"

Her eyes held his, and her lips curled enticingly. "I am here with *you*."

"Ah…the danger that lurks unseen…and whatnot."

"Yes." Her gaze lowered to their entwined fingers. "A touch

from you, Niall, and I am unequivocally turned upside down. Can there be anything more dangerous to a lady? That a touch from a man leaves her breathless with a craving she does not understand, and awakens impossible expectations in her heart?"

Devlin was bloody well captivated by her. "Is that how I make you feel?"

"Yes."

"That is fair, then. For days after I see you, I can still feel you beneath my skin. I am afraid to eat…to drink whisky or anything, for I do not want to lose the taste of your mouth from mine. Wickedly sweet and tart. A taste that promises exquisite sinfulness and such pleasure…"

She was taken so much by surprise that she could only stare at him. "Truly?" Fifi whispered.

"Truly."

• • •

Need broke over Ophelia, warm, rich, like honeyed heat.

This was not what she should be talking about with Devlin. She felt a sudden, aching wrench of emotion. Chatting about the night stars was a much safer and more agreeable topic for conversation, but there was a hunger in Ophelia's heart to know the man she lay so scandalously close to. To kiss him. To roll with him in the grass, wrapped in laughter.

To give him that taste of her that he did not want to lose.

Between her legs, she swelled and ached. *Touch me*, she silently pleaded. As if he heard her, with a long, indrawn breath, he lifted his right hand and laid it, tentative, against her cheek.

Ophelia got the sense he was almost afraid to reach out to her. Did he think she believed his caresses beneath her? She could not bear for him to think so. "Do you think I abhor your touch?"

"No."

"Then why do you seem…hesitant to hold me?"

"Is it not inappropriate to do so?" he asked with a small, amused curve to his mouth.

Terribly inappropriate. "Do you forget I vowed to be wicked in my pursuits?"

He made a small *tsk*ing sound, a sound of mockery and provocative amusement. His thumb slid against her cheek and down to her lips. There, he brushed it across her mouth. "How astonishing you think *this* is wicked."

"I *am* acquainted with its varied forms."

"Are you?"

"I recall your demonstration with my *cunny*."

He stilled. To Ophelia's shock, Devlin rolled her beneath him, keeping his weight on one of his elbows, and peered down into her eyes. He used his thumb to part her lips and then slid it against the inside of her bottom lip. He stared at her, his expression beautiful and savagely carnal, and she couldn't dismiss the awareness that Devlin was indeed dangerous.

But not to me, that silly and reckless heart of hers murmured.

"What is wicked, Fifi, is that I should tell you that your lips are perfect in their lushness, and I have dreamed about them on my mouth…my throat…my chest…and even my cock."

Color flooded her cheeks, for she had a good notion of what he meant by "cock." A dark, wanton feeling came upon her without warning, an aching fullness low in her belly. *Is this desire?* Ophelia surprised herself by laughing. "I think you are trying to shock my sensibilities, Niall."

"I suppose I failed abysmally?"

"I am no longer waiting, Devlin. I want to live a little...for myself. I have vowed to be wicked, even if it is once. And that means I get to do naughty things...*extraordinary* naughty things with my mouth. I daresay they might even involve cocks."

It was a wonder she did not choke on the crudely salacious word, but her taunt had the desired effect.

Niall faltered into remarkable stillness, a flush darkening along his jawline. Oh, teasing him was such fun.

"You delightful wretch," he murmured, dipping his head closer. Their noses brushed.

"A wretch, am I?"

"Note the distinction. I said delightful. I could have said bloody wretch."

He stroked lightly up and down the nape of her neck. He wanted to kiss her; she could see the craving in his eyes. Yet he did not lower his head. Ophelia had the sudden sneaking suspicion he did not kiss her to simply prove to himself that he could refrain from the desire. That he could control this... whatever this was.

The sudden awareness of that knowledge felt almost impossible to grasp. That would mean Devlin Byrne *desperately* wanted to kiss her, and that must be unacceptable to a man who at times seemed so controlled. That hunger crawling through him now must be a grave annoyance.

"You want to kiss me," Ophelia murmured daringly, brazenly, with utter provocation.

"That I do," he said, his mouth curving into a small smile.

"Then why don't you?"

"Is that another invitation, Fifi?"

"It was a question."

He lowered his face a little, looking at her from beneath his eyelashes. "I've already tasted the delight of your mouth, Fifi...surely you know where I want my tongue next, hmm?"

There was a teasing, provoking glint in his eyes.

The fiend indeed.

"I have wondered what it would feel like...to have you kissing my cunny. I thought it so wicked of you to plant the temptation inside me. Since that day at your home, every night I lay awake in the dark...I spread my legs...and my fingers hovered right *there*, but I am not brave enough to touch." The words felt like they came from somewhere and someone else. "But I think of your mouth there. How would it feel? Strange? Hot? Ticklish? Pleasurable?"

"Fucking hell!"

Suddenly, Ophelia was terrified. Of the way he made her feel...the way he made her hunger. And all from the merest touch. *Is he your slice of wickedness...?*

As she peered at him and the chain around his throat, she admitted she wanted him to be more than a slice. She wanted wickedness with him in its entirety.

"I am afraid," she whispered, taking a single step back in her thoughts. Yet she did not remove her hand from around his shoulders.

He froze, a spasm of anguish crossing his face before his expression shuttered. "You think me capable of hurting you?"

She pressed her trembling hand to her stomach, desperately seeking to stop the nervous flutters. "I am scared because…because I *want* you. I have never wanted a man before!"

It was so tempting to step off the precipice she hovered above.

Oh, God! I've already leaped.

His eyes gleamed with an unfathomable emotion. Then he laughed, low and soft, the sound decidedly mocking. "You are afraid that after I ravish you, I will want you to make an honest man out of me."

The words settled between them, heavy and fraught. The terrible irony did not escape her.

"I know I am not the kind of man a lady like you should take for a husband, Fifi." Though his expression was icily carved into stone, he tenderly brushed a kiss across her mouth. "Do not worry—I will not demand you do the honorable thing."

Not yet lingered unspoken, and she wondered if it was her fanciful thoughts.

I am courting you to my bed. That was a promise of an affair; nothing more. Yet she also had in her thoughts every word his mother imparted earlier. He cunningly tried to hide it, but Niall wanted all of her, and inexplicably, Ophelia wanted to give her entire self to him, even knowing it to be impossible.

She wanted to be his lover.

Ophelia did not want to deny the desire for him anymore. She did not want to think about any consequences at the moment. She simply needed to choose this for herself, so she did.

"Undress me, please," Ophelia whispered. A kiss of warning quivered down her spine, but she brushed it aside.

A charged stillness followed.

Their gazes held for endless minutes. She could not tear her eyes away from his brilliant gaze. The look in his eyes—savage lust and hunger—should have frightened Ophelia, for she had no experience in matters of the flesh, but her body throbbed with a deep, sweet ache of anticipation. She pushed herself up into a sitting position, shifted on the blankets, and stood, turning her back to him.

There was no movement between them, and the night echoed with their stillness. Wind rustled through the trees, and in the distance, a bird chirped. She heard when he stood and felt him behind her, a hard, hot, shifting wall against her back, at once comforting and intimidating. The sound of movement echoed; he was removing his clothes. Soft winds plucked the blades and leaves of the trees like violin strings, creating music around them. She heard it then—melodies in the night air.

A song from you to me…

She barely felt his hands as he undid the small buttons of her dress. Ophelia bit into her lower lip, aware of her rapid breathing. That he did not speak heightened her awareness of him, and she closed her eyes when his fingers lingered on the last button at her lower back.

The night air cooled her skin as he slowly tugged at the laces of her stay. The dress was pushed down to her arms, and he held it there at her elbows, a trap of sorts. He smelled her hair, and she swallowed. Still no words from him, and the feelings low in her belly tightened until they were painful. His fingers tightened on the crushed garment at her elbows. It was as if he struggled with hunger…and restraint…

"Do you know what I have imagined, Fifi…?" he said in a

rough whisper. "About you…and me…"

Her stomach filled with a thousand butterflies. "Tell me."

"You on your belly, your luscious hips sprawled over a cushion, your legs split wide so I can clearly see the pretty pinkness of your cunny…waiting for me to touch…and to kiss. The ways I dreamed of tupping you say I am too damn coarse for you."

Before she could protest, he delicately bit into the curve of her shoulder, the sting an erotic pleasure. Then he nudged the side of her face with his chin, like the great dangerous panther she imagined, curving her neck outward more.

"I've imagined taking you on your knees, your pussy wet with invitation, your arse arched while your elbows are low on the mattress. The pose would spread you wide, but you, my sweet, won't go blushing on me. You are too daring for that. I envision staring at the sensual arch of your spine, the roundness of your lush, plump arse. I admit to watching the sway of it many times when I saw you in the streets."

He stroked one finger over her derriere. "I've imagined biting those luscious globes, kissing it better…going to that valley with my kisses where you'll be dewy and so damn beautiful. You inspire fantasies of sweaty tangled limbs, writhing in ecstasy atop silken sheets."

She felt a primal twist in her belly.

The gown whispered from her body to pool at her feet, then her stays, drawers, and chemisette followed until she was gloriously naked, her hair tumbling over her shoulders and back, protecting her body from the night air. From his gaze. That finger stroked down from her buttocks to her thighs, slipping to her inner thigh. *Oh, God*. She gripped the edges of his trousers and held on at the sensations that

quaked through her belly. They were frightfully hot, needy…
almost desperately painful.

"I've been a right libertine, fisting my cock off nightly with
these images. You are a lady of quality. I am coarse and unfit
for you. I know it, but I cannot stay away from you."

"I do not want you to stay away," she whispered. "Never
that."

He groaned like a tortured man. "Fucking hell, Fifi, this
was not a part of the plan. Not today."

"But one day?" she asked, an ache rising in her throat.

His fingers brushed her throat as he drew the mass of her
hair back over her shoulder. "One day…when I was damn
well sure."

"Sure of what?"

He closed his eyes and pressed his forehead on top of her
head. "Until I was sure of you."

She made to turn around, and he clamped his hands
fiercely on her hips, halting her movement. "Are you sure of
me now, Niall?"

"I am even more uncertain," he said gruffly, running a hand
over her hips around to her belly in a motion of violent
tenderness. Up he went with both hands, his fingers exploring,
stroking, demanding, plucking at nerve endings over the flat
of her belly, the sides of her ribs, below her breasts until he
cupped the full mounds in his large hands.

His naked chest pressed against her back, his flesh imprint-
ing on every part of her skin her hair did not cover. Bare skin
to bare skin. Her skin felt engulfed in flames. Ophelia mewled,
the sound shocking and arousing her in equal measure. It was
instinct that had her reaching behind her…feeling for him. He
was still in trousers; however, the flaps were open. She slid her

hand inside them, exploring the hot, hard flesh within. She traced the length and thickness of it, blushing a bit. "What is this called?"

He tenderly kissed the slope of her neck. "My cock."

"Curious words…cock…cunny."

In response to her low murmur, his thumb found the taut, throbbing peak of her nipples, chafing back and forth in a delicious manner. A little sob of pleasure caught in her throat at that punch of sensation. In retaliation, she squeezed his thick length, and his breath hitched.

"Only the one word for this?" she murmured with dry amusement.

"Penis, lobcock, manhood, manroot, spindle, pulling prick… should I continue?"

She laughed, oddly amused and titillated. The touch of his mouth along the curve of her throat was just a whisper of sensation, yet it evoked a flame low in her belly. He was teasing, gentle, *dangerous*…for Ophelia had no will left in her to resist his caresses, only to be wicked and wanton.

Devlin teased her nipples, rolling each under his thumb before pinching down. Her breasts were released, and his hands started to roam. His touch felt impatient yet gentle, forceful yet seductive.

He spun her around, and the glimpse of him under the silvery wash of moonlight stole her breath. He was beautifully delineated with muscles that cut like marble slabs from his arms, over his chest, and to his stomach. As he cupped her cheeks, she found herself crushed against him, his mouth devouring hers with ravishing passion. Slipping her hands around his neck, she returned his kisses, all the feelings sweeping her up, vaguely aware that he dragged her down with him to the rumpled blankets atop the rug. In his kisses, she felt the echoes of the past and the yearning for a future. *I am fanciful*, she thought dazedly.

She whimpered, feeling the heat of him everywhere, like a searing brand. His hand on her thigh, sliding to her hips, her waist. He ran his palm along the length of her leg, a light stroke, from her ankle to her knee. When he touched her nipple with his tongue, she drew in a sharp breath and caught her lower lip in her teeth. The pleasure was sublime. Then he touched her wet, aching sex with a finger before sliding it deep. It was as if lightning pierced her belly. The sensations burned primal and wonderful, so much so Ophelia cried out, her voice rippling through the woodlands.

Everything felt fast yet so perfect.

She closed her eyes, and—oh, dear God, his tongue licked her sex. He actually kissed her…cunny! Her thighs…her belly…her entire body shivered as his tongue moved over her flesh. She moaned his name—Niall…Devlin—until they blended into a chorus of whispers and wanton pleas.

He chuckled, the sound one of low, masculine arrogance and appreciation, before his tongue stabbed against her nub of pleasure. He sucked it into his mouth, devastating her with the sudden thrill of exhilaration. She came up off the blanket, supporting her weight on her elbows to watch his dark head between her splayed thighs.

The picture they presented stole her breath. This was *indecent*…diabolical…wonderful torture.

And Ophelia wanted more.

With each skillful flick of his tongue, he unlocked her—he stripped her inhibitions and destroyed her ladylike sensibilities. She arched her hips more to his mouth, mindless sensation spearing from her sex to her belly. Ophelia gripped the blanket, biting into her lower lip. Something frightening was swelling through her body. It felt tight…and achy…and the center of the burning pleasure was the nub he sucked and licked with ease.

Her release came without warning—a violent, shuddering, powerful wave of joy that had her thighs trembling. It took her breath so she could not scream, only emit a sob of want, for she was still empty despite that devastating bliss. It was as if he knew, for he came up above her, blanketing her with his weight and powerful muscles. His fingers slid down her back and into the curve of her buttocks, dragging her roughly against his swollen cock. He reached between them with one hand, and then something hard and simply too large pressed against her opening.

"Fifi?"

"Yes?" she asked on a trembling whisper.

"Hold me."

Releasing the blanket that had been her lifeline in the sensual storm, she clasped his shoulders, hugging him close to her. A tight tension wound itself in the very air around them. He caught her mouth in a ravaging kiss, and at the same time his hips surged forward, going deep in one swift thrust.

It was sweet pain and wicked ecstasy. She could not distinguish between the two sensations. She bit his mouth, and he broke their kiss to whisper soothing, ridiculous nonsense that reached down inside and filled her with heady warmth. He withdrew and thrust, and Ophelia sobbed against his ongoing kiss. The pain was jarring, and where they joined burned. Somehow his fingers found her pearl, then pinched and stroked it, shocking her with the piercing, pleasurable sensations he forced through that small bundle of nerves.

She tunneled her fingers into the silky lushness of his hair, lifted her legs, and hooked her ankles around his hips, the move somehow taking his cock even deeper inside her. The sense of fullness was exquisite. He started to move, a wonderful, driving rhythm. He plunged deep and then deeper still, over and over, stirring emotions she didn't know how to absorb. Sensation upon sensation blossomed irresistibly through Ophelia, and she came apart in his embrace. Devlin hugged her to him, making three deep, hard strokes before he, too, shuddered and pulled from her, his release spilling on her mons and lower belly.

Bloody hell. Nothing would ever be the same again.

CHAPTER FOURTEEN

Devlin rolled to the side of her, and they lay beside each other, breathing raggedly and staring at the night sky. His mouth curved faintly with lazy satisfaction. Ophelia never dreamed coupling could be so ravaging *and* beautiful. Now she understood why so many ladies flung themselves over the abyss, embracing ruination. For this.

It struck her forcibly that she would now be considered ruined by others while she simply felt as if she had made a blissful choice for herself.

"I feel wet and sticky," she whispered, aware of the rivulets of sweat trickling between her breasts.

The night air suddenly felt balmy and suffocating. She pushed to her feet, watching the distant ripples of the lake. Without thinking about it, she dashed off toward the lake.

"Bloody hell!"

Laughing at that curse, she turned around to see Devlin loping after her. Ophelia laughed, hurrying her gait, aware of her hair flying behind her and into her eyes and mouth. He grabbed her about the waist just as she reached the edge; however, he did not draw her back or tumble them into the lush grass but allowed their momentum to take them forward into the terrifying darkness of the water. It was a cross between a scream and laughter that slipped from Ophelia, which was quickly cut off as they splashed into the lake. And not once did he release her. They sank, and she fancied the silvery moonlight perfectly sliced the surface of the lake, allowing her to see his expression as he securely held her to him.

I am cherished.

The thought rocked through her, and she clasped his shoulders as they kicked in unison to the top. Once they surfaced, the laugh rippled from her, and Ophelia laughed until he dipped his head and kissed her.

"You seemed frightened just now."

"I believe the enormity of our interlude had just sunk into my bones," she whispered.

The light cast from the moonlight shadowed the hard, savage contours of his jawline. His gaze slid over her face, serious and searching. "I protected you from pregnancy."

Oh, God! She had been so far gone it never occurred to her. Ophelia stared at him, something warm and sweet tumbling over inside her. He could have done it—gotten her with child, irrevocably forcing them together. Yet despite his cravings, he still thought of her first.

He was pure strength, pure heart

A whisper of sensation moved through her, and it felt suspiciously like she was falling...endlessly.

"Thank you, Niall."

Her words and her mouth trembled. He lowered his head, so now his forehead touched hers, and they were eye to eye. "Is this the harsh bite of regret?"

"Never." The fingers that touched his jaw also trembled. "People with regrets in their hearts will forever be lonely. I wanted you...I still want you; and months...years from now, I will feel no regret that I've been with you. Only pleasure and happiness, for this was my choice."

He chucked Ophelia under her chin and said, "Good."

She splashed water in his face and hurriedly swam away, knowing he would give chase. He easily caught her, and when he tugged her to him, she wrapped her legs high around his waist, shamelessly aware of her core pressed against the muscles of his lower stomach. "It is very dark," she murmured.

"Afraid?"

"There might be creatures we do not know at the bottom of this lake. That hide in the day but come out at night."

"Creatures other than fishes?"

"Yes, ones with tentacles, perhaps—snakes where their hair should be and maybe two heads."

"I do not believe you are jesting. Where has your good sense gone?"

"You, my good sir, lack imagination."

"I do not think—"

Something tickled beneath her left foot, sliding between her toes. Ophelia shrieked, cutting him off. It was the deviltry glinting in his eyes that warned her he was the culprit. "You beast!" she cried. "You odious, odious *beast*! You are beyond reproach. You might not know this, but I *live* for revenge. I could have died from your ill-chosen—"

His hands were suddenly buried in her wet tangled hair, his mouth devouring hers. In retaliation for her fright, she bit his lower lip. Ophelia gasped to find herself slung over his shoulders, her rump in the air.

"Are you a barbarian?" she groused, yet she was absurdly pleased at how they frolicked.

To her shock, he lightly slapped her derriere before tugging her down into his arms. Ophelia spluttered, and he laughed, the sound rich and masculine. The sensations that powered through her were fierce and intoxicating. It was sweet and gentle. It was hunger and satiation. Her hand rose of its own accord to smooth his brow, the hollow of his cheek. She kissed his lips, twining her hands around his nape. He waded with her to the steps leading out of the lake. Once they were on land, he laced their fingers together and strolled toward the blanket.

A sound of amusement escaped her. "We are casually walking across open lawns, *naked*. We are *terribly* outrageous!"

His finger stroked over her knuckle, and she looked down at their joined hands, wondering how he managed to infuse such sensuality into a mere touch.

"Go wrap yourself in a blanket. I'll be right back," he said, running off toward the cottage.

For a moment, she stood, admiring the perfectness of his well-sculpted buttocks and thighs bathed in moonlight. *Who knew I was so lascivious?* Another quality she possibly got from Sally Martin, considering how delicately proper her mother was. That tight, awful feeling that normally came when she thought of Miss Martin lodged low in her belly. Exhaling a shaky breath, Ophelia hastened to their mound, grabbed one of the blankets, and wrapped it around her body. Immediately, she was warmed. Devlin returned with another blanket, a comb, and a soft towel. He dried her hair with brisk movements, then helped her to redress in her drawers, stays, and chemisette.

He donned his trousers, and now they reposed on the padded carpet, his back flush against the stone, and she snuggled in front of his parted thighs. The pose was casual and indolent. Ophelia grinned, thinking how scandalous they must appear. With infinite care, Devlin pulled the comb through her hair, the faintest of tugs at her scalp. He worked her hair and fanned it open, so it formed a cloak around her.

Covering an indelicate yawn with her palm, she leaned back more into his warmth. "I am sitting in the open, dressed in only my drawers and chemise, with a man combing my hair. I daresay my friends will not believe a word of it."

"You plan to tell them *this*?"

She laughed. "Why not? Everyone is frightfully curious about what goes on between a man and a woman. It is a bit silly that most men know but we ladies are ignorant."

He tugged the blanket around her neck, and she snuggled down, leaning back in the crook of his neck, and stared up at him.

"I want to know all the secrets that go on between a man and woman."

He gave her a long, unblinking look before dipping slightly to kiss her nose.

A loud bark had them looking around to see his large dog bounding over. Conan planted his paw on his master's shoulder and licked his chin. Devlin drew one of his hands from the blanket and scratched behind his ears. "I missed you, too, boy."

The large body bounced off hers, as if he wanted her away from his master. Acting on impulse, she tossed her hand over his neck and hugged him, ruffling his hair. This was an invitation for the big brute to play, and with one shake of his body she was tumbled over onto the blanket. Ophelia laughed gaily, and Conan *woof*ed his reply.

She shifted so she could lean against the large rock, not minding that some of the edges dug slightly into her back. Man and beast romped for several minutes, and she watched them, hoarding the lovely picture they made. Devlin's laugh was beautiful, and she saw how much he loved his dog. Conan was more than a companion; he was family. Conan licked his master's chin before prowling away to sprawl on the lower end of the carpet, closing his eyes.

Devlin didn't hesitate to move closer, to rest his head on her thigh, his large body also splayed on the blanket.

"I see where Conan gets it from." Bending over, Ophelia kissed the tip of his nose. "I cannot imagine why I did that," she whispered.

A roguish smile creased his mouth. "It is because I am adorable."

His response startled a soft laugh from her. "Cats are adorable." She glanced at his large bullmastiff. "Maybe even Conan. But not you...you are something entirely different."

You are unquestionably dangerous to my heart.

His eyes locked with hers, offering a carnal promise she desperately wanted to accept.

"Tell me about you, Niall. I want to know you."

"What?" he murmured with sleepy amusement.

She traced her fingers over each scar: one in his brow, one right at the edge of his lip, two below his chin. "How did you get these?"

"Fighting."

"And why were you fighting?"

A fine tension entered his frame, and she wondered if he realized it.

She coasted her thumb along his eyebrow and cheekbone, her fingers trailing along his jaw. "Are you afraid to tell me?"

"No."

He said nothing else, and she feathered her fingertip over his brow, then kissed the scar.

"You should have told me you were paying in kisses. I would have been more amenable. That one came because another lad tried to steal my bread. I was hungry and damned cold. I did not want to give it up, though it was moldy, so I fought."

Her heart wrenched. She kissed his mouth in reward, and he growled his pleasure. After lifting her lips from his, she touched that scar once more. She could not imagine a life where she had to fight for food. Devlin had lived like this. Perhaps for weeks or years. It forcibly struck her how little she knew about this man who was now her love. How intimate they had been yet so far apart. "Someone stealing your food. Did this happen when you were in Newgate?"

The silence suddenly seethed with a tension that rattled Ophelia.

"How did you know about that, Fifi?"

Why did he suddenly have to sound so foreboding? His entire body was also locked in rigidity. "You do not want me to know this about you?"

"Answer me, Fifi."

How ice dripped from his tone.

She stared down into his face, which had become perfectly composed into nothing. "It was a fleeting mention from your mother. It does not make me think less of you," she whispered. "And I would never tell anyone."

A mocking curve lifted his mouth. "You believe I need your discretion?"

"I know no society paper has ever mentioned that you are an ex-convict," she said softly. "They do mention how shrouded your past is; they would not have given up the opportunity to tear into you like rabid wolves with the information."

"I spent two years, four months, and sixteen days in Newgate."

Said so casually without any of the horrors he might have suffered. Ophelia had read the arguments for calling for prison reform. The place they described in desperate need of change was hell, a place of despair and hopelessness. She stroked her fingers through his hair. "Permit me to ask the reason."

"I beat a toff with my fists. He raced his carriage down the street of Haymarket without any care in the world, and he crashed. A young girl's foot was stuck under one of his carriage wheels. We worked to free her, and the man...an earl took his whip to her in blame. She dared cross the street when he needed to race his curricle to win a bet. Nobs believe people like Poppy...me...children on the streets, the working class, are gutter slime they can use and abuse. I took the whip for her across my back..."

Ophelia recalled the vague knotted flesh on his lower back when she had clutched at him in ecstasy. "Then what happened?"

"I turned and slammed my fist into his mouth with all the anger and disgust fueling me. He toppled over into the dirt. A few other nobs held on to me until a constable arrived. I was arrested and sentenced to ten years in prison for daring to hit a lord. That earl went home, and Poppy lost her foot."

Oh, God. "Is she... How did she live after?"

"My friend Riordan took care of her and her family until I was out of Newgate. Poppy is like a sister to me, and we are still great friends today. One day you shall meet her."

"I would love to," she said with a smile. "How did you get out before your time?"

"Rhys Tremayne. He…he has an arsenal of secrets that he trades. It is the bedrock of his power and wealth in the underworld, where he is known as The Broker. He traded a precious secret for my release."

Unexpectedly, her heart thumped. Such a man existed. Might he be able to gather her information on Sally Martin? Renewed hope blasted through her. Pushing that aside, she directed her thoughts to this moment. "Was it after your release Niall was reinvented as Devlin Byrne?"

"A slight but necessary change."

"I see." She thought about the other rumors attached to his name, hungry to know truth from fiction. "I have heard whispers that you've fought duels."

"Four of them," he murmured.

"Why?"

"Some gentlemen believed my winning streak in the gambling den was achieved by cheating."

She was surprised they had actually met him on the field of honor when many in the *ton* believed only gentlemen had the right to defend themselves. "Did you kill them?"

A rough chuckle sounded. "I know I would have been hanged for it, even if the meeting was supposed to be about honor. I merely wounded their pride."

Those men must resent him for it. An odd sense of foreboding wrapped itself around her. "Many say that you have tried to penetrate the *ton*. Offering bribes and loans to secure invitations to *tonnish* events. But they keep you out."

"You are remarkably informed."

This was conversation overheard between her father and his cronies. "Is it true?"

"Yes," he said with dry humor.

"You do not seem to like or respect them."

"Some are decent gentlemen with honor. Many are like rabid wolves that viciously devour any sheep that stumbles. Most times the sheep are those more unfortunate than they are."

"Whyever would you want to be a part of the *ton*?"

"It is where you reside. For a long time that was important."

She stared at him with a keen sense of awestruck incredulity. She believed him, absolutely without question. A dangerous idea visited Ophelia, sinking like talons into her thoughts—*what if Niall still wants forever?* She shook her head, trying to clear the sensual haziness that still lingered and that ridiculous notion. They were only meant to be lovers for a time; nothing more. The things his mother spoke about were years ago. When he was a young lad, barely on the cusp of manhood.

Am I still at the end of your long, dark, painful walk, Niall?

Ophelia couldn't give in to the rush of yearning, the sensation his words aroused so instantly. She was aware of nothing but him. The beat of his heart underneath her palm, his masculine scent, the possessive…yet tender way he stared up at her.

Inexplicably, it took heart-thudding, breath-stopping courage to ask him, "Do you love me, Niall?"

Her voice had been a mere whisper, and she wanted to snatch back the words until she better understood why she needed the answer.

"No," he replied, his voice just as low.

Those words cut, deep and revealing.

Then he said, "Not yet."

Not yet. An indication that he allowed for the possibility of falling in love with her. Yet the possibility lingered that he might also never love her. *But what do I need his love for? We are not from the same world, and this must eventually end.*

The eyes that peered up at her were intent, soul searching. If possible, her heart thudded even faster. He smiled so faintly that it was barely visible. "Do you love me, Fifi?"

"Not yet," she whispered. Inside, she crumbled a little, for she was tumbling headlong into something she did not understand but craved with every part of her being.

"So we are in agreement. *Not yet.*"

"Yes." The word was tremulous.

"Should we kiss on it?"

"You find all sorts of excuses to put your mouth on mine, I see," she said, tenderly brushing a lock of hair from his forehead.

"Wouldn't you do the same if a certain lush mouth was the best thing you had ever tasted?"

Pleasure warmed her cheeks. "I am a firm supporter of the delight of kisses, but I daresay you've never drank sweetened chocolate or ate pineapple cake glazed with icing."

He caught her around the waist and pulled her against him, burying his face in her throat. He reached between their tightly fitted bodies. His hot, rough palm slid up her thigh, found her wet folds, and parted them.

"Hurry," she moaned. "I need you, Devlin."

With one long finger, he penetrated her. The shock of the sensation caused her to jerk. She was delightfully sore, but she was also soft and dewy. Ophelia gasped when his finger vanished and his cock pressed against her aching sex, and with an inexorable push, Devlin thrust his cock until he was buried deep inside of her. A low, rough sound came from the mouth still buried at her throat. A whisper of pleasure from her.

How long might I have this for?

• • •

Fifi slumbered deeply, her chest rising on even breaths. Devlin couldn't have slept well, even if he'd wished to surrender to the deep torpor pulling at him. He'd became gradually aware that there was a toe in his mouth and at least three more resting somewhere on his chin and lips.

Good God, what is this?

And such delicate little toes, too. With slow ease, he shifted his head, causing the toe to slip from his mouth, then sat up. Ophelia lay on her side, hugging his legs as if they were a lifeline. Her hip and thighs were slung over his lower body, with one of her knees pressing into his navel and her toes now resting somewhere in the crook of his neck.

He looked around, bemused. It should be impossible, given that after their last bout of tupping they had fallen asleep under the blankets with her snuggled into his side, her head rested comfortably on his arms. When had she moved her whole body, and where was the bloody blanket? The night had been unusually warm, but now there was a decided nip in the air. Spying the blanket at his feet, he reached down for it, careful not to jostle her awake. Devlin froze when she muttered and flung her body, her foot kicking him in the throat.

"Bloody hell," he growled.

Astonished, he stared as she scrambled up, her eyes still closed, shifted around, and flung herself on top of his chest, knocking his chin, slamming his teeth together.

"Mercy," he muttered, his teeth aching.

Pushing his tongue against them, he tested that none had been shaken loose with her tough head. She pushed a hand around his neck and wrapped around him like a vine. "Cold," she whispered in the crook of his neck.

Conan's eyes were open and staring at them, and he made a low chuffing sound deep in his throat, pushed to his paws, and padded off. Devlin chuckled, tugging the blanket up over her. She stirred, rousing halfway from sleep, then rolled toward him, nestling close and throwing her arm over his chest. At least thirty minutes passed before he gave up on sleeping. Fifi had shifted at least three more times, and now was in a position where her legs were flung over his waist, her upper body twisted away from him and one of her hands over his face. Surely that was her elbow stuffed in his mouth.

Devlin chuckled, untangled himself, bundled her in the blanket, and lifted her in his arms. He turned around and faltered. *Fuck*. Her cousin Lady Effie stood there, her eyes wide and her cheeks frightfully red. Clearly, she had come looking for her charge, and what did she find but a scene of blatant debauchery?

How had she found them? The path was not an easy one, and his family knew not to divulge it. They stared at each other for a long time.

She cleared her throat, squared her shoulders, and said, "I will not tell anyone about this."

Devlin knew of situations where a man was caught alone with a young lady in a conservatory, and within a few days they were wed. Of course, the man concerned had been a lord. And here he was, with a half-naked beauty wrapped in a blanket, and Devlin barefoot and only in trousers. But this…

this did not warrant any conversation with her father? A dark amusement rushed through him, and his mouth twitched.

"No demands for our immediate marriage?" he asked mockingly. "Your discretion is appreciated."

Lady Effie flushed, her eyes skittering from his to look beyond his shoulder. "The marquess would not consent to your union...and though Ophelia seems to have irrevocably lost all sense of herself, she would not marry without her parents' blessing and approval. Not that I believe she would go so far as to even request it of them."

Why did everyone see it fit to tell him that? Still, the words cut deep into his belly. "If that is her decision," he said flatly, holding her a little closer to his chest.

"I assure you, Mr. Byrne, you are merely a dalliance for my cousin, a rebellion... Crudely put, she is slumming."

He had just gotten a piece of her, and the world already wanted to take her from him. The denial bubbling inside him was violent and primal. She made a soft sound in her sleep, and he relaxed his hold around her body.

"I was charged with her safety, and I...I allowed her to convince me for a brief moment alone with you. When that moment turned into a few hours, your mother was kind enough to alleviate my distress by giving me the direction to this cottage."

Devlin stared for a moment at the stubborn lift to Lady Effie's chin before dipping his head in a nod. "Fifi will be with you within the hour."

"Lady Ophelia," she said tightly. "I am also not leaving here without her! I have already ordered your man to see the carriage ready. We will return to town post haste. If you wake her, I will see her into the cottage to get dre...dressed."

"I will do it," he said in a tone that brooked no refusal.

Devlin turned away and walked toward the steps of the cottage, Ophelia a comfortable weight in his arms. He had not meant for them to fall asleep under the stars. Hell, he had not even intended to ravish her so thoroughly. Not here, where anyone could come upon them. Yet it had happened, and he would not regret it.

Opening the cottage door, he entered. Devlin kissed her forehead, and she murmured sleepily. Another kiss to her nose, and then one to her mouth. She came awake smiling, and his heart trembled. Helping her down, he watched her wobble slightly, then glance around the cottage. The fire had died to embers, and he went over to the hearth, added a few logs, and quickly coaxed the fire to a blaze.

"Your cousin is outside."

Ophelia gasped. "Effie?"

"Yes."

She groaned but did not seem overly worried.

"Are you at all concerned she will speak of our…" The words to describe the best moments of his life eluded him.

"Indiscretion?" Ophelia murmured, tucking a wisp of hair behind her ears.

"Ah, is that what it was?"

"It was something wonderful," she whispered with a soft smile, her lovely eyes tender with an emotion he could not identify.

The hardness encasing his heart eased. Only a little.

He returned her smile. "I will help you as best as possible to dress. There is nothing I can do about your hair."

Several minutes later, she was buttoned up, stockings and slippers on. She stole through the door, no doubt to have a private word with her cousin before he joined them. Devlin took his time in making himself presentable before he killed the fire in the hearth and locked up the cottage. A quick sweep of the lawns outside only showed Fifi standing near the edge of the lake. The wind caught the skirt of her dress and blew it around her legs. It flung her hair from the loose chignon they had managed to cobble together and tumbled it to her shoulders and hips. A startled but delighted laugh came from her. She spread her hands wide from her body, lifted her face to the sky, and twirled.

She is happy.

Never-before-felt ripples undulated through Devlin's heart. He had just pleasured her quite wickedly. Dark amusement rushed through him. Should he ask her to marry, what would she say? No doubt his Fifi would be just as horrified as her lady cousin. It was a damn good thing he had no hopes of her being more than his precious lover.

He walked toward her. "Fifi."

She whirled to him, and he faltered. *Her heart could be mine for the taking.* He saw it in the soft, tender way she smiled at him. In the way hunger sparked in her eyes like a river of fire. The way she touched him just now, held him to her, opened herself to him.

From the first moment he had seen her again, he had wanted her in his life…in his bed. He would not dare demand more from her.

He was hardly invited to balls or political dinners. He lacked breeding and connections that were important to her family. He had understood at an early age that without money, there was no authority, no power, and most importantly, no choices in this world. He had money. But he also understood those belonging to high society were ruthless in treating those who did not belong to their circle like a cancerous cell— viciously cutting it away.

Devlin had barely penetrated the world she lived in, and he might never fully do so. Her world was glamorous and extravagant. His life was simple, and he worked hard. The people who were possibly friends of her family were the ones he blackmailed and dealt with ruthlessly to ensure certain bills that benefited the poorer class were passed. Devlin scrubbed a hand over his face, a spark of anger at himself burning in his chest. With a steady will, he drew on his cloak of indifference. It was dangerous to send his mind along the path to dreaming of more with Fifi. He was not that young fool anymore.

"What are you thinking that makes you scowl so frighteningly?" she asked, walking over to him.

"Where is your cousin?"

At his blatant sidestepping of her question, Ophelia canted her head, but she did not press him. "She is walking ahead of us. I asked her for privacy."

He arched a brow. "I am surprised she acceded."

Humor glinted in Fifi's eyes. "I confessed I was the one to ravish you, and Cousin Effie will understand my choices are mine to make."

He recalled the closeness he had observed between the two during the carriage ride and at dinner. Having nothing to say, he held out his hand to her, and, without hesitation, she took it. They started walking back through the woods toward the main estate. She glanced behind her and sighed wistfully.

"I do not wish to leave."

Another incremental easing around his heart.

"We can visit whenever you want."

"I would like that."

A commitment for future liaisons. It was a step, and he would hold on to it with ruthless hands.

Conan bounded over to them, surprisingly prowling by her side. His massive dog reached her waist, and without any showing of fear, she ruffled his head. Conan purred, and Devlin smiled.

I like her, too, boy. I like her, too.

CHAPTER FIFTEEN

Ophelia took a steady breath, then glanced up and down the avenue of Wardour Street. She saw no familiar faces or carriages, and, lifting a hand, she patted her well-coiffed blond wig. In the distance, the bell of St. Anne's Church rang. Deploring the anxiety twisting low in her belly, she lifted the knocker to the small townhouse. The door opened, and a plump woman of undetermined years she presumed to be the housekeeper framed the doorway.

"I am here to see Miss Barbara Fenley. Inform her Lady Starlight has called."

The lady seemed a bit uncertain; however, she stood back and allowed her entrance.

The hallway was small, the rolling carpet a bit threadbare, but the scents of lemon and beeswax were redolent in the air. Ophelia did not hand over her pelisse and hat, nor the walking stick she held, which hid a hidden blade. She had already taken a risk in calling upon this lady without Cousin Effie's hovering presence, and Ophelia needed to be careful.

The housekeeper led her down to a door and knocked. She opened the door when a throaty voice bid her entry.

"A Lady Starlight is here to see you, miss."

She stepped back, and Ophelia entered, her steps faltering. Devlin was seated in a high-backed chair near the windows, dressed in unrelenting black save for a yellow waistcoat, holding a glass of amber liquid between his long-tapered fingers. Exhilaration burst to life in Ophelia's bloodstream.

She should be quite out of good humor with the man, but her heart danced with happiness to see him, and silly as it was, she blushcd.

Struggling to banish memories of how wanton she had been with him, she moved farther into the room. He stood, one hand folded behind his back, and dipped into a bow. Their gazes collided when he straightened, and the heat in his provoked the fiery blush she'd hoped to repress. Unable to help her smile, she dipped into a curtsy, relieved he was here, though she had not expected to find him in Miss Fenley's parlor. Yesterday's visions of being attacked or taken advantage of had rollcd through her mind. With black humor guiding her, she had sent a note to Devlin.

Tomorrow I shall call upon a particular house in Wardour Street. If you are to receive the dreadful news that I've disappeared and should you wish to find me, start your investigation there.

Fifi.

The keenest sort of anticipation had held her for most of the morning and afternoon while she awaited his reply. When it came, shc had been considerably deflated.

Duly noted. Devlin.

It was terribly interesting that she had not told him the particular townhouse number or the identity of the person she would visit, yet he was still here.

"Good afternoon, Mr. Byrne," Ophelia said. "A most pleasant surprise to see you here. It is quite unexpected."

He fixed her with a baleful look. "With a grave, cryptic note in your flair, where else would I be?"

"And you knew precisely where to find me?"

"I am a man of unusual talents."

Another spurt of amusement shook her. "So you have been spying on me."

Without awaiting his reply, she turned her regard to the lady who stared at her as if she saw a ghost. "Miss Barbara Fenley, I presume? I am Lady Starlight, an evident moniker, but I am not at liberty to divulge my identity. I do hope for your understanding in this matter."

The lady walked over, her face pale and her eyes widening.

"Upon my word, you are the very image of her," Miss Fenley breathed, her eyes intent on Ophelia's face.

Her heart started to race, and her wits scattered. "I...I am looking for information on Miss Sally Martin. The investigator I hired said you were friends who worked together at Drury Lane."

Miss Fenley took her gloved hands between hers. It jolted her to note the emotions on the lady's face and the glistening of tears in her dark gray eyes.

"You are the very picture of Sally. Your face...is the same lovely shape. Only your eyes...and hair are different. Sally had the blackest hair I had ever seen on anyone."

The room spun around Ophelia; she withdrew her hands, walked over to the sofa closest to her, and sat. Miss Fenley rang for tea and biscuits that Ophelia had no interest in, but she took the time to gather her thoughts and desperately tried to calm her racing heart. After searching for so long in vain, she had not anticipated news.

"I suspect you know why I am searching for Miss Martin," Ophelia said when the lady took a seat opposite to her.

"I know who you are," she replied, slanting a glance at Devlin, who sat out of their earshot. "Her daughter. I never imagined this moment to be possible."

"Miss Fenley, do you know where I might find Sally Martin? Is she…is she alive?"

Her eyes softened. "That I cannot answer. Sally left London years ago, and she has never returned."

"Do you have any notion of where she is?"

"Sally mentioned her new home would be in Lincolnshire. After she sent me a letter to say that she had settled in, I've had no correspondence from her. She could be alive, abroad, or have gone on to her rewards. I am truly sorry I have no more information for you."

"Thank you," Ophelia said. "I'd hoped you could tell me more. Do you know anyone who might be aware of her whereabouts?"

Miss Fenley sighed, a tiny frown between her brows. "I am sorry I do not. I do have something I would like for you to have, however."

She stood, went over to a small writing desk, and picked up a locket before returning to the sofa.

"Sally left this behind. I am not sure if by accident or deliberately because it was a painful reminder of what she lost."

Ophelia took the small locket and opened it. A beautiful young girl with a babe snuggled into her arms stared back at her. Her heart painfully squeezed, and her throat ached. They did look remarkably alike. The tiny portrait showed Sally Martin wore her black hair in a tight coronet of curls, her eyes were sparkling, and a happy smile curved her mouth. There was nothing distinguishable about the child other than she seemed contented in her mother's arms. "Is this me?" she whispered.

"Yes, before she lost you."

The fury and shame of her father's action washed over her again. "I was not lost!"

Silence stretched for several heart-pounding moments.

"Your...Sally was so broken when her protector took you away. She screamed and cried until she was empty with loss. Nothing her friends said could pull her from her deep melancholy. There was a time I feared she would waste away. It was a cruel thing he did, taking Sally's child after his wife — "

Ophelia jolted as a raw, piercing emotion stabbed through her heart. "After his wife what?"

Miss Fenley appeared uncertain, and her gaze volleyed between Ophelia and Devlin, who looked on with bored civility.

She blew out a breath between pursed lips. "I am uncertain as to how much I can reveal with — "

Ophelia waved her hand in an impatient motion. "You can reveal everything," she said. "I trust Mr. Byrne."

Miss Fenley's gaze grew speculative. "I see."

"Do you, Miss Fenley?" Ophelia replied with crisp politeness, holding her regard steadily. "Please tell me about her, and I implore you not to mind my sensibilities."

She looked away briefly before continuing. "Sally and I were very good friends. We toured the city performing together. She met the marquess after a performance one night at King's Theatre. Sally was a vibrant soul who attracted many with her vivacity for life and her passion for singing. He was instantly smitten, and so was Sally, for he was quite handsome, rich, *and* charming. I warned her the marquess was rumored to be recently married. However, it did not halt her headlong rush into an affair."

Miss Fenley paused to sigh. "The very short story of it all was that Sally fell with child and dreamed about living happily with you and a protector who visited whenever he could. Even I envied her that arrangement, for he provided well for her and seemed to be genuine in his tendre. I was visiting Sally when…when he came for you. He… There was no warning. The marquess simply took you from the bassinet and left. Sally rushed after him, and when she begged him to know what was happening, he merely informed her he was taking his child and their liaison was at an end."

Ophelia sat frozen, hurt by the dispassionate manner in which Miss Fenley recounted Sally's ordeal.

"It crushed her, and it was as if she stopped living. Though he did not say his reasons, Sally suspected why he did it."

When Miss Fenley said no more, Ophelia leaned forward. "Why?"

"He had confided in her that his marchioness…she had lost her child on the birthing bed some months prior. She had sunken into deep despair upon receiving the report that she would not be able to have any more children, and for a long time, he feared she would not recover. Sally…she believed he took her child to replace the babe his wife lost. To provide her with the comfort and love of a babe, since she would never be able to have her own."

Everything inside her recoiled. How unspeakably cruel. Yet it showed his devotion and love to his wife. A desperate and selfish hope to heal her from the pain that shredded her heart while awakening an even more profound agony in another woman. Ophelia lifted trembling fingers to her mouth, and it was then she noted the back of the locket held an engraved name and numbers. "Who is Phelia?"

A smile trembled on Miss Fenley's mouth. "It was what she called you—a shortened name for Ophelia."

"So Sally named me," Ophelia said numbly, her heart pounding. Her father had not taken that, and suddenly she was thankful.

"Yes. She had you for a few months before…before you were taken."

So much awareness tumbled through her. Her mother had been given a child who she had not named, with the expectation that she would love that child as her own. Ophelia once again recalled those distant early years when she had hungered for a hug and warm words from her mother. There had been a time she thought the marchioness did not love her. A time when she tiptoed in her home for fear of irritating the marchioness.

The marchioness had only started loving her after thinking she had lost the only child she had. "And these numbers?" she asked hoarsely.

"Your birth date."

Oh, God. Her birth date? That would mean she was three and twenty, not four and twenty as she believed, and her real birthday was in a few days, not seven months ago. Fierce and complex emotions tore through Ophelia. She stood, dimly aware of her entire body shaking. A hand settled on her lower back, and she glanced up with a start of surprise. It was Devlin. She leaned into him, uncaring that they were observed with deep speculation from a woman she did not know.

"I…please, I need to leave!"

Miss Fenley hurriedly stood, but Ophelia was hardly aware of the words she spoke. Devlin bundled her outside into the cool evening air. The sky was painted in stark orange and vermillion hues as the sun lowered and night approached. They walked a few houses down until he helped her into a large conveyance.

"This is not Cosima's carriage," she murmured, glancing through the small window of the carriage toward where she had left that equipage.

"No. I've sent it back to her home."

Ophelia dazedly lowered the curtains. "I must go back to Cosima's so I can change from this pelisse and remove the wig."

"Fifi," Devlin said gently, tugging her into his arms. His lips slipped up to her temple. "Don't cry."

It was then she became aware of the wetness on her cheeks. "I feel so silly!"

Lips touched the corner of her eye. Hot and soft and comforting.

"Sally Martin is my mother," she whispered, pushing the small locket with the portrait into his hand.

"Ah," he said, barely more than a breath. "The resemblance is striking. This, however, does not tell me why you cry."

That only made her sob harder. "Did…did you hear what Miss Fenley said?"

"Not the full of it."

"Sally Martin wept for weeks, went into a deep melancholy…and almost died. My father…took me from her and never looked back once, leaving her in the ashes of her own torment and fears. Who is this man who acted so callously but raised me with such love and affection? Where is his honor?" Ophelia's fingers tightened on his coat. "I *hate* the pain I feel. I do not understand why the entire matter grieves my heart so. I do not want to feel so wretched, Devlin." A tear streaked down her cheek. She dashed it away with a furious swipe. "I feel silly!"

His fingers clamped on her chin and lifted her face so he could see her clearly. The instant he touched her, the tightness in her chest eased.

"Why do you feel silly?"

"Why does it hurt? My parents love me, and I love them. They are *good* people. I've led a very privileged life. I am overly indulged by Papa and Mama. They doted on me…even I can say I have been intolerably spoiled." She shook her head, the ache stabbing inside her chest, blooming to encompass her whole body. "But when I think of everything, Niall, I *hurt*. I cannot stop the hurt nor the feeling of fright that sweep over me. Why can't I stop it?"

Ophelia let herself be pulled, let him wrap his strength around her. She breathed, slow and deep, and he just held her, making wordless sounds of comfort.

"You've learned this thing about your father that is shocking, Fifi. I ken as parents they only show so much of themselves to their child. It is normal for you to grieve for the sense of safety that you lost, and quite normal for you to seek an understanding of everything. Do not judge yourself for wanting that safety."

She swallowed the tight lump in her throat. "I love my father and mother."

"The people we love can do things we do not understand, and we still love them despite the questionable nature of their actions."

"Growing up, sometimes I was so lonely and I longed for a sister to play with. I have other grandparents, perhaps other uncles, an aunt. I find myself looking in the mirror, wondering what part of me I got from her, and why is it so important to know! My mother often berated me for being too rash and impulsive. You think I got that from Sally Martin, perhaps?" The words seemed to stick in her throat. "I feel guilty, as if I am betraying Papa and...and my mother for searching for Sally Martin. For wondering if I have brothers and sisters."

"Rubbish."

A short, sharp, and very final word. Ophelia smiled. "I know you are going to tell me I have nothing to feel guilty about."

"Precisely, my sweet. It is your right to want to know about the woman who is your mother. In that, there can *never* be fault."

"I wonder if she lives. Or did she die from heartbreak?" Her gaze lowered to the locket once more. "The worrying about it has haunted me. My father will not tell me of her, and I...I..." Her throat closed.

"I will help you find her."

Her heart jolted. "You will?"

"Yes. I already have men looking into it."

Ophelia stared at him in astonishment, and then awareness bloomed. "I wondered at your knowledge, but I gathered Cosima told you."

"It was not a betrayal of your confidence. She thought it important I knew why you took the risk to mask yourself as Lady Starlight. I was also aware you asked questions about her."

"And without knowing who this woman is to me, you started searching for her?"

"Yes."

And Ophelia knew it was simply for her.

"I sold some of my jewelry and hired at least three investigators over the last few months, and the only connection they found is Miss Fenley, who has no more information."

"I will find her or discover the details of what happened," he said with calm confidence.

"Thank you." She raised trembling fingers to his lips, more than a little afraid of the strength of the feelings he'd aroused. She hugged him tightly, unable to deny the desire to feel his arms around her. He made her feel safe…cherished, and Ophelia inexplicably knew he would stand before any storm that came her way. His loyalty was unswerving, and she felt undeserving.

"Hold me tighter, Niall," Ophelia whispered. *And do not ever let me go.*

She nudged the side of his cheek with hers, wanting a kind of comfort from him that she could not evolve into words.

His arms closed more firmly around her, then he was lifting her, pulling her into his lap. Devlin cupped her cheeks and pressed their mouths together. Ophelia's entire body burst into flames. At a mere fleeting kiss on the mouth. A reminder of all the wicked, wanton things he had done to her only two days ago. Terrible, *wonderful* things she had allowed. Things she wanted again and again, and only with this man.

With a soft murmur of need, she thrust her fingers through his hair and tugged his head down for their mouths to meet. Ophelia clung to him, chasing the pleasure his mouth and his touch could bring her, burrowing into the comfort she found being clasped so closely to his chest.

The way they tugged at each other's clothes was frantic, heat burning wildly inside. Somehow she found herself straddling him, her thighs splayed wide and bracketing his.

Without breaking their kiss, Devlin gathered the skirts of her dress and pushed them high to her thighs. His touch as it dragged along her inner thigh swept like fire across her skin. Then he was there, at the place where she was already mortifyingly wet and aching. Devlin's fingers found her clitoris and rubbed it with quickening strokes. Ophelia went flame-hot with desire. Her fingers tightening in his hair, she moaned into their kisses even as she trembled in the cage of his arms.

Letting go of his hair, she pressed her hands between their bodies, searching for the thickness of his arousal. She found it. And squeezed. He hissed into her mouth, pulling away to breathe raggedly. Holding his eyes, she tugged almost savagely at the front of his falls, taking his cock into her hands.

"*Fuck*," he muttered against her mouth.

The word felt obscene, yet hunger bloomed through her in unrelenting waves. She could barely fit her fingers around his cock, and she marveled at how hard and silky he felt.

He hugged her so tightly to him, there was hardly any space. But he lifted her hips, moved his fingers from her sex, gripped his cock, and rubbed it in a tight slide over the folds of her cunny.

Ophelia mewled and bucked at the wicked sensation. He did it over and over until she was slick with desire.

"Take me," he muttered raggedly into the curve of her neck, raking his teeth when she arched her throat.

She began to lower her body, accepting him slowly, inch by torturous inch. The burn was simply wonderful. Barely taking him inside her body, she stopped and lifted her hips, coming off his cock. Then she repeated her motion, taking him only a small part into her sex, teasing him…tormenting them both with need.

His lips slid into her hair and nuzzled the side of her neck right over her pounding pulse. "You teasing wretch," he groaned, nipping at the underside of her jaw.

"*Delightful* teasing wretch," she whispered.

Devlin palmed her buttocks in his strong hands, lifted her until the tip of his manhood was poised at her wet entrance, then slammed her onto his cock. Exquisite pleasure and erotic pain. She cried out weakly into the crook of his neck.

"Ride me, Fifi."

The command was harshly sensual, and she responded with instinctive need, lifting from him slowly, feeling his thickness drag inside her sensitive channel and the reluctance of her flesh to let him go. She clung tightly to the feeling of having him inside her almost too much. But then there was that pleasure tightly woven right amid ecstatic sensations.

And his fingers…oh, God. His thumb caressed her nub, the calloused flesh exciting sensitive nerve endings. He pinched her clitoris, and the friction slammed such raw bliss into that small bundle that low in her belly, she whimpered. Another flick. Another moan. Then a ragged gasp. She was wet, embarrassingly so. Wild, vibrant arousal bloomed through her. With each thrust of his hips, each glide up and down his cock, the sensations only mounted. And his wicked fingers never stopped working her clitoris, driving her mindless with arousal.

The world dissolved, and nothing existed but Devlin. Her thighs shook, and she gripped his shoulders, anchoring herself against the wildness blossoming through her.

"Ride me harder, Fifi," he growled against her mouth. "Just like that, my sweet. Let me feel your cunny fucking us into exhaustion and bliss."

"Help me," she cried out, unable to find the depth and

rhythm the arousal in her called for.

As if he knew just what she needed, he complied, gripping her buttocks, taking control and using his strength so that she felt weightless. Devlin rocked her onto his cock hard and deep, over and over. It was too much. Too much pleasure. Too many sensations. Too many feelings. Oh, God, the emotions pouring from his kiss to her soul were everything. It was impossible to think with this much sensation overloading her. A sob tore as she unraveled, convulsing in his arms as pleasure shredded her.

With a groan, Devlin thrust deep, then pulled from her to release in a handkerchief that seemed to appear as if by magic.

Crumpling the silken cloth, he tucked it into his pocket, then gently eased her from him. A whimper caught in her throat at the sore feeling. Her body quivered with aftershocks, and Ophelia wanted to lean into his arms. Perhaps sleep there.

A bump in the road jarred her, and it struck her rather forcefully that she had just been intimate in a *carriage*. Suddenly she was overwhelmed, and with frantic hands she fixed her clothes and scrambled off his lap. It did not help that she was drowsy with contentment or that she felt as if something hidden had awakened inside her.

"Have you done this before?" *God*. She hated that her voice trembled and her eyes burned with tears.

"Tupped in a carriage?"

He reached for her, but she scooted over to the far corner on the carriage seat opposite him. Something dark and dangerous flashed in his eyes before his expression shuttered.

"Is that what we did? *Tupped?*" Ophelia did not understand why she felt as if a mere touch would shatter her into pieces that would never be able to be put back together.

"Tupped is one word for it," he said softly, his eyes penetrating on her. "Come here."

"No." God, she hated this secrecy. How long could they sustain being like this? For so long she had dreamed about a gentleman who aroused her mind and senses, and he could not court her with dances, or with a long walk in the park, or with flowers.

"Now, Fifi."

A fire of rebellion sparked in her heart, pushing aside the raw ache that had been building there. "You do not command me," she murmured softly.

Before she could gasp, he exploded into motion, dragging her into his arms and ravishing her mouth with violent tenderness. She bit into his lower lip, and he hissed.

"You forgot your promise to be my first in many things, hmm? I have not been with another woman in this way before. You... Everything is different with you. Even my damn senses seem to be lost when I am with you."

She dropped her forehead against his. "Is that not a good thing?"

"Only if it is mutually assured madness."

Devlin's body was a hard wall of heat, and she leaned in closer until no space existed between their bodies. "That I am here should tell you I am similarly afflicted."

"It does, doesn't it?"

How pleased he sounded.

Pulling back, he rapped on the roof of the carriage.

"What are you doing?"

"I am taking you to my townhouse."

"Are you mad?"

"Did we not just confirm the reality that we are both a little bit mad?"

She stilled the laughter rising in her throat at the outrageous comment.

"You are still in disguise, so it is safe."

Her heart pounding, she asked, "And what are we to do there?"

His eyes were raw and dark with emotions she could not identify. "You will use me however you want. This… What we did just now was not enough to soothe the emotions tearing at you. We need to do them all. Make love…tup…fuck it from your system."

The crude words shocked the breath from her body, but something wild rose up inside in answer, and a sob escaped her.

"You will use me until the hurt subsides." He dragged his thumb across her bottom lip. "It is high time I feel these wrapped around my cock."

Ignoring the arousal curling her toes, she sniffed. "I don't want to use you!"

His eyes darkened. "Then what do you want?"

"I want to love you!" The words tumbled from her in a fiery cry before she had time to process her thoughts. Startled, she held her breath. *I want to love you without judgment or thoughts of consequences.*

For several long heartbeats, he stared at her, and Ophelia looked back at him, astonished by her own words and the sweet but aching sensations twisting through her. *What do I even mean?* she thought with a hysterical flicker of humor.

"Would you marry a gentleman of my background and connections?" he asked softly, a thoughtful frown on his face.

He stole her breath. Her hands locked together in her lap

so tightly that her fingers were white. Everything felt off-kilter. "Are you asking me, Devlin?"

He glanced down at her hands, and an odd smile tugged at his mouth. "It's purely a hypothetical question."

"Then why do you ask it?"

"I merely wondered what your thoughts are on the matter."

A sinking sensation formed in the pit of Ophelia's stomach. "I have never given it any thought."

It was a hurtful truth simply because they were from different worlds, and she could not imagine what their lives would be like beyond this affair. Ophelia had not allowed her thoughts to wander along those pathways.

"That we are lovers alone was not even something I thought possible. With you…I am…I do not know who I am with you, Niall. I am bolder…*more* reckless. But I…I *love* being with you, yet I do not think beyond our moments together. Not yet."

Not yet.

His expression was inscrutable. Unexpectedly, something felt delicate. Breakable. Frightening. "Have *you* given it thought?" she asked, gripping the edges of the squabs.

"You are a princess of the *ton*, daughter of a powerful marquess. I am no one. What thoughts I give to the matter are fleeting, lacking in any true form." Before she could answer, he held up a hand. "It is not yet time for these conjectures."

"When will it be the right time?"

A gleam of interest lit the dark green of his eyes. "Perhaps weeks…months…when we have crawled into each other's skin and can hardly imagine where one ends and the other starts. Perhaps when we are finally fools in love, we might revisit it. When we no longer believe in 'not yet' but see the possibilities in everything and are willing to fight for more."

Ophelia stared at him in soft wonder. *When we are fools in love...* Her parents would never agree to it. Ophelia doubted even her friends would think it a prudent match. Yet the ripple that went through her heart was one of delight at the thought of forever in his arms.

Wait for me...

"What is love for you, Niall? A woman who accepts you unconditionally?"

"No."

"Then what?"

"A lady...a lady who understands there might be rough times in our lives, either because of my past or hers, but is strong enough to walk beside me through any storm. A lady who is strong enough to trust me with her emotions and well-being and knows she will be safe to cry on my shoulder always. Love with that woman will be passionate and hungry, but in the calm times, we also know that our love is still strong; we are simply slowing down. Love with her will be..." He raked his hands through his hair. "Chaotic but *beautiful*."

She felt genuine delight then. "And will you also trust her with your emotions and well-being?"

"Without hesitation."

"How curious. I always thought gentlemen were reticent when it comes to discussing sentiments."

A small smile touched his mouth. "Nobs can be foolish. What do you envision love to be, Fifi?"

"I... Love had always seemed so arbitrary. How does one convey love or even know what it is? A few of my dear friends are madly, passionately in love, and I admit I feel a bit envious of their surety. How do they know they found love? Was it the same for Kitty and Maryann and my mother? After all, I wanted to marry only for love, after witnessing my parents' contentment with each other. I thought it a grand thing, and at my coming out I declared only for love would I ever marry," she said with a soft laugh. "I was supposed to find it in the racing of my heart and tossing about at night unable to sleep because I could not stop thinking about my suitor."

Ophelia wrinkled her nose.

"That is why you remained unmarried?"

"Yes," she said simply. "I never met a gentleman who made my heart race. Not until you."

He stiffened but made no comment.

"But I cannot believe love is really about racing hearts." She looked away from him briefly, thinking about her father and the way he had hurt her heart and how he must have hurt his wife years ago with his indiscretion. "I think love does not lie. Even if it is painful and frightening, love is honest. Love is also about trust…faithfulness and loyalty to each other. I think most importantly…love must be in the kindness a couple shows each other, and there must be laughter in love."

All the things I have been slowly finding with you.

Thinking of her mother, who was truly a lady of extremely exacting propriety, who set such store on their reputations, Ophelia said, "Love is also dutiful and means taking into care the things that matter to those who love you."

She smiled at him, and his mouth curved in a beautiful grin as if they shared some secrets that only they understood at this moment.

"Come here, Fifi," he murmured.

She flung herself into his arms and buried her face at his throat. Her heart caught at the careful way he held her against him, his hands soothing as he rubbed circles on her lower back. She rubbed her cheek against the soft material of his jacket, able to hear the solid beat of his heart, finding comfort in its steady rhythm. "I'm sorry I fell apart on you."

"Are we not friends?"

"And lovers," she grumbled.

"Then never apologize to me. I'll always help you put back the pieces."

"I'll be there whenever you need me, Niall," she promised in the curve of his throat.

"Such a promise is not needed."

And though he said it tenderly, she heard the echoes of a man used to standing alone, a man used to fighting and crawling for the things he needed by himself. A hunger to know his life and what led him to this moment scythed through her. "Yet I still give it."

She felt the movement of his mouth to suggest he smiled. Ophelia was tempted to beg him to take her to his home, where she would crawl atop him and allow herself to drown away the pain in pleasure. *Using him.* With no promises of more, though she knew, deep in her heart, this man wanted her now and always. "Devlin?"

"Yes?"

"Take me…to music."

He was silent for long moments before he kissed the top of her hair. Fifi felt another curve of his mouth. Niall was smiling. Again.

Heat uncurled deep inside her.

"We are going dancing," he murmured.

CHAPTER SIXTEEN

Fifi's eyes were a spark of beautiful gold in the darkness of the Ironside Tavern and Pub on King's Street, one of the less affluent gambling dens. They had traversed the hallway and the wide-open area reserved for gambling and into a room reserved for dancing. It was a place where her class would never enter, and she stared around with her lips parted in awe, her eyes glittering with delight. The crowd was boisterous as they danced to a wild and beautiful Irish reel as several of his fellow countrymen stood on the sidelines, creating enchanting melodies from their violins and flutes. Ladies danced the lively reel with their dresses drawn up to their knees as they kicked and stomped with vigor, their elbows linked with their menfolk's, who led the charge.

"You want me to do *that* dancing?"

It was what she needed. Something raw and primal to burn away the emotions he could see still burning in her eyes. Fifi was hurt, confused, and perhaps a little bit frightened by what she had learned, and that edge of vulnerability in her gaze tore at him. It was his duty to care for her and see those torments eased. "Are you up to the challenge, my lady?" he said, dipping into an exaggerated bow. Devlin rose and tapped his feet in quick succession to the beat of the musicians' fiddles.

She looked suitably impressed. "Who taught you?"

He flashed her a grin. "My da."

Fifi bit into her lower lip and looked around.

"Scared?" he taunted with a grin. "Are we too bourgeoisie for you, my lady?"

A very unfeminine snort was his answer. With a toss of her head, she removed the pelisse, revealing a dark rose gown that clung alluringly to her figure. It was the perfect contrast to her vibrant blond hair and the subtle golden eye mask on her face. Even if someone here had interacted with Lady Ophelia, no one would be able to tell she and Lady Starlight were the same. There was a slight hesitation in her step when she moved forward, and Fifi looked back at him.

"You are safe," he said, tapping a finger over his heart.

Her eyes lit up, and with a wide grin, she moved to the edge of the crowd, immersing herself in the music, which seethed as if alive, filling the tightly packed space. The Iron Tavern was not as extravagant as the Asylum, and most of the patrons were honest, hard-working folks from his homeland who had opened up small businesses in London. The women danced lightly but with vigor, and the men tapped their boots hard onto the scuffed floor as they beat out the time of the music. As the dancing got wilder, the musicians played with greater enthusiasm. After hanging up his coat with Fifi's pelisse, he went up behind her and slipped a hand around her waist.

She tensed and peered up at him with wide eyes. Devlin lowered his head and boldly kissed the corner of her mouth. "Here we are free, my sweet. No cutting eyes upon us marring our enjoyment, hmm?"

She then seemed to note how closely other couples danced, how unrestrained everyone seemed, how bloody happy. His Fifi laughed. "Let's dance," she murmured.

He arched a brow. "You've figured out the steps so soon?"

"I am a quick learner, my sweet," she drawled, mimicking his endearment. "I know music. The sensation of it is in my soul. I feel the tapping of their boots beneath mine, I sense the rhythm in my fingertips, and most importantly..." She tapped over her décolletage with those fingers. "My heart is alive with the sounds from the fiddlers, the pipes, the stomping of their feet... Let's dance."

She wheeled away from him, impressively performing the rapid footwork of the reel. Fifi held each side of her dress and tugged it upward, revealing delicately stocking-clad ankles.

"*Scandalous*," he mouthed.

She winked and tossed herself into the dance with her entire heart. As she jumped, tapped, and laughed, it felt to Devlin as if everything around him went dark, and only Fifi stood in the light of his awareness.

He could see the sheen of sweat on her forehead, feel the bounce of curled tendril as it slapped against her cheek with each slap of her shoes to the hardened floor. Even her laughter slowed, the way she twirled, the way she unabashedly took the man who held out his elbows to her and twirled with the dancers. Every moment, every smile, every tip of her head revealing the beautiful lines of her throat seared itself into his heart. A memory not even death could steal from him. He was certain of it.

His "*not yet*" shattered, and he fell so impossibly deep in love with her, it hooked into him with violet passion and clawed its way up to his heart and set it to pounding.

His *a ghrá geal*.

Their gazes collided, and she lifted a hand and crooked a single gloved finger, beckoning him to come to her, her smile a teasing, provocative lure.

He went to her. It was impossible not to.

Devlin cupped her cheek and kissed her deeply, telling her without words that his "not yet" was over and he was waiting for her. He became lost in the rich taste of Fifi's sensuality as he slanted his mouth over hers. It was the hooting and hollering of the crowd that drew him back. She looked shaken, shocked…aroused. It was more than his kiss that shook her; she had seen something in his expression.

He tried to bring down the shutters, but then his Fifi sweetly sighed, and it spoke of longing. Color flooded her cheeks. "Devlin."

His name was a whisper that came out on a dark rush of need and want. And he heard it, over the laughter, the music, and the dancing. He closed his arms around her, painfully aware of every inch of her pressed into him. She put her hand over his heart again and looked up, such aching tenderness in her gaze that he felt compelled…owned.

She fucking turns me inside out.

Devlin spun her into the lively reel. They danced endlessly until she stumbled, clinging to him and laughing. Sweat glistened on her skin, and several strands of hair had loosened from the wig and enchantingly framed her face.

Almost two hours after entering the Irish tavern, they spilled outside into the night air.

"That was wonderful. Where to next?" she asked, laughing as he guided her to their waiting carriage.

Once they were inside, he drew her into his lap. He breathed in the scent at the curve of her neck, then kissed it. "Still not worn out, are you?"

She arched a brow in challenge. "Far from it."

"I know just the thing you need."

He rapped on the carriage roof three times, a signal to his coachman to return them to Mayfair. The coach lurched into motion, and, with a deft twist, he bore her down onto the large, padded seat of the carriage. The light from the lantern caressed her lovely face.

"Again?" she murmured, wetting her lips, anticipation gleaming in her gaze.

"Yes." And he would not stop until she dropped into a slumber.

Devlin pushed her gown to her waist, trailing his fingers over the silken stockings. Lifting one leg at a time, he put both over his shoulders—after pressing nibbling kisses along her inner thighs. "I am going to lick this sweet, pretty pussy of yours until you unravel for me, one orgasm after the other."

He watched the flush deepen in her cheeks, and her eyes gleamed with anticipation and something infinitely tender. "I think I like the sound of that."

He was thoroughly corrupting Fifi. "The next time I love you will be in a bed," he murmured. "And I will take hours to worship these sweet, lush curves."

She made a charming, feminine sound of pleasure. Devlin went straight to the center of what he wanted. He dropped to his knees and splayed her legs wide. He lowered his head until his lips were inches from her feminine heat, the scent of her wrapping around him. The heels of her shoes pressed hard into his back as she arched her hips at his silent urging. He spread her cunny open with his fingers, bent his head to her quim, and sucked her clitoris into his mouth with passionate tenderness.

Fifi shivered, a sob of pleasure escaping her.

"Shh," he murmured. "We wouldn't want the coachman and

his tiger to ken what is happening in here, do we?"

Her entire body blushed, and she shot him a carnal glare that promised retribution.

Devlin smiled. "I will give you the pleasure to suck my cock into that pretty mouth of yours and tease and torment me. But not tonight."

Then he licked her. She slapped a hand over her mouth, her body drawing like a bowstring when he did it over and over.

"That's it, my sweet. Remember, no matter how hot it gets… you must not make a sound, hmm?"

He kissed the inside of her thighs, right above the edges of the garter, adoring the smoothness of her silky flesh. Her skin felt so delicate, so different from his. So precious. Palming her lush arse in his hands, he held her to his mouth and fucked her to the edge of madness and exhaustion with his tongue. Her chest fell up and down in ragged bursts, and she kept her palm pressed over her mouth. Only muffled moans and whimpers sounded in the carriage. She found her release in shuddering waves several times, and Devlin stopped when she went limp with satiation.

He lowered her legs from his shoulders and fixed her dress before sitting on the squabs and taking her into his arms. She yawned, leaning her head into the crook of his shoulder, and within a minute fell into a deep slumber.

The carriage rocked and swayed, lulling her even deeper. Looking down at her in his lap, so trusting and peaceful, he felt that wrench once again in his heart. Devlin picked up the locket from the seat and stared at the date engraved there. Many things she had thought about herself had been upended, and for a lady cosseted from the harsh realities of life, it would have been a painful blow.

Hell, even more, even for a man like him who had endured many hardships to stand where he was today, such a piece of knowledge would have been difficult to swallow. That his mother was not really his mother or that his father could have acted in such a despicable manner. It was time for him to put this matter to rest. He would push his connections further and trade upon a few secrets to get the matter moving.

The carriage rumbled to a stop, and he glanced at his pocket watch. It was only a few minutes after ten p.m.

"You may leave. I will walk home."

His coachman, quite used to his love of walking, tipped his hat in agreement. The street was dark, and a soft misting rain had begun to fall. He covered her with his coat and, holding her carefully in his embrace, descended the stairs. An observer might think it strange, a man standing in the dark, deliberately in the shadows with a covered bundle in his arms. He did not wake her; moving with clandestine deftness, he went with her around to the side of the townhouse, walking deep into a garden.

There he found a side terrace door that was partially opened. Resting his shoulder against the wall to hold her weight to him, he used a hand to slide it open even farther. Devlin stepped into the dark coolness of the room, listening to the night and the household.

He jostled her slightly, and she murmured irritably. He smiled and whispered, "Where is your chamber?"

"The fourth door on the left of the second landing," she mumbled, then fell back to sleep.

Most of the servants were abed, if not all. He padded from the room, which revealed itself as a small parlor, and went out into the hallway. Devlin suddenly felt that this might be the only time he entered Fifi's father's home. Like a thief in the night, returning his daughter under the banner of secret.

At the landing, he walked down to her room. Once there, he shifted her, preparing to grip the latch when the door opened. *Bloody hell.*

"Ophelia, I have been waiting—" Her cousin broke off her rebuke and swayed.

"Compose yourself," he drawled, dark amusement rushing through him. "I'll not release Fifi to try and catch you if you faint."

"You are beyond reproach," she hissed furiously, stepping back and allowing him to enter. "How dare you do this, you *cretin*! To…to…" she spluttered, clearly overcome with outrage at his gall.

Ignoring the cousin, he walked over to the bed and deposited Fifi into the center, gently removing her shoes. It spoke of her exhaustion that she did not rouse when he shifted her around to remove her pelisse and the wig. He also removed the pins from her hair, fanning the dark tresses about her pillows. With the cousin's presence, he could do little about the dress. Thankfully, the design was not suffocating.

"Is she well? Why is she wearing a wig?" Lady Effie demanded a few feet away.

Fifi grumbled something and flung one of her feet across the bed. He smiled when she gripped a pillow and sent it sailing in the air to land on the carpet. All without waking. His smile widened. Sleeping with her for a lifetime would be most interesting.

"I swear if you do not answer me—"

He turned around. "She is safe. Only exhausted. Fifi—"

"Lady Ophelia to you!"

Devlin smiled without humor. "She will once again have your discretion in this matter."

Lady Effie narrowed her eyes. "Or?"

"Should you distress her in any way, I will ensure you know of my displeasure."

Her lips curled in a sneer, and she demanded scathingly, "And you think that is something for me to fear? From the likes of *you*?"

"Of course," he replied mildly.

Devlin was not sure what she saw in his expression, but she blanched and looked away. He left the room and closed the door gently, retracing his steps and leaving the house as he entered. Inhaling the crisp night air into his lungs, he turned up the collar of his coat. Not that it did much in protecting him against the rain. Hands deep inside his pockets, he walked along Mayfair toward his townhome, wishing he had Conan beside him.

Good night, Fifi.

• • •

How did you return me to my bedchamber? Considering the scandalous nature of my note, I shall be very circumspect in my salutation.

F.

It would have been too much of a risk to sign Fifi. His reply was pithy and infuriating.

Trade secrets.

Yours, Niall.

...

And what trade might that be?

F.

She had choked on her hot drink of chocolate at his reply.

Thievery.

Yours, Niall.

She hurried from the dining table to dash off a note to the dratted man asking for a more detailed explanation. Ophelia had expected another one line, but hours later, she got almost two pages of a letter. She now sat on her windowsill, her feet curled under her, Barbosa snuggled into her lap.

His reply began with…

A ghrá mo chroí,

She traced her finger over that line, wondering what it meant.

A few short months after meeting you, I journeyed to London determined to make my fortune. It did not take long for me to fall in with a gang located in St Giles. They taught me the tricks of the trade, picking pockets with a mere sleight of hand. Eventually, I was taken on a few missions, as they called it, to enter into our betters' grand townhouses and pilfer baubles, silvers, and candlesticks. At times we took food and blankets. But I learned there was always a window or a door left open in the bigger houses.

Ophelia sniffed, for she was guilty of sneaking out many nights into the gardens and perhaps on her return did not ensure the door or window behind her was properly latched. Curling her hand under her baby goat's belly, she lifted him against her chest. "Our Niall once stole from people."

Bloody hell.

It felt good to curse, even if silently. Lowering her gaze, she continued reading aloud to include Barbosa.

Alas, I was not a good thief, and I believe I lasted for three weeks. In watching another house to determine when to break in, I overheard servants talking about a watch stolen from a particular earl. It had belonged to his son, who had died in the war. I stole it back from my gang and decided to return it. I was caught in the act. That earl did not turn me over to the watch/ police but instead taught me to play chess.

"Chess—who is this earl?"

Her little goat bleated, and she laughed.

I returned daily to his home, sneaking inside through different means. I believed he was amused by my antics and perhaps a little bit lonely. I played chess with him for months. It made me think. And I decided I would be anything but a criminal.

That night as she slept, a sharp *ping* on Ophelia's bedroom windows had her jerking up in the bed. Another sharp *ping* sounded, and, shoving the warm comforter from her body, she pushed to the edge of the bed, parted the curtained canopy, and stood. Cautiously, she padded over to the window and nudged it open.

Someone stood below her windows, face lifted up, with a large dog sat at his side.

"Devlin?"

"You have many men doing this, Fifi?"

His face still held that faint, knowing hint of a smile.

"What are you doing down there? Anyone could see, and then we would be embroiled in a scandal!"

"Then you must be very discreet when you meet me

outside. Wear your mask."

"Frivolous wretch!" Ophelia choked on the air when he moved with stealth and disappeared. *I will not go*. Yet the desire to see him and just speak with him burned inside her chest like an unrelenting flame. She drew back from the window and simply stood in the center of her bedroom. A quick glance at the mantle showed the time to be eleven thirty p.m.

Her mama and papa had retired over two hours ago, and the household should be asleep, perhaps save for the house-keeper. Taking a deep breath, she hurried to her armoire and pulled out a simple day dress. Excruciatingly aware she wore no stays, Ophelia tugged the dark green dress over her che-misette. She rolled on some stockings and slipped her feet into a dark pair of shoes. There was nothing she could do about her hair, and it would be unconscionable to rouse her maid from her slumber. Ophelia undid the loose plait she'd worn to bed, allowing her hair to tumble down to her hips. Slipping on the gold filigree mask, she stared at herself in the mirror by the armoire.

She looked wild...and rebellious.

Whirling around, she moved with silent grace from her chamber, then down the long hallway and winding staircase. The hallways were empty, and nothing creaked or shifted in the dark. Using the servant's staircase, she made her way to the kitchens and slipped outdoors.

He was waiting there with his loyal hound. "Come with me."

"Where do we go?"

"Afraid?"

Ophelia stared at him. "You know I am never afraid when

I am with you." Though perhaps she should be. The pull she felt toward him seemed irrevocable. Being in his presence held real and dangerous temptations.

He thrust out his hand, and she took it, allowing him to pull her into the night and out into the street. An unmarked yet very elegant carriage waited. "This is not your regular town carriage."

"This I reserved for when I am doing dangerous, clandestine missions."

She sent him a scowl, and he merely smiled. He helped her inside, then hauled himself up, Conan bounding inside as well. The lantern's wick was turned low, and she could barely discern his expression. Ophelia did not understand the reckless madness of going with Devlin while not knowing where they headed. It was impetuous, outrageous, and scandalous. If they were caught, they could find no explanation that would save her reputation. She would be assuredly ruined, yet she did not voice these doubts.

In truth, the heavy weight that had sat on her stomach for the day had vanished. She felt…free. And safe. The awareness blossomed through her entire body, and she gripped the edges of the carriage seat. It was then she realized she had rushed out without donning gloves, and the night was chilled.

She wanted to talk about so many things with him, but there was something about the silence of simply existing together that felt peaceful. With a sigh, the last remnant of tension eased from her shoulders, and she leaned against the squabs. The large dog shuffled over to her, and Ophelia gently ran her fingers over his head. A soft growl came from him, and she paused. The great brute nudged her hand, and she supposed he liked it.

Devlin exited the carriage and helped her down. Conan jumped out in one great leap and trotted over to his master's side. They were at Somerset House at the river entrance. He led her through the arched opening. Ophelia looked around, noting the exquisitely crafted shallop, which seemed to wait on them manned by a crew of six. The boat was at least a seventy-foot beauty, with rich golden panels, and at the front, there was a white tent with a padded seat comfortably situated beneath.

Her father did not own one, but she was aware of many lords in the *ton* who traveled the river in their boats manned by their own liveried crew. A wind blew over the water, whipping her mass of hair about her. "Are we to go on the barge?"

"Yes."

A thrill of excitement went through her. "I did not bring a coat."

"I will keep you warm."

She looked at him from beneath her lashes, aware of the fluttering low in her belly. "Why did you bring me here, Devlin?"

"Why did you come?" He sounded genuinely curious and a bit fascinated.

"You know I trust you."

Holding her hand, he carefully escorted her down the steps and onto the barge. The men who waited to row their vessel were not in livery, but they bowed respectfully before taking their seats and gathering their oars. Devlin led her and Conan around to the front of the large vessel, toward the tent. Their vessel started to move, and Ophelia found that she did not mind the icy nip in the air. Then, she noted in the distance several more boats, smaller ones moving ahead through the inky darkness of the night. They barely made any discernable ripples, but as her eyes adjusted to the shadows, she noted there were at least a dozen smaller barges on the water before them.

"Happy birthday, Fifi."

She made a little sound of anguish. Somewhere inside of her shattered, but she did everything to not crumble. "I…I do not know what to say." *My birthday*. One that she might never be able to celebrate again.

"Say nothing. Look skyward and simply enjoy it."

"Skyward?"

"Yes."

She lifted her face to the night, noting the stars were barely out. Fireworks began to erupt and shoot to the sky in a dizzying and beautiful array. Ophelia gasped, her hand fluttering to her throat as she beheld the beautiful spectacle. Yellow, red, green, purple, and blue illuminations crackled and popped in the vast darkness, streaking left, then right, forming a fountain of light in the sky. The fireworks that speared to the heavens took her breath away. She had seen fireworks before at Vauxhall Gardens and during Guy Fawkes Night, but nothing like this.

The white lights intermixed with red and blue burst higher and higher in a dazzling display. Some burst straight up before exploding, others whirled in a spiral, and some shattered into thousands of sparks cascading in a glittering rainbow waterfall. Beneath that beauty, only white lights sparkled like a silver rainfall. The night became a shimmering enchantment.

She wondered if at this moment Sally Martin thought of her. Ophelia stood there, her hand in Devlin's as their barge floated behind the dozens of boats ahead of them. People walking on the streets stood and pointed, rushing toward the banks where they could see. Carriages stopped, and curtains were parted as people looked out in wonder.

Ophelia drank in the beauty of the night sky, and how the fireworks lit on buildings that had seemed so ordinary and grubby in the day, yet now appeared magical. They cruised past Lambeth Palace, Westminster, St Paul's, and even the Tower of London. And not once did the blazing display of fireworks pause.

Ophelia did not want to speak but just watched the beauty of the night, with Devlin by her side. Emotions twisted and churned inside as she inhaled the beauty he created for her.

I am falling in love with you...aren't I, Devlin?

• • •

Almost an hour later, they strolled toward the parked carriage in the distance. The street appeared empty despite the early hours, with only a few lamps to soften the darkness. A light fog had crept in, and she snuggled down closer into his coat. A quick peek at him did not show a man affected by the chill in the air. His steps slowed until they stopped.

Ophelia frowned, noting his countenance. "What is it?"

It was the stillness in how he held himself that alerted her to the danger. Her heartbeat staggered as only a few feet ahead, three men pulled from the shadows of the building and approached them. Ruffians with clubs or batons held in their grip. They might be bent on robbery or worse.

"Grab the bird; she's coming with us. Club the bastard," the apparent leader said to the stocky man to his left.

Devlin shifted, the movement smooth, dangerous. "Gentlemen, whatever you are after, we cannot help you this night."

The stocky man grinned, revealing missing teeth from the top row of his mouth. "It's three o' us and one o' ye."

Devlin arched a brow. "Nonsense; there are two of us. My companion's skills in fending off cutthroat are incomparable. I am certain should the need arise, she will acquit herself creditably."

She made a choking sound, and he glanced at her, his stare amused.

"Are you helpless without that walking stick of yours, my sweet?"

How did he know about that?

"My repertoire is limited to fencing rapiers, I'm afraid," she said shakily.

He *tsk*ed, the sound light and at odds with the promise of violence in his stare. His movements were a mere whisper, startling with their graceful swiftness when he positioned himself before her. "I am Devlin Byrne. How might I be of service?"

The soft words were etched in such menace her heart jolted. To Ophelia's utter astonishment, the men froze, then looked uncertainly at one another. No…they were scared. *Of Devlin?* They muttered vague apologies, turned, and ran away.

Devlin held out his hand to her. She took it, aware of the fine trembling in her limbs. She was with a man who had the power and influence to stop criminals with just his name. It shook her.

A quick peek at Devlin showed an inscrutable expression.

"Are you afraid?" he clipped. "I would not have allowed

them to lay a single hand on you."

"No…I…no. I knew you would have protected me, and though I am without my rapier, you should know I also plant a mean facer."

He made no reply, but his strides lengthened, and she hurried her steps to keep pace with him. "You are angry," she said softly.

"No."

She tugged her hand from his. "Do not lie to me. *Ever*. Even if you think you are protecting my sensibilities. What I enjoy the most about you…us…is how untarnished we are by the pretentiousness that I am overwhelmed with in the *ton*."

He stopped and faced her. His cheekbones were starkly drawn, and his eyes glittered with indefinable emotions. "I put you at risk by taking you here. You are a damn lady, and I am dragging you from your bed in the middle of the night like a damnable fool. You belong at fine balls, garden parties, and riding sidesaddle in Hyde Park with a gentleman of quality. They *could* have attacked. If you had been hurt…"

The thing that moved in his eyes then scared her, and she instinctively took a step back from him. "You would have defended my honor by killing them," she said shakily.

"Of course," he said so mildly she could only stare at him.

"I hardly know this side of you, Devlin. I…" She thrust a flying tendril behind her ears only to sigh in frustration when the wind whipped it back into her face.

"You know enough of me."

"Do I?" she said with an incredulous laugh.

"Yes. And what you do not know now, there is a lifetime to learn."

A lifetime. Her mouth dried. Ophelia made no reply but

slipped her hand in his when he held it out, almost shocked at her easy acceptance of every part of him that was slowly revealed to her.

A boy who had run from home, turned into a thief, was imprisoned, and reshaped himself into the man who silently walked beside her. This was a man who touched her with reverent awe but could use those same hands to ruthlessly protect. A man who could kill without regrets but also owned great kindness, for she knew of his philanthropic efforts.

"What are you thinking, Fifi? I can feel your thoughts whirling."

"I was wondering how long we might remain lovers," she said softly, knowing the day would come when it had to end and they would go back to their respective worlds.

"Do you want to end it now?" he asked mildly, as if her decision would have little impact on him.

Her belly tightened, and she told him the truth. "I do not want us to end." *Not yet*.

His shoulders relaxed, and he lifted their clasped hands to his mouth and kissed her knuckles. She pursed her lips when they walked past his parked carriage.

"I enjoy walking," he said abruptly. "After leaving Newgate, I discovered I do not like closed spaces."

"Was it difficult there?"

His fingers tightened on hers, but she bore the discomfort. "It was," he said starkly. "But I was a fighter. I survived until Rhys got me out. Every day was a battle. A battle for food, for the right to sleep unmolested, to protect my life and the little I still had. It was dark, cold, and overcrowded, and many of the others were sick and without hope."

Rhys Tremayne, Viscount Montrose. Ophelia did not

socialize with the man, but at that moment, she claimed him as a friend in her heart.

"I've read your guest article on prison reform," she confessed softly, recalling how her father and his cronies had mocked it, thinking it ridiculous that criminals were to be treated with dignity. "Several of those imprisoned are…"

"Children," he bit out, "whose crimes are hunger and trying to feed their families."

"Thank you for not hiding your past from me," she said. It was her turn to lift their clasped hands to her lips so she could brush a kiss against his knuckles.

"I have always thought about traveling. I wonder about other countries and sailing on the wide-open sea for weeks."

"That sounds lovely. Where would we go?"

"We?" he asked with a slight smile.

"Yes." A fantasy but one she was content to live within.

"We would go everywhere Fifi, anywhere our hearts want. We have the money to do it." He gently squeezed her fingers. "Have I told you I like walking because of the openness of the space around me?"

Ophelia wanted to hug and kiss him and away chase the memories of when he had been hurt and alone in his imprisonment. "And how far are we walking now?" she murmured.

"To your home."

"That, my sweet, is *miles* away."

"I ken. When you're tired, I'll drag you along."

Ophelia laughed. "I'll not get tired," she promised, shifting so they walked even closer together.

Walking…so simple but perfectly wonderful.

CHAPTER SEVENTEEN

Ophelia stared at the one line scrawled in Devlin's handwriting, hardly daring to breathe.

I've found Sally Martin.

They had not seen each other since that wild night on the barge, when she had walked beside him and Conan uncomplainingly until her feet hurt. When she had seemed tired, he hadn't dragged her along but had stooped, and she had hopped onto his back…giggling.

The memory of it brought a flush to her body.

It had felt prudent to stay away for a bit, to breathe without everything about him clouding her thoughts and judgment. The only thing she had learned from the exercise in restraint was that missing someone was not a light, joyous emotion. It was wrenching, and the feelings which had hooked inside her heart for him were more intense than anything Ophelia had ever felt before. But they were no longer frightening. No, she hoarded the sensations deep inside, never wanting them to leave her.

"Is everything well, Ophelia?" Cousin Effie asked in a tone that bordered on suspicious.

Ophelia folded the note and slipped it inside her reticule. "Everything is wonderful," she said with a small smile, discreetly scanning the crowd. They were in the gallery of the concert hall at the Hanover Square Rooms. The performance this evening promised to be a grand masterpiece of ninety-three sets, and she highly anticipated the performances highlighted for tonight's *Ancient Concerts*.

She was a frequent patron for the last four years, for the series of concerts performed consisted solely of music composed in previous generations. Many of Mozart's best-known symphonies and concertos had been played in this very assembly. Tonight she would absorb the gifts of Handel, Corelli, and Angelica Catalani with delight. Miss Catalani was one of the greatest soprano singers Ophelia had ever had the privilege to hear, and tonight she would perform *Le nozze di Figaro*.

The papers lauded her as one of the greatest bravura singers of all time, and when Ophelia heard the purity and power of her voice, she wished it could be her on the stage, sharing her voice with the world. She could attain such fame as Lady Starlight, but she had sensibly known it was not prudent to take her moonlighting so far. With fame came the risk of exposure and ruination. But how she had yearned for a vibrant moment. It did not escape her awareness that the longer she prolonged her scandalous affair with Devlin, the longer she assumed a similar risk of discovery and ruination.

"Why is he here?" Effie said stiffly, drawing Ophelia's attention from tonight's conductor. "He clearly does not belong."

"Who does not belong?" Ophelia searched for the object of Effie's censure and froze when she saw Devlin sitting a few rows above them to the left. A fierce joy leaped inside her, and she had to hurriedly glance away, biting her lower lip to dampen her smile.

"You were already conspicuous in your feelings," Effie hissed, displeasure marring her brow.

"Dearest Effie, you are entirely too preoccupied with the consequences of my interactions, or lack of them, with Mr. Byrne."

"And you place too little importance on social propriety."

"There are over two thousand seats here, and we do seem to be at capacity. I daresay no one noticed I was delighted to see a friend."

"A friend?" her cousin demanded stiffly, knowledge bright in her eyes.

"A dear one," Ophelia retorted, aware of the flush on her cheeks.

"Really, Ophelia, I thought you had better sense than to wear your emotions so on your sleeve—and for someone so disreputable."

She gripped her fan until her fingers ached. "Is there something objectionable about Mr. Byrne of which I am unaware? That I should be embarrassed to show my happiness in seeing him?"

Effie sniffed. "He is not of our set. Do you need another reason? I know plenty that the newssheets have mentioned over the last two years."

"Mr. Byrne is a gentleman of great character and fortitude. He does not deserve your contempt."

Effie's eyes widened. "Upon my word, surely you do not fancy yourself in love with…with *that* man?"

"It is my heart to love whom I choose, is it not?" she demanded with a tight smile.

Effie stared at her as if she were a creature. "I do hope you jest!"

Ophelia straightened her spine and set her unflinching regard on her cousin. "Why would I be ill-judged in this?"

Effie grabbed her hand and searched her face earnestly. "My dear, please do not disregard my words. If you love anyone, it should be someone charming and good-natured—

someone acceptable to our society. Very much like Lord Langdon, who clearly dotes on you and of whom your mother approves. Mr. Byrne is a clear despoiler who only sees you as a conquest."

"Effie, you do not know him, and I urge you to hold your tongue concerning Mr. Byrne."

"I know enough! And I urge you to disabuse yourself of the notion that he is acceptable for you. I have heard the rumors that once he labored as a dockside worker," she said in horrified accents.

"You have quite sunk beyond reproach if you are daring to think you are somehow superior to Devlin because you are the daughter of an earl, dear cousin."

Effie flushed, at least having the grace to appear discomfited. "I do not understand why you are so fiercely protective of him. I did not want to mention this before because it is so indelicate, but I…I know you and he to have a particular closeness. You cannot think something can come of it, Ophelia. It would be *unacceptable* by this family's standard. Surely you know this."

"If you are so confident that I know of my position in society and of my family's life, why are you bent on warning me? Trust that I know what I am doing, Effie."

"I cannot—"

Ophelia stared at her cousin's angry eyes and said mildly, "Let us not argue. I want to enjoy the concert. Nor will I speak to you anymore about Devlin, given your prejudices."

Ignoring her cousin's fulminating glare, Ophelia directed her attention to the concert, determined to enjoy her night, despite the dull throbbing in her heart. Surging to her feet, she excused herself, heading for the retiring room.

Near a large column in a pocket of shadow, Ophelia leaned against the wall and waited. She was well aware that what she was about to do carried a certain risk. Not even a minute later, Devlin strolled down the carpeted hallway, his expression mildly bored, his walk infused with masculine grace. How easily her heart started to beat. As if he could see her in the dark, he stepped into the shadows.

There was no greeting, as if he too understood this could only be a brief indiscretion to soothe the ache of missing each other.

"Fifi," he said, half laughing, half groaning, tugging her against him.

She gave a tiny, broken exclamation of pleasure as he took her mouth in a deep kiss, sending her senses in a freefall at the sensual shock. Confident they were hidden from prying eyes, Ophelia stood on tiptoe and tangled her fingers in his hair. She scarcely knew who she was anymore.

He broke their embrace and brushed his lips over her nose, then turned and walked toward the exit. Ophelia stood there watching him, a smile on her face and something entirely unknown wreaking havoc within her heart.

• • •

Hampstead Heath was a place Ophelia loved to visit with its hilly terrain, woodlands, and speckled ponds. Lord Langdon had sent an invitation to a picnic atop Hampstead Hill, which her mama had accepted on her behalf, with the expectation Ophelia would be happy about it. At first she had been upset, but then her mother had merely looked worried about how it would seem to call it off and she had relented. The earl had collected Ophelia and Effie some three hours prior, and they had met a few of his friends, four other ladies and three gentlemen. All of whom Ophelia did not normally socialize with, but all were considered the cream of the crop. Lord Heston and Lord Grantham were both heirs to marquessates, Lord Bramwell was a viscount, Lady Julianna and Lady Candace were daughters of dukes, and Lady Sarah, the daughter of an earl.

Lord Heston turned out to be of florid complexion, his interests seeming to be primarily horses and fox hunting. He was affable and laughed a lot but lacked other conversation. His greatest ambition was to take over from his father eventually as Master of Foxhounds. Lord Grantham, however, was tall, slim, and looked like he could be knocked over by a feather. He was certainly no Corinthian, but at least he did not affect the extremes of fashion and was accredited as an excellent dancer and a good conversationalist.

Lord Bramwell was a well-put-together man, and if you ignored his protuberant ears, he would be considered handsome. He seemed a little standoffish and did not speak to anyone while they walked.

The ladies were all pretty, and as a group, Ophelia suspected they had been chosen only on looks and pedigree. Lady Julianna had dark brown ringlets and a very pretty mouth. Unfortunately, the walk tired her, and that pretty mouth spent the time complaining about the unnecessary exertion. She seemed convinced that every insect on the heath was hell-bent on persecuting her.

Lady Candace was blond, curvaceous, and obviously made of sterner stuff, as she replied to Julianna's every complaint with, "Do stop moaning, Julianna. You're such a wet blanket!"

She did try at conversing with Ophelia but wanted to talk exclusively about the latest modes and what she intended to purchase on her next visit to her modiste.

Lady Sarah's hair was a luxuriant auburn, and she wore a bonnet with a deep brim to protect her alabaster skin. Lady Sarah considered Lady Julianna her best friend, so she rebuked Lady C for her criticisms of her darling Julianna.

They had hiked and chatted for more than an hour before picking their picnic spot atop a hill. Several picnic rugs and blankets with pillows and a decorative umbrella were set up by the accompanying servants. Ophelia lowered herself under a large willow tree with several low branches that provided a comfortable shade.

"My, this is lovely," Effie said with a smile.

Ophelia made a noncommittal sound as she watched the army of servants lay out the food baskets, serving trays, and utensils. A veritable feast of delicacies was laid out, and she accepted a glass of ice-cold lemonade from a footman.

"I am very glad you came," Peter said, smiling at her far too warmly. "My friends have wanted to meet with you for a long time."

The implication was that he spoke of her often. "The weather is lovely. Thank you for inviting us."

A quick frown chased his features, and he was too polite to point out he only invited her, not Effie, who had not wanted to come along. Ophelia had stubbornly insisted that her chaperone was very much needed, to her mother's annoyance.

"What a charming hat you wear, Lady Ophelia," Lady Julianna said, taking a sip of iced lemonade the footman had just served. Her eyes volleyed back and forth between Ophelia and Peter, and she realized Lady Julianna's interest was in Peter.

"When Langdon told us you were attending our little picnic, I mentioned to him I always admire the hats you wear. They are always so creatively eccentric. I have not seen that style in *The Lady's Monthly Museum*."

Everyone made some variation of a tinkling laugh, but Ophelia merely smiled and took a sip of her drink, having little to add to the conversation. A nice breeze ruffled the tendrils of hair that had been left to cascade down her cheeks.

"Lady Ophelia is wonderfully artistic," Peter said. "I've heard her play the pianoforte, and she is incomparable."

A slight red stained Lady Julianna's cheeks, and she briefly glanced away.

"I should invite you to one of my weekly salons and listen to you play," she said brightly. "We could also discuss where you buy your lovely hats."

"I believe it is the lady that is lovely, not the hat," Lord Heston said with a pointed stare her way and a supposedly charming smile. "I wonder how I never noticed you before. I am considerably distressed."

Ophelia gathered from the way the other ladies tittered it was some sort of compliment. "I never noticed you, either, Lord Heston," she murmured.

Peter cleared his throat, but she could tell he was pleased by her polite rejoinder.

Heston's smile was a bit tight when he replied, "Well, we shall have to rectify that matter, won't we?" He seemed very pleased with himself.

She arched a brow. "We will?"

"Yes. I am anticipating dancing with you at Lady Benoit's ball. I hear you are to attend."

The nature of his smile told Ophelia that she should be falling over her feet to confirm that she would be accepting his dance offers. Lady Sarah stared at him with softly wounded eyes, and Ophelia gathered they had some history between them.

"I do not dance at balls. I have not done so in years."

"Is that a refusal?" Heston asked, arching his brow, clearly challenged by the notion of a lady resisting his charms.

"It is," she said with a polite smile.

Effie laughed. "I cannot imagine why my cousin should jest with you in such a manner! She would be delighted to stand up with you, Lord Heston."

Before Ophelia could format a reply, Lady Candace interjected. "I recall a mention in society papers that you danced with Mr. Devlin Byrne recently. So you do dance at balls...perhaps just not with gentlemen of quality?"

Peter stiffened. "That was uncalled for—"

His quick defense was cut off by a large dog that bounded over. "Conan!" Ophelia cried, her heart instantly dancing a wild rhythm. Conan did not pay any of the alarmed gasps attention but butted his head along her chin in greeting. Her heart squeezed with mutual affection, and she rubbed behind his ears. A heavy purr rumbled in his throat, and the ladies gasped. Lady Sarah took that moment to scuttle closer to Heston on the blanket.

"Who does this beast belong to?" Lord Grantham cried, looking understandably wary. "I do not believe I have ever seen a dog this large."

"He certainly looks vicious," Heston said, slowly coming off the rug to stand. "Do have a care, Lady Ophelia; he might attack you."

She shot the man an incredulous stare. Conan was wagging his tail and even attempted to lick her chin. "He is not a brutish creature. I am certain that is evident, my lord," Ophelia said, kissing Conan's nose. "I fear he might have gotten loose from his master."

"And who might his master be?" Peter asked with a frown, looking about the area.

Her belly tightened. Ophelia glanced around for his master, her entire body burning when she spied him ascending the slight incline. He had not noticed her as yet. He was deep in thoughts, brooding almost, his gaze upon the view of the lower lands and London's skyline. He was dressed mostly in black, but his waistcoat was a worked damask of black with the pattern in shades of yellow. His sable curls were tossing in the slight breeze and framing his tanned face.

Ophelia glanced away at the quick clearing of Effie's throat. A glance at her cousin showed a face florid with embarrassment. Devlin chose that moment to notice her. Ophelia felt his gaze, way down inside her belly and in a secret place only he could touch. His stare was so intent, it felt disconcertingly like a touch. One of heat and want.

A sharp whistle rent the air, and Conan bounded away.

"Oh my. Who is that gentleman?" Lady Candace murmured, her tone rich with admiration. "He is terribly handsome."

A black scowl crossed Peter's face. "That is Devlin Byrne."

All the ladies gasped, and Ophelia felt the weight of their combined stares on her.

"Have I got dirt on my nose?" she drawled, though she hated how her heart pounded and the unexpected nerves shivering through her.

"How are you familiar with his dog?"

It was Peter who asked the quiet question. Ophelia glanced at him, not liking the hurt she saw in his eyes. It also irritated her. She had done nothing to injure him, nor had she given him any expectation. Nor did he have the right to question her. Her belly tightened as she wondered if her parents had encouraged him and perhaps that was why he still pursued her.

"Yes," Lord Grantham murmured, his dark blue eyes cutting into her. "How do you know the man's dog, enough so that this creature would run to you upon sight?"

"It is decidedly odd," Lady Sarah said, spite in her eyes. "Mr. Byrne is not of our set, and he is rumored to be associated with a most profligate gambling den. I suppose your familiarity came from dancing with the man, or is there something more we are not aware of? Do tell!"

While Effie looked ready to faint, everyone else seemed to wait with suspended breath for her reply.

A chilling reserve cloaked Peter's expression. "Has he been a bounder, Lady Ophelia? I assure you I will correct whatever wrong he has done."

She took a long, fortifying breath. "In all my interactions with Mr. Byrne, he has been a gentleman."

Peter's eyes narrowed. "That does not answer—"

"Yet it will suffice, my lord, for I owe you no other explanation," she said with polite civility. Ophelia stood, ignoring their expectations. "If you will excuse me."

From their gaping mouths, it was clear no one had anticipated her indifference. Effie hurriedly stood and grabbed her arm in a tight grip.

"Effie—"

"Do you dare to go over to him with so many eyes upon you?" she hissed beneath her breath.

"I had not thought it, cousin. However, I was walking away to breathe from all the intrusive questions that are not their business."

"Your friends—"

"I have only met them today. They are not my friends, Effie."

A flush worked itself up Effie's neck. "You are acquainted with Peter, and he could be more if you give him a chance to prove his admiration—"

Ophelia tugged her arm away. "Stop it, Effie!"

Her cousin swallowed down whatever rebuke hovered on her tongue and said, "Do not speak to that man publicly, and should he approach you, cut him!"

She flounced back to their party, who had watched their whispered argument with too much interest. Ophelia stood there, hating that Effie was right. A terrible feeling twisted low in her belly. Should Ophelia acknowledge Devlin in such a public space, her reputation would be tarnished. Her family's name had not endured a scandal or hint of impropriety, a state her mother was more protective of than even her father. She glanced over to where she had last seen him.

He stood, his attention seemingly overlooking the hill, his hand atop Conan's head, his silhouette one of stark aloneness. Her heart stumbled. As if he felt her regard, he shifted slightly so he could include her in his viewpoint. His lean, darkly handsome face was unrevealing, and the sunlight glimmered over the sharp angles of his face like beams of icy radiance. She took a deep, steadying breath and suppressed all the chaotic yearning pulsing through her. As if sensing where his master looked, Conan bounded back over to her.

She became painfully aware that everything she had done with Devlin since their very public dance had been done in secret. As if what they had was entirely sordid. God, he was her secret. A very dark yet precious one. Recalling her parents' plea to never accept an overture in public from Devlin Byrne again, Ophelia turned away, rejecting the advance of Conan, her throat aching fiercely.

Another whistle pierced the air, and without looking, she knew it had stopped the dog in his tracks.

• • •

The next day, her mother entertained morning callers in the drawing room with Cousin Effie thankfully at her side. Ophelia had excused herself to attend to household matters, except she faltered at seeing her father in the study, sitting behind his desk — a place she had not seen him in months. Pleasure warmed her that he was on the full path of recovery.

"Good morning, Papa," she said, walking farther into the room.

His eyes lit in welcome, and he reclined in the large wingback chair. "Your mother and I missed you this morning. We thought you would have accompanied us for a ride in Hyde Park."

She went around the desk, leaned in, and brushed a kiss to his cheek. "I had a slight headache and overslept."

Her father's intelligent eyes held an all-too-knowing expression, but he made no objection to her excuse.

"Is all well, Papa?" Ophelia asked, sauntering to sit in the chair facing her father.

He tapped his finger on the open ledger. "I have not been able to go through these ledgers in a while. Mr. Hunt has been doing an excellent job. And you, too, my dear. I can distinguish your handwriting from his, and your suggestions on running the household costings are well done. Your mother wishes to plan a dinner party. No more than fifteen guests. Cards will need to be issued right away."

She accepted the sheaf of paper from her father that held the names of those invited. All notable lords and ladies, mostly of her mother and father's set. One name snagged her attention. Peter Warwick, the Earl of Langdon.

Something in her expression must have betrayed her surprise, for her father said, "I understand you went on a picnic with the young earl yesterday."

She lifted her gaze from the list. "I did."

Her father considered her. "You are four and twenty, my dear."

"I am quite aware of it, Papa."

"Langdon is a *very* eligible catch, and he holds you in affectionate regard."

Ophelia sighed. "I cannot imagine why. I have given him no encouragement."

"Your mother is certain you have a tendre for him."

"We do not suit. Am I no longer encouraged to make my own match, Papa?"

He sighed heavily. "You are an intelligent, serious-minded young female who is also a beautiful and accomplished woman," her father said. "One day you will make an excellent match with a gentleman who is like-minded. I think that gentleman can be the earl."

Ophelia closed her eyes briefly. "What if I am not at all like you think?"

"Whatever do you mean?"

"What if I am so wild at heart and impetuous and adventurous and…"

His eyes flashed before his expression became inscrutable, and Ophelia knew then he was thinking of Sally Martin. Comparing his child with her mother. "Even if you are, Ophelia, you are responsible enough to temper all those for your family's sake."

For a raw moment she wondered if she had grown with another family—one from a lower class, where their connections and reputation did not rest on propriety—if she would be free to simply be herself. A swift kick of guilt followed, and she buried the complex tumble of emotions.

"He is a very handsome and good-natured young man," her father continued, oblivious to the hammering of her heart. "It is clear what his intentions are. Why are you not receptive to his courtship?"

Because I am falling in love with someone else. In fact, I am already undeniably, irrevocably his. The paper fluttered from her nerveless fingers to the carpet as Ophelia's "not yet" crumpled. She drew a deep, steady breath and fought for equanimity. "He is a likable gentleman with amiable qualities, but I have no tendre toward him."

"Your mother will be disappointed to hear that."

A few moments passed before she could speak. "I cannot fathom why. Mama has always maintained I should marry for love."

"You are four and twenty, my dear. Can we afford to continue holding on to that ideal? Within the blink of an eye, you will be thirty, a decrepit old maid who will be living with her parents still."

"Surely not," she said with a warm smile. "Six years is not a blink, and I most certainly will not be decrepit nor still living with you. I'll be traveling and experiencing the world." *With*

Devlin. Anticipation of such a life raced along her skin, burning with hot, sweet hunger. Then a surge of fright clutched at her heart, for she feared she dared for too much.

"Traveling the world? With what money?" Her father closed the ledger with a frustrated sigh. "I cannot seem to find the path to turn our fortunes around, poppet."

She stared wordlessly across from him, her heart pounding. "I have been studying the accounts, Papa. There are a few minor estates that you could sell and—"

"No. I'll not lose any more of the lands my father entrusted to me, and you must not worry your pretty head about these matters."

"This pretty head has ideas and has been managing this household and the accounts for seven months!"

His features softened. "And I am very grateful and proud of you, but it is *my* responsibility only to solve this matter."

With a sigh of frustration, she realized her father would remain stubborn on this issue. "Very well, Papa. I do have another matter I wanted to discuss."

"You?"

"There is a small art gallery in Derbyshire I would like to visit this weekend. *The Alchemist Discovering Phosphorus* will be on display for a brief time, and I cannot bear to miss it. I hope for your permission to travel down." Ophelia held his gaze, hoping she did not betray that she also planned to visit the home of Sally Martin, who lived in Aston-on-Trent.

"Cousin Effie will accompany you," he said, a frown puckering his brow, his attention no longer on her but firmly on a second ledger. "Some of our creditors have been settled, but I am not seeing from which accounts Mr. Hunt transferred the funds."

Ophelia's belly tightened with anxiety. Should he discover the crumbs of the twenty thousand pounds distributed in small pockets to cover pressing loans, she would have no explanation but the truth. That truth might see her banished from London for the foreseeable future.

Quickly she stood and excused herself. Strolling down the hallway, she heard her mother's laugh from the drawing room and smiled at the joy she heard in it. Hastening to her bedchamber, she opened the letter Devlin had sent her last evening.

Sally Martin lives in Aston-on-Trent in Derbyshire. If you wish for me to accompany you on this journey, I will.

Yours, Niall.

And she had dashed off her reply:

Please, accompany me. I cannot imagine facing it alone.

Fifi.

Instructions had arrived this morning for her to be ready tomorrow morning by the crack of dawn. He had been so prompt, outlining how far they would travel and the time it would take, considering the traveling speed of a carriage pulled by a team of four with regular changes. He had estimated they would arrive in Derbyshire in twenty hours with two resting stops to eat. With a soft smile, she folded the letters and slipped them into her writing desk.

Ophelia then sat on the window ledge and stared out at the back gardens, wondering if, with the prejudice of her parents, Devlin might ever be more than a brief affair in her life.

CHAPTER EIGHTEEN

They had been sitting in the carriage outside a large cottage in Aston-on-Trent for at least thirty minutes. The carriage was parked in the small graveled driveaway leading up to the main house. In the distance, Ophelia saw someone walking about the yard—a servant, perhaps. She did not understand her nervousness, for she was alone with only Devlin as her company. Early that morning, she had driven away without Effie as a hovering chaperone. Ophelia had left her a note, explaining she had to do something important and very private and regretted that she had to leave her behind for this trip.

Lowering the carriage curtains with shaking fingers, she stared at Devlin.

He sat on the seat facing her, his expression unreadable.

"You must think me a ninny," she said shakily.

"Never that. I believe it is normal to be nervous." He dipped his hand into the pocket of his coat and withdrew a flask. Uncapping it, he handed it to her.

"Liquid courage?" she asked with a light laugh. She was aware of a restless dissatisfaction, though she was not at all sure the reason for the discontent.

"Yes."

Ophelia took several healthy sips, the whisky burning a hot trail from her throat to her belly, unknotting the icy doubt. "I do not know what I am doing, Devlin."

"Come here, Fifi."

The ice loosened even more, and warmth flooded her limbs. Pushing from her seat, she went over to him but before she could sit beside Devlin, he pulled her into his lap.

"You wanted to know if she lived. She does. In that house right there. Only she is not Sally Martin anymore. She is Mrs. Sally Kent. She has a husband and three children."

Shock tore through Ophelia's heart. "She…she has more children."

"Yes."

Oh! She did not know what to feel or think. She swayed and he rested a hand at her lower back, rubbing his thumb in soothing circles. "Do you want to know about the children?"

"Yes."

"Two daughters. The eldest is one and twenty, and her name is Marianne. The other girl is seventeen and is called Jenny. The lad is thirteen and he is called Oliver."

Fifi pressed a hand over her chest. "Do you think she ever told them about me?"

He pressed a kiss to her forehead. "That I cannot tell."

"What if they hate me?"

"I'll gut them for it."

A shaky laugh escaped her. "I never knew you were this blood-thirsty."

"Multifaceted, my sweet," he said, kissing her nose. "Multifaceted. Now let's go outside."

Ophelia allowed him to assist her down. Her gloved hand clasped in his, they strolled a few steps from the carriage. Her steps faltered and she stopped and simply stared at the cottage. Inside lived people who were a part of her, yet she did not belong to them, and might never do. Ophelia could not impose and bring any sort of discord or unhappiness to their home. She might introduce worries and past pain Sally had not shared with her husband and children. It shook her badly that she had not thought about that in her drive to find the lady who had birthed her.

I have been selfish, and impetuous, and imprudent as usual. Taking a deep breath, she calmed the disquiet in her heart. Perhaps she should start by sending Sally Martin a discreet letter.

"I cannot go in there," Ophelia whispered, gripping his fingers tightly, yet he did not complain. "I might bring more pain than anything else."

"I understand, Fifi."

She nodded wordlessly and simply stared at the cottage for several long minutes. Devlin merely stood beside her, a silent protective force that she leaned against.

"Tell me, is her husband, Mr. Kent, is he good to her?" For she knew Devlin would have found out everything he could about this family before he told her about them.

"Yes. They do appear contented with each other."

Relief swelled in her heart. "I am glad. She deserves happiness after what happened to her."

Devlin's hair lifted in the slight breeze, and she had to curl her fingers to fight the temptation to touch.

"I wonder if she ever thinks of me."

"I believe she does."

"Then why do you think she has never tried to find me?" Ophelia whispered. "She knew who had me."

"He is a powerful man. It would have been foolhardy and dangerous for her to do so."

She nodded wordlessly, lifting her fingers to brush aside a swath of wavy hair curling on his forehead. "Thank you for doing this for me, Devlin."

"Thank you for allowing me the imposition."

Tipping onto her toes, she kissed the underside of his jaw in thanks. He closed his eyes, and his large frame shuddered. Stepping away, she smiled up at him. "I am ready to leave."

Arm in arm, they turned around, only for her to stumble to a halt at a gentleman who stood some yards away, staring at them. When he saw Ophelia, he removed his spectacles, polished the lenses with a handkerchief, then slipped them back on his face. He took a few tentative steps closer, his light blue eyes wide with disbelief.

"Are you..." He cleared his throat. "Are you Phelia?"

• • •

Devlin rubbed a thumb on Fifi's lower back, through the layer of her dress and pelisse. From the way her body relaxed and curved into him, he knew she felt his touch.

"Who are you?" she demanded.

"I...am Mr. Kent."

Fifi's face turned heartbreakingly fragile. "I...I..." She blew out a harsh breath. "I am not Phelia."

He hesitated. "It is shortened from Lady Ophelia. Is that you?"

They stared at each other, and Devlin could hear Fifi thinking.

"I am," she finally said.

The man closed his eyes in relief. "I never thought I would live to see this wound heal for my Sally," he said gruffly. "May I invite you inside?"

Her breath lifted on a harsh breath. "No. I must leave."

"Please, I beg of you to stay and meet her...meet your siblings."

Her hand pressed against her lower stomach as she breathed in roughly. "They know about me?"

"Yes, to a small extent. It would mean more to my Sally if she could meet you and see that you are alive and happy. It would mean so much to her if she knew that you know of her."

Ophelia looked up at him, and Devlin kissed the fierce frown from her brow. Her lashes fluttered close for a long moment, and he waited patiently while she gathered her courage.

"Yes," she murmured. "I would like to meet Sally Martin."

• • •

Ophelia muted all the chaotic emotions in her heart as Mr. Kent ushered them into a small but cozy parlor where a fire roared in the hearth, shaving away the evening chill. As he'd led them down the hallway, chatter and the clinks of utensils could be heard coming from a distant part of the cottage.

It had taken immense willpower to not turn and investigate. To see immediately for herself the brother and sisters she had.

Once they were comfortably seated, Mr. Kent excused himself. She rested her head on Devlin's shoulder with a sigh, thankful that he always seemed to be there whenever she needed him. The anxiety slowly leeched from her, and when Mr. Kent returned with a lady, Ophelia had little reaction.

The lady appeared younger than Ophelia had anticipated and was quite lovely. She entered the room laughing and chattering, and with a painful jolt, Ophelia realized Mr. Kent had not warned his wife to soften the blow.

"Now, Thomas, what is all the mystery about, and why must—"

She faltered sharply at seeing Ophelia and Devlin sitting on the sofa by the fire.

"I was not aware visitors had called," she said, glancing at the clock by the mantel.

Ophelia slowly stood, aware of the sudden fierceness of her heartbeat. This woman was Sally Martin. Her birth mother...who had yet to recognize her. "Hello, I—"

Sally Kent's eyes widened, and she swayed. Her husband rushed to her and gently clasped her from behind.

"Forgive me," he murmured. "I thought it best this way, but now I see I should have prepared you."

"Thomas," she gasped, sounding frightened. "Who is this?"

Before her husband could reply, she started to cry, great heaving sobs that rendered Ophelia motionless. Mrs. Kent pushed away from her husband and rushed to stand in front of her. Reaching out with a trembling hand, she attempted to touch her, but Ophelia stepped back.

Mrs. Kent flinched.

"I... Forgive me," Ophelia began hoarsely. "I..." With a dazed sense of shock, she realized her entire body trembled, and it felt as if she was sinking.

"Easy," Devlin soothed in a low voice. "I am here."

"You are my daughter," Sally Kent said faintly. "My *daughter*."

Ophelia stared at her for so long without blinking that her eyes began to burn. "Yes."

Sally gasped and clapped a hand over her mouth, her shoulders shaking on silent sobs. Such emotions glowed in her eyes—ones Ophelia could not understand and might perhaps never do.

"Did he tell you? Does he know you are here?" Sally asked.

"My father thought he was dying, and he told me your name. When he recovered, he would not tell me more and did not want me to find you, but I searched because I needed to see you," Ophelia said. "I am sorry for all the pain you endured."

Sally's lips trembled, and she firmed them. "Please, may I hug you?" she whispered. "Just for a moment…to see that you are real."

With a sense of bewilderment, Ophelia realized she did not want to hug her, simply because she did not understand how she was supposed to feel at this moment. There was relief that Sally Kent lived, relief that she was seeing her birth mother, but an absence of love and familiarity made her feel unmoored. The desperate pleading in Sally's voice propelled Ophelia forward, though, and she held out her arms.

It was Ophelia who hugged Sally Kent and murmured soothing nonsense to the heavily crying lady. Ophelia held her breath against her own emotions and offered whatever comfort she could give.

A few minutes later, they were seated on the sofa, Devlin and Mr. Kent departing the parlor to grant them a measure of privacy. Ophelia slowly told her of the journey it took to find her.

"Thank you for looking for me," Sally said, smiling tremulously.

Silence fell in the room as they stared at each other. Ophelia tentatively smiled. "I understand I have sisters."

"Yes, and also a brother."

"Do they know of me?" Ophelia asked.

"They do, but they do not know the story of how you were taken from me. They would love to know you; I am sure of it... as I would love to know you." Her eyes were shadowed when she asked, "Were...were you happy? Were you treated well?"

"My mother loves me, and my father indulges me greatly."

"I am glad to hear it." Sally plucked nervously at a bracelet at her arm. "I almost do not know what to say to you. I've missed you so much. Every day I thought of you. *Every day*."

Her throat aching, Ophelia nodded wordlessly, looking around the tidy parlor, unable to escape the sense that she did not belong there...with them, in their happy space. "Perhaps from time to time I could visit," she offered softly. "We might get to know each other."

"Please, I...I would love that," Sally said, sounding extremely relieved.

There was a loud commotion in the hallway, the door was pushed open, and three people spilled into the room. Mr. Kent had clearly told them of the matter, for they stared at her with varying degrees of shock.

They were lovely, and within their features, she saw a bit of herself. Over their heads, she saw Devlin, his eyes gleaming fiercely in the shadows and his face set in stark, inscrutable lines. If she wished it, he would whisk her away, uncaring of anyone else's wants. The tight knot in her chest simply disappeared, and she felt inexplicably safe.

Ophelia slowly rose to her feet.

"Hullo...I am Fifi."

• • •

Several hours after supping with Sally Kent and her family, Devlin's carriage rumbled away with Fifi to their cottage in Rochester. Once they had entered the equipage, she had laughed and then cried, and now she was in his lap, her face buried against his throat, muttering nonsensical apologies about crying all over him.

He held her like that until she fell asleep. She felt deeply conflicted about Sally Kent and her siblings; he could see it in her expression, in her tears. In the soft hitch in her breathing as she slept against him. He did not shift or move her, even when his shoulders burned and his arm deadened from her soft weight. None of that mattered. The only thing of importance was that she felt safe and comforted and that she was in his arms.

Leaning his head against the squabs, Devlin slept holding her close to his chest, only to rouse when the carriage drew to a halt. A quick look outside the carriage windows showed a night dark with rain clouds with barely any stars dotting the sky. They were also in Rochester, but the coachman had done as instructed and taken them to the cottage path and not the main house. He roused her briefly so they could safely exit the carriage. Once outside, he lifted her into his arms and started up the path. "I can walk," she murmured.

"I know." He simply wanted her in his arms.

"I am sorry, Devlin."

He slowed his steps and looked down at her. "Why?"

Guilt and some other emotion he could not decipher darkened her eyes. "At Hampstead Heath. I…"

He kissed her, stealing the words he did not want to hear. He already knew them, for they had haunted his soul that night as he slept. To be seen with him would be a stain against her reputation, and it had made itself evident under the harsh rays of sunlight atop that grassy knoll. What they had was a closely guarded secret, and he had known from the beginning it would be that way.

Could she give anything else to a man of his background and consequence? Devlin stared at her, knowing he would take Fifi in any way that he could. Swallowing the virulent curse that rose to his thoughts, he looked away. He had taught himself years ago to never settle. If he wanted something, he worked for it, achieving his needs at all costs necessary. Yet he did not feel as if he could apply the same principles to winning Fifi's love.

And why not? the ruthless heart of him whispered.

Slipping her hands around his neck, she kissed him back with sweet fervor. Their lips parted, and they did not speak until he reached the inside of their cottage. Setting her down on her feet, he watched as she faced him. Fifi did not speak but lifted a hand to her hair and started to remove the pins. Devlin felt like there was so much to say, yet his heart started to hammer inside his chest.

"Is this goodbye, Fifi?"

Her lashes swept down across her cheekbones, and her fingers hesitated on the string of her pelisse. Finally, she lifted her eyes to his, and it rocked him on his heels to see those beautiful golden orbs bright with unshed tears. He took a single step closer to her, lifted his thumb, and swiped a drop away.

"Are those tears for me…for us?"

Her breath caught, her hand pressing tighter to her stomach. "Yes. I keep…I keep wondering how long we can really remain lovers. Every moment I am with you, there is the threat of discovery."

There was a sadness in Fifi's eyes, one he did not feel he could touch or erase. She had held a similar expression that day on the grassy hills of Hampstead Heath. *Ah, fuck.* "I see. If you wish to end our affair, Fifi, do it. I always knew it would end."

"Would you let me go?" she asked brokenly.

"Yes." He scrubbed a hand over his face. *What a fucking lie.* "No. I would more likely kidnap you and whisk you to somewhere far from England."

Her eyes widened, and her lips parted with her alarm.

Devlin felt with bone-deep certainty this was their last time together. He fought against the jagged feelings of doubt. "Fifi, we do not have to stop being lovers. We have weeks, months, years left to us. I will protect your reputation, and I swear no one will ever discover us unless we want it. I know we are from different walks of life and—"

"I am falling in love with you," she whispered.

Fuck. Devlin stepped back three paces, as if he had been shoved. A shocking, insurmountable degree of emotions almost felled him to his knees. "Fifi—"

She tipped her head slightly to the side. "My 'not yet' is cracking at an alarming rate, Devlin, so it is time we ask ourselves the necessary questions. I *am* falling. And it's all the love. The one where my heart trembles upon seeing you, the one that makes me want to walk through a storm together, and the kind that is honest and loyal and is filled with laughter. I feel it growing with each moment with you, and it is frightening because the world I live in will roar at the very idea of us together. And while I might be able to live without that world, my parents, whom I also love, will never accept us being together."

He went to her and cupped her cheeks, then lifted her face and pressed his mouth to hers. Her lips parted to the incredible gentleness of his touch, the sweet yet fiery stroke of his tongue.

"I love you," he said roughly against her mouth. She gasped, and he caught the sound with his lips. "Never stopped, Fifi. Can never stop. I love you with every breath in me."

"It would be hard," she whispered.

Lifting her chin with two of his fingers, he saw the fright that she would crumple under the pressure of societal demands. "Sail away with me."

She clutched frantically at his jacket. "*Elope?* Are you mad?"

"Wonderfully mad. We established that some time ago, remember?"

She chuckled, but that uncertainty remained in her eyes, and she thumped his chest. "I cannot run away with you, Devlin, and you most certainly will not kidnap me!"

Well, hell. That was a massive wrench in all his plotting. Then... "I will speak with your father. That is the first step."

She looked almost ready to faint, and then her lush lips curved into a wide smile. "Marriage, then?"

"Is there any other way forward?"

"No."

"Then we agree. We will get married."

"How terribly romantic," she drawled, yet the sadness had faded from her eyes. Now they glittered with delight.

The tightness around his chest dissolved. "Should I recite a poem or sing a song?"

She lightly laughed. "Do you have it in you?"

He glanced at her, momentarily amused. "Once you need it, I'll find the words."

She held him tightly for a long time. "The only thing I need is you."

"Good answer. I was fretting you would have said yes."

Fifi laughed before she sobered. "If my father refuses you?"

Something dark moved through Devlin. "I'll come up with a notorious scheme to ensure his compliance."

"Devlin!" She gasped. "They…they are very important to me. No schemes or blackmail."

He stilled inside. After a moment, he said, not very easily, "So their approval is necessary?"

"Yes." She searched his eyes. "Do you blame me?"

It was in the highest unlikely degree that the marquess would ever accept his offer. *What, then?* "Never," he said, before taking her lips once more with his. "I am a fighter. Once you hold my hand and step forward, I will never let you go."

"I have dear friends who would never cut me from their lives for being with you. One is a duchess and the other a marchioness. That is enough connection, should I ever need it, and I doubt I will. There is more to life, and I want to reach for it…with you, Niall."

This time he did not allow her to step back but ruthlessly seduced her with one deep kiss after the other until she whimpered. Breaking off that tumultuous embrace, he kissed her brow, her eyelids, the tip of her nose, her cheeks, and finally her lips. Soft, slow, undemanding. He wanted to ravage her, yet also adore and worship her.

They removed their clothes in between kisses and whispering sighs until they stood naked before each other. Her wide eyes skipped over his body, stopped at his cock, then traveled down to his toes.

Her color considerably heightened, Fifi traced his lips with a single finger. "You are beautifully formed, Niall."

Sweeping her into his embrace, he kissed her while he walked her over to the small bed in the corner. Bearing her down, he trailed his fingers reverently over her quivering belly to her slit and found it wet with wanting.

"You are already wet for me, Fifi."

She gave him a brief, wondering look. "I cannot help it; with just a kiss you burn me alive."

"God, the taste of you," he whispered. "Sweeter than anything I've ever had."

Nudging her thighs wide, he settled between them while bracing his weight atop his other forearm. Dropping his forehead to hers, Devlin watched her eyes while he gripped his cock and pressed the tip against her quim. He tormented them both by rubbing the sensitive head of his cock over the slickness of her folds. Pressing hard against her sex, he started moving his hips in slow circles, then up and down he stroked, dragging along her clitoris with the head of his cock and then down where he wanted to sink deep. Her body reacted, going soft and pliant, her sex wetter. It was more pleasure than he could bear.

Fifi whimpered, hugging around his neck tightly, arching her hips to his.

"You are the devil," she murmured huskily, "to be teasing me so."

His eyes held hers as he split her legs even wider. "No more teasing," he said, thrusting deep inside her clenching tightness.

Instantly, Devlin felt the pleasure ripple through her, and it was enough to have him fighting his own release. With one hand curved around her back, the other holding her buttocks, he held her to him and chased their pleasure in a driving, sensual rhythm.

CHAPTER NINETEEN

Late the following afternoon, Ophelia jerked from the bed, a happy grin widening her mouth. After ringing the bell, with the help of her lady maid she dressed in a simple yellow day gown and caught up the mass of her hair in a loose chignon. Today she would write letters, one to Kitty and one to Maryann, telling them the news that Devlin Byrne would ask for her hand in marriage in the upcoming days.

It felt important she told her father that she had found Sally Martin and that she had spoken to her. Did she tell him that she had siblings? Two sisters and a brother, all younger and with features so similar to her it was remarkable.

Hurrying down the winding staircase, she became aware of muffled crying emanating from her parents' drawing room. Her steps faltered, and she frowned. Padding toward the door, she paused upon seeing Cousin Effie exiting the room. "Effie, is all well?"

Her cousin whirled around, pressing a hand over her chest. "You startled me."

The crying muffled and the distant sound of a man's voice echoed through the door. An uncomfortable pit formed in Ophelia's belly. "Is it Mother and Father?"

Effie hesitated, and that filled Ophelia with a greater sense of alarm.

"Yes."

"Is Mama crying?"

"They received some upsetting news. It is after one in the

afternoon. You overslept."

Ophelia fought back the blush, knowing which wanton activity had seen her exhausted and her muscles achy. Hurrying to the door, she touched the latch. "I must see to Mama."

"Ophelia," Effie said gently.

A quick glance at her cousin showed her eyes bright with tears.

"What is it?"

She held out a piece of newssheet. Irritated and frightened, Ophelia grabbed it and scanned the pages.

This author has it from a most credible source that the beautiful wallflower Lady O has been seen in the company of one D.B., a man of dubious character and business practices. Their relationship is of a scandalous nature, and a close source has confirmed that Lady O traveled alone *in a carriage with D.B for three days —*
— The Daily Gossip.

Unable to read any more, she lowered the sheet, her heart trembling. Whatever reputation she had was shredded in the *ton.* How could anyone know she sneaked away with Devlin to Derbyshire? She had been in disguise and...

An awful awareness pierced her. Ophelia lowered her hand from the latch and faced Effie. "You are the close source this article mentioned."

Effie lifted her chin. "I did what needed to be done."

"How dare you, Effie! You have cast slander upon my reputation!"

"*You* did that yourself, Ophelia, with your connection to Devlin Byrne. I told you on numerous occasions to end whatever is between you. And you refused to listen. The fact that you left for Derbyshire without me tells me it is because of that man!"

"And this is your way of severing my connection with a friend?" Ophelia demanded, unable to bear the pain creeping into her heart. "You decided to ruin me in the eyes of society."

"That is not what I did," she said firmly. "I simply did enough to force you to your senses!"

She stared at her cousin in appalled shock. "My life is my own, Effie. It is not yours to manipulate because I have not fallen in line with how you believe I should behave. How do you dare act in such a manner?"

Ophelia struggled to accept that her cousin would truly take steps to ruin her simply because she wanted to keep her away from Devlin.

"I have also told your parents everything."

"What?"

"I told them of your close connection to Mr. Byrne and my suspicions that your connection with him is of a scandalous and intimate nature, and that without a doubt you were with him in Derbyshire."

Of course, revealing her secrets to society would not be enough; Effie had involved her parents, for they were the final authority in bending Ophelia's will. Sorrow clutched her throat at the choking sounds coming from behind the door. Her mother was sobbing as if her heart was breaking.

"You did not save me, Effie," she whispered. "I was always careful in my interactions with Devlin. *Always*. All you've done is bring gossip and scandal with your actions and pain to my family...to *your* family."

Effie's chin lifted, and her eyes flashed. "Yes, I did save you from the clutches of a predator. You will eventually thank me! Because I did this for you...and only for you. You would not heed my advice, and this was the only path I saw to sever this obsession you have with that wretched man. He would have been your irrevocable downfall. I *saved* you."

"You know the power of scandal...how the pain of airing sensitive matters for public consumption would ravage our family. You are *inexcusable*. I will not forgive you."

Walking away from her cousin, Ophelia gently knocked on the door and opened it. She straightened her back as she entered the drawing room to face her parents. Unable to run away from the brewing storm, she knew she must see them. Stifling her cry, she stared at her parents. Her mother sat in her husband's lap, her head resting on his shoulders, heartbreaking sobs sawing from her throat.

Guilt and pain clawed up inside Ophelia. This scene was so unimaginable, so frightening. A sound of anguish escaped her and settled in the room. Her mother's head snapped up, and she hurriedly wiped at her tears, standing and smoothing down her gown.

"Ophelia," she said hoarsely, her eyes red and swollen. "I... my darling...I am sorry..."

With a sense of shock, Ophelia realized her mother found it hard to look into her eyes. "Why do you apologize, Mama?"

Her mother lifted her head with regal pride and took a shuddering breath. "I am so *very* sorry."

Her father stood, took his wife's hand, and placed it atop his.

"We know the truth," he said quietly. "You did not visit an art gallery in Derbyshire but traveled with that man...Devlin Byrne to find Sally Martin."

Ophelia sucked in a harsh breath. "How do you know this?"

Instead of answering, her mother said, "I never intended for you to find out in this awful, wretched manner. I..." She waved at the scattered, ripped-to-pieces paper littering the silver-and-blue carpet.

With a jolt, Ophelia recognized pieces of all the letters exchanged between her and Devlin. She met her father's accusing stare without flinching. "You searched my bedchamber and writing desks."

"After what Effie brought to our attention, do you think we would not?" her father growled. "That our daughter could act in such a reckless manner is beyond the pale and a grave disappointment."

They had found that letter with the simple line, *I've found Sally Martin*, and all the other letters with the instructions on how Ophelia should meet him in secrecy.

"Did you...did you find Sally Martin?" her mother whispered, clutching her husband's hand.

Ophelia was tempted to lie and spare her the pain. But she couldn't. "Yes. I met her."

Her mother went chalk white. "*How* did...how did you know of her, Ophelia? Was it this Devlin Byrne who told you? Effie has accused him of acting most incorrectly and without respect to you."

She hesitated, torn by conflicting emotions. Her father

held his wife to his shoulders as she cried, yet still he had not revealed to his wife that her daughter had long known the truth of the whole sordid matter. The faith she held in him, the one that had already cracked, now shattered, the pain so acute silent tears streamed down her face.

"I've known for several weeks," Ophelia said hoarsely.

A profound stillness blanketed the room.

"You knew?"

"Papa told me a few months ago when he…when he was abed, with the thoughts that he would die. He only told me he took me from the arms of Sally Martin when I was a babe. Papa would not tell me any more, so I searched for her."

"You reckless, willful creature!" her father slung at her with anger. "I told you to leave it alone!"

"I could not know that you stole me from someone… someone you left in the sweat of her tears, someone you left powerless to fight you…someone who possibly mourned the loss of her child daily! I could not sleep, Papa, without knowing who she was or if she lived. Do I look like her? Am I like her in temperament? Do I have another family? She was not just a mistress you discarded. You had the power to tell me. I *begged* you to let me understand, and you ignored my confusion and fears. Do not blame me for acting. I am your daughter. I am most certain you knew I would not let it alone, given I have heard all my life about my willful and contrary nature!"

Her father's shoulders pushed back as if he braced for condemnation. His wife did not lash out at him but sank onto the chaise longue, burying her face in her hands, her shoulders shaking.

"How you must hate me."

The words were muffled, but Ophelia heard her. "Hate you?" She hesitated, torn by conflicting emotions. "Mama…" She was stricken silent. All the pain and guilt and doubt suddenly fell away from her, and she breathed in deeply. It must have been terribly painful for her to lose her child and then the hope for more. Then to live with her husband's actions. How incredibly strong she must have been to raise Ophelia with such care and love…with such compassion and patience, all with the dread that one day she might uncover it and not love her mother anymore. That awareness stabbed her clean through the heart. Ophelia felt undone. "I *love* you. *You* are my mother."

The marchioness looked up, her eyes searching Ophelia's face almost wildly. "We stole you and kept you from your real family—"

"Papa took me from her, and it caused her great pain. I cannot fully know what made Papa act in such a callous disregard for someone else, but I cannot dismiss that you provided me with a wonderful life filled with rich happiness. I was well loved by you, Mama. I cannot imagine trading those memories for *anything*. My rebellious temperament and love of music and singing were not inherited from you, but you taught me so much more. Mama, you taught me temperance… how to be gentle and kind…and how to love. I cannot…I *cannot* ever regret that you are my mama."

Her mother surged to her feet, rushed over, and drew Ophelia fiercely in her arms. She hugged her mother for several minutes while she sobbed. Her papa looked on, his face stoic, except his hand gripped the edge of the gilded chaise until his knuckles whitened.

Her mother stepped away, wiping the tears from her

cheeks. "We will fix this. Our family is powerful, and we will not acknowledge the rumors or pretend there is anything to be ashamed of! We will not confirm them should anyone ask, and we will go about our business as if that dratted scandal sheet spoke of another family. As it stands, many will speculate that *Lady O* is you, but they cannot know with utmost certainty."

Walking over to the marquess, she took the handkerchief he held out and delicately dabbed beneath her eyes.

She masked her inner turmoil with deceptive calmness. "Mama...Papa...how have you reconciled taking me away from Miss Martin?"

They stared at her before walking over to sit side by side on a sofa. Ophelia took the seat opposite her parents and clasped her hand before her.

"Your mother is blameless," her father said gruffly.

She made to protest, and he squeezed her fingers gently.

"I was a young and foolish man whom your mother forgave for his base stupidities. I knew I was in love with her when we married, but I had not ended my liaison with a lady I had taken to be my...my mistress some months prior."

Her mother trembled so fiercely, Ophelia whispered, "Papa, I know the truth of it. Mama lost her child, and...I replaced that pain."

Her mother flinched as if struck. "You are my daughter. It took me some time to realize it, but I love you, Ophelia."

"I know, Mama. I know."

Her mother took a deep breath and said, "We must discuss this scandal sheet."

"Cousin Effie is their source," she said. "She feared my friendship with Mr. Byrne and believed this was the way to sever the connection."

"That means you have been sneaking from this home to… to meet that man," her mother said. "All the encounters your cousin told about are the truth."

She blinked away the tears. "I… He is my friend." *More, so much more.* "Mama—"

Her mother lifted up a palm. "No. We do not have time for arguments and recriminations. We must immediately plan how to salvage your reputation and this family's honor. What I do fear is the rumor will run amok and tear apart your reputation. Should you marry, and marry well, it would do much in protecting you. Marriage will most certainly put the brakes on those wagging tongues and newssheets who will print more of this…*rubbish*! You must marry, and it must be done quickly."

Her father's eyes caught her. "I have sent a note to Lord Langdon that you have accepted his offer. Marriage is to be immediate by special license."

A most awful sensation pressed against her belly. "I cannot marry Peter," she said. "I have promised to marry—"

"Do you dare say it?" her father roared, his face darkening with anger. "When you know perfectly well an alliance with that man is most objectionable?"

It took courage to face her parents' inevitable disappointment, but she lifted her chin and said, "I will only marry Devlin Byrne."

There. It was out in the air.

"That man is not interested in marrying you, Ophelia," her mother said with a sigh. "He is interested in your connections."

She almost laughed at that ridiculous assumption. "Mr. Byrne will call to speak with you, Father—"

"I will never accept that man's offer. How dare he believe

he could even approach me?"

"Papa… I am of age and do not need your permission."

Her father stared at her as if she had lost her mind. "Have your senses taken their leave? The man is nothing but a common thug of uncertain, most certainly filthy origins. You are my daughter. Such a match is unpardonable and will never be condoned by your mother or me. I will only approve a match with the earl or some other suitable gentleman."

The revelations fell like blows. It did not matter how good or wonderful Devlin was. To her parents, he was unsuitable simply because his blood was not blue.

"He is brilliant," she said hoarsely. "He is shrewd…ruthless, yes, but it is tempered by his kindness and his honor. He sponsors many children to get an education who would be denied because of their class and opportunities. A proper education that will see them claw themselves from poverty to owning land and property. He helps those who wish to become tradesmen, and he donates thousands to charities that provide proper care to orphans. He is not a man to show disdain but a man to admire…a man to love."

Her father scoffed. "Do you dare say you love this person?"

A thrill of frightened anticipation touched her spine. "Yes." Ophelia looked at them. "Is that not what you always wanted for me? For me to love the man I marry, and that he would love me in return? Or did you intend for me to *only* love and marry a man that has blue blood and a title? Did you mean for me to find a gentleman's worth in his connections and standing in the *ton*? Did you mean for me to own a heart filled with prejudice? I cannot believe you mean for me to reserve kindness and love and civility for only a gentleman of consequence and aristocratic blood."

Her parents were briefly stunned into silence.

Her mother surged to her feet. "Ophelia, darling, you have always lived in the boundaries of society's acceptance. Can you imagine your life without it? People would stare and whisper and speculate on your life. You would be cut from the invitation list of almost everyone. Society does not accept this man. And if you marry him, they will not accept you, either."

"Then society will just have to carry on without me in it!"

"And what about us?" her mother said quietly.

"Mama, I would *never* leave you."

"And do you think we could accept you calling on us once you are Mrs. Byrne?"

Ophelia recoiled, and her throat ached. "Are you saying I will not be welcome, Mama, should I marry the man…the man I love? That you and Papa would sever all acquaintance with me?"

Her mother paled. "You cannot love him. He is simply an exotic creature who has turned your head for a brief spell. Forget that man, and we will speak of this no more!"

Her parents, united, hand in hand, walked out of the drawing room, leaving Ophelia alone with her crushed hopes and an aching, terrified heart.

CHAPTER TWENTY

Devlin approached the marquess's townhouse only an hour after he'd seen the scandal sheets. He'd understood then there was not a moment to lose. In his experience and understanding of the *ton*, the marchioness would move swiftly to protect her family's reputation and consolidate their alliances in the face of the latest scandal. That would mean offering up Fifi to the most connected bidder.

He was certain that this would be an unpleasant interview, if the marquess even agreed to speak to him. There was a deep stillness inside of him as he waited for someone to open the door. The sounds of banging and rushing around came from within the house as if some crises were being dealt with. The house was not the quiet, conservative dwelling of a marquess and his family at present. If pandemonium reigned, then perhaps there was a crisis caused by Fifi telling her parents that she wished to marry a commoner. He smiled ruefully at that thought and masked his expression as the solid door cracked open.

"Will you inform the marquess that Mr. Devlin Byrne is here to see him?" he asked the butler who had opened the door.

"I will inquire whether my lord is at home to you…sir," he said.

The pause before reluctantly saying the word "sir" was just a trifle too long, and the door was then firmly closed. There was some considerable wait before his return, and Devlin's keen ears heard raised voices coming from within the house. He thought he heard the words, "How dare the bounder call on me; the man is an utter scoundrel…" and he suspected the explosive utterance had been the marquess, who must have yelled them at great volume.

He could pick out the muffled sounds of more speech, but the words were quieter and could not be distinguished from the stone steps of the townhouse. Devlin let it wash over him. It was not the first time he had been refused entrance to a grand house.

He waited, taking two paces back and forth on the top step, counting his steps—he was reaching two hundred—when the door opened again. The same butler stood there and sniffed before pompously saying, "My lord will grant you a brief interview…Mr. Byrne."

With grim amusement, Devlin noticed the replacement of the word "sir." He stepped inside, and the butler closed the door behind him, taking his damp coat, hat, and umbrella. The butler showed him down a corridor and knocked on a door.

"Mr. Byrne to see you, my lord," the butler intoned pompously.

Devlin entered, and the butler closed the door behind him. Seated at a large mahogany desk was the marquess. He had clearly got his temper somewhat disciplined, and the empty brandy glass on the desktop suggested he had swigged a measure to control his fury. The pinpoints of high color on Fifi's father's cheekbones proved that attempt had not been entirely successful.

"Well, what do you want, man? This intrusion into my privacy is beyond intolerable," were the first words the marquess uttered.

"I want to seek your blessings on the union of your daughter, Lady Ophelia, to myself," Devlin stated, knowing that whatever answer he would receive from this blustering, irate man would not be positive.

"Refused! I'll never permit my daughter to marry scum of your ilk. Now be off with you. This interview is over!" The marquess was trying hard not to shout the word, but he was failing.

Ah, Fifi, he thought, closing his eyes briefly. Devlin never wanted to do anything to cause her pain. This would hurt her.

At his silence, the marquess stood, trying to intimidate Devlin.

"My daughter will be marrying the Earl of Langdon."

How certain he sounded. Ice congealed inside Devlin's chest as he stared at Fifi's father. "Am I truly so unsuitable to be Fifi's husband?"

The man slapped his hand on the desk. "Yes!"

"I make her happy," Devlin said simply. "With me, she will always be cherished and protected."

Something quick flickered in the man's eyes before his lips flattened. "Lord Langdon will also love and protect her. He already made his offer, which was accepted, and he is even now waiting on Ophelia in the drawing room. Your presence has rudely interrupted a happy occasion."

"She will never marry him."

The marquess's mouth curved into an unpleasant smile. "You have no notion of their close friendship."

Raw silence coated the room for a precious moment. "Is there anything I can do for you and your wife to grant your blessing?"

"By God, there is nothing," the marquess snarled, clearly

aghast at his gall.

"I offer my fortune for her hand."

The marquess staggered and stared at him as if he did not know what to make of him.

"All of it," Devlin said. "And it amounts to over two million pounds."

"You have clearly taken leave of your damn senses," the man spluttered. "The answer is still no."

"I am willing to lower to my knees and beg you if that will sway you."

"My God, man," the marquess sneered. "Have you no dignity?"

"I am willing to sacrifice anything for Fifi. For you see, since she is of age, she does not need your permission to marry me, my lord, but your blessing seems important to her. I presume it will make her happy, and that is the only concern of mine," Devlin said softly without flinching. "Money…pride…dignity… nothing is as important as her happiness. I came to respectfully ask your permission, as we will be family, whether you wish it or not."

He seemed as if he stared with some sort of understanding, and then it died.

"I'll never accept it; she will be dead to me," the marquess said. "Ophelia knows her duty and would not deign to marry so low…" The marquess hesitated as if less sure of himself and resorting to bluster.

Something cold and ruthless moved through Devlin. "I had hoped that you would be a sensible man over this. I hoped you might love your daughter enough to care about her happiness. I have bought up most of your debts and mortgages simply to ensure I could ruin you completely at one word to my man of business."

The marquess paled, but Devlin remained unmoved when he leaned forward and braced his hands against the table. "However, Fifi would not like that. She loves you, so I...must tolerate your prejudice. It will be a wedding present to my bride and I will settle the rest of your debts before we wed."

Devlin turned and strode toward the door, gripping the handle to open it.

"How dare you, you absolute scoundrel. I forbid it; you will not marry Ophelia. Get out, get out, get out before I have you thrown out!" All vestige of self-control had disappeared from the marquess's face. "As if I would allow my daughter to marry a man from the gutter!"

Devlin stared back at the marquess, the coldness throughout him growing deeper by the second. "I want to imagine a life with your daughter as my wife. Some might sneer; others might try to look down their noses at us, and by default, you might be caught up in that. However, Fifi has a spine and heart of steel, and she is not bendable. Not by people's opinions that do not matter to her. My wealth will, however, matter, as will my influence over their debts—gambling and otherwise—and I promise anyone who hurts her will rue the day. When I tried to make myself into a man of wealth and influence for Fifi, it was not only to buy her all the houses, dresses, country homes, and seaside resorts she wishes. It was also so that my reach would be unfathomable to those who dare think they can hurt her. You can give your blessing knowing she will be sheltered from society's storm with a man who would give his life for her...or live knowing that if you make a move to thwart our union, one day she will disappear from under your noses, and *never* will you see her again, for I will take her far away from all of this."

The marquess had faltered into remarkable stillness, and the gaze that stared at Devlin hinted of the marquess's own ruthless nature.

Devlin allowed his mouth to curve into a humorless smile. "Do not bother to show me out. I know the way."

• • •

It was utterly and wretchedly ridiculous that Ophelia had been locked inside her chamber. Pacing the carpeted floor, she silently raged.

She had bounded up the stairs after a fierce back-and-forth on the merits of why she cannot marry the earl, and to her shock, a few minutes later, she had heard the key turned in the lock. Her mother had spoken through the door, informing her that the earl would be stopping by soon and she should make herself presentable for an audience. It had almost been an hour since her maid whispered through the door that Devlin had come to call. Ophelia had not been able to warn him what he would be walking into. With a shake of her head, she realized he would very well know it, for he had always lived outside the acceptance of society.

The key turned in the lock, and she whirled around to see Effie.

"Lord Langdon is awaiting you to take a turn about the gardens. Tidy your hair and—"

Ophelia rushed past her cousin and down the stairs, aware of her bare toes and her hair flying behind her. Was Devlin still here? Hastening down the hallway, she skidded to a halt to see Peter coming from the library with her father. They were smiling and shaking hands.

"Lady Ophelia!"

Surprise flared in her mother's eyes, and disapproval in her father's, no doubt at her state of dishevelment.

"Forgive my manners, my lord, but I cannot speak with you just now."

Her father smiled tightly. "Lord Langdon would like a word with you in private in the gardens."

A word with her in private. To propose marriage—one which her father had clearly already approved.

"Where is Devlin?" she asked, painfully aware of the stuttering of her heart.

Her father's eyes cut to the earl and then back to her face. "I do believe you mean Mr. Byrne," he said with icy precision.

"Yes, Mr. Byrne."

The marchioness lifted her chin. "Your father has made it clear he is not welcome in our home, and the utter gall he showed in calling upon us is too much to even speak of."

"Mother—"

"I believe he will be away from England for the foreseeable future. Good riddance," her mother said with feeling.

Ophelia stumbled back as if she had been pushed. "He *left*?"

"Yes," her father clipped with chilling civility. "Let us retire to the drawing room. I am certain you are alarming Lord Langdon with this display."

She had forgotten that the earl lingered in the hallway, and a quick glance revealed his intense stare upon her. Ophelia pressed her hands over her face, desperate to hide the piercing agony cutting through her. Tears slipped through her fingers.

How could he have given up on her so easily? Devlin had simply left. Why had she not answered him when he asked her if she would sail away with him? Perhaps he did not think she loved him, when she desperately wanted to spend her years with him. Why hadn't she told him, instead of saying her "not yet" was cracking?

"What else did he say?"

"Ophelia—" her father began sternly.

Peter came over to her. "Mr. Byrne came for the same reason I did: to save your reputation…to ask for your hand in marriage," the earl said with soft contemplation.

"He was, of course, refused," her father said with a scoff of incredulity. As if he could not believe the man's daring, even though she had forewarned him.

Ophelia choked on a small laugh. Devlin had done it the gentleman's way. How much it must have taken to approach her father to ask for her hand, knowing the contempt he would face. What must her father have said to him that he would leave without speaking to her?

"What did you say to him?"

"I told him the truth of it. Should you marry him, you would no longer be a part of this family."

"You cannot mean that, Papa," she whispered.

Harsh resolve was stamped on his face. "He is a commoner, Ophelia."

She appealed to her mother. "There are many people in the *ton* who have married below their station, Mama. *Many*, and they are still welcomed in society even if it is strained. It is your innate prejudice I am resisting. And that is what I am hoping you will see. It is not society's acceptance I hope for. Hang society. I will be so scandalous and original and outrageous many will still send me invitations to their balls and drawing rooms. My friends will never forsake me. It is your acceptance that is important to me. Do you understand? It is *yours*."

In the face of her heartfelt plea, her parents remained silent. Mama's eyes were glistening with tears, but her father's mien was icily composed.

"Will you not say something, Mama?" Ophelia inhaled on a ragged breath. "You would force me to make such a painful choice?" And of course they had every expectation that she would go to the garden to have an amiable talk with Peter and then accept his offer. She'd always had a steadfast loyalty to family and friends, yet never to her own wants and needs.

"The man you claimed to love walked away with little fight for your hand. Have you considered that, young lady?"

A sharp pain lanced through her chest. How long did it take for dreams…hope…and love to die? Ophelia turned away from her father, staring at the door. She shook under the piercing loss she felt. *How could you leave me so easily?*

Once you hold my hand and step forward, I will never let you go.

She faced her parents with a small smile. "Mama…Papa…I cannot imagine a world without Devlin by my side as my husband. You've had your story…your grand love, and it was frightful and complicated and also beautiful. I will have mine, and I will not have you interfere with it. It does not mean I love you less as my parents; however, since you are forcing me to choose…I will always choose Devlin Byrne."

Ophelia whirled around and ran toward the door.

"Ophelia!"

The shocked tones of her mother did not stop her, but she

skidded to a halt with her hand on the latch, profoundly afraid that she might open the door and he would not be there. It was raining, and he could have gone to his carriage for shelter, and his coachman might have carried him to the vast open world where she might never find him again. The fear was irrational…or perfectly acceptable, given the depths of her feelings for him.

The butler stood stoically to her left, unmoving, his face a mask of polite professionalism.

"Clarkson," she whispered. "How long ago did he leave?"

He cleared his throat. "At least thirty minutes, my lady."

"How did he…how did he seem to you?"

"Frightfully cold and indifferent. I have never seen such empty eyes."

Her hands slipped from the latch, and she dropped her forehead to the door, uncaring that it hurt.

"But I believe he is still standing outside," the butler gently said.

Ophelia's head snapped up with such force her neck hurt. Looking up at the butler, she saw he stared straight ahead, and she wondered if she had conjured the words in her desperation.

Gripping the latch, she could not bring herself to open it. With a sense of mortification, she realized her heart could not withstand another disappointment. Uncaring of the appalled shock of her father and mother and the look of stupefaction on the earl's face, she ran to the chair in the hallway and shoved it to the door. Clarkson politely helped her, and Ophelia hopped up, peering through the stained glass at the upper door.

And looked straight into the eyes of Devlin Byrne.

She was so shocked, she quickly dipped from his sight. Why was he just standing there, watching her door? And why was she hiding from him? The ridiculousness of it all shook a gasp of laughter from her and more wretched tears.

Wait for me…Fifi. Devlin was waiting for her. *God.* He would have waited for hours, days, if necessary, until she came from her townhouse, she knew. Her heart shook so fiercely it was a miracle she did not faint. Ophelia jumped down, dragged the chair away, and opened the door.

He was not there. Her chest tightened painfully. "Niall!"

He seemed to emerge from the night shadows of the sleeting rain like the prince of darkness himself. He held a large black umbrella over his head, a faithful Conan at his side. His gaze was bleak and dangerous.

"You are soaked to the bones," she said, aware tears still ran down her cheeks. Ophelia hated tears, but she could not stop them.

A brief silence passed in which he did not move. Then he took one step closer.

"Why were you here?" she asked.

"I asked your father for permission to marry you, promising I had enough wealth that you can live as a duchess for ten lifetimes. Promising to love and cherish you forever, Fifi."

She licked her lips. "And he said no."

A single dip of his head.

"And you were leaving?"

His eyes stayed on her face for a very long time. "I was thinking."

"Now is not the time for brevity, Niall," she whispered. "What were you thinking about?"

"Will you marry me, Fifi, without his blessing?"

Her father's shout of outrage was heard over the harsh pattering of rain and, incredibly, over her heartbeat.

"The common, wretched vulgarity of this man's audacity! You will return inside at once, Ophelia!"

Instead of obeying her father, Ophelia took a single step over the threshold and into the sleeting rain. Yet Devlin did not move, and though she longed to fling herself into his arms, she had to spare her parents in this at least. One or two scandals were enough.

"I feel I have been waiting all my life for this moment to love you," she said. "I feel no regret in knowing you…I feel no regret in loving you…and I do love you most astonishingly. 'Not yet' crumbled a long time ago. I want to take your hand and step forward."

Devlin jerked, the umbrella shaking, before he stilled. Then he smiled, and it was the most beautiful thing she had ever seen.

"I will marry you," she said with a light laugh. "And I promise to love and cherish you for all my lifetimes."

"Over my dead body will you marry this man," her father snapped, perilously close behind her.

Something dark moved over her lover's face, and his eyes gleamed. "I will arrange your wish, Lord Shelton," he commented in a tone of polite boredom.

"Papa," Ophelia gasped. "He teases you. In time you will come to understand his black humor, even appreciate it and love it as I do."

A choking sound came from behind her, but she paid it no heed. Suddenly, a sob burst from her, and she ran down the steps and into his arms, pulling herself close to him.

He pressed a kiss of violent tenderness to her forehead.

"Who would I be if I didn't meet you, Fifi?" he murmured harshly. Yet the touch against her cheek was impossibly tender. "Who am I without you?"

He gave her the umbrella, and once she held it, Devlin lifted her into his arms and walked her toward his carriage, away from the shocked stares of her mother and the spluttering of her father. And yet she couldn't help laughing and crying.

"Are those happy tears?" he demanded gruffly.

"The happiest." Her voice was muffled against his waistcoat.

She shifted in his arms, tucking her head against the corded muscles of his throat.

"I have a special license in my top pocket."

She squeezed him so tightly he grunted. "Let's find a vicar to marry us tomorrow." When he pressed a kiss to her forehead, she felt his smile. "Devlin…I waited for you."

"I love you, Fifi, so damn much."

"I love you, too… Now take me to our cottage."

She smiled faintly. And so did he.

EPILOGUE

8 WEEKS LATER...

Despite the decided nip of the early autumn air, Ophelia did not wear a pelisse for their games on the lawn. The excitement and vigor of playing ninepins with her friends was enough to work up a sweat and keep her warm. If that did not work, the kisses that Devlin stole when he thought no one was looking did enough to delight her blood and had her flushing with wicked heat.

"Yes!" Maryann cried as she rolled the heavy ball along the bowling green toward the jack in the distance.

Emma, Fanny, Charlotte, Poppy, and Mr. Noel Baker cheered when she got her ball very close to the jack with her first throw.

"Come, Charlotte," Maryann said, tipping back her head and laughing before pushing her spectacles atop her nose in that charming manner of hers. "It is your turn."

A footman bowed and handed Charlotte the ball. Maryann sauntered over and grinned at Ophelia. The balls were marked with different colors to indicate to which player or team the ball belonged.

"What do you think our husbands are so busy chatting about? Perhaps how to trounce us in cricket, which is up next."

"Or Poppy and Mr. Baker's wedding which is in a few days." Ophelia smiled. "It could also be about Robert Peel's acceptance of the invitation to our dinner party next weekend.

The man is apparently keen to speak with Devlin after the articles he wrote on how to make the streets of London safer."

Ophelia felt a swell of emotions squeeze her throat. She and Devlin had been married a few weeks earlier by special license. After Ophelia had gifted her father with the paperwork to show all his debts had been discharged, he and her mother had grudgingly—or so he admitted—attended their small yet beautifully intimate wedding.

However, on the day, she had seen the pride written large upon his face and the tears in her mother's eyes. Afterward, the scandal sheets had seen it fit to talk about their alliance for days, but Ophelia had not allowed it to bother her. Still, she had been happy to leave for their country home in Dorset, another impressive manor house that had stolen her breath, and she had quickly fallen in love with her new home.

"It is good that Devlin has such influential friends," Maryann murmured. "It might remove the sting that your parents still feel."

Ophelia nodded. "Though Mama writes, she does not mention when they will visit. However, I am pleased they attended the wedding, even if a part of their capitulation was merely to avoid more rabid speculation and scandal."

She and Maryann shared an amused smile and cheered Charlotte when she knocked their balls away on her third try.

"Have you gotten a letter from Fanny?" Maryann asked with a slight frown.

Ophelia waited until the footman passed with the tray of chilled lemonade before she replied. "I did!"

"She has infiltrated Viscount Derrick's townhouse on the pretense of acting as his housekeeper! A lady pretending to be a housekeeper. I could not credit it, not even for one of us sinful wallflowers."

Ophelia blinked. "In the letter she sent me, Fanny said upon reflection that dressing as a man and acting as a valet might seem safer. The man her parents all but sold her to would have a more difficult time finding her if, as the viscount's valet, she traveled with him in disguise."

"Ah, he is the viscount who wrote the sensational travel memoirs. His fiancée also ran off and married that American. The scandal was all over town last year." Maryann took a sip of her drink, deviltry glinting in her eyes. "Do you think Fanny knows that as the man's valet, she will have to assist him with bathing and dressing?"

They collapsed in a heap of mirth as they imagined Fanny's shock and reactions.

"Surely she *must* know," Ophelia said, laughing still.

Maryann glanced up, and her eyes widened. She hurriedly placed her glass on the lawn chair and dashed off in the direction of her husband, who strolled toward them, and leaped into his arms. Ophelia chuckled and walked in a more sedate saunter toward Devlin, her heart hitching in her chest.

God, she loved him so much.

"What, no run and jump into my arms, Fifi?" he drawled, his green eyes gleaming with rich love and desire.

"No," she said, smiling and slipping her hands around his neck. "However, you will be greeted with this." She tipped atop her toes and perfectly fitted their mouths together.

Such unladylike hollering came from Emma and Charlotte that Ophelia dissolved into laughter, ruining their kiss.

"Your friends are incorrigible."

"I know."

"I think that scream to kiss you again is from Poppy,"

Ophelia said, laughing.

His mouth caught hers in an even deeper kiss, and she sighed, returning his passionate fervor, uncaring of their audience.

When they broke apart, they said in unison, "There is something we must discuss."

She searched his expression, which was mild yet inscrutable. Pressing her hand over his heart, Ophelia said, "What is it?"

"A letter was delivered to me just now. It is from your father."

"Oh!"

Devlin kissed the tip of her nose. "He has invited us to stay in Derbyshire. I am open to this invitation."

"Very good of Papa." Ophelia smiled, a lightness entering her heart. "He misses me."

Devlin chuckled. "What did you want to discuss?"

She slid the hand that rested over his heart upward until she traced a finger over his chin. "I have been thinking about babies," she whispered.

Her husband froze. "Babies?"

She smiled tenderly, "Yes. I want some."

He cleared his throat, his somewhat shocked expression morphing into a wicked grin. "Well, we have been working quite diligently on them twice a night and sometimes once or twice in the day. Or did you not know that was how they were made?"

She thumped his shoulder and started to laugh.

A heavy *woof* sounded in the distance, and she turned to watch Conan racing with a new dog, Hera, whom Devlin had recently rescued, with Barbosa prancing underfoot.

They had been in their carriage a few weeks ago when Devlin knocked on the roof and jumped out. When Ophelia had looked out the window, it was to see her husband coming from the woods with brambles in his hair and a wounded dog in his hands. Hera's foot had been broken, and it seemed her owner had simply left her, or they had not been able to find her. Devlin had taken such care of her with the aid of the local doctor, who had set the bone, and then named her Hera. Conan had not been jealous at all but licked Hera's face several times as if to reassure her. Ophelia greatly admired his generosity and giving, protective nature, and had also fallen in love with Hera.

"They are quite happy together, aren't they?" she asked. "To think I was worried Conan might not accept his new lady companion."

The dogs paused and seemed to rub their noses together before tearing off toward the woods.

"I think Conan is in love," she said, grinning.

"More likely, he is chasing a rabbit," Devlin said drily.

Ophelia laughed and looked up at him. He had not been watching the dogs at all but had been staring at her the entire time.

"I am thinking about babies," he said gruffly. "A little girl with your eyes and smile, and a son."

Happiness filled her heart. "But first, we *must* do some of that traveling you've wondered about. Our own grand tour of the continent and sailing on the wide-open sea for weeks"

"That sounds wonderful my *a ghrá mo chroí*."

Ophelia loved his endearments, especially this one which meant my heart's beloved. She took a deep breath. "I also want to give you something."

Devlin lifted a brow. "What has you looking so nervous?"

She dipped into the pocket of her dress and removed a carefully folded handkerchief. He took it when she held it up to him and slowly opened the material. Devlin stilled for the longest time as he stared at the ring of vines he had given her so many years ago.

He lifted his regards to her, and her breath seized at the poignant emotions espied in his brilliant gaze. "You also kept yours."

"I did," she whispered.

"I love you," he murmured, the joy in his eyes raw and real.

She swallowed past the lump in her throat and, brushing her mouth against his, whispered, "I love you, too, my husband. I love you."

ACKNOWLEDGMENTS

I thank God every day for loving me with such depth and breadth.

To my husband, Du'Sean, you are so damn wonderful. Your feedback and support are invaluable. I could not do this without you.

Thank you to my wonderful friend and critique partner Giselle Marks. Without you, I would be lost. Thank you for all the amazing feedback and the messages that encouraged me to write in the face of my illness.

Thank you to my adopted children, Liam and Zuri, who were so understanding and loving through a very difficult period in my life. They understood that whatever energy I had to give would have to go into my work. You guys are amazing.

Thank you to Stacy Abrams for being an amazing, wonderful, and super-stupendous editor. Your thoughtful feedback and supportive patience helped me to finish this book.

To my wonderful readers, thank you for reading *A Scoundrel of Her Own*. I hope you enjoyed Ophelia and Devlin's journey to love and happily every after as much as I enjoyed writing it.

Special THANK YOU to the Historical Hellions, who always root for me, and to everyone who leaves a review—bloggers, fans, friends. I have always said that reviews to authors are like a pot of gold to leprechauns. Thank you all for adding to my rainbow one review at a time.

AMARA

an imprint of Entangled Publishing LLC